BECAUSE NAUGHTY CAN BE OH SO NICE®

NE LTD

By Nicole Edwards

The Alluring Indulgence Series
Kaleb
Zane
Travis
Holidays with the Walker Brothers
Ethan
Braydon
Sawyer
Brendon

The Austin Arrows Series
Rush
Kaufman

The Bad Boys of Sports Series
Bad Reputation
Bad Business

The Caine Cousins Series
Hard to Hold
Hard to Handle

The Club Destiny Series
Conviction
Temptation
Addicted
Seduction
Infatuation
Captivated
Devotion
Perception
Entrusted
Adored
Distraction

The Coyote Ridge Series
Curtis
Jared

The Dead Heat Ranch Series
Boots Optional
Betting on Grace
Overnight Love

By Nicole Edwards (cont.)

The Devil's Bend Series

Chasing Dreams
Vanishing Dreams

The Devil's Playground Series

Without Regret
Without Restraint

The Office Intrigue Series

Office Intrigue
Intrigued Out of the Office
Their Rebellious Submissive

The Pier 70 Series

Reckless
Fearless
Speechless
Harmless

The Sniper 1 Security Series

Wait for Morning
Never Say Never
Tomorrow's Too Late

The Southern Boy Mafia Series

Beautifully Brutal
Beautifully Loyal

Standalone Novels

A Million Tiny Pieces
Inked on Paper

Writing as Timberlyn Scott

Unhinged
Unraveling
Chaos

Naughty Holiday Editions

2015
2016

Chasing DREAMS

DEVIL'S BEND
Book 1

NICOLE EDWARDS

Nicole Edwards Limited
PO Box 806
Hutto, Texas 78634
www.NicoleEdwardsLimited.com

Cover Image by: © Piet Mall/Stock4B/Corbis
Cover Design by: © Nicole Edwards Limited
Editing by: Blue Otter Editing www.blueotterediting.com

ISBN (print): 978-1-939786-13-5
ISBN (ebook): 978-1-939786-14-2

DEDICATION

To my amazing mother and my wonderful mother-in-law:

There will never be any way to show just how much I love you both, but please know that you mean everything to me.

Thank you so much for your love and encouragement.

CHAPTER ONE

"Tessa."

At the sound of her name, Tessa Donovan glanced up from the beer she was pouring. Not that she needed to. She knew exactly which man owned that sexy country drawl.

"Awww, hell!" she exclaimed, glancing down to see a mess of foam as it poured over the edge of the glass she was filling.

"Well, don't get *too* excited that I'm here," Eric Lancaster, the only other bartender that The Rusty Nail employed, said with a cocky grin as he headed her way.

"I blame you, Mr. Lancaster." She grinned sheepishly as she grabbed a towel and wiped the overflow off her hands.

"You can drop that mister shit right here and now," Eric teased. "Keep it up and I'll start callin' you ma'am."

"Okay, buddy. No need to start with the threats," Tessa joked, returning her focus to the new glass she grabbed, paying attention this time as the foam lifted to the top. Once full, she slid it over to the man at the end of the counter as she called out to him, "Hey, Tex, put your hands on the beer, not the lady. You know she's married, right?"

The stranger who'd bellied up to the bar half an hour ago had the decency to blush. Didn't stop him from hitting on the bar bunny though. The very same bar bunny with a wedding band on. Tessa glanced down at his hand. Great. He had one on too, and it wasn't from a matching set. Lovely.

As Eric made his way behind the bar, Tessa grabbed another glass, filled another beer, and passed it over to another waiting customer. Story of her life.

"Ow!" Tessa hollered when Eric swatted her on the ass, as was his usual greeting. "Don't let your ol' lady see you doin' that."

"She might just be jealous that I got to touch your ass, you know that, right?" Eric's sexy rumble echoed around the bar.

Glancing over at him, Tessa smiled. If it weren't for the fact that Eric was more like her brother than her own brothers sometimes, she might just get excited. Okay, no. That wasn't true either. She'd grown up with Eric, and since he was actually married to her best friend, Isabelle, Tessa knew more about him than she cared to. Probably no attraction to be had, no matter the case.

He was a decent guy though.

"You're probably right on that one," she said, making Eric laugh.

The sexy rumble that followed caused more than one head to turn at the bar. Eric had that effect on women … er, *other* women. He turned heads. In fact, Tessa was pretty sure he was almost personally responsible for the sheer volume of ladies who flocked to The Rusty Nail on a nightly basis. It was just a good thing that Izzy — Eric's lovely bride — was one of the most confident women she knew. Had Eric belonged to Tessa, she couldn't guarantee there wouldn't be at least one cat fight each and every night.

"You see Adam yet?" Tessa hadn't seen her older brother all day, and that was unusual, especially for a Friday night.

Since Adam was in charge of the entertainment, he generally stopped in early to ensure there weren't any problems with arrival, setup, that sort of thing. Considering the band wasn't there yet, and they were closing in on seven o'clock, Tessa figured it was safe to say there were problems. If not, then this was one band that could use a course in time management. She would not be responsible for the chaos that would ensue if the main attraction did not show up on time.

"He texted me earlier. Said he had to run an errand," Eric explained as he grabbed a bottle of vodka and began rolling shots out as they were ordered.

The bar was quickly filling up, and Tessa knew it was because of the night's entertainment. She personally hadn't believed Adam when he'd said he'd booked Cooper Krenshaw, but from what her brother told her, he was actually excited to play there.

Right.

Why one of the biggest names in country music wanted to play her bar, she had no idea, but she wasn't in charge of the music selection, so she didn't ask. She wasn't the swoon-worthy type, which meant she wouldn't be swept off her feet by his overwhelming presence either. From the looks of it, she might be the only one though.

"Care if I take a few minutes?" she asked Eric when the walk-ups slowed a short time later. Although it was still early, Tessa had been running solo for the last hour, and they were busier than usual.

"Take all the time you need." He grinned and she could've sworn she heard several sighs from a few of the ladies seated at the bar.

"Thanks." Tessa pulled off her short apron and tossed it onto the shelf beneath the bar before sneaking out. She made a beeline for the back door, hoping for some fresh air before the place filled to capacity as was expected tonight. In fact, she had called in extra backup to man the doors because she was pretty sure there would be a line of people waiting to get in even after they hit maximum capacity. Thankfully, she had a family full of cousins who weren't too proud to help out when needed.

Before the solid steel door could slam behind her, Tessa was inhaling the humid September night air, letting the warm breeze slide over her overheated skin. It wasn't long before some of the tension in her shoulders eased.

Her brother Adam gave her a hard time about wanting to be outside rather than upstairs in the private office that they rarely used. Tessa couldn't explain it, but she'd rather be inhaling the country night air than the stale, bittersweet fumes that lingered on the inside.

At least out here she could think. Inside, with the whoops and hollers of the crowd, she could barely pay attention, much less focus on anything other than serving drinks to her customers. The sheer volume of people overwhelmed her, even if she did enjoy the interaction most of the time. Tonight, it seemed that her feet were already pissed off at her, and her shift had only just begun.

Leaning back against the corrugated metal, she gave one foot a rest by propping it flat against the wall at her back before alternating to the other. It was on nights like tonight that Tessa wondered why she hadn't become an accountant. Sure, it might be stressful in its own right, but at least she'd be able to sit down. Then again, that would probably make her crazy too.

At twenty-nine, she should've been used to the constant hustle, smelling like beer, *and* her aching feet. She and Adam had acquired the bar from their late father — a man neither of them had known all that well — six years ago, and after some careful consideration and a long talk with her husband, Richie, she'd opted to give it a go.

It could safely be said that a twenty-three-year-old did not come equipped with all that much wisdom when it came to running her own business, but no one would've been able to tell her that at the time. Hell, for years before that, no one could tell her *anything at all*, so it wouldn't have mattered much then either.

Just the thought of her late husband made her heart ache. Seemed life had taken a turn some years ago, and Richie's death was only part of the heartache Tessa had experienced. To this day, she missed him dearly. He had been a police officer, killed in the line of duty when he was only twenty-six years old. She had been twenty-five, and they'd just settled into life together, married only fifteen months when he was taken from her.

Here she was, four years later, slinging beers and dodging more than a few wandering hands night after night in the place she'd come to feel was her second home. The Rusty Nail was nothing more than an eight-thousand-square-foot remodeled old barn that had at one point been a feed store years and years ago. At that time, it had received an enormous overhaul, which included an exterior facelift of metal walls and reinforced steel beams on the inside to support the roof as well as bear the weight of the two-hundred-square-foot office upstairs. Not much had changed after her father had purchased the place and converted it into a bar until Adam had come along and set up the stage.

Speaking of the stage, she could only hope the band showed up soon, because there was an excellent chance things were going to go from bad to worse if they didn't. If Adam left her to handle the fallout like he had the last time, she was going to give him a piece of her mind, followed by a good swift kick in the ass.

Glancing down at her watch, Tessa realized she had a few more minutes to spare, so she pushed off the wall and headed back inside. She disappeared into the restroom, using the free minutes to take care of business before washing her hands and pulling her hair up into a ponytail. While she was standing in front of the mirror, two women slammed in through the door in a flurry of giggles followed by "Ohmigod! Ohmigod! Ohmigod!"

Tessa didn't turn to face them, but she could see them through the reflection in the mirror. Since they were effectively blocking the door, she waited for the ladies to move on so she could sneak out and get back to work. She smiled at her reflection, trying not to laugh at their giddy excitement.

"Ohmigod! Did you see him? He *winked* at me! Winked!" one of the ladies squealed, the other jumping up and down by her side as though this were the biggest news to hit Devil's Bend since Jessica Sanderson told the *Devil's Bend Gazette* that she was having triplets.

"He's going home with me tonight if I have anything to say about it!"

"Oh, he will. Maybe we'll just surprise him. You know, tag team," the blonde woman exclaimed, giggling between words like a schoolgirl.

Figuring she wasn't going to be able to outlast their elation over meeting another famous singer, Tessa turned around, smiled at the ladies before squeezing past them and out the door. Once she was in the dark, narrow hallway, the familiar noises and the perfume-slash-cologne mixture assaulted her senses, and she pasted on another smile as she turned the corner.

"Holy crap," she muttered to herself, pushing through the wall of bodies as she tried to finagle her way back to the bar.

An influx of women had descended upon them during her short reprieve. Tessa sighed as she wove through the commotion, realizing that tonight was going to be one of those nights. If anyone ever thought men were high maintenance in a small country bar, they clearly hadn't met the women Tessa had. Especially when there was supposed to be a hunky, big-time country music star in their presence.

With her back to the stage, she made her way through the throng of people to the bar on the other side of the room, smiling at Eric as she approached. "What the hell happened while I was gone?" she asked, not expecting a response.

"You have *him* to thank," Eric said, nodding his head in the direction of the stage. Due to the sheer volume of people filling every available inch of floor space, not to mention her height deficiency, Tessa couldn't see who he was referring to, but she could pretty much guess.

"Hey, can we get some beers over here?"

Tessa glanced over, nodding her acknowledgement to a table of women who looked as though they'd prepped themselves for prom. *Wow.* This guy certainly had quite the following.

"Why didn't you come get me?" she asked, grabbing her apron before turning toward the first customer she came to.

Within seconds, Tessa felt frazzled. Unlike Eric, who was standing a couple of feet away, looking as cool and confident as ever although the oversized bar with its hardwood top scarred from years of customer abuse — her favorite part of the entire place — was completely engulfed by people.

"What? You think I can't handle this?" Eric laughed and, once again, heads turned. Geez, these women were easy.

"Hey, Katie!" Tessa had to raise her voice over the din of the now-overcrowded section. "Can you check on that table? They want beers, and Miranda is not here yet."

Katie Clarren was one of the two waitresses that Tessa employed. Young, beautiful, and almost too smart for her own good, Katie was also one of the best servers she had. Not too long ago, Tessa had been under the impression that her younger brother, Jack, actually had an interest in Katie. According to Katie, she didn't have time for dating, although she seemed flattered.

As it turned out, Katie was juggling college and another part-time job outside of the bar, so her days and nights seemed to be full. Considering Jack's history with women, she was actually grateful for Katie's busy schedule. No need to have another broken heart left behind in her brother's wake.

"Sure," Katie said sweetly, her long, silky black hair swinging behind her as she nodded energetically.

For the next few minutes, Tessa didn't have a chance to look up from the horde of people demanding drink after drink. Just when she was beginning to think she would need to call in some backup, a gruff voice echoed through the speakers, causing the noise to dim as everyone turned toward the stage.

"Howdy, y'all." The deep southern drawl, followed by a rough, raspy chuckle, silenced the rest of the chatter.

Tessa spared the voice a glance, but she couldn't see over the sea of heads standing around, so she returned to pouring beer, taking money, and making change.

The disembodied voice continued talking, and Tessa smiled at the sweet, sexy drawl that drifted through the room. He gave a brief introduction, followed by casual conversation with a few people in the audience, and Tessa decided immediately that she liked the intimate sound of his voice. Especially his laugh. Hearing his voice in person was a lot different than on the radio.

Managing a bar in the middle of nowhere, Tessa had the pleasure of meeting a few hopefuls, but not generally any who actually had made a name for themselves. Tonight's entertainment was an exception. Granted, in the last year, Adam had raised the bar on the talent he brought in, but to have set it this high, Tessa was amazed.

Screaming and carrying on from the cowboys and cowgirls reacting to Cooper's presence was once again quickly building to a dull roar, and Tessa forced herself to tune out the noise. Over the years, she'd become successful at drowning out the steady rumble of voices and music, mainly because her sanity required her to. She couldn't help but wonder what kind of guy could garner this much enthusiasm.

From what she knew of Cooper Krenshaw, thanks to the stories Adam had told her, he was an old friend from college. Even though Cooper had made it big in the country music world, Adam still kept in touch with him on a regular basis. Adam never had given her a viable reason why Cooper was in Devil's Bend though. Seemed odd that he was just passing through their tiny neck of the woods or that he was craving the scenery. And she seriously doubted his busy schedule would allow him to make the trek this far south to play here.

But she didn't really need a reason, and based on the scene in front of her, the crowd was more than thrilled that he'd made an appearance. The women obviously liked him if their screams and catcalls were anything to go by. Tessa knew *of* Cooper Krenshaw, had seen pictures in magazines, but since she wasn't much into music — country or otherwise — she couldn't have named even one song of his. Most of her downtime was spent listening to the comforting serenity that being outside in the country afforded her. After nights like this, her eardrums thanked her for it.

Listening to him chat and laugh with the fans, Tessa realized she could get on board with this guy's voice. Very sensual. Seductive even.

"All right, all right. I'm sure you're tired of listenin' to me ramble. I'll get on with it." The voice somehow managed to calm the group again, and the deep, rusty chuckle that followed had Tessa's head popping up. Despite her disinterest, his voice had a strange effect on her.

"This is something new I've been working on in my spare time. Let me know what you think," he continued. A few brief guitar strums followed, and then the crowd was eerily quiet. The sound always surprised her.

As all of the heads in the room turned to face the stage, Tessa realized they'd stopped demanding alcohol, and she shot Eric a smile, noticing he still didn't appear ruffled. He was a patient man, she would give him that. Considering he had to put up with her best friend, Izzy, on a daily basis, he had to be.

Knowing he could handle what few customers they might have in the next minute or two, Tessa snuck out from behind the bar and over to the long wooden shelf along the south wall that was a catchall for empty beer bottles. Not seeing Katie anywhere, she decided to help the girl out by disposing of what she could while the masses were engrossed in the man now crooning out a slow, country love song.

Grabbing a handful of bottles, Tessa eased through a few cowboys lining the outer edges of the room to one of the large barrels used for trash. Interesting how they couldn't seem to find it on their own, she thought to herself. Tossing the bottles in as quietly as she could, Tessa looked up, noticing the man on stage for the first time.

She couldn't see much of his face, which was in the shadow of the black Stetson sitting low on his head and covering most of his features as he looked down at the ladies in the front row. What she could see was an incredibly well-developed torso, clad perfectly in a dark gray T-shirt that clung deliciously to a set of well-defined pecs.

It somewhat baffled her how many hot, well-built cowboys graced her stage week after week. A dime a dozen they were. It was just unfortunate that they all came with an ego the size of Texas and more baggage than the TSA handled in a week.

CHAPTER TWO

Cooper Krenshaw could've performed all night in a place like this. The scent of sawdust and hardwood drifted up as a handful of people at the edge of the stage began slow dancing on the cramped dance floor, making him smile as he belted out the tune, enjoying the happy faces he could see peering up from the floor below. The last time he'd played for a crowd this small had been several years back at a rodeo down in Austin, which seemed like an eternity ago.

These days, his songs were blasted through amphitheaters and stages that would rival most football stadiums, and they lacked the intimacy he found in a place like this. In fact, it had been his last concert in Chicago that Cooper had found himself escaping as soon as his last set was complete because he couldn't seem to shake that disconnected feeling. Without even talking to his manager, Cooper had set out on the road, nowhere bound. He hadn't known where he was headed until he'd reached the Texas border. It was then that he'd given his buddy Adam Dryden a call and beaten feet toward Central Texas.

Having met Adam during his first year at the University of Texas, he'd managed to keep in touch with him through the years despite the chaotic lifestyle Cooper found himself wrapped up in. Something had clicked between them from the moment they'd met, and keeping in touch with Adam had given Cooper a way to ground himself to his roots. A gentle reminder of where it'd all started.

Their conversation hadn't been a long one, but when Adam had mentioned he was looking for some local talent to play his small-town bar, Cooper had found himself aching for something a bit more relaxed than an arena filled with screaming women and known Adam's proposal was right up his alley.

That's how he'd ended up in Devil's Bend, Texas, for the last week and a half. Until tonight, he'd been hiding out at a modest motel when he wasn't checking out the local real estate.

This small-town setting was a far cry from what he was used to but undeniably more in line with where he had come from. More in line with what had sparked his interest in the early stages of his career. In his early twenties, once he'd been picked up by a record label, he'd been blown away by the attention and chaos, inspired by it even.

Not so much anymore.

At thirty-one, after nearly eight years on the road full time, Cooper was ready to slow down. Significantly. After just a few minutes on stage, he realized this was more his pace these days. Not that his manager would agree with him, but then again, Marcus Evergreen didn't think he could do much thinking for himself anymore at all.

"What'd you think?" he asked the crowd when his song came to an end. The group erupted in catcalls and whistles, clapping and laughter, and the excitement seeped into his blood. Truthfully, he hadn't felt that heart-wrenching rush of adrenaline in quite some time.

Glancing around the room, Cooper made eye contact with both women and men, smiling as the group began tossing out suggestions. As was usually the case, most of the requests seemed to go back to one of his early albums, back when he'd had fun doing this night after night. It seemed as though some of what he'd valued had been lost along the way. Probably one of the reasons he was working his way back to his roots once again.

A shrill voice caught his attention, and his eyes darted back to the area closest to the bar. Before he could pinpoint where the sound came from, his gaze had landed on a stunning blonde maneuvering her way through the swarm of people. When the woman stopped and looked up at him, their eyes met for a brief second before she abruptly turned away, fleeing deeper into the crowd. Thanks to his position on the stage, he managed to track her until she slid behind the bar, leaning up to talk to another man standing there.

"Play 'Cowgirl in my Dreams,'" one woman shouted from close to the stage, and Cooper tore his eyes off the mystery woman in the back, glancing over to where the request had come from.

"Yes, ma'am." Readjusting his guitar, Cooper started the song, falling back into the music, letting himself get lost in the memories of a different time. This was what he'd been searching for these last few months. This was exactly what he was looking to find again.

Forty-five minutes later, Cooper was ready for a break. And a beer. Not necessarily in that order either.

He informed the group that he'd be back shortly, secured his guitar in an area at the back of the stage, and moved down the steps. The instant his feet hit the hardwood dance floor, he was inundated with women flocking to his side, an influx of chatter making his head pound. They didn't seem to mind that they were invading his personal space, hanging on him even as he tried to keep moving.

With a smile on his face, he worked his way through the group, trying his best to answer questions, offering a couple of hugs, posing for more than a few pictures before he finally reached the bar. He just wanted a beer. And maybe a few minutes of quiet. He wasn't going to get the latter, but from the looks of it, the former was on its way thanks to the man behind the bar nodding in his direction.

A beefy hand clapped him on the shoulder, and Cooper turned to see who it was, coming face-to-face with Adam Dryden.

"Hey, man." Holding out his hand, he waited for Adam to shake it before tipping his hat slightly on his head.

"How's it goin'?" Adam asked, having to speak louder just so Cooper could hear him.

A group of women was trying desperately to get his attention, and Cooper was doing his best to be polite. He'd gotten used to the demand on his time, but he found it difficult to turn his attention away from someone he knew personally for a group who assumed he owed them his undivided attention.

"Why don't we go to my office?" Adam offered, and Cooper didn't hesitate before nodding his head in agreement.

Grabbing his beer bottle from the bar, he fell into step behind Adam. Sheer determination was the only thing that got them through the crowd, but once they did, Cooper found himself following his friend up a set of stairs at the back of the room. Just when he thought they were going to have company, a hulking man insinuated his bulk between the gaggle of women and the cramped stairwell.

"Mr. Krenshaw will be back down shortly, ladies," he told the group, making Cooper smile.

Mr. Krenshaw. *Shit.* That was funny. At thirty-one, he certainly didn't feel like a *mister.*

At the top of the dimly lit stairwell was a door that read "Private" on a plaque haphazardly glued to the wood. Adam used a key to gain access, and Cooper followed him, successfully shutting out the majority of the noise once inside.

"Damn, man. You sure know how to draw a crowd," Adam stated as he moved across the room to a large window. He twisted a plastic stick and the cheap wood blinds turned, offering them a view of the scene below.

"It's a curse." The words tumbled out before he could think better of it.

Okay, so truthfully, it was a blessing, but Cooper wasn't feeling it these days. The words were an honest reflection of his mood, but he'd grown accustomed to keeping a filter on his thoughts until recently. Cooper hoped he sounded as though he were joking, but for some reason, he wasn't all that worried whether Adam knew the truth. He *was* beginning to feel as though it was a curse.

He wasn't sure when he'd stopped being grateful for all of the fame that came along with his career, but in recent months, he was finding it harder and harder to want to keep moving forward. Instead, he found himself wanting to sneak out early, disappear on his own, and find the solitude that had been lacking in his life for years.

His manager told him it was a phase that he'd be over soon. Cooper wasn't so sure that was the case. Sure, he was thankful for his success, especially after he'd worked his ass off to get where he was, but Cooper was beginning to feel disconnected. As though he wanted more, but wasn't sure what that *more* even was.

Hitting the big time and becoming a country music star might've been his original intention when he was a teenager, but he hadn't known what all it entailed. Somewhere along the way, he felt as though he'd lost a part of himself. And despite all of the fans and the interactions, he couldn't seem to shake the feeling of being alone that had started haunting him lately.

Cooper moved up close to the window, standing nearly shoulder to shoulder with Adam in the confined space, downing half of his beer as he took in the silence while watching the overabundance of bodies below. His eyes landed on the woman he had glimpsed earlier. She was moving gracefully as she worked behind the bar, and he found himself once again staring at her.

She was short, much shorter than most of the people standing around her. He couldn't see much more than the snug black T-shirt that clung to her rather impressive curves, but he found himself trying to get a glimpse of the rest.

She looked like a country angel with her curly blonde hair pulled up into a ponytail at the back of her head, the long strands falling down and over her shoulders. He couldn't make out much of her features from this distance, but it was her dazzling white smile that captivated him. She was laughing with the man behind the bar, serving up drinks as if she were born to run the crowded place.

"You meet my sister yet?" Adam asked, pulling Cooper from his visual assault of the cute bartender's sultry smile.

"Haven't met anyone, actually. I got here late, so I had to rush up on stage. The Realtor you referred me to decided tonight was a terrific night to show me another house."

Adam just nodded, his attention once again on the folks below. "What'd you think of it?"

Cooper was beginning to relax again as he watched what was going on down on the main floor. There were still people coming in the door, and he was beginning to wonder just how many people the place could actually hold. He couldn't imagine they'd be able to squeeze more than a couple hundred people between all four walls, but from the looks of it, they had almost twice that.

"This one is a little worse for wear than the one you mentioned. It needs more work, but I'm definitely interested. Don't think the price can be beat. Luckily, I'm kinda handy."

"A fixer-upper, huh?" Adam smiled at him, then returned his gaze to the scene below.

Fixer-upper was an understatement, but for the price, Cooper could see himself making some serious progress on the house. It wasn't like he wouldn't have some extra time on his hands.

And the land…

The property was almost double that of the one Adam had told him about. Hell, the two hundred forty acres were more than worth it. He had plans for the land, which was the main draw of the property in the first place.

Movement at the front of the room close to the bar caught Cooper's attention, and he looked over to see two men going chest to chest.

"Awww, hell. I'll be right back," Adam said with a groan, obviously seeing the melee that was about to erupt below.

As much as Cooper wanted to enjoy the solitude for a few more minutes, his instincts told him to follow Adam. The last thing he wanted was for a brawl to break out in his friend's bar because of him. This happened more often than he wished it did. With this many women around, cowboys often had a hard time controlling themselves. Testosterone was a heady thing.

Dropping his now-empty beer bottle in the trash can by the door, Cooper followed Adam, matching his fast pace as they made their way back to the main floor. By the time they reached the group, Cooper realized that the guy and the woman who had been manning the bar earlier were already attempting to break up the fight.

"Not here, you don't!" The sweet Texas twang of the woman's words, heard loud and clear over the music battling for attention in the overhead speakers, pierced something deep inside of Cooper. He watched as the angel in blue jeans stepped right between the two oversized men as though she were six feet tall and bulletproof.

"Fuck off, dickhead!" one of the men shouted to the other over the top of the blonde's head, ignoring her altogether.

Cooper took a step closer, praying like hell this woman wasn't about to get knocked out by one of these assholes. His protective instinct suddenly kicked into high gear as he watched her attempt to stay right in the middle.

"Uh-uh. Not in here. This is your last warning, damnit!" The sassy cowgirl's voice rose even louder, her drawl crystal clear, and despite her irritation, Cooper found he liked the sound of her voice as well as her spirit. A lot.

That's when the shoving match ensued, and much to Cooper's dismay, the cowgirl was pushed out of the way. Hard.

As the fists began flying, he watched her stumble backward. Somehow he managed to reach out and grab her before she crashlanded on the concrete floor at his feet. As grunts and groans echoed in the small area, Cooper grabbed the girl, pulling her out of the chaos, trying his best to shield her as the punches landed, neither of the men caring who got in their way.

Suddenly, a shrill, ear-splitting whistle sounded, and to Cooper's surprise, the rumble of voices died instantly. The two idiots stopped throwing punches, but neither of them moved far.

"Get your asses out of here," the giant of a man said, his tone frighteningly calm as he moved closer to the two men who were now sweating, bleeding, and breathing as if they'd just run a marathon … in quicksand.

It took Cooper a minute to realize he was still holding the girl, her petite body pressed tightly against his as they stood on the sidelines staring back at the cowboy who'd managed to halt the fight with a whistle.

"Jack," the woman said breathlessly, successfully wrenching out of Cooper's arms and moving away.

Before she walked away, she turned to look at him, her pale green eyes meeting his as a blinding smile tilted the corners of her full pink lips. Cooper tipped his hat slightly at the same time he felt something strange and exciting stir up inside of him, rendering him speechless as he smiled back.

"Damn," he groaned, turning away from the crowd and moving back to the stage. The least he could do was provide some entertainment, and hopefully, by the end of the night, he'd have a chance to talk to the angel in blue jeans.

CHAPTER THREE

When they first walked out of the building, Tessa fell into step with her brothers at the same time two women began yelling obscenities from directly behind them. As much as she wanted to say something, she kept her mouth closed. No matter what she told them, the ladies weren't likely to listen to reason anyway. Luckily, it only took Adam one piercing glare in their direction before they stopped their yapping.

Escorting the two hot-headed men over to Shane, one of their cousins who worked at the bar most frequently, Adam and Jack left them with instructions to ensure the men got home safely — and that meant they weren't going to get behind the wheel of their own vehicles.

"You've got seriously good timing, you know that?" Adam asked Jack as they made their way back inside.

That he did. It seemed one of her brothers, usually Jack, was always having to come along and break up one fight or another. For the most part, they occurred at least once, sometimes twice on a Friday or Saturday night. Especially when they booked the more popular talent. Although Tessa was pretty sure they had never had anyone bigger than Cooper Krenshaw on their stage.

As Tessa made her way back to the bar, she looked up to see him on the stage, his guitar in hand while he successfully distracted the crowd. A sudden flush of heat traveled from the base of her skull right down her spine when her eyes met his from across the room. Not five minutes before, she'd somehow landed practically in his lap, and her body had immediately taken stock of the feel of his hard body against her.

Something she hadn't felt in … well, since Richie.

While Cooper had been off with Adam during his break, Tessa had received an earful about the country music phenom from a group of women standing around the bar, attempting to capture Eric's attention since the superstar was nowhere in sight. Not that Tessa would trust anything she heard, but then again, since most of the chatter was about how nice his ass appeared in the Wranglers he wore, she could pretty much check that out herself.

Not that she would.

Okay, so she did.

And they were right.

"Is that Cooper Krenshaw?" Jack asked Adam as her brothers stood along the back corner of the bar where the sound system control panel was discreetly hidden.

"The one and only," Adam answered easily, sounding entirely too proud of himself.

Tessa watched her baby brother as he moved behind the bar, grabbing a bottle of Southern Comfort from the shelf. Jack was the youngest of the three, and although they all had the same mother, she and Adam had a different father. For whatever reason, she found that she was closer to Jack than she was to Adam. Tessa was only a year younger than Adam, but she was three years older than Jack, and needless to say, she'd been an overprotective older sister. It wasn't until Jack hit his twenties that he had taken over the protective role.

Tessa listened to her brothers as she tried to help out with the drinks; all the while, her mind drifted back to the brief interlude she'd just shared with the famous country music star. Her body still tingled from where Cooper had touched her. It was the first time in a damn long time that her body actually craved the attention of another human being.

Considering she'd spent the better part of the first year and a half after Richie died grieving rather than living, Tessa hadn't had much time for intimate relationships, nor had she wanted any. After one failed attempt at another relationship about a year ago, it hadn't been until recently that Tessa even realized when the opposite sex was around her. At least not in any way that mattered.

In Cooper's case, there was something in his touch, albeit brief, that felt familiar yet exciting at the same time. And oh, holy moly, he smelled so good. She would admit that she might've leaned against him a tad longer than was necessary just so she could sniff him.

Working to try and forget all that had happened a few minutes ago, Tessa got wrapped up in passing out drinks while listening to that provocative voice that filtered through her bar. Thankfully, by tomorrow, all thoughts of Cooper Krenshaw would be a thing of the past, and she could get on with her life.

No need to start dreaming about anything more now.

Especially about things even farther out of her reach.

Morning for Tessa didn't begin until roughly noon on most days, but that was because she tried to get the required eight hours of sleep, and going to bed at four o'clock in the morning meant the day was halfway over by the time she crawled out of bed.

She was a creature of habit, so it didn't matter what time she woke up, the first thing she did each and every day was make coffee and sit on the front porch while Havoc and Harmony, her beloved Siberian Huskies that she had rescued from the animal shelter just over a year ago, frolicked in the yard in front of the house. Ever since she'd brought them home to live with her, they'd preferred to be outside as opposed to inside. Just like her.

So, this morning wasn't much different than any other morning, with the exception of the dream that Tessa could not seem to stop thinking about. It continued to stream through her mind as she listened to the birds chirp and her dogs rumble and growl as they played in the grass just a few feet away from the steps she was perched on.

For the life of her, Tessa couldn't get Cooper Krenshaw out of her head. Remembering the way it'd felt when the tall, dark-haired cowboy had wrapped his arms around her, keeping her from stumbling right on her ass the night before was becoming annoying in its own right. Not only that, but that strange, bubbling sensation in her tummy when she pictured him in her mind wasn't doing her any favors either.

The man was sexy, she'd have to give him that much. His face was a mishmash of rugged, chiseled features that, when blended together, made one of the most handsome faces she'd ever seen. A strong, angular jaw with that scruffy stubble that was just a smidge darker along his jawline. His perfect white teeth were framed by lips that looked like they were made to kiss.

But what had captured her almost instantly were his eyes. Light brown and so bright they were almost gold. And he wasn't perfect, which probably made him all the more appealing. His nose was slightly crooked but just barely noticeable unless, of course, one was staring at him the way she had been. And Tessa could've stared at him for hours.

It wasn't hard to imagine why he was a country music sensation either. That voice.

Oh, and did she mention he was tall? So very tall. At least compared to her.

Tessa hadn't inherited her height from her mother or father the way her brothers had. She was roughly five foot four while both of her brothers towered over her. The same could be said for the dark-haired stranger from the night before. Cooper was taller than she'd imagined him being, not that she had actually imagined him at all. From his perch on the stage, he hadn't appeared unusually tall, but if she had to guess, the attractive cowboy was at least a couple of inches over six feet. However, it was possible that her brain was only making him seem larger than life because of the way her body had responded to the innocent hold he'd had on her the night before. Yep, that had to be it.

Since the moment she'd walked through her front door in the wee hours of the morning, Tessa had battled the urge to Google him just to see what kind of dirt she could dig up on the man. Thankfully, she'd thought better of it. It wasn't like she was ever going to see him again.

He was a passing fancy, every woman's fantasy, and probably a fly-by-night lover, at that. Who knew what he had done when he'd left her bar a few hours before dawn. Although he hadn't been with anyone when he'd finally called it a night just a few minutes after closing time, that didn't mean there wasn't a flock of women who had offered to make sure he was tucked in safe and sound when his head finally did hit the pillow.

Tessa tried to shake off the thought of the good-looking cowboy. Finding a man wasn't on her priority list. And yes, that list was actually long.

Not that the list was going according to plan, but she refused to deviate from it. For so long, it'd been all she had. After Richie had died, she went back, added more to the list, and made up her mind that the only thing that mattered was accomplishing the dream she'd had since she was younger. And if she had any intention of getting to that goal, she didn't have room for one-night stands, especially with the likes of Cooper Krenshaw.

Tessa's cell phone rang from somewhere inside the house, and knowing that her little brother, Jack, would be checking on her as he did every day, she hopped up from the steps and hurried inside. Havoc and Harmony were by her side instantly, pushing their large, wet noses into the house before she could stumble in after them.

The phone stopped ringing mere seconds before she reached it, but Tessa looked to see who it was anyway. Adam. *Odd.* She rarely heard from him so early in the day, especially after the kind of eventful evening they'd had the night before.

Her brother was known to sleep away most of the day, but that was usually thanks to his extracurricular activities that typically took up most of his early-morning hours. Unlike Tessa, Adam didn't avoid the opposite sex. Nor did he have a problem with the love 'em and leave 'em code of ethics that he had apparently inherited from their absent father.

Before she could dial her brother back, her phone chirped, signaling an incoming voice mail. As she attempted to fill the dogs' food bowls, Tessa juggled the phone in one hand and tried to fend off her eager animals at the same time.

"Cool it, Havoc. I'm working on it," she informed the sixty-pound Husky insistent on nudging her with his powerful body. It was well past their lunchtime, which meant he was overly ornery at the moment.

"Hey, sis. I hope you're awake. I'm on my way over. If you know what's good for you, you'll have coffee ready when I get there."

Tessa smiled as she dropped her phone onto the counter, putting the final scoop of kibble into Harmony's bowl as she did. She couldn't imagine what could possibly bring Adam over at this time of day. He should've been passed out for at least another couple of hours.

Although he sounded fairly reasonable in his message, Tessa rushed to the kitchen and put on a fresh pot of coffee just in case. Adam could be awfully demanding when he wanted to be, and considering he wasn't a frequent visitor to her humble abode, Tessa wanted to be prepared for the worst.

Ten minutes later, she heard the sound of tires crunching on gravel out front. With a fresh cup of coffee for herself and one for Adam, she moved toward the front door just in time to see none other than Cooper Krenshaw climbing out of the passenger side of Adam's pickup.

"What the hell?" she muttered to herself as she watched the handsome cowboy move easily up her driveway just a few steps behind Adam.

Harmony and Havoc realized they had company about that time and went barreling through the screen door, their tails wagging with excitement. Neither of them barked like she anticipated, but then again, they were familiar with her brother.

It wasn't Adam she was worried about though. If they knew what was best for them, they would keep their distance from the cowboy who was now leaning over to pat them both on the head.

Again … *what the hell?*

∞ ∞ ∞ ∞ ∞

"That's Havoc, and that's Harmony," Adam stated as two oversized dogs rushed out the front door and right up to his legs as Cooper followed Adam up the path to the house.

The way their hind ends wagged furiously, Cooper didn't think he had anything to worry about, but he moved with caution anyway. They were some big animals.

Two seconds later, he was trying to balance on his haunches while the dogs licked at him furiously, both eager for him to put his hands on them. Cooper obliged them as he looked up at the old farmhouse in front of him.

He still didn't know why he was here — wherever *here* was — but after Adam had shown up at his motel room out of the blue, banging on the door and rousing him from an intensely erotic dream, Cooper figured he had nothing better to do.

After a quick breakfast at the congested café in town and a brief, rather uninformative conversation with Adam, Cooper wasn't sure what to expect. He'd felt as though he were being interrogated while he forced eggs and bacon down his throat, answering question after question from his buddy.

Do you plan to stay in Devil's Bend? Will you continue to tour? Are you looking for something else to do? Would you be interested in helping out at the bar? What do you think of managing musical talent?

Those were just a few of the questions Adam had thrown his way, and he wasn't sure whether they were trick questions or not, but apparently Adam seemed satisfied with his answers. That still didn't explain why they were here though.

Pushing back to his full height when Adam summoned the dogs with a whistle, Cooper looked up on the porch, and that was when he saw her.

The angel in blue jeans. Only she wasn't wearing jeans at the moment. *Holy hell.*

And he was pretty sure he liked her with fewer clothes on anyway. With a strained effort, he tried not to ogle her. And he had to focus to keep his mouth from hanging open.

He couldn't help but watch as Adam embraced the woman in a hug that said they knew each other. From the looks of it, they were fond of one another based on the way the woman stared up at him lovingly. Considering he hadn't talked much with Adam, aside from the barrage of questions that morning, Cooper's first assumption was they were more than mere friends.

"Cooper, meet Tessa. Tessa, meet Cooper. Blah, blah, blah. I need more coffee," Adam introduced in a rush as Cooper made his way up the front steps.

Tessa, as Adam referred to her, laughed sweetly, and Cooper couldn't help but smile. Removing his hat from his head, he held out his hand to the woman he'd dreamed about the night before and steeled himself to touch her again. Their hands met, her small, smooth fingers sliding into the palm of his hand, and Cooper had to clamp his teeth shut to keep from groaning.

Damn, he liked touching her.

A sudden strange, possessive instinct surged up in his gut, which was odd considering where they were. It wasn't a reaction he expected at all, but he tried to attribute it to the night before.

"Nice to meet you, ma'am," he finally said when he located his voice. Their hands touched for longer than was probably customary, but Cooper found he didn't want to pull away. "You too." Her sweet voice sent another chill racing through his bloodstream, only this time, it forced the blood farther south. As though it were natural, Cooper kept his cowboy hat resting in front of his now-interested cock in the hopes that she wouldn't notice.

When she pulled her hand away, Cooper let her go, but he allowed his eyes to linger for a while longer.

She was wearing a thin black tank top and a pair of tiny white shorts that put her trim, tanned legs on display. If he were acting like the gentleman that his parents had raised him to be, Cooper would've looked away, yet he found himself glancing down, his gaze slowly traveling upward, until his eyes narrowed in on the pebbled tips of her nipples that were now clearly visible through the soft, threadbare cotton of her top.

She must've realized what he was looking at because she quickly recovered, glaring up at him before crossing one arm over her chest and holding her coffee cup with the other. She must've realized that Adam wasn't there to save her, and her reaction made Cooper chuckle. It wasn't often that he saw something other than pure, unadulterated lust written all over a woman's face, especially the first time he was introduced to her. What he saw on Tessa's pretty face resembled anything but, which, ironically, he found he enjoyed immensely.

When she turned and walked into the house, Cooper followed, very aware of three things: the woman walking away from him, the intriguing sway of her hips and her cute little ass, and the man staring back at him from the doorway to what appeared to be the kitchen.

"I'm surprised the two of you didn't meet last night," Adam said between sips of his coffee.

"How do you know we didn't?" Tessa asked, sounding oddly irritated.

"Coop said he didn't meet my sister," Adam admitted, turning to follow Tessa into the kitchen.

Sister.

A sudden, not to mention overwhelming, river of relief flooded Cooper. This intriguing woman was Adam Dryden's sister. They looked absolutely nothing alike.

"So what brings you by so early in the morning?" Tessa asked Adam, seemingly oblivious to Cooper standing just a few feet away.

Early? Morning? Shit, it was after noon already.

"Why don't you offer our guest some coffee, sis?" Adam smirked before walking out of the room, leaving the two of them alone once again.

For some reason, Cooper was beginning to get the impression that Adam was doing that on purpose.

CHAPTER FOUR

Remembering her manners became more and more difficult as the minutes passed. Ever since Cooper Krenshaw had shaken her hand, then blatantly leered at her body, Tessa had been in some strange state of shock. Then again, the guy was probably used to getting any woman he wanted, so the come-hither look he'd perfected probably got him pretty far in life.

Too bad for him, she wasn't interested.

Damn it.

She was *so* interested her body was doing crazy things.

Her hormones were out of whack, her blood was churning in her veins, and her head was spinning from the intoxicating scent of the man. And yes, he smelled even better today than he had last night. That could've been because they were lacking the nauseating mixture of various other perfumes, colognes, and the pungent smell of beer. Or it could be because Cooper Krenshaw smelled like hot, virile male.

Either way, Tessa continued to remind herself that she wasn't interested. She wasn't interested in one-night stands. Wasn't interested in a week-long affair. Wasn't even interested in a brief romance, because ultimately, in the end, Cooper Krenshaw would be moving on to bigger and better things.

Above all else, Tessa had no desire to spend time with a man she couldn't keep, nor did she have any interest in what came with country music stardom.

And why the hell did she keep referring to him as Cooper Krenshaw? The man had a first name, and she was pretty sure he didn't go by both first and last. Or maybe he did. Hell, what did she know?

Shit.

At the moment, she didn't know anything. Her brain was a tangle of lust and hormones, and she was quickly becoming exceedingly irritated with herself. Sort of like her frustration with the women in her bar when they threw themselves at the nightly entertainment, well known or not.

"Would you like some coffee?" Tessa finally asked, trying to sound as though it were an afterthought to offer. She didn't want this man to drink her coffee. She didn't want him to sit on her couch. She didn't want him to steal her heart and...

Oh, what the hell was she thinking? *It's just coffee.*

"Yes, ma'am," he said in that dark, rich tone that made her pulse thump rapidly.

"No need to call me ma'am," she told him, not bothering to look up as she poured his coffee. He didn't answer, but she knew he'd heard her.

Without another thought, Tessa handed him the cup and turned to walk away, letting him know that the cream was in the refrigerator and sugar on the counter should he need it. The proximity was too much. She needed to get away, preferably outside where she could smell the sweet, lingering scent of the country and not the potent scent of Cooper Krenshaw.

Cooper, damn it. His name was Cooper. He was just a normal person like the rest of them. It didn't mean a thing that his voice was crooning all over radio stations worldwide or that his face was well known on the front cover of magazines. And it didn't matter that he'd won an award, or probably twenty, for his music.

A few minutes later, the three of them were sitting on the front porch, Adam perched on the wood railing, Tessa in the lone wicker chair, and Cooper on the porch swing. She much preferred the swing, but the possibility of him sitting beside her was a risk she hadn't been willing to take, so her choice of seating had been calculated for her self-preservation.

Now that they were all seated, no one was speaking. There was no rushing her brother, but Tessa sensed he wanted to talk. Not only because he had shown up at her house at an ungodly hour after a particularly long night but because he looked as though he had something on his mind. Rather than pelt him with questions, Tessa chose to focus her attention on Harmony and Havoc, who were once again frolicking in the yard like puppies.

"Coop's gonna buy Old Man Deluth's farm," Adam said out of the blue, and Tessa damn near spilled her coffee in her lap.

What the fuck?

"What do you mean, he's gonna buy it?"

"Just what I said," Adam answered, one eyebrow cocking as he looked back at her before his gaze transferred to Cooper.

That wasn't even possible. Cooper could not be buying the Deluth farm because Tessa was buying it. She'd been paying Old Man … er … Jerry Deluth for several years, a little at a time until she had enough for the down payment so she could take over the rest of the payments. It was an agreement they had made a very long time ago, before...

Before Jerry had passed away two months ago.

Tessa frowned as she peered at Cooper. She'd still been making the payments like clockwork.

Surely, Adam had to be wrong.

First of all, why would the famous country music star want to live in Devil's Bend? For some reason, that did not sound like a good idea, and Tessa knew it wasn't just because of her intense attraction to the man.

Hold up … that wasn't the point. Regardless.

"I wouldn't say it's much of a farm anymore," Cooper added, grinning at Adam. "Maybe one day, but right now, it's more of a shamble of a house and two hundred forty acres of weeds."

Tessa smiled despite herself at the way he enunciated the words, sounding very much like he was born and raised in the South. And definitely not from Texas. She wondered if he'd come by his drawl naturally or if it had been developed for his country music persona.

Realizing she wasn't supposed to be smiling, she forced her attention back to Adam. "When did this happen?"

"Talk to him," Adam told her. "He's the one buying the place."

"But…" Wait. No. Tessa was not going to mention the fact that she had a stake in that place. After all, she'd never told Adam that she was buying it for a reason. And thankfully her brother Jack had kept her secret as well. She wasn't looking for a handout, and she knew all too well that Adam would've tried to jump to her rescue, especially after Richie died.

35

There had to be a mistake, and as soon as she got the chance, she was going to call Luanne Deluth Rosenbough and talk to her.

"What do you plan to do with it?" Tessa asked, glancing Cooper's way briefly. Her throat felt tight, and her eyes stung from unshed tears, but she fought them back. She refused to get emotional until she had all the facts.

"It needs some work, and it'll probably take me some time to build it up, but ultimately I'd like to turn it into a fully functioning farm. As a side venture, I'm looking to build an equestrian center. I've always wanted to use horses to work with disabled children and adults."

Tessa knew her jaw was hanging open, knew she shouldn't stare at him as though he'd just admitted that his dream was the *exact same dream* she'd been chasing ever since she was a child, but she couldn't help it.

"Hey, that's funny. Tessa wanted to do that when she was a kid," Adam offered.

She *still* wanted it, but Adam didn't know that.

So if Adam hadn't said anything, then that left… Had Luanne told Cooper what Tessa was planning to do? Was this some kind of joke? Or payback?

Tessa had to force her jaw to relax when she realized she was grinding her teeth together.

"Really?" Cooper sounded as though he was hearing the news for the first time. Didn't mean she wasn't still suspicious of what his overall objective was. What were the odds that he'd come to Devil's Bend, bought the property she was in the process of buying, and planned to build the exact same thing? Something was off here.

"So, *what?*" Tessa realized she sounded frustrated. "You bring him all the way out here to tell me he wants to run a horse farm?"

Adam frowned down at her, and Tessa bit the inside of her cheek as she turned to stare out into the yard. Yes, it was somewhat of a sore spot that she spent her nights slinging beers in a bar, even if she owned said bar, while others were out making their dreams come true. She might not be able to make her dream come true overnight, but she was working on it.

"No, I brought Coop out here because I wanted to know what you thought of him handling the entertainment at The Rusty Nail."

Tessa stared up at Adam once again, confusion replacing the frustration from moments ago.

"You want him to sing in the bar every night?" Turning to face Cooper, she asked him, "And you'd want to do that? I thought you were a big country star."

Adam laughed, pulling her attention back to him. "No, I don't think Coop would be interested in becoming a permanent nightly fixture at The Rusty Nail. He, however, would be good for business."

"What are you talking about? You handle the entertainment. Why would we need him?" Tessa stared at her brother, trying to comprehend what he was telling her. Or rather, what he *wasn't* telling her. She knew there was something, but for the life of her, she couldn't put it together. The look on his face told her she wasn't going to be happy with his news.

"I'm going into the police academy." Adam's calm tone sounded as though he were trying to soothe her, which meant...

And then his words registered.

Police academy.

Tessa's heart stopped beating in her chest and she felt faint. Somehow, although her body was hardly cooperating, she managed to put her coffee cup on the railing beside her, because she wasn't interested in wearing what was left in it. Staring up at Adam, she couldn't get a single word out of her mouth.

"Tessa..." Adam began, sounding as though he were going to start explaining.

"Don't," she demanded harshly. "Don't. I... I don't even know what to say."

Pushing to her feet, Tessa forced her legs to move, forced herself to go inside before she lost every ounce of her decorum right there on her front porch in front of God and everyone.

And Cooper Krenshaw.

∞ ∞ ∞ ∞ ∞

So maybe Cooper wasn't the smartest man on the planet, but he knew immediately that what Adam had just announced to his sister was not a good thing. As for why, he had no idea.

"Shit," Adam said, pulling his ball cap down low on his head before taking it off altogether and turning to face the yard.

"I'm going to take a wild guess on this one, but I don't think she took that well." Cooper's statement was met with silence, and he allowed it to settle around them for a few minutes.

Not only was he uncomfortable being there, Cooper was confused as to *why* he was there, and the answers didn't appear to be forthcoming. Had Adam thought that bringing him along would lessen the sting of that blow? If he had, it damn sure hadn't worked.

"Richie died in the line of duty," Adam explained, although Cooper had no idea who Richie was. Not knowing what he was supposed to say to that, Cooper kept his mouth shut.

"Richie was her husband," Adam finally explained long seconds later.

Oh, shit. Well, that explained it all too well. Adam had just informed his sister that he was going to do the exact thing that'd gotten her husband killed? *Shit.*

Cooper wanted to ask Adam why he'd thought it was a good idea to do this. Or better yet, why Adam had thought it was a nifty idea to bring Cooper along when he announced his intentions? How in the hell had he gotten caught in the middle?

"I need to talk to her," Adam stated, but he didn't move from where he stood.

That would probably be a smart idea, Cooper thought to himself. It was a good thing that the filter was back in place, because he knew for sure that he shouldn't get in the middle of this any more than he already was.

Adam suddenly turned and faced Cooper, a pained look on his face. Pulling his ball cap back on, Adam said, "I've wanted to do this my whole life. I was actually going to go into the academy with Richie, but when my stepfather got sick, I decided not to go."

Cooper knew that Adam's stepfather had been sick several years back, but he wasn't aware that his illness had derailed Adam's future. Nor had he been aware that Adam had a brother-in-law. He'd known Adam had a brother and a sister, both younger, known he had grown up in a small town and that he wasn't close to either of his parents. The distance over these last few years hadn't kept them as close as they had been during those two semesters that they'd roomed together in college.

That was probably mostly Cooper's fault, because when he'd ventured into the music industry full time, he'd essentially left most of his friends behind. He and Adam talked from time to time, at least once every three or four months, but obviously not enough that Adam felt close enough to share those personal parts of his life. On top of that, Cooper knew Adam well enough to know the man didn't share much of himself with anyone.

"Do you think she'll ever be okay with it?" Adam asked, and Cooper merely stared back at him. How would he know? Cooper had never known the type of loss that Tessa had obviously experienced, but he couldn't imagine it would be easy to deal with.

A second later, the screen door opened, and Tessa joined them on the porch, her eyes red and puffy from crying. Cooper had a sudden need to go to her, to pull her against him and shield her from all of the pains of the world.

He kept his ass planted on the porch swing.

"How about I go take a walk?" Cooper offered when neither sibling spoke.

"No," Tessa whispered. "Please stay. I'm sorry for…"

When it looked like she was going to cry again, Adam moved toward her and pulled her against his chest, holding her close. "I'm sorry, sis. I know how hard this is for you, but I need to do this."

The silence returned for a few minutes, and Cooper was beginning to feel even more uncomfortable sitting there. He was an outsider looking in, and he felt as though he hadn't been invited to witness what was transpiring between the siblings.

When Tessa spoke, Cooper immediately looked away.

"I know you need to do this," she sobbed against Adam's chest. "This has been your dream. I get it."

When Tessa pulled back, the movement caught his attention, and Cooper glanced over, noticing the tears once again streaming down her pale cheeks as she continued. "I wouldn't want to get in the way of that. Doesn't mean I won't be scared every minute of every day."

Adam sighed and pulled her back against him, leaving Cooper once again sitting on the porch swing feeling like a third wheel who clearly shouldn't be there.

"When are you going?" she asked, taking a step back and staring at Adam, her hands scrubbing away the wet streaks on her face.

God, the woman did something to him. There was just something about her that made Cooper want to grab her up and ease some of her pain. Even when her eyes were swollen and her nose was red from crying, Tessa Donovan managed to steal his breath.

Forcing himself to look away, he stared out into the yard, watching the dogs napping in the shade of an enormous oak tree as he listened to the conversation.

"The next class starts next week. I've been accepted, so I don't want to wait," Adam informed her but then paused.

"What aren't you telling me?" Tessa asked.

Unable to not look, Cooper glanced over at Adam again. The man appeared as though he had some more unpleasant news to give Tessa, and Cooper wished that the damn porch would open up and swallow him whole. He did not want to be there for any more unpleasant news. Hell, he didn't think he should've been there for any part of it at all.

Adam smiled sadly as he looked down at his sister. "I'm going to Dallas."

"What? Why? Why not Austin?" Tessa questioned him, her eyes wide.

Okay, so Cooper could guess at this one. Austin was obviously closer to Devil's Bend than Dallas. Like, thirty minutes, as opposed to three hours.

"Austin doesn't have any openings for a while. I'm ready to do this, Tessa," Adam said, taking her hands as he shifted on his feet. "When and if I make it through the academy, they'll hire me on. At that point, I've got to give it a couple of years, but then I promise, I'll be back."

"First of all, there is no *if.*" Even as Tessa spoke, Cooper could see the tears reforming in her eyes, but somehow she managed to hold them back. "I'll miss you."

"I know you will. Which is why I want Coop here to help you out at the bar. He'll be here permanently, and I know him; he'll get bored."

Bored?

Cooper noticed that Tessa didn't look his way. Not that he expected her to. If she had, she might've seen the surprise on his face. At least he understood the reason behind the random questions Adam had fired off earlier at breakfast.

Cooper contemplated what Adam was saying, and he fought the urge to smile. He wasn't so sure he'd ever get bored with all the work that would have to be done on the house he was in the process of buying, but he got the impression Adam knew that. Instead of interjecting, Cooper sat quietly, continuing to watch the exchange between Tessa and Adam.

There was a series of emotions that played across her extremely expressive features, but Tessa didn't say another word to Adam. She stood there, her arms crossed over her chest as she regarded her brother for long moments. Cooper wished he knew what was going on in that pretty head of hers.

"So, when do you plan to start?"

Realizing the question was directed at him and that he'd been busted while he was mentally noting every detail of her sweet, lithe body, Cooper glanced up to see Tessa studying him.

"When do you *want* me to start?" he asked.

He had to admit, it felt a little strange to be accepting a job offer of this sort, especially when his regular life in Nashville was still up in the air. But it didn't mean he wasn't looking forward to it.

Whether or not he would admit it to anyone directly, Cooper wasn't just looking for a place to start over. He was looking for something that was missing from his life. Recent events had changed his course, and he needed something more than what he was currently getting. According to Marcus, happiness came with a price, but it seemed like the more he paid, the less he got.

Stardom had its downsides, and one of them was the loneliness that came along with it. He wasn't referring to the women necessarily either. They were a dime a dozen, but that novelty had worn off years ago. No, Cooper was referring to the interaction with other people on a much more intimate level. Unless he was with his parents, Cooper rarely spent time with anyone who actually knew him. And that included his manager, who seemed to think he knew what was best for him, despite Cooper's frequent disagreements.

"How about tonight?" she asked, glancing back and forth between him and her brother. She was obviously changing the subject, and Cooper was grateful for that.

"Tonight's good." He was in the process of buying the Deluth farm, which meant he had some time to kill before he could actually move in and get started. Working at the bar would help him to get familiar with the people in town, as well as give him something to do with his spare time. And the bonus was that Cooper now had an excuse to spend more time with Tessa.

"It's settled then." Adam's smile looked both satisfied and concerned, but Cooper didn't say anything more.

There would apparently be plenty of time to figure out how this was supposed to work.

CHAPTER FIVE

Cooper wasn't sure what Adam's idea of settled was, but clearly it wasn't the same as his, that was for damn sure.

Several hours later, he was sitting on a stool in The Rusty Nail, doing absolutely nothing except talking to anyone who approached him. When he had asked Tessa what it was that he could do to help out, she'd flat-out told him to do what he did best. When he'd simply stared at her, she had followed it up by telling him to find a chair and look pretty.

He'd laughed it off at first. Until he'd realized she was serious.

The bar was slowly filling up, although he noticed they didn't have quite the impressive turnout as the night before. There wasn't an act on stage, but Cooper's mind was whirling with possibilities. If he was going to be in charge of the entertainment, he was going to ensure that every Friday and Saturday night had live music. Why the hell shouldn't they have someone on stage drawing in the crowds? There was plenty of new talent who would love the opportunity to play in front of these people. And he had a few friends who would surely get a kick out of playing in the small-town bar.

To his surprise, he'd found out that The Rusty Nail was only open Thursday, Friday, Saturday, and Monday nights. When he asked Adam for the reason, he was told that they didn't bring in enough business during the week. Devil's Bend was a small town, and it was saying something that they managed to draw in a lot of their patrons from the bigger neighboring towns. Based on Adam's explanation, Tessa liked the part-time schedule.

"Hey, handsome." A sultry voice sounded from behind him, and Cooper turned to see a tall, willowy brunette standing within just a few inches of him.

Cooper smiled at her, giving her a slow once-over. Before she said another word, he was already predicting how this conversation would go. Had he been just a random cowboy in a bar, he'd at least have the pleasure of going through the preliminaries with a woman, but he doubted this conversation was going to go that way.

When the brunette's hand quickly trailed up his thigh, he couldn't hide his grin. Too easy.

"What do ya say we get outta here for a while?" she asked, batting her fake eyelashes and letting her hand wander freely as though he'd actually invited her to touch him.

"Why would I want to do that, ma'am? I just got here." Considering he had nothing else to do, he figured he might as well indulge her for a few minutes. After all, he didn't want to be rude. He just wasn't interested.

It wasn't that the woman wasn't pretty. She was. But based on her wandering hand, he could tell there was another man who thought so too, if her wedding band was anything to go by.

She giggled, and Cooper fought the urge to roll his eyes.

"But I think I could find us a place a little more private, if you know what I mean."

What? No dinner and drinks? No candlelight and romance? A night out at the movies? Shit, Cooper knew chivalry wasn't dead, but based on some of the come-on lines he got, he was beginning to wonder whether courting a woman was even necessary anymore.

"I'm not sure I do," he told her.

The crease in her forehead told him that she wasn't used to rejection, but Cooper had no intention of going home with any woman he met. Not tonight or otherwise. He'd spent the better part of the last decade doing exactly that, and look where it'd gotten him. Right here on this barstool with another random woman looking for a quick hookup.

"Lacey, you know your husband's gonna be here soon. He ain't gonna be too happy that you're on the prowl, and I'm not looking for another altercation tonight."

Saved by the bartender.

Cooper noticed Eric watching the woman with the wandering hand carefully from across the bar top. The look on his face said he wasn't at all impressed with whatever she was up to. It didn't take long for her to get the hint, and Cooper watched as she marched away, putting a little sway in her backside as she did.

"Thanks." Cooper turned back to face the bar, grabbing the beer Eric placed there.

"No problem. You'll want to watch out for that one."

Cooper didn't need the warning, but he tipped his hat at Eric anyway.

"So, I figured there'd be paparazzi chasing you down by now," Eric said, leaning his forearms on the bar.

"Let's just say I'm MIA at the moment." Cooper hadn't even told his manager where he was going when he'd disappeared. His phone was currently turned off for the simple reason that he didn't feel like explaining himself. And because he was pretty sure Marcus had outfitted it with GPS.

When he'd woken up that morning, shortly after he'd told Adam he'd meet him at the café in half an hour, he had made a half-assed attempt at checking his voice mails, but Marcus's messages quickly became repetitive — he was ruining his career, he was walking away from fame and fortune, he couldn't be serious — so he had deleted them all and hadn't thought about them again until now.

"Well, considering the word is out that you were here last night, I figure it won't be long before the country is aware of where you are. I can only assume it ain't gonna be pretty."

No, it probably wasn't, but for the time being, no one would know that he was staying in Devil's Bend, just that he had been seen there. Not that he actually gave a shit. The only thing he wanted to do was sit right on his bar stool and look at the cute bartender who was doing her damnedest to avoid him at all costs. Cooper found it amusing that she barely spoke to him, although he was almost certain he had caught her sneaking a peek a time or two.

"You're not being hounded by the locals either?" Eric asked, obviously trying to make conversation.

Grinning, Cooper glanced over at Tessa, then back at Eric. "Not much, no. I signed a couple of autographs this morning at the café down the road, but for the most part, they kept their distance."

"Interesting," Eric said as though contemplating what that meant.

Cooper knew it meant that either people didn't recognize him or, being this was a small town, they were just used to keeping to themselves. He let his gaze stray down the bar to land on Tessa, who was watching him. When their eyes met, she instantly turned to face Eric.

"I'm gonna take a break," Tessa said, not looking back at him.

Cooper kept his gaze trained on her as she moved out from behind the bar, then he followed the sensual sway of her hips with his eyes as she moved toward the hallway at the back. He thought about giving her some space … for all of about fifteen seconds.

Not wanting to miss the opportunity to talk to her, he informed Eric that he would be back and headed in the same direction she had. He wasn't sure whether she had disappeared into the restroom or out through the exit door, so he opted to check the latter. He was interested in talking to her, but following her into the bathroom was pushing it a bit too far. A quick peek out the door told him that his luck hadn't run out on him yet.

"Hey," he greeted, closing the door behind him quietly so as not to alert anyone inside that someone had gone out.

Tessa looked somewhat startled, but she quickly masked her expression, her eyes darting away. When she didn't say anything, he moved closer, standing directly in front of where she was leaning, one booted foot flat against the wall. She still didn't look at him.

"Hey, you okay?" he asked, tipping her chin until she had no choice but to look him in the eyes. Surprisingly, she didn't pull away as he expected.

Her soft green gaze met his, and Cooper's heart squeezed in his chest when he realized there were tears in her eyes.

"What's wrong?" Not that he expected her to talk to him, but he couldn't very well leave her out here when she appeared so upset. She probably wanted him to, but Cooper wasn't built that way. If she asked him to go, he'd go. Until then, she was stuck with him.

"Nothing," she said with a forced smile.

So she clearly wasn't going to open up. Then again, why would she? She didn't know him. Still, he made it his mission to try and remove those tears that were threatening to fall.

"Ahhh, I get it," he said, forcing himself to sound serious.

"You get *what?*" Those brilliant sea-green eyes fixed on his, and her curiosity got the best of her.

"If you're worried about that ol' married gal inside, you don't have to."

That made her laugh at least.

"Trust me, I'm not worried about Lacey. She's been around the block more times than a school bus. I'd warn you away from her, but who you spend your time with isn't any of my business."

"What if I want it to be?" The question came out before he gave the words permission to escape.

"Well, don't." Clearly a warning.

Cooper still had his finger and thumb on her chin, and he wondered if she even noticed. He damn sure did. Where his fingertips touched her skin, a flash of heat sparked just beneath the surface.

"Why not?"

Tessa pulled away from him then, pushing off the wall and putting distance between them. Cooper didn't move away, but he didn't move toward her either.

"Because I'm not interested in a fly-by-night fling."

"Fly-by-night? Who said I was going anywhere?"

"That's what you famous types do, ain't it? You're just around until the next big break," she answered, looking away.

Cooper wondered whether she actually knew this from experience or if she was simply assuming. Knowing that she probably had met her fair share of country music up-and-comers, he couldn't help but wonder if she'd encountered that in the past. He knew she had been married, but years had gone by since her husband had passed away, so it was possible. By the way she tried to keep herself emotionally distanced from those around her, at least as far as he could tell, he couldn't determine for sure.

"What if I told you I was here to stay? What would you say then?"

"I'd say have a great life."

All of the emotion he'd witnessed earlier was long gone now. There were no signs of the heat he'd seen in her eyes when they'd been standing in her kitchen either. No, this woman had clearly made up her mind that she wasn't going to give him the time of day.

Good thing for him, he loved a challenge. Now he just needed a plan.

♥ ♥ ♥ ♥ ♥

Tessa was doing her best to pretend she wasn't affected by Cooper. Ever since he'd walked outside, she had been painfully aware of his presence. When he'd touched her, she'd half expected her knees to buckle, leaving her a puddle of lusty goo on the concrete at his feet.

Except she was still pissed at him. It didn't help that she hadn't been able to talk to Luanne, but Tessa fully intended to as soon as she could. She wasn't sure what was going on, but she had made a pact with herself that she would not jump to conclusions until she had all the information. Yes, that was new for her, but she was willing to give it a shot.

For now.

Between the news that Adam was going to Dallas for the police academy, Cooper Krenshaw might've actually stolen her land right out from underneath her, and to top it all off, she seemed to have some strange attraction to the man, she had plenty to worry about all in her own head.

Truthfully, she had snuck outside to have a few minutes by herself. Away from Cooper specifically. Even tonight seemed odd, and she knew Adam wasn't gone yet, but picturing Cooper taking her brother's place for the last hour didn't make it any easier to accept that Adam was about to leave. For the academy.

Police officer.

The idea made her heart ache again, the loss of her husband feeling like a fresh wound in her chest just thinking about it. Through the years, the pain had lessened, the mourning had gotten easier, but she still missed him.

She didn't want to cry, but she had found herself close to it when Cooper had joined her. Part of her was thankful for the distraction because the last thing she wanted anyone to see was her weakness. Especially not this famous superstar who would likely be hightailing it out of town next week after realizing what it meant to work a real job. Hell, running a bar wasn't easy.

And then the man had the audacity to think that she would be jealous of a woman hitting on him. Not in this lifetime. If he wanted to go home with Lacey, or any other floozy in the bar, that was his prerogative. As for her, she didn't have the time or the energy to spend on a relationship, even if it were a one-night stand.

She could tell by the look in Cooper's shockingly golden-brown eyes that he was gearing up for some sort of challenge. Tessa had no intention of explaining why she wasn't willing to get caught up with the likes of him. Been there. Done that. Got the T-shirt and burned it. Not doing it again. That was the point in her life when she'd realized she would never find a man who could replace Richie. Never.

"I'll see you inside," she told him, abruptly turning to the door and hoping like hell he wouldn't move closer. As strong as she was, for some reason, Tessa wasn't able to resist this man when he was close because her damn hormones went on strike.

"Hey," he called out before her hand made it to the doorknob.

Squeezing her eyes shut, Tessa inhaled slowly. Held it. This was not going to go well; she could feel it.

Before she could turn around, she felt the heat of Cooper at her back. When his strong hands came down on her shoulders, she fought the urge to melt into him, to soak up some of his strength at a time when she so desperately needed it. Against her will, she turned around slowly and nearly lost the tears she fought to hold back when he pulled her flush against him and held her close.

His arms were strong and warm, his heartbeat a soothing anchor in the turmoil that had become her life. And damn it all to hell, he smelled fantastic. Pressing her cheek against his chest, she gave in to him momentarily. She could've tried to come up with excuses as to why she was willingly letting Cooper hold her, but she knew they'd all be a lie. She wanted him to. That was the simple truth.

She had no idea how much time had passed, but the next thing she knew, Cooper was pulling back slightly, his hands cupping her face as he tilted her head back. He stared down into her eyes for what felt like an interminably long time, and she held her breath, aching for this man to give her something more. Something that she needed but wasn't willing to ask for.

"I want to kiss you," he whispered.

Tessa's heart pounded painfully against her chest. She didn't turn away, but she didn't give him permission either. The smart thing for her to do would be to turn and walk away. Hell, maybe even run. He was a man who had walked into her life and uprooted it in ways she'd never imagined. This attraction she had for him was only part of it.

"If I kiss you, Tessa, I won't be able to stop," he warned, but she found her gaze straying to his lips.

Please, please, please, let him kiss me.

Oh, hell. What was she saying? She didn't want… Before she could finish the thought, Cooper's velvet-soft lips were on hers, and her breath escaped her in a rush.

He was gentle yet firm, his big, warm hands tilting her head slowly as he seemed to be monitoring her reaction. Her body relaxed instantly, and she knew he felt it too because as soon as a sigh escaped her, his hands moved down lower, pulling her body against his. When his tongue slid slowly over her lips, Tessa found herself opening for his kiss.

And the fireworks that exploded behind her closed eyelids nearly knocked her off her feet, a blinding collision of colors melding together. Kissing him was like coming home for the first time in years. The comfort and familiarity were there, although this man was no more than a stranger to her. But something in him had connected with something in her.

The low rumble that echoed in his chest only added fuel to the fire, and Tessa found her arms were sliding up over his chest to wrap around his neck and pull him closer. His Stetson was nearly knocked off when she latched her fingers into the silky hair at the nape of his neck.

As far as kisses went, this one was the equivalent of an unpredicted hurricane, sweeping over her and knocking her sideways, leveling everything she held near and dear.

Sweet mercy, the guy could kiss.

Minutes passed before either of them attempted to come up for air, and by the time they did, Tessa was practically trying to climb his body. She was both embarrassed and shocked at her behavior, but when she tried to pull away from him, Cooper's arms locked around her.

"Don't run from me, please," he whispered, his voice so rich and sultry she let the tone settle her nerves.

Momentarily.

Their eyes met, and Tessa fought the urge to cry again. What the hell was wrong with her? She wasn't supposed to be kissing this man. He'd never be able to give her what she needed — no one could — and she had no desire to give in long enough to find out for herself.

"I can't do this," she said firmly, forcing him to release her. "Please. I just can't."

Without looking back, Tessa fled back inside her bar, sneaking into the relative safety of the bathroom. It was the only place she would possibly find solitude for long enough to get herself under control. And she desperately needed to.

By the time the night was over, Tessa had managed to successfully evade Cooper at every turn. She had to admit, when he'd gone up on stage and surprised the customers with a thirty-minute set, she had been enthralled. Again, this man had a voice that captivated her. Not that she would let him know that.

The few times she'd caught him looking her way, Tessa managed to pretend she didn't see him. She was just having one problem with that. She did see him. Everywhere. Even when he wasn't near her, she saw him. That kiss had rocked her world, and she feared she would never be able to forget it, no matter how hard she tried.

"Can I walk you out?" Cooper's deep, panty-melting drawl oozed over her as she wiped down the last of the glasses and put them in their place beneath the bar.

"I'll be here for a while. Thanks though." That was a monumental lie, but there was no way she wanted him to walk her out.

In fact, she wanted to pretend she didn't know him. She hadn't had this kind of reaction to any man in a very long time, and she continued to remind herself that she shouldn't be having a reaction to him. It had to be because he was famous. Maybe she was star struck.

No. No, that definitely wasn't it. Tessa didn't get star struck. She had learned no matter how big or how small their stardom reached, their egos exceeded that tenfold. If there was a possibility of her ever settling down again, it undoubtedly wouldn't be with the likes of Cooper Krenshaw.

"I'll wait."

Tessa flinched from the sound of his voice. He was much closer than he had been, and she hadn't realized he'd snuck up on her.

"How much longer you got? Can I help?"

Good Lord. Could the guy just take a hint? Why did he have to be the perfect gentleman?

"I'm not going to sleep with you." Tessa slapped her hand over her mouth as she turned to look at him, her eyes wide with horror because her thoughts had just tumbled right out of her mouth.

His chuckle reverberated through every molecule in her body, and Tessa found she liked that too.

"Well, I'm sorry to hear that. It's a good thing I wasn't asking, or you might've bruised my ego a little bit."

She couldn't help but smile at his reaction to her verbal blunder.

"I'd still like to walk you out. I promise it doesn't require either of us to get horizontal."

His words produced a vivid image in her mind, and it had nothing to do with them being horizontal and everything to do with her plastered against the wall while this big, sexy cowboy was pressed between her thighs.

Damn. It was definitely time to go home. Alone.

Figuring she wasn't going to be able to talk her way out of it, Tessa finished up the last glass and then removed her apron, tossing it beneath the bar. At least she'd have tomorrow off, which meant she would be able to officially get Cooper out of her system.

CHAPTER SIX

"Come in, Tessa," Luanne Deluth said in a curiously fake accent when Tessa arrived at her house on Sunday afternoon.

It was a fact that Luanne was born and raised in Devil's Bend; however, somewhere along the way, she'd adopted some variation of a northern accent. She sounded awkward and confused because she was dropping her *r*'s as well as mixing in a few *y'all*s. Tessa wasn't sure how her husband even understood what she was trying to say.

Ignoring the need to tell her to remember her roots, Tessa simply walked into the house, letting the screen door slam behind her as though it were an accident. It had taken some pleading, but Luanne had finally relented and agreed to meet with her. If that weren't a sign that something was going on, Tessa didn't know what was.

"Thanks," she said, matching the saccharine sweetness in Luanne's tone although she honestly wanted to grab the woman by the hair and ask her what the hell was going on.

It wasn't a secret that Tessa and Luanne didn't get along well. They had grown up together, graduated in the same class, but for whatever reason, as of their freshman year of high school, their friendship had turned to loathing. For various reasons, Tessa had always made a point to stay out of Luanne's way.

"Have a seat. Can I get you something to drink?"

"No, thanks," Tessa replied, lowering herself onto the pretentious little couch in the awkwardly designed living room. She had to admit, the place looked like it was straight out of a magazine and equally homey too. She had to wonder whether Luanne had removed plastic covers from the furniture before Tessa's arrival. Probably not. Knowing Luanne, she would've left them on because she wouldn't want Tessa to touch her things.

"What can I help you with?" Luanne asked, primly lowering herself into an ugly side chair and crossing her legs like a debutante on display. Damn, this woman was absolutely nothing like her father, nor was she anything remotely close to how Tessa remembered her either. They hadn't spoken to each other in years, not since Luanne had married Jacob Matthew Rosenbough *the Third* about five years prior.

"I wanted to talk to you about your dad's farm," Tessa stated, figuring she might as well get right down to business. No sense beating around the bush when Tessa would much prefer getting the hell out of Dodge as soon as possible.

"In case you haven't noticed, the farm belongs to me now."

Oh, she'd noticed all right. Biting her tongue to keep from being sarcastic, Tessa forced a smile. "I'm sorry, I meant *your* farm."

Luanne nodded, her perfectly coifed hair never budging an inch. She must've used plaster to keep that thing in place.

Shaking her head to regain her focus, grateful that her own hair actually moved, Tessa continued. "I was wondering whether you'd received my last payment."

After some research, Tessa had found out that her last two checks hadn't been cashed, which meant either Luanne hadn't received them or she purposely hadn't cashed them for whatever reason. Based on the fact that Cooper Krenshaw believed he was about to become the new owner of the Deluth land, she had to assume the latter was the case.

"What in heaven's name are you talking about?" Luanne asked, her real accent coming out in spades. That was an easy tell. When the woman was lying, she obviously had a hard time keeping up the rich socialite front. That and the way Luanne's jaw ticked, a clear sign the woman was hiding something.

Figuring it wasn't in her best interest to get defensive, she decided to explain the situation. "Your father and I had an agreement," Tessa began. "I've been paying him every month for the last several years until I could come up with the entire down payment on his land. At that point, I was going to take possession of the house and continue paying him the agreed-upon price."

Luanne cocked an eyebrow, but Tessa could tell that the confused look was for her benefit. "I'm sorry, Tessa. I don't know about any agreement that my father made. He wasn't very good about keeping records," she said snidely, "and when he passed away, everything was willed to me."

Tessa clamped her jaw shut, breathing in through her nose and trying to rein in her temper. This was not going to go well if she lost it. Instead of arguing, she waited for Luanne to continue.

"And besides the fact that my father was much too generous with you over the years, I've actually sold the land to a really nice man who was willing to pay a much more reasonable price." Luanne smiled greedily. "I'm sure you've met him."

Wait. More reasonable than what? If Luanne didn't know about the agreement, how would she know what was considered *more* reasonable?

To Tessa's surprise, Luanne didn't actually elaborate on whom she'd sold the land to. Because Cooper was famous, she figured Luanne would be all about bragging around town. But Tessa didn't need Luanne to give her the details; she already knew.

"I'm confused," Tessa said, pretending Luanne hadn't out-and-out lied about the agreement between Tessa and Luanne's father that she'd initially claimed she didn't know about. "I've got an agreement."

"And that agreement is null and void now that my father passed away. If I'd had my way, he never would've made a deal with you in the first place."

Well, the truth was out at least. Not that it made her feel any better. Tessa clenched her hands at her sides, but she didn't move. "So, where's my money?"

"Oh, honey, don't you worry your pretty little head. I don't need your money. You'll get back every penny."

So Luanne did know about the money. Did the woman not realize she was revealing her lie? Or maybe she did it so often that she didn't even notice.

But despite Luanne's lies and her deceit, Tessa didn't want her money back. She wanted the land. She had plans for that land, and she was almost in a position to make her dreams come true. What was she supposed to do now?

"Since I was able to sell the land for almost twice as much as what my father was going to sell it to you for, I think it's safe to say your offer no longer holds my interest. Unless, of course, you'd like to make another offer. But keep in mind, the person who is purchasing is willing to pay cash. Up front."

Tessa felt defeated. It wouldn't matter at this point what she did or said. She couldn't even afford a lawyer to fight Luanne. If Cooper was willing to pay twice what Tessa had agreed to, she would never be able to afford it. Not to mention, she hadn't even been able to come up with the down payment in cash, much less the full asking price.

Realizing she was beating a dead horse and she was only going to get herself worked up, Tessa decided enough was enough. Her temper was hovering on the brink of explosive, and the last thing she wanted was for Luanne to see how defeated she felt.

Standing, Tessa headed toward the door without saying another word. It was that or she was going to scratch the woman's eyeballs out. Her emotions were churning like a violent, straight-line wind, and any minute, it was going to start swirling, taking out everything in her path.

Fifteen minutes later, Tessa was pulling into Charlie's Restaurant. After leaving Luanne's, she'd called Jack and asked him to meet her. She wasn't sure why she needed to talk to her younger brother, but she knew, if anyone could, he'd be able to put this entire situation in perspective. She couldn't call Adam because he had no idea that she had even been trying to buy the land, and she didn't want to put him in the middle. Since Cooper was his friend and the man who was buying the Deluth farm, she felt as though he might not understand.

"Hey, sis," Jack greeted as he approached the table she was sitting at. "Uh-oh, what the hell happened?"

Tessa loved her baby brother. He was actually more protective of her than Adam, and that was saying something. She watched as he eased down into the booth across from her, his muscular body folding into the seat awkwardly. There was a reason he'd garnered the nickname "Tiny" in high school. Of course, she didn't dare call him that because Jack had always hated that name, but at six foot six inches, he wasn't necessarily small.

"Did you know that Luanne was selling her father's land to Cooper Krenshaw?" she asked, forgoing any pleasantries.

Jack's eyebrows shot downward as he stared back at her. "What? I thought you were buying the land."

Tessa had told Jack about the situation a couple of years before when she'd wanted to rent the house she was currently living in, which happened to belong to Jack. He'd grown up in the house, and when his father had met their mother, they'd bought a bigger place just on the other side of town. After Jack had graduated from high school, his father had given him the house, but for reasons Jack wasn't willing to talk about, he'd never moved back there.

So when Tessa had needed a place to stay, she'd felt compelled to explain why she wasn't looking to buy a house at the time, and since they'd all been so worried about her because of Richie's death, she had told Jack everything.

"Well, it looks like that isn't the case," she whispered, fighting the urge to cry.

"What about the money you paid him?" Jack asked, his voice lethally low.

"Oh, Luanne assured me I'd get it back. Said she was getting twice as much as Mr. Deluth was willing to sell it to me for."

Tessa had been close to Jerry Deluth, helping him out for years when he needed it. After all, he had been the reason her entire life had taken a radical shift in course when she was a teenager, so she'd felt as though she'd owed him. Because they'd spent so much time together, Tessa figured he'd been inclined to make her such a good deal. Now that he had passed on, she knew there was nothing she could do about it.

"Have you talked to Cooper? Does he know?"

Tessa hesitated, staring over at her brother. "No, I don't want him to know."

"Why the hell not? Maybe he'll back out and you can still get it," Jack argued.

"First of all, Cooper plans to open an equestrian center."

"Are you fucking serious? Did Adam tell him about your plans?"

"Not that I can tell, no. After talking to Luanne, I didn't get that she did either, but I don't know for sure."

"Don't you find it strange, Tess?"

Yes, she did. She thought it was more than a little coincidental that Cooper had descended on their small town with the same end goal as her. She didn't answer; she just shrugged.

"Hey, Tess. Jack. What can I get you two?" Miranda Wynter asked when she approached the table.

Tessa forced a smile, hoping her friend wouldn't notice that something was wrong. Miranda spent her days waitressing at Charlie's, and on Thursday and Monday, and sometimes extremely busy weekend nights, she helped out at the bar. It went without saying that the two of them were close, and Miranda would likely bombard her with questions if she thought Tessa needed someone to talk to.

"You hungry?" Tessa asked, turning to Jack.

"Was that rhetorical?" He laughed and then turned his signature grin at Miranda. "Have you ever known me not to be hungry?"

Miranda laughed, her eyes lingering on Jack for a surprisingly long time. Forgetting all of her worries momentarily, Tessa stared up at her friend. The woman she'd known since grade school looked like… She looked like she was crushing on Tessa's younger brother.

Oh, hell.

Jack didn't seem to notice, because he glanced between the two of them, gifting Miranda with the million-kilowatt smile before saying, "I'll take a cheeseburger and onion rings, if you don't mind."

"I'll have the same," Tessa added. "And two sweet teas."

"Sure thing." Miranda grinned as she jotted the information down on a well-worn notepad. "Be back in a minute."

"So, you're not gonna tell this guy that he's stealing your land?" Jack asked when Miranda walked away.

"I think she likes you," Tessa whispered, ignoring Jack's question.

True to form, Jack peered around the room, looking hopeful, but when his eyes met hers again, he just looked confused. "Who?"

"Miranda."

There was a dark cloud that appeared in Jack's midnight-blue eyes, but he quickly shifted it away. "I seriously doubt that."

Tessa tilted her head, studying her brother for a minute. She didn't think he would hide anything from her, but she had to wonder. Knowing that if she pressed him for details he would just shut down, she dropped the subject.

"Why don't you want to talk to Cooper?" Jack asked again, reminding Tessa why they were there in the first place.

"Technically that land wasn't mine. Yet. And I'm not sure what the point would be. It's not like he wouldn't buy it anyway."

"You don't know that."

Okay, so she honestly didn't know that, but for some reason, Tessa didn't want to interfere. Maybe that made her chicken or weak or whatever, but part of her held out hope. The simple fact that Cooper Krenshaw had the money to build an equestrian center, and he planned to work with disabled kids… How could she argue with that? It was her life's dream, and just because she was financially hindered didn't mean Cooper couldn't do the same thing she had planned, only sooner.

"So…" Jack started after a few seconds of silence, obviously realizing like a loyal brother should that she didn't have more to say.

And the way Jack was looking at her now, Tessa didn't need to be a mind reader to know where the conversation was headed. Not that she was finished talking about Cooper and the land, but she knew this subject was touchy. She could see the concern etched in Jack's ruggedly handsome features.

"Yes, I talked to Adam," she told her younger brother flatly, swallowing the golf-ball-sized lump that automatically sprung up any time she thought about what Adam was going to do.

"And you're okay with it?"

"It's not my decision," she explained sadly.

It really wasn't either. Yes, if she had her way, Adam wouldn't go anywhere near the police department, but that's because she was being selfish and didn't want anything to happen to him. There were plenty of families who felt the same way about those they loved in that line of work. She was sure they all prayed the same way she had, hoping that their loved one came home every single day.

The more she thought about it, the more the tears threatened, and Tessa was tired of crying. "He'll be a fantastic police officer," she told Jack. "I know this is what he's always wanted. I'll pray for him every single day, just like I did for Richie."

"What do you think about him going to Dallas?"

Before Tessa could answer, Miranda walked up to the table carrying their drinks. "Who's going to Dallas?"

"Adam," Jack explained. "He's been accepted into the Dallas Police Academy."

Miranda's cheerful demeanor took a drastic turn as she glanced back at Tessa. The only thing she could do was nod her head. Miranda had been right there with her when Richie had died, so the woman knew exactly how hard this was on her.

"Well, tell him that I wish him luck," Miranda said, and if Tessa wasn't mistaken, the words were said on a sob.

Losing Richie had been hard on everyone, including their friends. By the time Tessa was a junior in high school, they had all become a tight-knit group. Even though Richie and Eric were just a little older, they had still hung out even after they had graduated, spending their days and nights doing all the things foolish teenage kids did. Or rather, everyone had been trying to reel Tessa in.

Before Tessa could ask if Miranda was all right, the waitress darted toward the back of the restaurant, leaving Tessa and Jack staring after her.

"Do you need to go talk to her?" Jack asked, his head turned away as he watched Miranda disappear down the short hallway that led to the kitchen.

"I'll give her a little while." Miranda wouldn't welcome Tessa's questions right now. If there was anyone more closed off than Tessa, it was Miranda.

"Do they have something going between them?"

Tessa glanced at her brother as though he'd just lost his mind. Hadn't she just told him that Miranda was crushing on him? Was he really that dense? Figuring it wouldn't help matters to remind him, she just said, "Not that I know of."

"Well, speak of the devil…" Jack mumbled.

Tessa turned around, fully expecting to see Adam walking in the front door of the restaurant. Instead, she got an eyeful of intensely sexy cowboy as Cooper sauntered into the room, his hat in his hand as he made his way to the long counter, where a couple of others were seated. He didn't see her at first, so Tessa turned around abruptly, hoping he wouldn't notice she was there at all. She wasn't sure she could handle him at the moment, and she certainly didn't want Jack giving away anything they had been talking about.

"Don't worry," Jack whispered as he brought his glass to his mouth. "Your secret's safe with me."

"Tessa," Cooper greeted as he approached the table, startling her. "Jack."

"Hey, man. Join us," Jack offered, much too easily.

When he didn't budge in his seat, Tessa knew that she was going to have to slide over if Cooper was going to join them. Which meant she was going to have to sit very, very close to the man.

Please let him say no. Please let him say no. Please...

"Thanks. You mind?" Cooper asked Tessa, and the words set on repeat in her head died a slow, painful death.

"No, not at all," she mumbled, grabbing her tea glass and sliding toward the wall, allowing him enough space to join her in the booth.

Glancing down at her glass of tea, Tessa suddenly wished she had asked for something stronger. Like a bottle of tequila.

Or maybe two.

CHAPTER SEVEN

The last person Cooper expected to see when he walked into Charlie's Restaurant was Tessa. In fact, he'd just been thinking about her, so it was almost as though she had materialized right out of his thoughts. Not that he minded in the least. She was a sight for sore eyes, and being that he wouldn't get the pleasure of seeing her at The Rusty Nail because they were closed on Sunday, he welcomed the few minutes he would get now.

After all, since the moment he'd kissed her, Cooper had thought of little else. He was bombarded with memories of that kiss, and he welcomed all thoughts of her. Hell, he relived the first time he'd met her more than he probably should. So, when Jack invited him to join them, he couldn't resist.

"How's it feel to be back in Small Town, USA, again? I'm sure it's a lot different than being on the road, touring and all that," Jack stated as soon as Cooper had moved into the booth beside Tessa.

He glanced over, noticing she was eyeing her tea glass as though she would be able to morph the amber liquid into something else.

"I'm getting used to life in the slow lane." Leaning back, Cooper hooked his arm at the top of the booth behind him, casually letting his hand rest close to Tessa's shoulder between them.

"Do you think you'll enjoy being on the other side of the fence when it comes to music? Adam said you're handling the entertainment at Tessa's bar."

"That's the plan. Right now I've been ordered to sit around and look pretty," Cooper said, peering over at Tessa. He noticed the way she grinned slightly as she continued to study her glass.

"Look pretty?" Jack questioned. "That's not easy for you, is it?"

Cooper laughed, liking the way Jack said what was on his mind, unlike so many people who spent their time trying to kiss his ass and make him feel important. He didn't want to feel important. He wanted to feel as though he contributed to something. Something more than other people's wallets.

"I'll admit, I'm not good at it," Cooper added.

"Not true," Tessa mumbled, and Cooper slid his arm behind her on the booth, still being careful not to touch her.

"What was that?"

"Nothing," she said, peering over at him while using her hair to shield most of her face. He still managed to get a peek at the bright pink blush that suffused her cheeks.

He let it go, but he kept the information filed away for later. So it would seem she might actually be attracted to him more than she was letting on. Although based on the way she had kissed him back, he wasn't sure he should be all that surprised.

"I hear you're buying the Deluth farm," Jack commented as Miranda brought another glass of tea and set it in front of Cooper.

After saying thank you to the waitress, Cooper turned his attention to Jack. "That was the plan. I thought it was all a done deal initially, but the woman who owns the property called my Realtor a few minutes ago and told her there was another offer on the table. Said I might want to reconsider the price if I really wanted the land."

"What?" Tessa jerked as though someone had hit her before turning to face him more directly.

At her passionate reaction, Cooper focused on her, watching her expression change from shocked to angry and then back again.

"Something wrong?" Cooper noticed that the pretty blush was gone, and reflected in those crystalline green eyes was something more like fire.

"You didn't offer more money, did you?"

"Not yet, no."

"Don't." The single word was a command, and Cooper suddenly wondered what she knew that he didn't.

"Why not?"

Cooper studied her as she looked over at her brother. He followed her gaze, noticed the way Jack cocked an eyebrow as though giving her some sort of signal. Apparently Cooper was right because she sighed. Before she said anything, Miranda brought out two plates, setting them in front of Jack and then Tessa.

"I'll have yours in just a minute," Miranda told him and then turned away quickly.

"You didn't order anything," Tessa commented as she glanced up at him.

"I don't have to these days. Seems I've become a regular in here, and they bring me the same thing every time."

"Would you order something different?" she asked, a cute smile tipping her lips.

Cooper laughed. "No, probably not. I guess they've figured out I'm a man of routine."

Tessa turned her attention back to her food, but she didn't start eating.

"Go ahead. Don't wait for me," he told them both.

Jack dug into his food as if he hadn't eaten in a month, and Cooper tried not to stare. He had so many questions running through his head, most of them having to do with the land and what these two knew that he didn't, but he didn't want to interrupt their meal. Luckily for him, he didn't have to wait but a few minutes before Miranda was back with a plate containing chicken-fried steak, mashed potatoes, and green beans.

"Can I get you anything else?" she asked the three of them. When everyone said no, she moved on to the next table.

"So, one of you want to give me more details on the land? Or do I have to guess?" Cooper asked before he put the first bite in his mouth.

He noticed Jack didn't stop shoveling food in his mouth, his cheeseburger never getting too far away from his lips. Cooper figured the guy was making sure he didn't have to talk. Tessa, on the other hand, wasn't eating much of anything. She was pushing her onion rings around on her plate, flattening them with her fork.

"Finish eating," she told him. "Then we'll talk."

Cooper nodded, realizing he wasn't going to get any further with the conversation until Tessa was willing to talk anyway. Doing as she said, he resumed eating, and the three of them talked mostly about the bar and the events of the night before — which were rather mundane for a Saturday night, according to them.

Once Jack was finished, he looked over at Tessa and then back at Cooper before he spoke. "I just realized I had something to do," he blurted. "I'll get the check on my way out."

"Wait!" Tessa called to him, but he was already climbing out of the booth.

Cooper noticed the wry grin Jack sent Tessa. "I'll catch up with you later. Let me know if you need anything."

"Dammit," Tessa muttered, snapping a bite of food in her mouth.

"I see he bailed on you," Cooper joked. "What are you going to do now?"

If she had her way, she'd probably knock him out of the booth and onto the floor. When his teasing didn't get a rise out of her, he grew concerned. "I take it there's a problem?"

With the booth on the other side now empty, Cooper knew he should move, but he didn't want to. In fact, he wanted to stay right where he was for the duration. Sitting close to Tessa, inhaling her sweet fragrance, and listening to her mutter obscenities under her breath was making his body stand up and take notice. Yes, he was even turned on by her irritation.

"Only if you consider Luanne Deluth a problem," Tessa said, not looking at him.

"So you know about the other offer too?"

"I don't think there is another offer," she admitted.

"Why would you think that? Do you know her?" Now Cooper was thoroughly confused. Tessa must have realized it too, because she continued, not looking at him though.

"I went to see Luanne," Tessa began, with another long sigh as she paused to wipe her hands on a napkin. "I had an agreement with Jerry Deluth, Luanne's father, before he passed away a couple of months ago."

"What sort of deal?"

"To buy the property."

That got Cooper's attention. Pushing his plate away, he decided he did need space. This conversation didn't sound like the intimate one he'd have preferred to have with Tessa over dinner. Once he was situated across from her, he rested his forearms on the table and waited for her to continue.

"I had a verbal agreement with Jerry to buy the land. We agreed that I'd come up with twenty percent down and then I could take possession of the house and continue paying out the rest of the note."

Cooper didn't take his eyes off her. He noticed the way she wrapped her arms around herself as though trying to hold herself together. "Go on."

"Apparently, now that he's gone, the agreement he and I had is null and void. At least that's what Luanne told me a little while ago. She said you were paying her double what Jerry was charging me, and she wasn't going to pass up an offer like that for my measly price."

Fucking hell. Cooper didn't like the sound of this. It wasn't that he didn't want the property, because he did. Even at the price he'd agreed to, but something was off here. What were the chances that he had stumbled on some property that Tessa was in the process of buying — without a legal, written agreement?

"I would bet that she's using me to try and get more money out of you," Tessa offered. "I was having a hard enough time coming up with twenty percent, and that was at half the price you agreed to. As it was, I could barely afford what I was paying Jerry monthly just for the down payment."

"What about the money you've already paid?" he asked, still wary of how this all had come about.

Another sigh, then Tessa sipped her tea, although her glass was practically empty. He waved Miranda over to refill her glass while he waited for her to continue.

"Luanne said she'd give me my money back. Said she didn't need it."

"Did she?"

"Not yet, no. I just talked to her right before I came over here."

Well, that explained the phone call he'd received from his Realtor a few minutes before he got to the restaurant.

"What were you planning to do with the land?" he asked, having a feeling there was more to this story than Tessa was telling him.

Finally, she looked up at him. When their eyes met, Cooper saw the sadness in hers. His stomach clenched painfully at the sight.

"I was going to build an equestrian center," she said softly.

"Seriously?" he asked as he leaned back, crossing his arms over his chest. He realized he looked as skeptical as he sounded.

"Yes," Tessa answered firmly, her eyes locked with his. "Quite the coincidence, don't you think?" she asked snidely.

He'd have to agree. And yet he still wondered whether he was the butt of someone's joke here. Was there a conspiracy to try and get more money out of him?

"I thought someone had told you and you were messing with me. I've had plans for that land, and if you don't believe me, I've got the designs to prove it. Not only was I going to build an equestrian center to provide equine therapy to both the disabled as well as troubled youth, but I wanted to build a farm that would give the troubled kids a place to go. I've grown up around horses and figured it was the best of both worlds."

Holy shit. Still leaning back, Cooper stared across the table at Tessa, noticing the way the soft waves of her hair fell over her shoulder, resting just above her breasts. God, the woman was beautiful, and for some reason, when she looked vulnerable like that, his protective instincts kicked in. He was pretty sure she wouldn't want to know that though.

"Why troubled teens?" he asked, his curiosity getting the best of him.

Tessa's expression turned stony. "That's a conversation for another time."

Figuring that pushing her would only make her get up and leave, he decided to take a different route. "So what do we do about it?"

"*We?*"

"Yes, we." Cooper smiled. "It sounds like we've got a few things in common, and I'm not here to step on any toes. Maybe we can work out a deal."

"What kind of deal?" Now it was her turn to sound disbelieving.

Not that he blamed her for not trusting him. After all, it looked as though he'd waltzed right into her life and stolen her dream right out from under her.

Tessa wasn't sure what Cooper was angling at, but she was a bit surprised. Truthfully, she had expected him not to care one way or another about what she had put into the land so far. Not that the money was her greatest concern. Sure, she wanted her money back if she wasn't getting the property, because she could certainly use it to put toward something else. But the Deluth land was something she had wanted for a long time. Not only because of the price but because of the location. She would be able to stay in Devil's Bend. Something she fully intended to do.

This was her home.

"What if we go talk to Luanne together? See what happens when we play her game?"

"Together?" Tessa wasn't sure that was a good idea. What if Luanne decided not to sell to either of them?

"Or I'll go talk to her. See if I can persuade her to my original price."

The disappointment swamped her. She knew she shouldn't have gotten her hopes up. She doubted from the beginning that he would be willing to take a step back and take his money elsewhere. The selfish part of her hated that he was coming in and stealing her dreams out from under her. Not that she'd gotten very far. Not yet.

"Okay, so I take it you don't like that idea either," he said before she could answer. "How about this? We go about our business, I let my Realtor know that I'm still thinking it over, and we give her a couple of weeks. See if she comes back to me and agrees to my original price."

Tessa knew it honestly didn't matter one way or the other. Even though she wanted the land for herself, she knew the next best thing was for Cooper to get it. There was nothing to say she could even get an equestrian center up and running anytime in the next decade. It wasn't like it was a cheap endeavor. Not in the least. Cooper would certainly have the means to do it much sooner than she would.

"I think that's a smart decision. If she is playing us, then she'll surely get back to you. However, if there is another buyer," she told him, "which I seriously don't think there is, but it's still a possibility, you might lose the land."

"I'm not going to lose it," he countered. "I'll top the price if I have to, but I think you're right. I think she's trying to see what she can get out of me."

Tessa genuinely wanted to believe that. Not because she wanted Cooper to get taken by the likes of Luanne, but it seemed way too coincidental.

"Now, I've only got one stipulation," Cooper added, and Tessa met his eyes once again.

"What's that?"

"A date."

Tessa cocked an eyebrow. "Luanne's married. I'm not sure she'll date you. Then again, I don't know her all that well."

Cooper laughed, but she had expected him to. Tessa knew what he was getting at, but she truly didn't want him asking her out. She liked him. Despite the fact that he was interrupting her entire life in more ways than one, she still liked him.

Too much.

"With you."

Damn. How was she going to get out of this one?

"How about this? We give Luanne two weeks. If she calls you about your original price, I'll go out with you. If not, we'll leave it at that."

"Hmmm," Cooper said, looking as though he were pondering her suggestion. Tessa could only hope that, no matter what, Luanne would realize the error of her ways, because Tessa was almost positive that she wouldn't survive even one date with Cooper.

"Deal." Cooper held out his hand for her to shake and Tessa stared down at it.

Her brain took a second to realize what she'd just done, and then she lifted her hand and met his, enjoying the firm grip of his touch much more than she should have.

Yep, she had evidently just jumped in over her head.

CHAPTER EIGHT

It was hard to believe, but two weeks had passed since Tessa and Cooper had had their conversation at Charlie's Restaurant and just as many days since she had hired him on at the bar. There were no other encounters of the kissing kind during that time, which was both a relief and a disappointment. Tessa knew she shouldn't want him, but the more time they spent together, the more he was growing on her.

On top of that, The Rusty Nail was running seamlessly. There were new faces last Friday and Saturday night, all of them drawing enormous crowds, sometimes more than her bar could handle. Cooper didn't seem to have a problem with it. In fact, he had already told her that next week, the acts would be even bigger.

And, as if that wasn't enough, she had managed to get through her first phone call with Cooper's infamous manager who, honestly, was an asshole. She'd had the pleasure of talking to him on Monday night when he'd called the bar directly. According to him, Cooper wasn't answering the phone and it was urgent. At least they hadn't been busy because Manager Marcus had refused to let her get off the phone with him.

Much to their dismay — her and Eric — they hadn't gotten to hear the showdown between the two men because once Cooper had been informed that Marcus had called her, he'd gone outside to call him back. Tessa had no idea what Cooper had told the man, but they had yet to hear any more from Marcus the Manager.

No love lost there.

Cooper was a little more relaxed, although she wasn't sure that was even possible. It seemed as the days went by, he became more and more comfortable in Devil's Bend, and he was still just as anxious to get the land as he had been in the beginning. As far as she knew, he hadn't heard from Luanne though.

Every night they were open, Cooper was right there beside her, working his magic and making the crowds go crazy. If he didn't have someone on the stage, he would sometimes jump up there for the hell of it. Tessa enjoyed those moments, especially when Cooper let himself go. The man was a sight to see up on that stage.

The fans were still bombarding him, but they were at least trying to be polite about it. Tessa wasn't sure that would ever slow down; after all, he was famous, so it did make sense that people would want to meet him. So far, they'd been able to manage them easily.

"Hey! Can I get a beer over here?" Tessa looked up to see Cooper walking toward her, a huge grin on his face. For some strange reason, she felt the urge to smile back.

It could've been because the man was sinfully attractive with his dark hair and glowing golden eyes. Or possibly, that body that looked good enough to eat in those damn dark Wranglers that showcased one of the finest asses she'd ever seen. Not that she was attracted to him or anything. She'd gotten over that about thirteen days ago.

Okay, so she was in denial too.

She was still doing a damn impressive job of pretending though. They had managed to work side by side each night and had even shared a few casual conversations, which gave her a glimpse into his life.

He was looking for something, obviously, which was why he'd ended up in Devil's Bend. Tessa just wasn't sure he was going to find it. He seemed to be running from his own life. The problem with running was that you generally didn't end up where you wanted to be either. She kept waiting for Cooper to announce to them all that his tour bus was waiting outside and he was riding off into the sunset.

Without thinking about it, Tessa poured him a beer, knowing that he preferred draft to bottle thanks to his frequency in the place. When he approached the bar, she passed it over and beamed at him. His grin was contagious. "Why're you so happy?"

"Why wouldn't I be? I just received a phone call from my Realtor. You know what that means?"

Tessa shook her head, though she still smiled because that devious grin on his face was infectious.

"It means no more motel rooms for me."

Thank God he didn't mention the date. After all, they'd agreed if Luanne called him first, Tessa would go out with him. And clearly, he must've received an agreement on the original price. For some strange reason, she wanted to walk around the bar and wrap her arms around him. She was a sucker for that sort of emotion, and he seemed genuinely happy.

Even if his happiness was at her expense.

"I take it she went with your price?"

"She actually came down a few thousand. Seems that playing hard to get works out sometimes. We should celebrate," he stated after she was smart enough to keep her feet glued to the floor where she was.

"I just gave you a beer." Tessa laughed. "What more could you possibly want?"

"Dinner." The smile was still on his face, but there was something else lingering in his golden eyes. Heat maybe? Since she felt it too, she was hard-pressed to be able to deny what she saw there.

"With who?"

"You, of course."

"Sorry, cowboy. I've got a bar to run."

"You do. But I also know you happen to have Tuesday night off. What do you say?"

Tessa didn't say anything. She wasn't sure what to say. Tuesday was still a few days away, but her nerves didn't seem to understand that. The smart part of her brain told her she needed to say no. The other part wanted to jump up and down like a giddy schoolgirl and announce to the bar that Cooper Krenshaw wanted to take her on a date.

Before she knew what was happening, Cooper was leaning over the bar, mere inches from her face, and Tessa could hardly breathe. His eyes were glowing with what appeared to be elation, but worse than that, she couldn't take her eyes off his mouth. If she just leaned forward a fraction of an inch, she would be close enough to feel the heat of his breath against her mouth. If she moved a fraction of an inch more than that, she would get to confirm yet again that those sensual lips were as soft as they looked.

Damn. Damn. Damn.

Tessa managed to lean back slightly while trying to hide her reaction to him.

"One dinner. That's all I ask."

"You're telling me that if I go to dinner with you one time, you'll leave me alone indefinitely?"

"If that's what you want, then yes. One date."

"You just said dinner, now date. Which is it, cowboy?"

"Date. After Tuesday night, when I return you to your front porch, if you decide that you don't want to go out with me again, I'll leave it at that."

Tessa had to think about it for a minute. Oh, who was she kidding? There wasn't any thinking involved. She was merely fantasizing about what it would feel like to taste his lips again.

Rather than speaking, she nodded her head. She didn't trust her voice. Based on the look on Cooper's face, he didn't need the words.

"Perfect. I'll pick you up at five on Tuesday. Be ready because I've got plans for us," he told her and then grabbed his beer and sauntered off across the bar, leaving her to stare after him.

Tessa wanted to be angry with herself for giving in to him. There was just something about him. He was enigmatic. Charming. And, of course, he smelled so damned good. One night, Tessa had even searched on the Internet and come up with the answer that it was pheromones that caused her to be so drawn to his scent. She knew it had to be something because no one should be able to smell that delicious.

She allowed herself a few more seconds of admiring his ass before she turned back to what she had been doing before he'd walked up. And she would get right back to doing it … if she remembered what it was.

∞ ∞ ∞ ∞ ∞

Score a point for the cowboy, Cooper thought as he forced himself to walk away from Tessa.

Not only had he finally signed a firm contract on the house, he'd scored a date with the woman who managed to insert herself right smack in the middle of his mind and taunt him when he least expected it.

And if dreaming about her wasn't enough, he was also waking up with his dick hard enough to hammer nails into concrete. Of course, he'd been playing it cool when he was around her. Or he would like to think he had anyway. Tessa was skittish, and he knew he had to take his time with her. He wasn't looking to rush anything, so he had all the time in the world. If only his dick would feel the same way. Before it was over, his balls might be cobalt blue, but Cooper was pretty sure it would be worth it.

Making his way up onto the stage, Cooper set his beer on top of the stool and grabbed his guitar. The Rusty Nail might not boast live music every night, but this was what he'd been missing these last few years. He wanted to sing, and this place gave him that opportunity. On his nights off, or during some of his spare time, he would write the songs, practicing in his motel room. So far, no one had complained, but he was thrilled to be able to move into his house to get more privacy.

According to the Realtor, he wouldn't have to wait long. Everything was going to move fast because he was paying cash. In fact, she'd told him that all of the paperwork would be ready and waiting for him first thing Monday morning. He was counting down. As soon as he signed the papers and the electricity and water were turned on, he'd be moving in.

Not a minute too soon.

Obviously it helped that he had ignored Luanne's first call a week ago. And then he'd had his Realtor call her back late last week to tell her he was concerned with her new price. Apparently the woman realized her luck had run out, and as of yesterday, the ball was back in his court. Now that it was Friday, everything seemed to be waiting for the beginning of the next work week.

"Bear with me, folks," he spoke into the microphone, glancing out at the few people scattered throughout the bar, his eyes landing on Tessa. "I've been working on this one recently. Not yet finished, but I'd be glad to hear what you think. It's called 'Angel in Blue Jeans.'"

74

A couple of people clapped, making Cooper smile. Closing his eyes, he got lost in the music for the next few minutes, trying to feel out every word. By the time he was finished, there was another round of applause, and to his delight, Tessa even joined in. He wasn't sure what it was about her, but to know she liked what he did made it all worthwhile. Of course, the song was about her, but he didn't think she would appreciate knowing that. Yet.

Over the course of the last few weeks, he'd learned that he much preferred the sincerity of the handful of people he had come to call friends in this small town over a stadium full of people in an unfamiliar city. Many of those who came out to see him night after night he was now on a first name basis with.

"Thank you, thank you." He grinned at the crowd, keeping his eyes locked on Tessa's. In her cowboy hat, her tiny tank top, and those hip-hugging jeans, she made his mouth water. Not that he was trying to think about what she would look like with all of those clothes removed, but he couldn't help himself at times. Like now.

Realizing he was seconds away from embarrassing himself with a hard-on that even his jeans wouldn't be able to conceal, Cooper turned his attention back to the group. At least he could get distracted for a few minutes.

By the time three o'clock rolled around, the bar was empty. This had become his routine, working on his laptop after closing while Tessa, Eric, and Katie shut everything down. Tonight he'd been engrossed in a project. A surprise for the bar he'd become so fond of.

One of the pluses of being in country music, the number of friends he had made was endless. And he wasn't just talking about acquaintances. He'd built some relationships over the years, and he knew the people he kept close would support him through a time like this, and at this moment, he needed all the help he could get.

Not only was he looking to get some solid entertainment on board at the bar, but he was also looking for some volunteer work on his farm. That was still a couple of weeks away, but once he got the stables up, he fully intended to get the ball rolling with the equestrian center. That was his main goal, and his friends would make the end result that much sweeter.

"I'm gonna call it a night," Eric told Tessa, who was standing behind the bar, wiping down the countertop.

"I don't blame you," she answered, sounding tired. "Katie's already gone, so can you lock the door on your way out? We'll go out the back door."

"Yes, ma'am." With that, Eric swatted Tessa on the ass with a towel as he passed her.

Initially, Cooper hadn't been all that fond of the gesture, but once he'd learned that Tessa and Eric went way back, and, in fact, Eric was married to Tessa's best friend, he'd seen a different aspect to their relationship. They were friends, that was obvious. Cooper knew that he wouldn't walk away with his junk intact if he swatted her on the ass like that.

Damn, but he wanted to.

His dick stirred, making his jeans damned uncomfortable as he thought about his hand on Tessa's ass. In his mind, she was naked, the sweet, rounded curves of her ass filling his hands as she rode him fast and hard. *Shit.*

"You plan on staying here all night?" Tessa questioned, pulling him from his thoughts at the perfect moment. If he had let his imagination wander any further, she'd be laid out on the bar top, stark naked while he...

This was *so* not helping.

"I didn't realize you were ready to go," he told her, trying to stall while he got his body under control.

"There's nothing left to do here."

Well, Cooper would have to disagree with that.

"Hey, come here," he told her as he stood.

Without waiting for her, he moved to the sound system that was hidden in a panel on one end of the bar. He ran through the menu of songs until he found the playlist he was looking for and then hit play.

Moving back to Tessa, he took her hand and pulled her out onto the dance floor. She was smiling up at him, and the carefree look on her face was so rare it stole his breath.

Pulling her in close, Cooper removed her hat, placing it on the edge of the stage before sliding one hand in hers, the other around her waist. With their bodies aligned so intimately, he had to look down to see her, but even with their height difference, they fit together like puzzle pieces. He prayed she didn't feel the effect she had on him, but he couldn't very well help it. They had been doing this figurative dance for more than two weeks now, and honestly, Cooper was looking forward to getting his hands on her again. Even innocently.

Although his hands weren't thinking anything innocent at the moment.

"Are you trying to tell me something, Krenshaw?"

"Me? I don't have any idea what you're talkin' about," he replied, smiling. Cooper knew she was referring to the song, and yes, he could never go wrong with Conway Twitty.

"You think you're sly, don't you?"

Sly or not, Cooper didn't want to move from where he was. They danced slowly around the floor, two-stepping although their feet barely moved. This was as close as they'd been since the night he'd kissed her, and the feel of her soft, smooth fingers entwined with his, the crush of her breasts against his torso, were exactly how he remembered. Better even.

While the song referred to laying her down, Cooper was perfectly content with being upright. Hell, he wasn't particular about how they went about it, he just wasn't sure he'd be able to keep going another minute without kissing her. When the next song he had selected queued, Cooper knew his control would be shot in less than thirty seconds.

CHAPTER NINE

"Let me guess. You and Jason Aldean are friends?" Tessa asked as she stared up at the man whose arm was wrapped around her back, the heat of his hand scorching her skin even through her shirt.

"And what if we are?" He smirked.

They were so close not even a breath would fit between them, yet Tessa's body was screaming for more. Not that she would ask. It wasn't what good girls did, and quite frankly, Tessa was bound and determined to be a good girl. She'd spent the majority of her life being just the opposite. And for some reason, with Cooper, she didn't want him to know that side of her. Despite her better judgment, she didn't want to send him running. She had a feeling he'd decide to do that on his own before too long.

The way his intense brown eyes watched her made her mouth go dry. When she used her tongue to moisten her bottom lip, she felt his body tense, and suddenly, Tessa prayed he'd get the hint. If he didn't kiss her soon, she was almost certain her body would spontaneously combust.

He picked an incredibly fitting song, and suddenly, not talking anymore sounded like an extremely good plan to her too. When Cooper leaned closer, pressing his lips to hers, Tessa held her breath while praying he would lose the perfect gentleman act for at least a few minutes. She wanted this man to sweep her off her feet.

Seconds later, that's exactly what he did.

Suddenly, they weren't moving anymore. They were both rooted in place, their hands had taken up the part of their feet as they touched and tasted as though they'd been waiting for this day.

She had.

Tessa lost her ability to think when Cooper's tongue slid into her mouth, his taste sending her body into hyperspace as she wrapped her arms around his neck, looping her fingers into the soft, silky hair at the nape of his neck, just beneath his cowboy hat. When Cooper pulled her even closer, his hips subtly grinding into hers, she moaned.

"Lord, woman, if you keep doing that, I'm going to forget how to be a gentleman," Cooper said breathlessly.

Tessa stared back at him. At this point, she didn't give a damn what they did, but if he didn't put his mouth back on hers, she might just scream. "You talk too much."

That mischievous, crooked grin sent tingles racing through her bloodstream, taking brief breaks along the way to explode in her belly and then linger between her legs.

"Well, you don't have to tell me twice."

Tessa squealed when Cooper lifted her off her feet, forcing her to wrap her legs around his waist, the evidence of his arousal pressing intimately between her thighs and causing her to groan seconds before his mouth was once again on hers. This time, Tessa knocked his hat from his head and held him in place, not allowing him to get away from her until she got her fill. Based on the way he kissed, she wasn't sure if she'd ever get enough.

Her back hit the solid wall, and yet she still didn't allow him to get away. She couldn't stop, couldn't let go, because she wanted more of him. Her body had a mind of its own, and she was grinding herself against his erection, his groans matching hers as he pressed her firmly against the wall, his hands bracketing her ass as he held her in place.

"Do you have any idea what you do to me?" he asked when they both came up for air a few minutes later. "What you've done to me since the very first time I laid eyes on you?"

"I've got some idea," she whispered, her eyes darting from his lips to his eyes and then back again. Tessa watched his mouth, her brain on a single track with one destination in mind, and she feared that, if she allowed him to keep talking, they weren't going to get there.

Cooper's mouth returned, but this time he sent sparks of fire trailing down her neck in the path of his lips as he kissed and sucked her skin, making her damn near come apart at the seams.

The intelligent part of her brain told her that she shouldn't be doing this, but the other part, the part ruled by her hormones, told her not to care. She'd spent too long waiting for him to kiss her again. She had gone without for even longer, and just having his hands on her would probably be enough.

"Darlin', as much as I don't want this to stop, I fear if we don't, you won't like me all that much in the mornin'." Cooper's words were a breath against her ear.

"I don't care about liking you. As long as you keep doing that." Tessa groaned, her head falling back so he could have better access to her neck.

"See, that's where we differ," he said with a chuckle between kisses. "I'm very interested in you liking me."

Cooper's lips were close to her ear once again, and a shiver raced down her spine. Tessa wasn't sure she was going to survive this. She wasn't a virgin by any means, but never in her life had a man's voice appealed to her so much. Not to mention his hands on her.

"Well, I can assure you that I like what you're doing," Tessa whispered back to him, turning her head so she could bite his earlobe with her teeth. The guttural growl that rose from his chest had moisture pooling between her legs.

"That's a start. I plan to do so many more things to you that I want you to like."

Tessa could hear the "but" in his tone. He was going to stop, and she so didn't want him to. She didn't even want to think about what that said about her.

"I'd just prefer we had a place that was a little less … public. One where I could take my time, because I want to run my tongue over every inch of your body."

Oh, God, yes! Tessa's body tightened at his words. If he actually said something dirty to her, she couldn't promise that she wouldn't have a mind-blowing orgasm right there, fully dressed.

"And?" Her question was meant to spur him on.

"And what?" Cooper pulled back, and she could once again see his mischievous grin. "Tell me what you want me to do to you, Tessa."

Oh, how the tables had turned and absolutely not in her favor. Tessa didn't have a problem telling him exactly what she wanted, but she knew from experience that could very well backfire in her face, and she wasn't looking to be the talk of the town over the way she had let loose with a guy.

He must have realized she wasn't going to answer him, because Cooper's mouth once again pressed against hers, his tongue lightly tracing her bottom lip as she moaned in pleasure.

"When I get you somewhere private," he began, trailing that exquisite mouth across her jaw, "I'm going to tell you all the things I plan to do to you. As I do them."

Holy hell. Tessa wanted to take him back to her place. One night of sexual bliss was all she needed to cure the dry spell, and she would have Cooper Krenshaw out of her system.

"But not tonight." Cooper pulled back, looking into her eyes, and that glimmer of passion said he knew what she had been thinking.

Tessa groaned half-heartedly. She was grateful that the man seemed to have some sort of restraint, because she was quickly learning that, with him, she had none.

∞ ∞ ∞ ∞ ∞

Cooper wasn't sure how much more of her he could handle before he was reduced to a horny teenage boy who couldn't control himself.

He was holding Tessa in his arms, her body pressed against his, her legs wrapped around his waist, and even through his jeans, he could feel the heat of her sex against his aching cock.

As much as he wanted her, he wasn't willing to give up one night of what would probably be the most mind-blowing sex of his entire life if that meant she would walk away from him indefinitely. No, Cooper had more in mind when it came to this woman. He wanted so much more than one night. Hell, he wasn't sure thirty nights would be enough, but he was willing to try.

Letting her slide down to her feet, Cooper kept her pressed between himself and the wall, keeping his hands planted firmly on the sweet, rounded curves of her ass. Lord, the woman had the most amazing ass.

"Tuesday night, I'm going to pick you up at your house. I'm going to take you out like I planned. And then…" He freed one hand so he could tilt her chin up to meet his gaze before he continued, "And then, if you still want to see where this leads, it'll be your call. Until then, you'll just have to resist."

Her tempting smirk and simple nod didn't tell him anything, but he knew she would be thankful in the morning. Hell, his dick wasn't all that happy with him, but Cooper had learned a long time ago to stop thinking with his dick.

"You ready?" After reaching down and retrieving his hat, he twined his fingers with hers as he took a step back, keeping his eyes pinned on her. She was the sexiest woman he'd ever laid eyes on, and with her hair tousled, her lips swollen from his kisses, Cooper wasn't sure he would be able to walk away when they made it to her truck.

She nodded again as she grabbed her hat off the stage, still not saying a word, but he didn't push her. Instead, he held her hand firmly in his and led her to the back door, then waited for her to lock up. Once they reached her truck, he stopped her before she opened the door. Backing her up against the cool metal, Cooper once again pressed his mouth to hers, but this time he didn't go for gentle. He wanted to make sure she understood how much he wanted her.

When her arms came up around his neck once again, he couldn't resist pushing his hips against hers as he claimed her mouth. His blood had turned to lava in his veins, and he was so hot he wouldn't be surprised if his skin started to melt, but it was a risk he was willing to take. Her kiss was so much more than he'd anticipated, and the hungry way she delved her tongue into his mouth told Cooper that there was a wildcat beneath that cool, reserved exterior. He had sensed it earlier, but he also detected the way she had held back from him.

If he had anything to say about it, she wouldn't be able to hold back. Cooper wasn't a gentle lover, and with Tessa, he was beginning to wonder whether he'd met his match.

When they both came up for air — something they seemed to do a lot — Cooper cupped her face with his hands, holding her so that she couldn't look away. "I doubt I'll be able to sleep tonight."

"No one said you had to," she retorted, sounding somewhat frustrated.

"Trust me, darlin'. I want you more than you'll ever know, but I'm not looking for one night. If I was, I'd have buried my cock in your pussy right there against the wall in your bar." Cooper let the harsh words escape, wanting her to understand that the need was just as great for him as it was for her.

He was a gentleman when he was supposed to be, but when it came to Tessa and him behind closed doors, he wasn't going to promise her soft music and candlelight all the time. He wanted everything she could give him, and in no way was he just referring to sex.

The shiver that made her hands tremble told him that his coarse tone didn't bother her. In fact, if he had to guess, she very much liked it.

"I'll see you tomorrow. Get some sleep." He pressed his lips lightly against hers again. "You're going to need it."

CHAPTER TEN

Going back to his motel room was certainly Cooper's original plan; however, when Tessa took a right turn out of the parking lot of The Rusty Nail, rather than a left that would lead her back to her house, he decided to follow.

He had a feeling she was going to stop for breakfast or an unusually late dinner because she had mentioned that to Eric earlier in the evening. Considering Cooper had kept her at the bar longer than usual, he figured it would only be fair for him to pay for her meal. Not to mention, he'd get the opportunity for a pseudo-date without having to ask her.

Since Tessa seemed completely against dating him, although she had relented to the bet they had made, Cooper was willing to take his chances whenever the opportunity presented itself. Like tonight — or rather, this morning.

Fifteen minutes later, his suspicions were confirmed when she pulled into the parking lot of IHOP just off of the interstate in the neighboring town. Since Devil's Bend didn't have any options that were open that late, her choice made sense to him.

Parking directly beside her truck, Cooper climbed out at the same time she did.

"Are you stalking me, cowboy?" she asked sweetly as she made her way to the sidewalk that surrounded the building.

"I was just wondering the same thing about you," he said seriously.

The confusion that passed over Tessa's face briefly almost made him smile. "You're the one following me if I do recall."

Well, she had him there.

"Since we're both here, we might as well eat, don't ya think?" Taking Tessa's hand, Cooper led her to the front doors of the restaurant and then held one open for her. Once she was inside, he followed and then instructed the hostess they needed a table for two.

When they were seated with their menus in front of them, Cooper smiled, waiting for her to look at him, which she managed to avoid for a painfully long time.

"You're relentless," she told him as she glanced down at her menu, smiling.

"That's me," he replied as he skimmed the menu, thrilled to know she still sensed him there even when she pretended to not be paying attention.

"So, are you a regular here as well? Are they going to bring something out before you ever order it?"

Cooper laughed, enjoying the way she liked to tease him. It had been quite some time since he had been on a real date with a woman. One who wasn't more curious about his music career or the people he knew than who he really was.

"Nope. But if you'd like to join me for breakfast every morning, we can change that."

Tessa's face flushed, and she looked down at her menu again. He heard her mumble something along the lines of "Cowboy, you can't handle me every morning," but he didn't say anything. He could show her just how much he could handle if she wished to dare him.

The waiter arrived to take their order, and they rattled off what they wanted. A few minutes later, they were sitting quietly while Tessa fussed with her coffee, adding cream and sugar. Cooper took his black, so he remained silent, waiting patiently until she was finished.

"Do you go out to breakfast a lot after work?" he asked just to make conversation.

"Every now and then, Eric and I will stop somewhere. On some nights that Miranda works at the bar, we'll stop afterward, especially if things were hectic. Just some time to unwind."

"So why tonight? Alone?"

"I knew I wasn't going to be able to sleep," she said, and her honesty had that strange sensation surging through him. Cooper liked how open she was with him, although sometimes he didn't think she meant to be.

"You weren't gonna be the only one," he admitted as he watched for her reaction.

There was a minute or two of silence, and then Cooper realized she wasn't going to talk if she didn't have to. Considering there was so much he wanted to know about her, he figured he'd start tonight.

"Does your mom ever stop by The Rusty Nail?"

Okay, so jumping in with both feet might not have been the way to go based on Tessa's horrified expression, but Cooper decided he would let the question hang until she answered with something.

"I don't want to talk about me," she finally said when the silence was almost suffocating.

"I didn't ask about you. I was asking about your mother," he explained.

"Same difference," she retorted.

"Not really, no."

Another round of silence sat heavily between them until, finally, Cooper saw the moment Tessa surrendered.

"My mother rarely leaves the house," she said softly, her hands wrapped tightly around the coffee mug in front of her. "She's been that way since I was a child."

"She doesn't work?"

"Not now she doesn't. When I was younger, before she met my stepfather, she did."

"What did she do?" Cooper knew he had to keep the dialogue going, or Tessa was going to shut down on him, and he truly wanted to get to know her.

"She was a secretary for a law firm. For a while after she met Michael, Jack's dad, she continued to work. It wasn't until after they got married that she decided to quit."

"Are you close with her?" Because the question was a little more personal, Cooper didn't expect her to answer.

"No." There was a long pause before Tessa continued. "My mother was diagnosed with depression many years ago. After she met Michael. Up until that point, we had no idea what was wrong with her. My dad left when Adam and I were kids, and for the longest time, that's what I thought was wrong with her. But then she met Michael and she seemed happy. For a while. And then it was like a vicious cycle. Happy. Sad. Happy. Sad. Over and over and we didn't know how to fix it for her.

"Finally, Michael took her to the doctor. Since he's quite a bit older than my mother, he was worried that she regretted marrying him even after she assured him that wasn't the case. Jack was in high school before we found out she had depression. So, needless to say, she and I lost a lot of years in between."

That explained a lot. Cooper knew that Adam wasn't close to his mother either, and truthfully, he hadn't expected such an in-depth answer from Tessa. "Is she better now?"

"When she takes her medicine, she is." Tessa looked so lost and so sad Cooper wanted to rip her out of her seat and wrap his arms around her.

"See, and that's why I don't like talking about me," Tessa added. "My life story's not all that interesting, and I don't want your pity."

Cooper grabbed Tessa's arm when she would've jumped out of her seat and walked out on him.

"Sit down," he demanded, keeping his voice low.

Tessa lowered herself back down in her seat and stared at him as though he'd lost his mind. He was beginning to think he had.

"I'm sorry. I want to get to know you, and I haven't yet learned what the banned topics are."

Tessa seemed to relax as she resettled herself in the booth, but she didn't say anything.

"I'm not trying to pry, Tessa. I think this is how this is supposed to work."

"How *what* is supposed to work?" she asked.

"You know, the whole dating thing. Aren't we supposed to get to know each other?"

"We're not dating," she said abruptly.

Cooper couldn't suppress the grin. He loved how feisty she was. "No need to get defensive," he teased. "We're just having breakfast."

He was saved from any rebuttal from Tessa because the waiter decided to bring their food out. Cooper was grateful for the interruption. The fire seemed to be smoldering in Tessa's eyes, but he knew she needed a minute or two.

But then, he was pretty sure he was going to be in for it.

Tessa hated talking about herself. Hated talking about her mother and their issues. And above all else, she hated dating. Well, the last part wasn't necessarily an issue because until Cooper, she hadn't been on a real date in … well, forever.

Not that they were dating. Nor would this be classified as a date, if, in fact, the two meant different things.

Tessa occupied herself by staring at her food, moving the eggs around her plate with her fork until Cooper cleared his throat and she glanced up at him.

"Eat."

She wanted to tell him to make her, but then she realized how childish that sounded even in her own mind. And that made her smile, which in turn made Cooper smile. As her appetite slowly returned, Tessa tried to come up with some questions for him since he obviously now knew more about her than she did him.

"What about your parents?" she asked when he put his fork down to take a sip of his coffee.

"What about them?" He didn't seem fazed by her question as he watched her like a hawk watches its prey.

"Are you close to them?"

"Yeah, we're close," he said, his answer hesitant.

Tessa wasn't proud of the fact that she wasn't close to her mother, but she never held it against anyone else. Izzy's parents were still married, and they doted on their daughter as much as Izzy would let them. And of course, there were Richie's parents, who were still together but had moved out of Devil's Bend shortly after Richie died. They still called to check on Tessa frequently, but as time passed, she had stopped answering their calls. It was too hard to talk to them because they were a vivid reminder of what she had lost. She often wondered if it was a relief for them that she'd all but disappeared from their lives. She knew they wouldn't say as much, but she still had to wonder.

Wanting to get away from the depressing thoughts, Tessa shoveled a forkful of eggs in her mouth as she pondered her next question.

"Do you see them often?"

"At least once a month, sometimes more, depending on my tour schedule."

Tour schedule. For the past couple of weeks, things had been so normal with Cooper around she'd actually forgotten what he did for a living. Somewhere along the way, she'd gotten used to him being at the bar, and the reminder that he wasn't a permanent fixture in town was like a punch to the throat.

"Do they come to your shows?" she asked, suddenly wanting to get off of this subject. Off of any subject, really. Tessa was scared to get to know Cooper better, scared that she would like him even more than she already did, and that would make it more difficult to keep herself distanced from him.

Which she definitely had to do.

"When they can, they do."

Cooper must've sensed her discomfort, because he leaned forward and placed his hand on her arm. Tessa just stared at the place where he touched her for what felt like a long time.

"I didn't mean to upset you," he said softly. "I just want to get to know you." Cooper paused, and Tessa dared to look up, her eyes meeting his and holding. "You're a lot like your brother, you know that?"

"Which one?" Tessa knew exactly which one, but the question just came out.

"Adam. He doesn't share much with anyone."

"Adam has his reasons," Tessa said abruptly. She didn't know all of what Adam kept inside, but she absolutely understood his need to keep his feelings and experiences to himself. "And I've got my reasons."

"I get it," Cooper said softly. "It still makes me crazy. When we were in college, getting information from him was like pulling teeth. Kinda like with you."

Cooper laughed, and the sound eased some of her tension, causing her to laugh too. She knew he was right about Adam because she had thought the same thing in the past. Not that she felt it was a bad thing that they didn't share their life stories with everyone. Tessa knew how easy it was for someone to hurt you if they knew you. Trust didn't come easy, and unfortunately, she and Adam had learned that early on with their father.

"I'm sorry. I'm sure it's easy for you because you're in the spotlight all the time, so you're used to sharing your deepest, darkest secrets, but I'm not."

"See, that's where you're wrong," Cooper said gruffly, the warmth of his hand disappearing from her arm and leaving her chilled all of a sudden. The look in his eyes matched the temperature as it plummeted due to the cold chill that ran down her spine.

"Being in the spotlight makes it difficult to keep anything private. The things people learn about me don't usually come from me or from anyone who knows me."

Tessa suddenly wanted to do anything to erase the anger from Cooper's face. She didn't want to see him upset or mad, and she knew that her own defensiveness had resulted in this night going so terribly wrong. With a small smile, she reached over and touched his arm. "This not-really-a-date isn't going all that well, is it?"

For long seconds, Cooper just stared at her. Long enough that Tessa's stomach started to churn. Just when she pulled her hand back, Cooper's deep, rumbling laugh echoed through the entire restaurant, and Tessa responded with a laugh of her own.

"I'm just glad this isn't really a date," Cooper said when he settled.

"Why's that?"

"Because you still owe me one date," he replied smoothly.

Well, damn. Now he got her on a technicality.

Sneaky bastard.

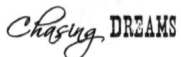

CHAPTER ELEVEN

By the time Tuesday evening rolled around, Cooper was giddier than a teenage boy on prom night hoping to get laid for the first time. And despite his body's desperate ache, he found he longed to spend some uninterrupted time with Tessa. Maybe a chance to talk like they had at breakfast, although he would certainly ensure he didn't pick the wrong topics this time.

Suffice it to say, he was more interested in talking as opposed to just the possibility of sex. He wanted to say that as far as the sex was concerned, he could take it or leave it. However, if it were actually a multiple-choice question, he would absolutely pick sex. No questions asked.

Either way, he just wanted to see Tessa again.

He hadn't bothered to tell her anything about where they were going, so when she called him at three o'clock to ask about what she should wear, his anxiety level had ratcheted up at least one hundred notches. Luckily, he managed to keep a firm grip on his man card by not running straight to her house, and he'd gone over to his new house — *new to him*, which was certainly the only thing new about it — to take care of a few things.

With electricity and water on, he had opted to head back to the motel and pack up his things, followed by a trip to the big box department store just outside of town. He wouldn't have any furniture until the movers delivered his things on Thursday, but it wasn't like he didn't know how to rough it for a night or two.

Now that he was pulling up to Tessa's house, the rest of his concerns and priorities flew right out the window. The only thing he could focus on was seeing her.

He was greeted in her front yard by her two dogs. The ones he'd seen the last time he was there, but neither of them seemed any more worried that he was walking up to the house this time than they had last time, so he took that as a good sign. Figuring it couldn't hurt to butter them up a little, he squatted down on his haunches and gave them each a rub when they sauntered his way.

The front door was only a few steps away, but for him, it seemed like a mile. In all honesty, aside from their impromptu breakfast at IHOP last Friday, Cooper hadn't been on a real date in longer than he could remember. He'd had his fair share of women over the years, but much to his dismay, he never had to work for it. They were generally waiting for him, some of them even managing to sneak on his tour bus a time or two. And weren't those just fun times waiting to happen. No challenge whatsoever.

But with Tessa, he didn't have to worry. The woman was undoubtedly a challenge, and he loved that about her.

As he watched the stunning woman through the screen door as she made her way toward him, all of the women from his past faded away, and he felt like a damn virgin standing naked — even though he was fully dressed — in front of a woman for the first time. Then she smiled at him, and he thought he was going to have to sit down.

"Hey," he greeted, realizing he didn't sound all that sure of himself, but shit, he could barely form coherent thoughts, much less words.

The cowgirl was standing not three feet in front of him in a white cotton sundress, her sexy, tan legs beneath the hem that rested just above her knees. Her pink toenails peeked out from her sandals, and all of a sudden, his entire body went hard. Lord have mercy, he wanted to know what she had on under that damn dress.

"You ready?"

Tessa nodded, but her smile didn't fade, so Cooper accepted that she was still speechless after their phone call earlier. Not only had he told her what she should wear, he also told her what he'd *like* for her to be wearing — which had consisted of absolutely nothing. Needless to say, the conversation after that had been laced with enough sexual innuendos that he'd worried he wouldn't be able to sit down for a couple of hours.

He pulled open the screen door and waited while she locked up the house, and then he followed her with his hand pressed firmly on her lower back. When they reached his truck, Cooper opened her door and then waited while she climbed inside, shutting the door behind her. He took his time walking around the truck, trying not to seem too excited, but if the smile on his face was anything to go by, then Tessa clearly knew he was anxious for this night.

"Where're we going?" she asked as they were backing out of her driveway a minute later.

"Well, if I told you, it wouldn't be a surprise, now would it?"

"You didn't say anything about surprises," she retorted as she leaned casually against the door, the weight of her gaze heavy on him as he drove.

"I meant to."

Her throaty chuckle lit him up from the inside, and Cooper suddenly wondered whether what he had in mind was actually a smart idea or not. Taking her to a public restaurant probably made more sense than taking her to a secluded place where he didn't have to worry about anything other than enjoying her company.

"What's that smell?" Tessa asked, turning toward the backseat, where the delicious aroma seemed to be coming from. "Is that food?"

"I sure hope so because I'm starved," he said, not taking his eyes off the road.

"So you aren't taking me to dinner?"

"I thought I'd bring dinner to you," he answered easily.

Tessa turned back around, peering out the window to see where they were going. She knew the town like the back of her hand considering she'd lived there her entire life. It was clear based on the landmarks that they were headed south toward the Deluth farm, better known as Cooper's new house.

Tessa wasn't sure exactly how she felt about that. She was having a hard time convincing herself that she should be upset that Cooper had upended her dreams so easily. In fact, she feared she was actually starting to like the guy more than she should.

For the better part of the afternoon, she had ridiculed herself for her reaction to him the other night when they were at the bar. Had he not shown the type of restraint that she obviously didn't possess, she would've had sex right there in the middle of her bar with Cooper Krenshaw, and this date would probably not even be happening. And then she had risked sending him running in the opposite direction by opening up to him when he had asked about her mother. That hadn't been her smartest move. Tessa, as a rule, did not open up to people, so she didn't know what had happened between them that night. Thankfully, she had her thoughts back under control, locked up safe and sound, which meant she didn't have to worry about tonight.

So this morning, once she had finally talked herself back off the ledge and decided she wasn't going to cancel on him, she had primped in front of the mirror more times than she was willing to admit. To find out that he wasn't even taking her out, she was a tad bit disappointed but oddly relieved at the same time.

Was he expecting her to sleep with him? *Was* she going to sleep with him? If the other night was any indicator, it was highly likely that she would take him right there in the bed of his truck if he just kissed her once. Except now in the bright light of the day, that option didn't seem so simple anymore.

For the last several hours, she had thought of nothing else except this man, and she'd come to a conclusion. She was far more attracted to Cooper than for just his incredible body or his country charm. Or his deep, soothing voice.

There was something else about him that appealed to her on many levels, the least of them being sex. Although she wouldn't deny that they could probably create one hell of a science project just by the chemical reaction the two of them created when they were together.

For the last two weeks, he'd been the perfect gentleman, and she'd been a hot, ogling mess. Ever since the first night he'd walked into her bar, put his arms around her in order to keep her on her feet, Tessa had to admit that she was seriously intrigued by the man — despite her many reasons not to be.

At first, there was no doubt that it had all been based on physical attraction. However, that appeared to be morphing into something deeper. Sure, she would've preferred to keep her interest on a more superficial level, but Tessa knew, ultimately, she wasn't built that way. And the more she learned about him through their various conversations during slow times, the more she found herself liking him. In the same sense, he was somehow getting her to open up to him about things she didn't talk to anyone about. And yet he wasn't running away.

Cooper turned the truck down the dirt driveway that led to the farmhouse sitting several acres off the road, and that's when the butterflies erupted in her stomach. Tessa wasn't sure what she was so nervous about, but whatever it was, the closer they got to his house, the worse it got.

"Now, don't go panickin' on me, darlin'." Cooper's voice was gentle, and Tessa wondered whether he could feel her apprehension in the congested confines of the truck cab.

"What are you talking about?" she asked, trying to appear unaffected. She wasn't sure she succeeded, but thankfully Cooper opted not to challenge her. Figuring she should keep the conversation going so that she had less time to think about what it actually meant to be alone with him, she asked, "When do you plan to move into the house?"

"Already done."

Tessa snapped her head in his direction, trying to determine whether he was serious or not. "You just closed on the house yesterday. How'd you manage that?"

"Technically, I don't have anything in the house. I just brought the things I had with me. The movers will be here on Thursday with the rest of my stuff."

"You know, I never did ask, but where'd you live before this?" Tessa realized there were a lot of things she didn't know about this man.

"About twenty minutes outside of Nashville." When Cooper didn't elaborate, Tessa realized they'd parked in front of his house. She stopped asking questions so she could help get the items from the backseat.

They didn't say anything more until they were walking up onto the front porch, each of them carrying a large plastic sack filled with small containers of food.

"If your furniture isn't here, where do you plan on eating?"

"I was thinking on the porch if you don't mind. If I had my way, it's where I'd have supper every night. Come on, I want to show you the view from the back."

Tessa slowed, staring at Cooper's back as he continued to lead her toward the rear of the house. She admired how his muscles flexed and bunched as he moved while she was still processing what he'd said. Was she being overly sensitive or was it too coincidental how much they had in common?

Shrugging off the thought, she followed Cooper around the wood-planked wraparound porch, noticing the areas that were in desperate need of patching. Much of the wood was rotting, and some of the planks were broken in half. Her heart ached at the memory of her time spent there with Mr. Deluth. Over the last year, she'd spent more and more time with him, trying to convince him to let her help fix the worst of what was broken, but he'd always seemed more content just to spend their time talking.

"Watch your step. I think this'll be my first project, trying to get this thing back to its original glory."

Tessa wasn't sure this old farmhouse had ever been really glorious, but she certainly understood its appeal. She had always loved old country farmhouses and actually had hoped one day to own this particular one. In the meantime, she was renting her current house from her brother Jack. Considering Deluth's land had been the prime location for what she'd spent her life dreaming about, she knew finding something else wasn't going to happen anytime soon.

But tonight she didn't want to think about that.

When they arrived at the back of the house, their apparent destination, Tessa noticed that there were two plastic chairs and a diminutive plastic table sitting in the middle of the porch.

"I have to admit, I'm jealous of this porch, Krenshaw," Tessa said, going for casual.

At the moment, she was feeling anything but, and she wasn't sure why that was. Just being with him, alone like this, was so incredibly intimate she wasn't sure she was going to be able to eat with all her nerves churning in her belly.

"Yeah? It's a little on the neglected side, but the promise of what it could be was what appealed to me."

"I know exactly what you mean," she mumbled, hoping he didn't hear her. For as long as she could remember, she'd loved this old house. Especially the solitude to be found on the property.

Taking the bag from her hand, Cooper set up the food on the table after signaling for her to take the opposite chair. She noticed the chair was new, even having the stickers attached to it, and she smiled.

"I tried to think of everything. I don't have any furniture on the inside, so I figured this would do. Not that I need anything more than that porch swing over there. It seems more than adequate for a bed if you ask me."

Tessa looked over her shoulder at the swing he was referring to, and had she been drinking something, she would've choked. The dilapidated swing appeared to be hanging by a thread as opposed to the two rusty chains that actually secured it to the wood rafters. Jerry had never wanted to replace it for as long as she could remember.

"Don't worry, I checked. It's stable. It'll do for a while."

Tessa wasn't sure she believed him, but she nodded her head anyway.

When the food was laid out between them, the plastic utensils and the paper plates within reach, Tessa looked up at Cooper. "This is great, by the way. I was worried you'd be the fancy type, and I won't lie, I'm not big into that stuff."

"I think I knew that," he replied, grinning.

"What are you trying to say, Krenshaw?" Tessa tried to sound stern, but her smile probably gave her away.

"We're a lot alike. I'd much prefer to sit out here all night as opposed to wine and dine in some fancy restaurant. I'm claustrophobic in social scenes like that. I like wide-open spaces. I don't think Marcus ever truly understood that."

Tessa knew he was referring to his manager, and she noticed the frustration that lingered briefly in Cooper's eyes. For the last couple of weeks, she'd overheard bits and pieces of several of his phone conversations, and although she only ever heard a few words, she sensed that he still wasn't happy with Marcus or what he was telling him.

"Do you plan to just walk away from your career?" she blurted as she watched him scoop potato salad onto his plate.

Cooper's eyes met hers, his lips a thin line as he seemed to be trying to read her intention. Smiling, she made an effort to lighten the mood. "Don't worry, I'm not planning to go talk to the tabloids."

He smiled back, but it didn't reach his eyes. Feeling as though she'd overstepped and invaded his personal space, she followed up with, "Sorry. We can talk about whatever you want."

"No, I'm good. Where you're concerned, I'm an open book."

Tessa wasn't sure she wanted him to be an open book, because that would mean he would expect the same from her, and there were too many things that she shied away from talking about. Her history was one of them.

"I like this," he said as he motioned with a tilt of his head toward the fields, "but I don't want to give up my career altogether. Maybe slow down some. I want to do something more. There's a part of me that is constantly looking for a challenge. I think I found that here."

Tessa wondered whether he was referring to the potential of the farm or her.

"And you're up for the challenge of a farm?"

Cooper tilted his head, as though studying her again, and Tessa fought the urge to squirm.

"It'll be the biggest challenge of my life, no doubt. Not only will it take a tremendous amount of time, but the back-breaking work will keep me occupied." Cooper paused, his gaze still intently focused on her. "Financially, I can help in a lot of ways, such as getting the center off the ground, but I know it won't be enough for me. Being able to work with children and horses and to see the benefit of them together, that's where the true reward is."

"What made you want to work with kids?" she asked.

There was a distant sadness in Cooper's eyes that made Tessa's heart ache in response, but for the first time, he didn't answer her. *Open book, huh?* Well, it looked like he had some things he wanted to keep to himself, so Tessa didn't feel so guilty about not sharing her life story with him just yet.

Changing the subject, she asked, "So, you don't want to stop performing?"

Cooper forked potatoes in his mouth, his gaze intently focused on her to the point she was about to start fidgeting when he finally spoke. "No, I don't want to stop altogether. The fans are the reason I keep doing what I do. But, honestly, I like The Rusty Nail," he replied, sounding serious.

"So, what? You're going to give up all the world traveling and just sing at a small-town bar a couple of nights a month?"

"I'm thinking about it."

She had to break the eye contact, fearful that he would see the lust that was slowly building inside of her as she watched him eat. Luckily, the food looked wonderful, effectively redirecting her attention.

Cooper hadn't skimped on dinner. According to the napkins, he'd ordered from Charlie's Restaurant: roasted chicken, potato salad, and corn on the cob. She remembered he was a man of routine and couldn't help but think that this was definitely not his normal meal.

"Would that bother you? Me hanging around your bar indefinitely?"

Tessa grinned. She couldn't lie to the man. "I kinda like you hanging around."

"Well, that's good because if I have anything to say about it, I'll be hanging around for a long time."

They ate in silence for a few minutes, both of them glancing out over the landscape as the night descended upon them. When they were finished, Tessa helped Cooper clean up the mess, using a large black trash bag to dispose of the containers since he didn't yet have a trash can.

When he disappeared inside the house for a few minutes, Tessa moved over to the rickety porch swing and decided to test it out. There was a new cushion on it, probably the ugliest one he could possibly find too. The dark red with even darker blue flowers was not at all appealing to the eyes. She liked the idea of him planning ahead for their date though, and the longer she was there, the more she liked the idea of being somewhere that no one would interrupt them.

Getting comfortable, Tessa gazed out at the acres of empty space in front of her. There was no denying the jealousy she felt when it came to the land and the fact that Cooper had purchased it. It was the perfect place to build an equestrian center. She could almost picture where the barn and the stables would go, as well as the various areas that could be sectioned off for events. And despite the fact that she didn't own the land outright, it was as though she now had the opportunity to live her dream vicariously through Cooper.

She wanted to believe that she wouldn't harbor any ill will toward the man for having the opportunity she knew she'd never have, but she wondered whether that was even possible.

CHAPTER TWELVE

Cooper managed to clean up what he could and then grabbed two beers from the refrigerator. He wouldn't let Tessa know that the beer was the only thing he had stocked up on prior to picking her up. Considering the refrigerator had seen much better days — probably back in the seventies when it was new — he wasn't all that keen on putting anything else inside. Thankfully, his refrigerator would be delivered later in the week, and he would be able to donate that one to someone else who could put it to good use.

Making his way back outside, he let the screen door slam behind him, the loud slap making him smile. It reminded him of growing up, running through the house and right out the back door, his momma yelling at him not to slam the door seconds before it did just that. God, he missed her even though he talked to her practically every single day. Sometimes more. That was probably the only thing about being in Texas that he found disconcerting. He had always been close to his parents.

Realizing he was on a first date — although technically, it was officially their second — with a woman he actually wanted to know more about, Cooper shook off the train of thought.

When he walked back outside, he found Tessa sitting on the swing, her legs curled up beneath her as she stared out at the overgrown fields that surrounded the house.

"What are you thinking right now?" he asked as he approached, handing her one of the beers.

"Huh?"

She was stalling, so he merely smiled at her, letting her know he'd caught on to her game. "I can tell you're lost in thought. Where'd your mind go?"

"Nowhere," she lied and Cooper frowned.

Figuring they knew each other better than most first date couples did, Cooper went ahead and sat on the swing beside her, wrapping his arm across the back and around her shoulder, easily pulling her up next to him. He loved the way she felt against him. The soft skin of her bare arm brushing against his, the sweet smell of her hair, it was a combination that brought out his protective side in a bad way. Then again, everything about her seemed to do that.

"See the old barn out there?" he asked her as she settled against his side, sighing as though she'd resigned herself to his questions.

"The one that's falling down?" She giggled.

"That'd be the one." Cooper took a swallow of his beer, then rested the bottle on his knee. "I'm gonna tear it down and build another one. I want to push it back a hundred yards or so. Get it farther from the house."

"I'm assuming it'll be bigger?"

"Yeah. I'm hoping to stable at least six horses and have more animals, so I'll need a place big enough to store stuff. At first, it'll probably seem like overkill. I'll probably only start out with two or three horses, maybe a dog or two."

"I think that's a smart move. See where it goes."

Cooper heard the sadness in her tone. According to everything he had learned since arriving in town, Tessa had the same dream he did. Although hers was probably more thought through … planned out.

"Would you do it differently?"

Tessa glanced up at him, her pretty green eyes sparkling as though he'd found the one thing she loved to talk about. He suddenly really wanted to get her input.

She turned back to look out at the fields and said, "The first measure of business should obviously be clearing the land, ensuring the outer fences are in shape. Check the barbed wire, get all of that repaired. I don't think you'll have to worry about a bunch of garbage to be hauled off, with the exception of that barn."

That was one thing about the property that Cooper had been happy about. The land was entirely fenced, and based on what he'd seen, the majority of it was in decent shape. Only a few sections needed to be rebuilt, but certainly manageable.

"Got it. Clean and repair first."

Tessa peeked up at him briefly. He ran his hand slowly down the side of her cheek, encouraging her to continue.

"From there, I'd probably start out small," she continued, resting her head back against his shoulder, sipping her beer before holding it in her lap. "Obviously dispose of that." She nodded with her chin toward the barn. "Depending on what you're planning to replace it with, that could take some time."

"I'm not looking to take a lot of time," he informed her. Not that he flaunted his money, but he had enough to do what he wanted to do and then some. "It'll probably be the first thing I really focus on. I'd like to see it up in a couple of months, if possible."

"That's definitely possible, but again, that depends on the size," she stated. "From there, assuming you'll build the stables at the same time, you should start out with three horses, maybe four. If you're hiring a trainer, you'll have some help in taking care of them. They're a lot of work for one person, so you'll be busy just with their upkeep. Are you going to hire someone to help?" she asked, lifting her beer to her lips again.

Cooper glanced down, watching as her lips touched the edge of the bottle, the way she tipped it up just a little before moving it back to her lap and sliding her pretty pink tongue over her bottom lip. He suddenly had a craving to lick that bottom lip himself.

Maybe it was the fact that they were somewhere private for the first time since he'd met her, maybe it was just being outside with nature, or maybe it was simply the woman… Any way he sliced it, Cooper hadn't felt this content in a long time. For years, he'd been going ninety miles an hour, never slowing down. But here, in this place, with this woman, he felt as though he had a chance to enjoy it.

"Do you think I should hire someone?" Lifting his gaze back to the rapidly darkening expanse of sky in front of them, Cooper listened to the crickets as they chirped loudly around them.

"I don't think it's a bad idea. You can check in with the high school. They've got an agriculture program and might have some kids looking to learn."

Cooper liked that idea. A lot. Apparently Tessa Donovan had done her homework. It confirmed for him that she'd been telling him the truth from the get-go.

They sat in silence for a few minutes, neither of them needing conversation to make things comfortable. Cooper loved sitting outside like this. With nature being the only sound disrupting the breeze flowing across the acres of tall grass. Other than the light from the kitchen spilling through the screen door and spraying a soft, buttery glow over the wooden planks of the porch, it was now almost totally dark. There weren't any other lights in the distance, no other houses within miles to disturb the perfection of the evening.

"Why haven't you done this yet?" he asked, using his hand to gesture toward the barn in the distance.

When Tessa flinched in his arms, her soft body no longer pliant, he tightened his arm around her, unwilling to let her run from him. She didn't have to answer the question, but he didn't want her to go. Not yet.

"You just seem so passionate about it, especially when you talk."

Tessa tried to pull away again, but Cooper held her tight. "Don't."

"Don't what?" she asked, once again trying to sit up straight.

"Don't run away. I'm sorry. Forget I even asked."

Long seconds passed before Tessa eased back against him, but Cooper noticed that she wasn't relaxed anymore. Her body was rigid beneath his arm, her shoulders tense. He lowered his head toward her, pressing his lips against her hair and inhaling her sweet, fresh fragrance.

He could get used to this. Get used to this woman. Although he hadn't known her all that long, Tessa was the type of woman he'd been looking for. Sweet, honest, maybe a bit too apprehensive though. She had all of the characteristics of a woman who could withstand a long-term relationship if she'd give herself another chance. Something he was looking for, more so now than in previous years.

Ever since he'd hit thirty, Cooper had been looking for long-term. Maybe not actively pursuing women for a happily ever after, but he had kept the thought in mind when entertaining the women he came in contact with.

From the minute he'd stepped off of the stage in Chicago, Illinois, Cooper had known he was ready to slow down. To settle down. And as he'd walked out of the concert arena, he'd decided there was never a better time than right then. He'd found himself heading south soon after that.

A year ago, he had wanted to believe he had found his happily ever after; although the circumstances hadn't been within his control, he'd figured fate had been dealing him a surprise hand. Unfortunately, he'd learned soon enough that his life had just taken an off-road detour, and he'd been forced to find his way back to his original path.

Now that he was in Devil's Bend, he felt like he had finally found the place he was meant to end up, and no matter how much Marcus threatened him, Cooper wasn't going anywhere. Was it possible that he had found everything he was looking for? Could Tessa be the woman?

"Have you considered a petting zoo?" Tessa's sweet voice drifted over the sound of cicadas chirping in the towering oak trees.

Cooper laughed, and this time Tessa did pull away. Completely. She pushed up off the swing, sending it rocking wildly until he managed to still it, moving to the edge.

"Where're you going?" he asked, looking up at her as she paced away. "Come here, Tessa."

When she stopped abruptly, Cooper held his breath, waiting to see what she would say.

"Why'd you laugh?" she asked, her voice suddenly sad.

Choosing not to spook her, Cooper remained where he was, placing his empty beer bottle on the porch beneath his feet.

"Come here, Tessa," he repeated more firmly, his eyes never leaving her. Okay, so she was definitely skittish, even more than he'd thought. They needed to work on that knee-jerk reaction of hers.

He wasn't sure whether she won whatever internal struggle she was having or not, but Tessa finally turned to face him, and he locked his gaze on hers. There wasn't an ounce of the sadness he had detected in her tone written on her face. No, she looked more pissed than upset, but he was ready to remedy that.

He tilted his head slightly, lifting one eyebrow as he waited for her to give him a piece of her mind, or worse, turn and run. Cooper might be laidback, he might be easing into the slow life, but he wasn't a patient man, for the most part. With Tessa, he realized he wasn't going to have much of a choice but to adapt.

She took a few steps closer, putting her beer bottle on the table. When he lifted his eyebrow once more, she moved even closer. Once she was within feet of him, he put his hands on her hips and pulled her closer, causing her to stumble. She righted herself by placing her hands on his shoulders as he looked up into her face.

"I wasn't laughing at you, Tessa." He kept his voice firm, making sure she understood that he preferred talking to running. "I was laughing because of how perfect you are. Or rather, how ironic it is that we have so much in common, yet we're so different."

Tessa's expression didn't change, but she wasn't trying to pull away from him, so Cooper considered that a win.

"I'm sorry if you thought I was laughing at you. I promise, I wasn't. I'm not surprised that you've come up with a million ways to make this place into something only dreams are made of. You've managed to consider all of the possibilities."

Tessa didn't say anything as they stared at each other, the defining moment upon them. If she was going to put up a wall every time he did something she didn't like, they weren't going to get anywhere.

"I don't want you to run," he admitted openly, his hands involuntarily gripping her hips more firmly. Being this close to her made his body hum and his brain buzz. "I'm going to say and do stupid things from time to time. Bear with me."

"I don't want to run, but…" Tessa left the sentence hanging between them.

"Then stay. Right here with me." Cooper allowed his voice to drop, brown eyes locked with green as he willed her to understand what he was feeling.

"I could ask the same from you," Tessa whispered.

His brow furrowed as he tried to understand what she was telling him. Apparently she realized his confusion, because she continued.

"It seems to me that you're the one running. From your career, from your fans. Who's to say you'll stay here? Why would I even want to believe you would?"

Cooper let go of her hips, forcing himself to his feet as he moved away from her. Was Tessa right? Was he running? The thought pissed him off, because that was the last thing he wanted to do. He didn't run. When things got tough, he wanted to believe that he would stick it out, but maybe Tessa was right. Shit. Maybe he was just being selfish again.

"This isn't easy for me," Tessa stated from behind him, but Cooper didn't turn to face her.

He wanted her to keep going. To explain herself. Based on what he knew about Tessa Donovan, she was a strong woman. She ran a bar practically by herself, and she had made her way in life. She had big dreams, but something had gotten in the way of them. Was it just money? Or was there something else holding her back? Those were the questions that he pondered at night when he thought about her. She intrigued him, unlike any woman before her. He wanted to know everything about her, and not just the feel of her silky skin beneath his hands.

Although there was that.

"Maybe I should go," Tessa said, sounding even farther away, although he could still feel her standing behind him.

Unwilling to let her walk away, Cooper turned. The woman stole his breath when he looked at her. That simple, white sundress highlighted the smooth, tan skin of her arms, even in the darkness. The soft yellow glow from inside the house backlit her, making her look like an angel. He wanted this angel. He wanted to believe he'd found her for a reason.

Moving closer, Cooper kept his gaze pinned on hers, not allowing his eyes to roam over the gentle swell of her breasts or the subtle curve of her waist. When she licked her lips, his gaze faltered, and he glanced down, wanting to suck on her bottom lip, to taste her the way he had before. He wanted to get carried away.

"I assure you, I'm not running. Not from my career or anything else. I came here for a reason. I'm just not sure what that reason was anymore." Cooper was beginning to think he'd been lured to Devil's Bend for this woman.

"Come here," he whispered, standing just a few feet away from her. He wasn't going to push her, but he wasn't sure he could keep his hands off her a minute longer.

She moved closer, causing him to hold his breath, the eager anticipation running amuck in his bloodstream. When she was within touching distance, Cooper forced his hands to remain at his sides, refusing to touch her. Not yet.

"I'm not interested in casual, Tessa. I haven't been interested in casual for a long time. I'm old enough to know what I want, and playing games ain't it." His honesty surprised even him. The way her eyes widened said he'd stunned her as well.

"What do you want?" she asked, sounding unsure of herself.

"Right now? I want you." He wanted to pick up where they'd left off the other night.

"Tell me," she whispered, obviously reading his mind.

"I want to peel that damned dress off of you and run my lips over every inch of your perfect skin. I want to sink to my knees and bury my tongue between your legs, to lap your sweetness until you scream my name. I want to risk getting splinters in my ass while you ride my cock right here on the back porch."

Tessa's breath hitched, she bit her bottom lip, but she didn't run from him this time. Cooper could see the pebbled tips of her nipples through that soft fabric of her dress, and he wanted to untie the thin straps that kept her hidden from him and suck her into his mouth. What he wanted from her was intense. It had been since the moment he'd laid eyes on her. He wanted to learn every inch of her body by taste and touch. But he wasn't willing to get anything less in return. He needed her to know his intentions.

"Do you understand me, Tessa?"

She nodded her head as though she did, but Cooper wasn't so sure. Taking another step closer, he closed the gap between them, tilting her chin up so she had to maintain eye contact.

"Then I want to wake up in the morning with you in my arms. I want to feel your body pressed against me, the heat of your skin as I roll you over and slide inside of you." He swallowed. "I'm not looking for one night, Tessa."

"I'm not looking for forever, cowboy," Tessa stated, her tone laced with what sounded like fear.

"No? And how do you know that?"

Cooper wasn't necessarily looking for forever, but if it found him, he wasn't going to walk away. He had never found forever, not in all of his thirty-one years, and by God, he wanted something of his own. He wanted a house, a wife, babies. He wanted the whole nine yards, and he would be damned if he was going to let his career hinder him anymore.

"I just know. I've been down that road."

She'd been married, he knew that. Based on the stories he had heard, the man she'd married had been the love of her life. He had died and left her all by herself.

Cooper understood that he would never be able to replace that man, nor did he want to. But he knew for a fact that there was a passionate, intense woman hiding behind those walls, and he had a sudden desire to tear down every one of them.

He planned to start tonight.

CHAPTER THIRTEEN

Tessa refused to listen to the naïve heart that was pounding like a bass drum in her chest. This was a man who made his living writing songs that made people fall in love.

She wasn't looking for love, but she was quickly warming to the idea of all of the tantalizing things he was offering when it came to physical gratification. However, when she'd told him she'd been down this road before, she wasn't lying. Both the heart-melting love, which she'd had with Richie, and then the erotic moments stolen between two lovers, which she'd experienced with another man a couple of years after Richie died.

And aside from the love she had shared with Richie, Tessa had sadly learned that nothing was sacred.

Sex, even with astronomical, top-of-the-Richter-scale orgasms, usually came with a price. As much as she wanted to let loose and go wild with Cooper — something she'd done more when she was a foolish young woman than any time in the last few years — she felt her self-preservation kick in.

She had learned the hard way that she couldn't give in to that reckless side of herself anymore because once her passion ran high, she did stupid things … like fall in love. That possibility had been stolen from her when Richie had been killed by a strung-out drug addict. She didn't have it in her to risk forsaking herself for another man. Even a man like Cooper.

"But you haven't been down that road with me," Cooper said, making her skin prickle with goose bumps.

Just the rich rumble of his voice sent chills racing down her spine. That and the way the night cloaked them in darkness, adding another degree of mystery to the man who was quickly getting under her skin.

She had to remind herself that she hardly knew this man. Just because he'd walked into her bar, singing sweet country love songs, did not mean he meant them for her. And even though she did know some things about him, she still wondered what he was running from. Was it his career? Had he really gotten burned out? Or was there something more that he wasn't telling people? Based on the pieces of the one-sided conversations she had heard, Tessa wasn't so sure he hadn't disappeared off the country music map for a reason other than the one he was giving her. And he was keeping those reasons to himself.

"Same road," she muttered. *Different guy.*

When Cooper's fingers grazed the bare skin of her shoulder, she couldn't repress the shudder that rippled through her. Still staring into his mesmerizing brown eyes, she watched as they darkened, a compelling hunger reflected there. Oh, the things this man could do to her body. She didn't doubt his ability to make her body scream and beg for more, she just got the impression that he might want more from her than she was willing to give. And it had nothing to do with naked, writhing bodies.

Tessa wasn't interested in love.

She wasn't interested in romance.

Dinner on his back porch, just the two of them alone, promised so much more for her than wine and roses and fancy, expensive restaurants would have. It gave her the opportunity to explore those more powerful feelings that fluttered through her. And she had known that was a risk she was taking as soon as she'd realized he was bringing her to his house.

Her hesitant, uncertain heart knew better than to let her hormones make decisions for her. Right now, the term *vulnerable* was an understatement, and she'd do well to remember that.

She wasn't the type to fall in love quickly. Her brothers teased her that she should've been a man with her convoluted ideas of sex. Sex did not equal love. Nor did she want it to. But that didn't mean she couldn't get caught up in the moment.

And yes, exploring a night in Cooper's arms sounded like heaven to her. Waking up the following morning with his warm, naked body beside hers, now that scared the shit out of her.

She didn't have more to give.

She compared all of her experiences to the love that Richie had showed her. Although he hadn't been her first sexual partner, he had been her first true love. Her best friend. Mad, passionate sex hadn't been in Richie's repertoire of skills, but the lovemaking between them had been good. Heartwarming. Then again, she had known explosive, no-holds-barred sex, and she had learned that her emotions ran hot, made her do stupid things.

Not that she was promiscuous anymore, because Chad Harper — the only man she'd been with after Richie — had pretty well put the nail in that coffin a long time ago, but that didn't mean she wasn't a healthy, sexually motivated woman. She just wasn't willing to let her heart get involved. As far as she was concerned, Richie would forever hold her heart, so it wasn't up for grabs.

Cooper leaned in, his warm breath tickling the sensitive skin just beneath her earlobe. "Take a chance with me, Tessa. One chance. I promise, you won't be sorry."

She doubted that. Her fight-or-flight instinct was kicking in, and she knew she should run and hide as fast as possible. Only she couldn't get her feet to move. Her hands were defying her direct orders as well. Her palms flattened against the hard, muscled wall of his chest, desperately aching to feel her fingers against his bare skin.

She could so get lost in him. One night. That's all she needed. Except she would have to see him every day, and the way her body responded, she knew she wouldn't be able to control herself. If he was expecting sweet and innocent, she wasn't sure she could give him that. No matter how badly she wanted to be that woman, she just wasn't.

If Tessa was going to go all in, per se, she wanted wild, hot, passionate sex. All or nothing. Without the nuisance of that something more that he said he was looking for.

"I'm not interested in anything more than sex," she blurted, confused at the lack of filter on her mouth, but not at all sorry she'd said the words out loud. He deserved to know, after all.

Cooper took a step back, still looking down at her. He slid his hands through the strands of her hair that had spilled over her shoulder. He twined them around his fingers, pulling her forward as a thrilling tingle penetrated her scalp.

God, she wanted him to pull her hair. How fucking crazy was that?

"All right. We'll leave it at sex for now. But I'm warning you, Tessa, I'm not a man who gives up easily," Cooper stated firmly, keeping a tight, spine-tingling grip on her hair.

Tessa wanted to believe him; however, the very fact that he had ended up in Devil's Bend rather than chasing his country music dream made her wonder how much truth was in the statement.

"So you're willing to give me one night?"

"I never said anything about one night." Cooper leaned down, his lips hovering dangerously close to hers, his hands sliding up until he was cupping her jaw, tilting her head at the perfect angle that would align their mouths if he decided to kiss her.

God, why wouldn't he just kiss her? Then she wouldn't have to think anymore. "But nothing more, Cooper. However long it lasts, you have to remember, I only want sex."

Cooper nodded, his lips pressing down on hers, and she pushed up on her toes, forcing him even closer, opening her mouth to let his tongue tangle with hers, and the world began to spin.

He tasted like beer and man and heaven all mixed into one, and Tessa found herself suddenly addicted to his taste. Sliding her palms up his chest, she had to reach to wrap them around his neck, but once she did, she pulled him down closer, taking the reins and deepening the kiss.

The growl that rumbled in his chest sent vibrations straight to her clit, and Tessa found herself practically climbing him. She wasn't a wisp of a thing like most of the women he was probably used to, but Cooper didn't seem to have any problems handling her.

When his mouth separated from hers, Tessa groaned, the loss of his taste making her body work harder to touch him, to ensure he didn't disappear. His firm lips began trailing scorching-hot kisses down the underside of her jaw, then he moved on to nibble her neck, and Tessa was almost positive she was going to come right then and there.

"Do you want to take this inside?" he asked, his mouth never leaving her skin.

Tessa shook her head. She didn't want to go anywhere. This was right where she wanted to be. Under the stars, with this man, right here on his back porch without another soul within at least three miles.

"I'm going to have you naked in under a minute. Are you sure about that?"

"Positive," she answered, holding his head tighter, forcing his mouth closer to the vulnerable area between her neck and her shoulder. God, she loved what his tongue was doing.

She felt the ties at the back of her neck give, the rasp of the strings tickling her skin when he pulled them along with him as he stood to his full height, stealing his wondrous lips away from her eager body. Staring up at him, she watched as his eyes widened, the once golden-brown darkening.

"You're beautiful," he whispered, lowering her dress until her breasts spilled forth, unbidden without the bandeau top.

The late summer breeze was warm against her skin, but her nipples puckered painfully beneath the scrutiny of his gaze. Tessa wouldn't consider herself ugly, but she would never go so far as to say she was beautiful. Only, when Cooper looked at her, she felt as though she were a princess and he had never found another woman quite so exquisite.

He continued to lower her dress until it bunched across her ribs, just beneath her sensitive, swollen breasts. Warm hands cupped her, lodging her breath in her chest. Splendid warmth enveloped her, her thighs clenching as her pussy began to throb with anticipation. Closing her eyes, she prayed he'd get on with it.

Tessa squealed when her feet left the ground, her body lifted and turned until her butt was resting on the railing that surrounded the porch.

"There," Cooper said, sounding pleased with himself.

Oh, hell! Cooper's fiercely hot mouth surrounded one of her nipples without so much as an introduction, the suction sending electric shards of pleasure ricocheting from her nipple to her clit. She couldn't stifle the moan, couldn't keep from pulling his head closer as she bowed her back, trying to force him to suck harder. The sharp tug of his mouth had her praying he would never stop.

Disappointment took up residence where the pleasure had been seconds before when he pulled away, her breast falling from his mouth with a sinfully delicious pop. He wasted no time before unleashing the same treatment on her other breast.

"Cooper," she moaned, holding him to her. "Don't stop. Please, don't ever stop."

Reckless.

The thought flitted through her mind, but the pleasure was too intense, too all-consuming that she couldn't focus on anything other than the way he teased her nipple with his tongue.

This time he bathed her entire breast, licking the underside, then lapping at her nipple with gentle swirls of his tongue. She tried to focus on the intensity of his mouth, but his big, warm hand was sliding its way up her thigh. When his finger dipped beneath the elastic edge of her panties, she was afraid she was going to shatter right then and there.

"You're wet."

It wasn't a question, and Tessa didn't feel the need to say anything because her body was doing all the talking for her. She spread her knees farther apart, gripping his shoulders to keep from tumbling backward off the railing as he slowly penetrated her with one finger.

"Cooper!" *Oh, God.* She wasn't going to last. It'd been too long. "Please! Oh, God! Please!" Grateful that they were so far away from civilization, Tessa didn't try to restrain herself. She wasn't sure she would've been able to if she'd had to.

"Tell me, Tessa." Cooper's tone was firm, demanding, as he stood tall, looking down at her, his finger sliding ever so slowly inside of her, curling to the perfect angle that made her womb contract. "Tell me, darlin'."

She was momentarily stunned by the abrupt shift in his demeanor. The laidback, country boy had taken a backseat to the dominating man before her. She had no idea what she was supposed to tell him. Her brain had gone offline, granting all of the decision making to her body, and her nerve endings were suddenly in charge.

"Do you want me to make you come?"

The way he spoke had more sparks exploding inside of her. This was what she needed. What she wanted more than anything. She didn't want to make love. She wanted to get wild. Go crazy. She wanted her body to soar, and the way he continued to fuck her with his finger was doing wondrous things to her insides.

Cooper lifted the hem of her dress until the cotton rested on her thighs, his tan hand between her thighs, her plain white panties pulled to the side as his finger moved in and out. Tessa couldn't tear her eyes away from the sight.

"Two fingers?" Cooper's words came out as a question, but Tessa watched as he retreated before sliding two long, thick fingers inside of her, making her scream from the delicious ecstasy that tormented her.

"Harder," she begged.

"Not yet. I want to watch you come just like this. You're so fucking hot, Tessa. The way your pussy pulls at my fingers."

Cooper's thumb entered the mix, slowly flicking across her clit, and Tessa threw her head back, holding on to his shoulders as her orgasm ripped through her. She had to clamp her teeth closed as a scream tore from her chest.

Long seconds later, her body relaxed. Thankfully Cooper was holding her once more, because she would've easily slid right down to the floor, or worse, fallen off of the ledge she was perched on.

Not that she would've cared either way.

∞ ∞ ∞ ∞ ∞

Cooper wasn't sure he'd be able to move. His cock was like an iron rod, painfully squeezed behind the zipper of his jeans. The discomfort probably the only thing keeping him from going off like a rocket.

The way Tessa had responded to his touch, completely uninhibited, was a hell of a lot hotter than he'd expected. This woman knew what she wanted when it came to pleasure. Knew how to take what she needed.

Honestly, he hadn't expected that. In the short time he'd gotten to know her, Tessa seemed more than a little reserved, thwarting most of his attempts to get close to her. Clearly not the case, and it was another thing he found so damned appealing about her.

Having had his share of women over the years, never had he been with one who made him feel as though he were experiencing the same pleasure she was. Never had he realized that giving could be as appealing as receiving. Until now. Until her. Cooper wanted to make her come in a thousand different ways, and he had no intention of slowing down now.

Pulling her down from the rail, he gave her a second to get her feet beneath her before he let her go. "Don't move," he ordered before turning to go inside.

With hurried movements, Cooper grabbed the sleeping bag and the single pillow he'd purchased earlier before returning to the back porch. To his relief, Tessa was still standing where he'd left her, her dress still bunched beneath her full, luscious breasts.

Spreading the sleeping bag out over the deck and tossing the pillow down, he beckoned Tessa over with a crook of his finger. The smile she dazzled him with had his jeans once more constricting as his dick pulsed.

"I thought you were willing to endure splinters in your ass?" she teased, her sultry laugh hanging on the warm breeze.

"We're not at that point yet," he told her as he eased her dress down her torso, then over her bottom before letting it slide down her legs to the floor. Her tiny white panties were the next to go.

Cooper went to his knees then helped her down until she was sitting in the center of the blanket. It took him a minute to free her feet from the sandals, but once he did, he took his time looking at her. Tessa was perfection. Her curly blonde hair wild around her face, golden skin glistening with perspiration. He continued looking his fill, letting his gaze travel over her breasts, admiring the dusky pink tips, still puckered, then over her gently rounded belly to the soft curls between her thighs.

"Why am I the only one not dressed?" she asked, drawing his eyes back up to hers.

"Because I'm not done with you yet. Trust me, we'll get there. For now, I want to feast on your pretty pussy." Cooper loved the way her green eyes darkened when he told her exactly what he wanted to do to her. He sensed she was turned on by the vulgar words, which only spurred him on further. "I want to slide my tongue deep inside of you until you're screaming my name again."

And heaven help him, when Tessa had screamed his name as she'd come, he'd damn near fallen to his knees.

"What're you waiting for, cowboy?"

Fuck.

Cooper didn't need to be told twice. Easing her legs farther apart, he lowered himself to the floor, shouldering his way between her thighs, inhaling her sweet, musky scent. When she moved, he looked up the delectable curve of her body to see she was propping herself up on the pillow.

So she wanted to watch, did she?

Cooper took his time, running one finger through her wet folds, grazing her clit every so often before separating her swollen lips and baring her completely to his gaze. She was pink and wet and so damn perfect his mouth watered with the need to taste her. Unwilling to rush, he used the tip of his tongue to glide down the outer portion of her labia, down, then up, stopping at the swollen bundle of nerves before flicking his tongue sharply.

"Oh, God!" Tessa's scream split the air and a surge of satisfaction filled him.

Sucking her clit into his mouth, he teased her gently before releasing her, sliding his tongue lower until he reached her entrance. One hard thrust of his tongue had her hips bucking beneath him. He reached up, gripped her hipbones, and held her in place as he began fucking her with his tongue. He increased the pressure, alternating between relentlessly flicking her clit, then returning to bury his tongue in her sweet, warm pussy.

He wanted to slide his cock inside of her. Wanted to feel her heat envelop him. It wouldn't take much before she pulled his release from him, but he wasn't willing to end it just yet. Although Cooper was pretty damned sure he wasn't stopping at only one time. Not tonight anyway.

"I need to feel you inside me," Tessa begged. "Please, Cooper. I want to feel you."

He couldn't resist the thought of her wrapped around him, but he wasn't willing to let her have a break.

Pushing himself up onto his knees, Cooper met her gaze. "Play with yourself," he ordered. "I want to see how you use your fingers to fuck yourself."

Tessa didn't hesitate, and once again, Cooper was desperately trying to muster up enough control to hold out a little while longer. Pushing to his feet, he kept his gaze locked between her thighs, watching her fingers as she slowly slid one deep into her pussy, her moans filling the night and making his dick throb.

"You're so pretty, Tessa," he groaned, his body hard and his brain fuzzy. He knew he was standing for a reason, but it took him a few seconds to remember he was supposed to be getting naked.

Time stood still as he managed to remove his clothes in record time, barely remembering to grab the condom out of his pocket. Rather than move closer, he rolled the condom on, then began stroking his cock, his gaze roaming back to her face. The way she watched him made him want to move faster, to give in to the release that was beckoning.

What he wouldn't give to feel her mouth wrapped around his cock. Her sweet, soft tongue teasing him. A tortured groan escaped, and he noticed Tessa smile. She was an angel with a devilishly naughty side. He liked that. Really liked that.

He nearly fell to his knees when she crooked her finger, inviting him closer while her other hand continued to thrust slowly, sinfully.

She was going to be the death of him.

Lowering himself to his knees once again, Cooper leaned over her, propping himself on his forearms, purposely leaving space between their bodies. Tessa pulled her arm up from between her legs, her eyes darting down to his mouth. When she teased his bottom lip with her finger, the same one she'd been fucking herself with, he slowly sucked it into his mouth.

"Let me feel you," Tessa whispered as he bent closer to nibble her bottom lip, his cock resting between her thighs, the heat of her tormenting him.

In one swift move, Cooper flipped them, rolling her over until she was straddling his hips while he took the brunt force of the ungiving planks beneath them.

"Ride me, Tessa."

Her eyes once again widened, but she didn't falter as she leaned forward on one arm, using her other hand to guide his erection right to the heart of her.

Fucking hell.

So damn tight.

Cooper gritted his teeth, groaning as her body pulled him deeper, the tight walls of her sex squeezing him until he wasn't sure he'd be able to breathe from the sheer ecstasy of it. He didn't have time to think before she was lifting off him, then lowering. Over and over again. Her lush, perky tits directly above his face as she took him deeper inside of her.

"Fuck!" The word escaped on a pained breath as he fought to hold on, not willing to come just yet because he didn't want it to be over. "That's it, darlin'. Fuck me."

Tessa smiled down on him, her eyes glazed over with lust as she continued to ride him, faster, harder. Gripping her hips, Cooper met her thrusts, burying himself to the hilt inside of her, reveling that she was taking his full length.

"You feel so good," she whispered. "So good."

Cooper pulled her forward, crushing her breasts against his chest as he held her hips immobile, grinding his pelvis upward, lifting her, then pulling her down on his cock. They were both sweating, the evening breeze doing little to dampen the desire burning out of control.

"Yes! Fuck me, Cooper. Fuck me harder!"

Cooper lost his last vestiges of control, her words shattering his mind as he began thrusting harder.

"Come for me, Tessa. Fuck, baby. Come for me." He wasn't beyond begging. He refused to come until she did, but he couldn't hold on much longer. The velvet grip of her pussy on his cock sent waves of sensation to the base of his spine. With each bone-jarring thrust, his balls tightened, his muscles contracted.

"Cooper!"

Tessa's scream was the only warning he received as her body clamped down on him, pulling him deeper, milking his release from him. Not to mention, shattering something deep inside of him.

Something he wasn't sure would ever be the same if she decided this wasn't enough for her.

CHAPTER FOURTEEN

By the time the sun penetrated her sleepy brain, Tessa had been rolling over, attempting to get away from the intrusive light. Expecting to feel the softness of her mattress, she groaned as pain shot through her hip from the hard, ungiving ground beneath her. Peeling one eye open, she noticed she was not in her bed but rather outside. Memories of the events from the night before raced through her mind, her body immediately overheating. A full-body blush consumed her as she remembered exactly what they'd done.

"Good morning." The deep, melodic rumble teased her eardrums, and Tessa leaned back against the warm body behind her.

Before she could even respond with her own morning greeting, Cooper lifted her leg, slipping his cock between her thighs from behind, easily sliding inside of her. Apparently her dreams, or maybe just her subconscious knowing he was there beside her, had been enough to prepare her for him first thing.

"Oh." Tessa let the word linger on an exhale, enjoying the full sensation of him inside of her.

Although he was almost painfully thick, her body had finally acclimated to the delicious intrusion, and she began rocking her hips backward. Her head lifted as his bicep tightened beneath her ear, his hand coming to rest on her bare breast, gripping it.

"I want to wake up like this more often," he grumbled in her ear. "So wet, so tight," he panted. "Never enough."

Tessa knew just what he was saying. The way they had given in to each other several times through the night, she still wanted more of him. The seductive friction of his steel-hard length as he burrowed deep inside of her had her gasping for breath.

When he leaned over her, effectively rolling her onto her stomach, Tessa's breath hitched. He was behind her, his hard body pressed against hers fully, his hips rocking as he began fucking her harder. The morning sun was bright, yet she didn't worry that anyone could see them. At the moment, she wasn't even sure she would care. She just wanted him to continue.

Cooper's thrusts abated as he lifted her hips until she was on her knees, the thin sleeping bag not nearly enough to relieve the pain from the hard wood beneath them, but the divine sensation of him sliding back into her dissolved most of her discomfort.

"Can you come for me again, darlin'?"

"If you keep doing that—" Tessa's breath hitched, a moan disrupting her sentence. "Oh, God, yes." And that's all it took. The sharp, sudden tremor in her womb erupted outward as he slammed into her over and over again, sending shards of electricity through her veins as she hurled herself over the edge into mind-numbing bliss.

Two hours later, Tessa was back at home, standing beneath the warm spray of her shower, her aching muscles reminding her just how much pleasure Cooper had bestowed upon her the night before. Ever since she had asked him to take her home, scared she would wear out her welcome, she'd been trying to think of anything other than how in tune their bodies had been. She didn't want to remember how wild she'd gotten with him, how her inhibitions had all but disappeared as he'd told her exactly what he'd planned to do to her, right before he'd followed through.

He must think she was easy. That thought was like a bucket of ice water being dumped over her head, forcing the heat from the memories to disappear instantly.

It didn't matter that Cooper had seemed disappointed that she didn't want to stay longer. It didn't matter that he'd offered to come inside and help her christen her shower. None of it mattered when she thought about the repercussions of what she'd done.

What happened when she pissed him off? What happened when she pushed Cooper away, and he retaliated against her? If history were to repeat itself, which she feared it would, he was going to spread vile rumors about her through their small town.

Just like Chad Harper.

Only people would listen to Cooper.

Tessa moved under the water, hoping the warmth would penetrate the chill that had taken up residence in her body. Chad was the only man Tessa had been with since Richie had died four years ago. He was also the sole reason she knew she'd never be in a relationship again if she could help it. He was also the reason she didn't have sex. Not even casual one-nighters.

As he so kindly reminded her, she was out of control when it came to what she wanted. He'd told his friends how she'd begged him to fuck her. Repeatedly. Which she had, no doubt. During the throes of passion. Between the two of them. Never had she expected him to share their intimate moments with anyone else. But he had. Oh, how he had.

She'd learned her lesson. Considering she and Richie had been young, their sex life had still been enough to satisfy her. Tessa had learned a little too late that not all men were like Richie. Not all men knew how to keep their personal lives private.

For months after she'd tossed Chad to the curb because of his verbal abuse, Tessa had had to fend off men who were looking for a good time. She had idiotically thought she was falling in love with Chad. They had only dated for a couple of months, but he'd filled a void that Richie had left when he'd died.

As it turned out, she was just a means to an end for Chad. He had been an up-and-coming country music singer, and he was more popular in his own head than he was anywhere else. But Tessa had honestly liked him. He was handsome, charming. He was also a notorious flirt. And he was using her to play at The Rusty Nail, trying to lay the groundwork for his future stardom — which had never come.

Needless to say, the very first time she'd been approached by one of Chad's buddies, she had known then and there that what had happened between them surely hadn't stayed between them. Another reason to add to the long list of his shortcomings.

Apparently, her breaking up with him had been a blow to Chad's ego, and rather than acting like a rational adult, he'd turned on her. A man who had professed his love for her on more than one occasion had turned on her so fast her head had spun.

Before she'd even known what had happened, rumors were spreading about how easy she was. How she had begged him to have sex with her on their second date. It didn't seem to matter that he was lying, nor did it matter that she had never been with another man since her husband had died. The rumors had spread and Tessa had vowed never to let it happen again.

Until Cooper.

It was as though he flashed one of those flirtatious, lopsided grins and her panties fell off. And last night, she'd given in to the pleasure her body sought so desperately. She'd wanted to savor every second she was with him. Only she should've known better. She should've thought about the repercussions.

When he'd left her on her front porch, he hadn't seemed happy. He had kissed her quickly on the lips, then disappeared down the steps, leaving her to stare after him. Or maybe that's just what she'd expected. Either way, regret was eating a hole right through her.

The water in the shower began to chill, and Tessa quickly turned it off, reaching for the towel she had tossed on the closed toilet seat. She wrapped the plush cotton around her, but she couldn't seem to ward off the bone-chilling cold that had replaced any warmth from the night before.

Why did she do this to herself? Why did she compare every man to Chad? Or to Richie, for that matter?

She didn't have the answers, didn't think she would ever have them. The only thing she knew for a fact was that she wasn't willing to let herself get close to Cooper. She should probably clarify that — she wouldn't get any closer than she already was.

What had happened between them last night would live in her memory forever, and hopefully, it would always remain between just the two of them. Tessa wasn't sure what she'd do if she had to relive the painful lies all over again.

Geez, she really needed to get out of her funk. And soon.

Grabbing her cell phone, she dialed Izzy's number, knowing that her best friend would be her only saving grace at this point.

∞ ∞ ∞ ∞ ∞

It'd only been three hours since Cooper had dropped Tessa off at her house, yet it felt like days since he'd last seen her. Although he had busied himself by running to the hardware store and picking up a truckload of wood to repair the deteriorating porch and had actually forced himself to work on it, he couldn't keep his mind from drifting back to the night before.

He'd had to start working on the front porch to avoid going to the back of the house because the memories were even stronger there. Cooper could still see Tessa sprawled out beneath him, feel her sharp nails as they dug crescent shapes into his shoulders, hear the soft, gasping moans that had the blood rushing south in an instant.

Cooper had no idea what fascinated him so much about the woman, considering they seemed to be at separate places in their lives — him wanting to settle down, her not looking for a relationship of any sort, aside from perhaps friends with benefits. It didn't stop him from wanting her. Wanting to get to know her and not just what made her body burn. He wanted to know what made her smile, made her laugh. What made her so jaded.

Whatever was going on with her, she didn't seem interested in sharing with him. This morning was proof because as soon as they'd made love with the early-morning sun shining down upon them, she'd practically raced to get away from him. He had been confused, but not necessarily surprised. They hadn't talked much on the drive to her house, and when he'd walked her to her door, she had barely been able to look him in the eye. The last part was what did him in.

Cooper could accept her need to keep things casual, even if he didn't agree with it. However, he wasn't willing to be a notch in her bedpost any more than he'd want her to be one in his. No matter how many sexual partners he'd had in his past, Cooper had never been able to look at a woman that way.

Truth be told, he was never with nearly as many women as the media liked to proclaim. Mainly for that reason. He found that most of the women he met were interested in one of two things: being able to brag about their conquest, or eager to get their hands on his money. Some were even interested in both. He'd gotten used to the expectations, and yes, he had used sex to take the edge off from time to time. But things were different with Tessa. Significantly different.

There was chemistry there, obviously. But there was something more.

Taking a break, Cooper headed inside, checking his cell phone to see if he'd missed any calls. He hadn't. He grabbed a bottle of water out of the cooler he had filled with ice during his trip into town and stood at the back door, staring through the screen. He purposely avoided glancing down at the floor, or the railing.

Shit.

Wiping his forehead with the back of his hand, Cooper tried to think of something other than Tessa. The problem was, he couldn't. He didn't want to. He was acting like a damn woman, and it was beginning to piss him off.

Before he could give in to his frustration, his cell phone rang, and his heart leaped right into his damn throat. Picking it up from the table, he glanced at the caller ID and groaned.

"What's up?" He greeted the one man he wasn't interested in talking to at the moment.

"Coop. Where're you at, man?" Marcus asked the same question he'd been asking for days. Cooper didn't understand why Marcus didn't just track his cell phone to pinpoint his exact location.

"At home."

"Home? As in Nashville? Why the hell didn't you say so?" Marcus's tone had turned upbeat quickly, and Cooper couldn't help but smile.

"Not Nashville," he answered, trying his best to hide the amusement in his voice. He wasn't proud that he found satisfaction in being the downturn in Marcus's day. Okay, so maybe he was proud.

"What the hell are you talking about? When are you coming back, Coop?"

"I'm not," he answered honestly.

"Come on, man. If this is depression or some shit, I know we can get you some help. I just need to know when you're coming back. I've got people starting to ask a lot of questions."

Cooper frowned. This was the problem with Marcus. He never listened. Not that Cooper was much of a talker, but when he did, he expected the man who claimed to have his best interests in mind to actually listen to him. "It's not depression."

Marcus's voice lowered, sounding more than a little irritated. "You know you've got a contract, don't you?"

"Yep," he answered, not giving a shit about the contract. He had one album about to release and one more he'd signed on to do. At this point, he wasn't sure what that meant for him or the album, but he wasn't interested in thinking about it at the moment.

"So, what? You're just going to run away?"

Damn it. Why the hell were people saying that? Cooper wasn't running.

"I've got some things to take care of. I need some time."

"How much time?" Marcus asked, relief threaded through the words.

A year? Ten, maybe? Hell, Cooper had no idea. He had no intention of throwing himself headlong into the fray at this point. He'd just bought a damn house, and he was actually beginning to feel more normal. It was a feeling he'd missed for so long he barely remembered what it even felt like.

"I've got to go, M. I'll call you in a couple of weeks, and we'll figure out what comes next."

"Godammit, Coop!"

With that parting shot, Cooper disconnected the call and tossed his cell phone back on the table. The call had successfully managed to disengage all thoughts of Tessa, but now he couldn't help but wonder whether he actually was running or not. If so, what from?

More important, would he be running again?

CHAPTER FIFTEEN

"I still can't believe it. Cooper Krenshaw sang at The Rusty Nail?" Izzy declared as the two of them sat on Tessa's front porch, drinking wine and watching the dogs play in the yard.

Thankfully, the instant Izzy had realized Tessa needed someone to talk to, she'd come over. Then again, the two of them had always been like that. Ever since they were teenagers.

"He did. You should've been there. It was wild," Tessa mentioned, not turning to look at Izzy. She knew her face was red because her skin was flaming hot as thoughts about the night before danced in her brain.

"But he's still here, right? He didn't just sing and leave town?" Izzy asked.

Because of so many things going on, Tessa hadn't had much time to just sit and talk to Izzy lately, and based on her best friend's questions, she realized how far behind they were in playing catch-up with what was going on in each other's lives.

"He's still here," she confirmed.

"Have you talked to him?"

Yes, among other things, Tessa thought to herself.

"Adam brought him over the next day and officially introduced us."

"And?"

"And what?" Tessa shot her best friend a questioning look.

"Tessa Lynn Donovan, I know you're hiding something from me. You better spill it and spill it quick."

Tessa laughed. She loved how passionate Izzy got when she felt as though someone was holding out on her. In this case, it was true, but Tessa wasn't willing to share anything that happened between her and Cooper with anyone. Not even her best friend.

Although Izzy had stood by her when Chad had gone from sweet boyfriend to spurned dickhead, Tessa still had a hard time trusting anyone with her most private thoughts.

"No way!" Izzy exclaimed, pushing back on the porch swing and sending it rocking as she pouted.

From her perch on the side railing, Tessa smiled at her friend.

"You aren't really going to hold out on me, are you?"

"I am."

"You have to at least tell me about him. Why's he still here in Devil's Bend anyway?"

Tessa sipped her wine and stared back out at the yard where Havoc and Harmony were crashed beneath the shade of the old oak tree.

"From what I can tell, I think he's looking for something to do on the side." Which was true. "He bought the Deluth farm though, so I think he's planning to stay for a while."

"Are you serious?" Izzy's swinging motion stopped abruptly as she sat upright and stared at Tessa. "Cooper Krenshaw moved here? Like, permanently?"

Tessa was surprised that Izzy asked that question first. Her friend had known full well that she was trying to buy the Deluth land as well. She had to fight the urge to sulk because her *best friend* had missed the entire point of her comment. "I don't know about permanently, but yep, he bought a house."

For any normal person, buying a house would probably mean putting down roots. But for a famous country music star who owned at least one other house that she knew of, it probably wasn't the same. He could very well be planning to build his equestrian center and then leave it to be run by others. She didn't know. Then again, she could just be letting her negative thoughts take hold.

Did she want him to stay? The question was hard for her to answer. That meager piece of her heart that was yearning for something she felt was out of her reach said yes, she'd like to have the opportunity to get to know him. See if whatever this was between them actually went somewhere.

Then there was her jaded side. The part of her that she kept closed off from anyone and everyone, including her best friend and her brothers. Tessa didn't want anyone to know how vulnerable she actually was. It wasn't a becoming trait, as far as she was concerned, so she tried to keep it buried down deep.

As far as she could tell, Cooper might be willing to stay for a while. After all, getting the farm up and running smoothly wasn't going to be an easy task. He was looking at months of work at minimum. She knew he had ambitious plans for the farm, but considering he was currently running from his singing career, she had to wonder whether this was something he did often. He didn't seem like the type to jump from one place to another, but she honestly didn't know much about him. Hell, apart from knowing his body intimately well, Tessa didn't know much about him at all.

"Eric tells me he's helping out at the bar? That true?" Izzy asked, pretending to be interested in the answer, but Tessa could feel her excitement.

"He's handling the entertainment."

"What about Adam?"

Tessa felt the sadness stirring to life in her heart. She hated that her older brother had already left to go to Dallas, but the fact that he was pursuing his dream should've made her happy for him. If she weren't scared senseless that she'd lose him too, she might be.

"He's off to the police academy in Dallas," Tessa stated, wondering how in the world she hadn't already filled Izzy in on everything that was going on lately. And despite her questions, Tessa knew Izzy was up to speed on everything that was going on in Devil's Bend, but she liked to pretend she wasn't.

"Dallas? I thought he was trying for Austin?"

"He was. They don't have any space right now."

"Does that mean Cooper's gonna be working for you for a while?"

Tessa didn't know what that was going to mean. Hell, come tomorrow, he may not want to have anything to do with her. She forced her thoughts to remain in the moment instead of drifting back to the most amazing night she'd ever had.

"Are you dating him?" Izzy asked suddenly, and Tessa instinctively turned to face her, much faster than her casual answer would support.

"Why would you ask that?"

The mischievous grin on Izzy's pretty face told Tessa the answer before her best friend said a word.

"Because of *that*," Izzy exclaimed as she pointed at her. "Your reaction. You *are* seeing him. Wow. Tessa Donovan and Cooper Krenshaw."

"It is so not like that," Tessa said with a hysterical laugh.

"So tell me how it is then."

Tessa felt the scrutiny of Izzy's gaze. She also felt her friend's concern.

"I don't know what it is." At least that was the truth.

As of that morning, from the second her eyes had opened, Tessa knew she was getting in over her head. No matter her reasons for wanting to keep Cooper at a distance, more so for self-preservation than anything else, she found herself thinking about him constantly. Not only was last night the absolute hottest thing she'd ever experienced, she couldn't deny the connection she had felt.

"If he sticks around, I could see myself dating him. For a while."

The long pause between them held a wealth of meaning, but Tessa hoped Izzy would keep her thoughts to herself. Her friend meant well, and she had always been there for Tessa when she needed her, but Tessa still never shared her most intimate thoughts with anyone.

"Honey, I know you've been hurt. And I know you miss Richie, but he isn't coming back."

Before Tessa could respond, Izzy continued. "And as for that asshole Chad, he wasn't worth the air he breathed. I think you squashed his ego, and he didn't know how to deal with it. But he was an anomaly. Not all men are like that," Izzy stated, leaning forward on the swing, reaching for Tessa's hand.

Tessa gave in to Izzy's sympathetic gesture, but it only had minimal impact on her concern. The very idea of being painted with such a brutal, vicious reputation was more than she could stand. Even though the rumors hadn't been true, they still hurt. She had managed to disassociate herself with relationships in general just to avoid the stigma that would come along with them. She had learned early on that the catty women in their small town enjoyed harassing her when they thought she might even remotely be interested in a man. Not that she was.

No, Tessa had kept herself isolated from any and all relationships. She hadn't even gone on one single date in the year since she and Chad had called it quits. Considering Chad still lived in Devil's Bend and he still enjoyed harassing her from time to time, probably to remind her that he was still there, she wasn't interested in drawing his attention any deeper. Lucky for her, Chad feared Jack, which helped some. Mostly due to her younger brother, Chad gave her a wide berth these days.

"Look at me, Tessa." Izzy squeezed her hand, and Tessa steeled her resolve as she faced her friend. "Do me a huge favor, would ya?"

"What's that?"

"Give this guy a chance. He may not be what you're looking for, but until you give it a shot, you'll never know. No one is ever going to replace Richie. But this guy isn't Chad either. He deserves a chance."

Tessa nodded and glanced out at the dogs still snoozing in the shade. She'd give him a chance. At least a shot at a casual, no-strings-attached, friends-with-benefits romp. That way, if and when the world came crashing down around her, her heart would at least be spared.

The sound of an engine in the distance had Tessa releasing Izzy's hand and turning to see who was coming toward her house. Since she lived at the end of a long dirt road, she knew whoever it was had her house in mind for their destination. She just couldn't imagine who it could be.

"Oh. My. God!" Izzy exclaimed, jumping to her feet as the big gray truck came rolling to a stop close to the house. "Is that him?"

The smile that tipped her lips came without warning. Her heart fluttered strangely in her chest. Both because of Izzy's enthusiasm and more so at the fact Cooper had come over. The idea that he wanted to see her as much as she secretly wanted to see him did odd things to her insides.

Like a crazed lunatic, Izzy set her wine glass on the railing before she darted out into the yard, jumping up and down like a teenager with a crush.

"You're Cooper Krenshaw!" she screamed as he slid down from the truck.

Good grief. The man looked freaking hot. Those damn tattered jeans encased his powerful legs, drawing Tessa's eyes right down his body. Then back up. The white T-shirt he was wearing formed perfectly to the hard chest and sculpted abs beneath. She vividly remembered what the man looked like naked, and heat suffused her face as she tried to force back the naughty image.

As though Cooper knew Izzy, or at least women like her, he put his brawny hands on her shoulders and practically held her so she'd stop hopping up and down. When he grinned knowingly up at Tessa, a shiver ran down her spine.

"Nice to meet you. Let me guess. You must be Isabelle."

"Izzy. Yes. I'm… Oh my God! You're Cooper Krenshaw," Izzy squealed and then turned toward Tessa. "And he knows my name!"

Tessa laughed, but she didn't move from her front-row seat. She wondered whether this was how Cooper was greeted by women everywhere. It was clear that her very married best friend had a major crush on the country superstar.

Tessa couldn't necessarily blame her, she thought to herself.

∞ ∞ ∞ ∞ ∞

Cooper laughed at Tessa's friend's reaction. He attempted to keep the tiny thing from plowing him down, but her excitement made him laugh. The moment he'd seen Tessa and the other woman sitting on the front porch, he had contemplated turning around, not bothering to stop. Except he wouldn't be able to do it casually because there was only one way in and one way out, which meant Tessa would obviously know he had changed his mind.

Looking at her now, her pretty blonde hair swept up on top of her head, just a few loose strands blowing around her face, he wasn't sure he would be able to make himself leave without talking to her.

"Oh, my." Izzy's voice pulled Cooper from his trance, and he turned to look down at the fiery red-headed woman standing in front of him. She had finally calmed down, thank goodness. "Would you look at the time? I've got ... a ... thing. Yep, I've got a thing to go see. *Do*. Whatever."

Cooper laughed again, noticing Tessa's beaming smile as she sat on the front porch railing watching them.

"Yep. Thanks for the chat, Tess. I'll call you later."

Cooper was fascinated by the woman's joy. The way she held her pinky and her thumb up to her head, resembling a telephone. And just like that, she was skipping away like a teenager.

That's when Cooper realized there weren't any other vehicles in the driveway. He turned to see which direction Izzy was going, and she had already set out at a run across the field that separated Tessa's house from her next-door neighbor. He grinned again.

"What brings you by, cowboy?" Tessa asked as Cooper turned to face her, his entire body hardening at the sultry sound of her voice.

"Oh, you know. Just out and about. Was in the neighborhood."

Tessa chuckled, and Cooper moved closer. He found himself trying not to make any sudden movements because the last thing he wanted was for her to panic and run inside, similar to the way she had done just that morning when he was backing out of her driveway.

"In the neighborhood, huh?" Tessa's voice had a raspy undertone that drove him absolutely mad. Especially last night when she'd been crying out his name as she'd come.

"Yes, ma'am." He moved closer until he was up on the porch, his body just inches away from hers. She turned to face him, continuing to sit on the railing that surrounded her narrow front porch, and he was immediately assaulted with memories of the night before.

When he stepped between her jeans-clad legs, she was forced to look up at him. He couldn't think of a single thing to say, but his body was begging him to get even closer. Just another inch.

"I'm going to kiss you now," he warned her, unable to stop himself. And that's exactly what he did.

Without waiting for permission, Cooper leaned down until his lips met hers as he cupped her head, holding her still while he slid his tongue in her mouth. When her soft moan made it to his ears, Cooper pulled back slightly, meeting her gaze. "Did you miss me?"

He could've sworn a frown turned down the corners of her mouth, but then suddenly she was smiling. "Maybe. Did you miss me?"

"That's why I'm here," he explained. "I didn't think I could go all night without seeing you."

Cooper had finally had enough of himself and known he needed to get out of the house. At first he hadn't had any idea where he was going, but when he'd ended up driving down Tessa's street, he hadn't questioned himself. Since the minute he'd left her that morning, she'd been the only thing on his mind. He had the bandaged thumb to prove it.

"What happened?" Tessa asked, sounding calmer than he expected a woman to be as she took his hand in hers and held it out.

"The hammer jumped right out of my hand and landed on my thumb."

"Hmmm, maybe I need to teach you how to use a hammer correctly." Tessa's eyes danced with mischief, and Cooper leaned in again, stealing another kiss.

"I'm more than happy to be your student. Anytime, anywhere." *Here and now would be good.*

"I'd hate to put you to shame," Tessa joked, her smile actually reaching her eyes that time.

"That right?" Cooper loved Tessa's flirtatious side. She didn't show it often though. "So what do you say we go get a bite to eat? I promise not to keep you out too late tonight. Unless, of course, you'd like me to."

"What were you thinking?"

Cooper honestly expected her to come up with an excuse as to why she couldn't go out with him, so he hadn't actually thought everything through. After that morning, the way she had all but run inside her house when he'd dropped her off, he knew she wasn't going to be an easy woman to get close to. Those vulnerable moments like the night before aside. It had taken a considerable amount of effort to get her to relax enough around him, but Cooper wasn't complaining. The reward was so worth the effort.

"How about we run into town and grab a burger." He was willing to make this simple if it meant he could spend time with her. "I could eat," she said with a shy grin.

"Good." Pulling her down from the railing, he leaned in and pressed a kiss to her lips before turning her toward the house. "I'll wait right here while you get ready."

The look on Tessa's face said she was surprised by his actions. Exactly what Cooper had been going for. If he really wanted to push it, he would follow her inside. But as much as he would like to get intimately familiar with her bed, he knew Tessa wouldn't hang around long if she thought he was only after sex, even if she claimed it was all she wanted. Which he wasn't. Sure, he was aching for another round with her, but he was slowly learning how to be patient.

"Go on now," he told her as he swatted her on the butt, making her jump.

"Give me five minutes." Tessa's words trailed behind her as she disappeared into the house. Cooper would give her all night if she would just ask.

Half an hour later, they were pulling into one of the busier diners in the neighboring town. Tessa had mentioned that they had the best burgers, and Cooper wasn't one to argue, so he'd let her give him directions.

Taking her hand, they walked inside together. Surprisingly, the restaurant was fairly busy for a Wednesday night, but not nearly as jam-packed as the restaurants Cooper was used to.

They found a booth in the back, and Cooper gave Tessa some space, opting to sit across from her. He would much rather sit beside her, but he knew not to push his luck. She seemed nervous, but the fact that she had agreed to go out with him was a good sign.

They didn't have to wait long before a harried waitress approached their table, sparing them a minimal glance as she took their drink orders and rattled off the specials. Once she disappeared, Cooper turned his attention back to Tessa, watching as she perused the menu.

"So what's good here?" he asked, never bothering to open his menu. He'd already resigned himself to a cheeseburger. He was just making conversation.

"Depends on what you like," she said, not looking up at him.

"You," he whispered, and Tessa's eyes shot up to meet his.

"What?"

"I like you, Tessa."

The pretty blush that infused her cheeks made Cooper's heart thump wildly, but oddly enough, the feeling wasn't sexual. The woman stole his breath in so many ways, and when she lit up like that, he couldn't help but want to wrap her in his arms and never let her go.

"Well, I'd suggest you go with the cheeseburger and fries, but whatever," she said with a strangled laugh.

He continued to watch her until the waitress returned. This time the woman actually glanced at them, and Cooper noticed the instant she recognized him. Hoping she wouldn't make a big deal out of it, Cooper took control of the situation. "What are you gonna have?" he asked Tessa directly.

"I'll have the cheeseburger and fries. Oh, and a chocolate milk shake."

"I'll have the same, only make my milk shake a sweet tea."

"You're Cooper Krenshaw," the woman said, her mouth hanging open. She never even bothered to write down their order, just continued to stare at him.

"Yes, ma'am," he replied with a grin. "Do you need our order again?"

"No. No, I got it. Two cheeseburgers and fries. One chocolate milk shake and a sweet tea."

Glancing down at her name tag and then back up at her face, Cooper grinned as he said, "Thanks, Rose."

"Sure," she mumbled, turning away briefly and then back to stare at him. "Oh my God! I can't believe you're here."

"Hey, Rose, is Ron in the back?" Tessa asked, effectively redirecting the woman's attention.

"Yeah, he's here," Rose said with a huge grin. "Hey, Tessa. Sorry, I swear I wasn't trying to be rude." The waitress's apology sounded genuine.

"No problem," Tessa replied sweetly.

When Rose trotted off, Cooper looked at Tessa. "Who is Ron?"

Tessa's brilliant smile had him answering with one of his own as they stared at each other.

"Ron owns this place. I know. I know. You thought Charlie did." Tessa laughed. "Charlie is actually Ron's son and no, he doesn't work here."

When Tessa glanced in Rose's direction, Cooper frowned. "Sorry about that, by the way."

"I get it. You're famous. I figure half the people in here are fans of yours, even if they don't necessarily know what you look like. How do you handle that everywhere you go?"

"It doesn't happen as often as you'd think," he explained. "In Nashville, it's a regular occurrence to see someone out and about. For the most part, I just try to keep a low profile."

"Has it happened much since you've been here? In Devil's Bend, I mean?"

"Not really. I've been stopped a few times when I'm in town, but I think, for the most part, people are giving me my space. It's nice to be where I'm treated like a regular guy." Cocking his head in the direction Rose had disappeared, Cooper grinned. "And even Rose's reaction was tame compared to some I've encountered."

"Does it bother you when people approach you like that?"

Cooper had to ponder the question for a minute. In truth, it didn't bother him at all. He felt like a normal person, so when someone recognized him and wanted to say hello, he mostly just went with it. Only when it encroached on his time did he get bothered by it, which honestly wasn't often. "It's still flattering," he admitted.

"If that's the case, what made you run from Nashville?"

The wording of Tessa's question hit him like a brick to the back of the head, surprising and painful at the same time, and her interest in his answer made him curious.

"I'm not running from Nashville," he said through gritted teeth. He took a deep breath and leaned back in his chair. "Sorry. I guess I'm just having a hard time seeing it the way everyone else is, that's all."

"How do you think they see it?"

"I get it," he told her. "I left suddenly, and I'm hiding out. Or at least they think I'm hiding out. But I'm not, Tessa. Right now, right here is where I want to be. As much as I like the limelight, as grateful as I am for the opportunity to do what I love, it isn't all it's cracked up to be."

"So you're saying it's hard work to do what you love?"

"Yeah, it is."

"Did you ever think it wouldn't be?"

Cooper couldn't help but wonder what was spurring all of Tessa's questions. He suddenly felt like he was under a microscope and she was digging for something specific. He never was one to circumvent the difficult questions, so he opted to go for the truth. "I always expected to work for what I wanted. I didn't expect to get so far away from what I started out doing. That's what I miss."

"Playing in the small-town bars?"

Cooper chuckled. "That's part of it, but not all. I miss the fans, I miss getting in touch with what they want. I've spent the last few years letting other people make all of my decisions for me. I want to regain some of the control, I guess."

Rose interrupted their conversation when she brought their drinks, but she didn't linger, and for that, Cooper was grateful. "So, what else you got for me?"

"What brought you to Devil's Bend?"

He had expected that question before now, but he actually hadn't given it much thought. "I'm not sure what brought me to Texas," he explained. "But as soon as I found myself here, I called Adam. He's the reason I came to Devil's Bend."

"But you came to Texas on your own?"

"Yeah, I did."

"Are you originally from here?"

"I'm from a small town in Tennessee," he admitted. "I grew up there but came to Texas my freshman year of college at UT."

"That's how you met my brother." It wasn't a question, but Cooper nodded his affirmation anyway.

As much as he liked the idea of Tessa getting to know him better, Cooper couldn't help but wonder whether she was actually trying to deflect from herself tonight. Not that he blamed her after their impromptu conversation over breakfast the other morning hadn't gone so well.

Little did she know, but he was almost at his quota of personal information for the night. At least until she offered up some of the same answers for herself.

After all, it was only fair.

CHAPTER SIXTEEN

Tessa was on a roll, and as long as Cooper was willing to answer her questions, she didn't feel the need to stop asking them. That was until he pinned her with that look. The one that told her she wasn't going to like the spin he was about to put on this entire conversation.

Yes, she knew early on that if she bombarded him with questions, he'd eventually get to take a turn. That was why she hadn't let a single second pass before she asked another. Hell, part of the time, she barely had time to process his answer before she was looking for something else to ask.

Apparently she wasn't fast enough.

"I think it's my turn."

Darn it.

"Your turn for what?" Her rule of thumb: always play dumb; it helped to confuse them.

Thankfully, Rose chose that moment to arrive with their food, her gaze still glued to Cooper as she set their food on the table and went through the motions of making sure they didn't need anything else. Tessa was pretty sure she could've asked for anything at all and Rose would've agreed to go get it for her. Instead, she chose to keep quiet, quickly tossing French fries in her mouth so she wouldn't have to answer any questions if Cooper decided to throw a few her way.

Unfortunately, that didn't last long.

"So, I know you grew up in Devil's Bend," Cooper commented, grabbing the ketchup and pouring some onto his plate.

"Yep," she mumbled, her mouth full.

"You've never lived anywhere else?"

"Nope." See, this wasn't so bad. She could do this if he kept asking closed-ended questions.

"What about college?"

"What about it?" Tessa could see the irritation in his eyes, but she couldn't help herself. She didn't want this conversation to turn on her. She remembered all too well what had happened the last time they'd tried this. As much as she liked being in Cooper's company, she certainly didn't want to give him a glimpse into her life. If she did, she risked getting too close to him.

"Where'd you go?"

Paying attention to the food on her plate, Tessa swallowed hard. "I didn't."

"Why?"

There were many reasons, but none she cared to share with him. Not that he was going to be pleased with her deflection, but Tessa honestly didn't want to go into this.

"Tessa," Cooper said quietly, pulling her attention to him.

His sparkling brown eyes were so full of interest Tessa felt like a jerk for trying to avoid him. No, it probably wasn't fair that she'd asked him a barrage of personal questions but didn't want to sit on the other side of the interrogation table, so to speak.

"Do we have to talk about me?" she asked, just as quietly.

"I want to know you."

God, why did he have to sound so sincere?

Swallowing hard, Tessa pushed her food around on her plate. She recalled Izzy's statement from earlier: *Give this guy a chance.*

"Richie and I fell in love in high school," she began, which wasn't necessarily true, but close. Tessa wasn't going to tell Cooper that she'd been a wild child, one who had ventured far past smart ideas and into extremely reckless territory, and that was actually how she'd met Richie.

"I had no idea what I wanted to do with my life, so he went to college while I stayed back here and worked. At the time, Jack's dad had just had his second heart attack, and Adam had already started his first year at UT. And because he wasn't always here, I felt obligated to stay here with Jack. Not to mention, I didn't have the money to go. Neither did my mother."

"What about your father? Where was he?"

"Who knows. The guy was unreliable. He left when I was two, and he wasn't much on being a father after that. I think I probably saw him ten times my entire life even though he lived just a couple of miles away."

Tessa hated talking about her father. No matter how she tried to spin the story, she never could rationalize his behavior. He hadn't had anything to do with either of his kids, nor had he helped out her mother much financially. It wasn't until he'd left The Rusty Nail to her and Adam when he'd died that Tessa even felt as though he'd acknowledged he had kids.

At first, she'd been defiant, not wanting anything from the man. Except Richie had managed to calm her down — something he'd gotten used to doing — and after they'd talked about it, Tessa had decided she would take over the bar. And she was still grateful to him for that because, at this point, it was the only thing she had.

"What about your parents? Where do they live?" Tessa asked, hoping Cooper would take the hint before he started asking about her mother again. She wasn't sure she had it in her to talk about Sheila tonight.

"They live in Tennessee. Probably two of my biggest fans," Cooper said quietly.

Obviously her sad story was weighing on him. She truly didn't want this date to go that direction like the first one had, so she smiled and decided to dig further. "I'm sure they're proud of you."

Cooper's smile actually reached his eyes, and the golden-brown orbs lit up with pride. "They are. My dad's not a big fan of Marcus though."

"Well, I could never imagine why," Tessa remarked, grinning. "I have to say, I'm not his biggest fan either. When do you think he'll show up to drag you back kicking and screaming?"

Cooper's face hardened, his mouth a thin line, an immediate response not forthcoming. Tessa knew she'd opened her mouth and inserted her whole boot. Grabbing her milk shake, she made herself appear interested in the other patrons in the restaurant, hoping he wouldn't be too angry at her.

"I'm not going back, Tessa," Cooper said sternly, drawing her eyes back to his face. She couldn't come up with anything to say, so she just watched him. "I want to be here, even if you don't believe that yet."

Did she believe it? Had he given her any reason not to? Tessa wasn't sure. The only thing she knew for sure was that she enjoyed his company, liked talking to him, and did want to get to know him better. Even if that street went both ways.

Nodding her head in understanding, Tessa pushed her half-eaten burger away. "Richie and I had only been married for a little over a year when he died. I was so hurt and so angry at him for leaving me. That's all I could think about for the longest time. My grief consumed me. I had never been so thankful for The Rusty Nail and my brothers until then."

Cooper's eyes stayed locked with hers, but he didn't say a word, so Tessa continued. "I spent the next two years focusing only on managing the bar. Adam finished two years of college before he came back home. He was supposed to go to the police academy with Richie, but he stayed home to help with Jack's deteriorating father."

Tessa expected to see pity in Cooper's eyes. Her story wasn't an exciting one, and yes, she'd had her fair share of grief. More than her fair share actually. But she didn't want anyone feeling sorry for her. But that's not what she saw when she looked at Cooper.

"You're a strong woman, Tessa."

Most of the time, she didn't feel strong.

"So, what do you do in your spare time?" Cooper questioned.

Tessa let the relief flood her. She could talk about this. "If it's outside, you'll probably find me there. When I'm not at the bar, that is," she answered simply. "The dogs and I spend a lot of time out and about. I volunteer as a youth counselor at our church." The last part was something she didn't necessarily care to elaborate on, more specifically, what had gotten her into that particular area.

"And for the last couple of years, I spent a lot of time with Mr. Deluth, hanging out with him, helping with his garden when he wanted help. Or simply talking to him."

"And that's how you and he came to an agreement on the land?"

"Sort of. I've never purposely kept my dream a secret." Tessa left off the *except from Adam* part. "I want to help people, and I love working with kids. I was just a kid when I first fell in love with horses, and I never grew out of it. I've volunteered at the high school's Ag barn a few times to help them out. Both the horses and the kids have brought me such joy, I guess I figured I could have the best of both worlds."

Cooper pushed his plate away and stared back at her, his forearms resting on the table in front of him. Tessa could feel his full attention focused on her, and she fought the urge to squirm in her seat. She continued, "Jerry and I were talking one day, and I told him what I wanted to do. We'd been on the back porch, staring out at the rickety old barn that was falling in on itself. That's when he mentioned his property would be perfect for what I wanted. I explained to him that I didn't have that kind of money, so we worked out a deal. I'm not sure I ever would've had enough for the down payment, but I was trying hard."

"And then I waltzed in and stole it out from under you." Cooper's tone had turned bitter, surprising Tessa. She sat up straight as her eyes roamed over the hard lines of his face, too startled to continue.

"Goddammit, Tessa," he growled, his voice low. "How the hell did you let me do that?"

All of a sudden, the sweet, laidback country boy was nowhere in sight, and Cooper Krenshaw was more than a little pissed off. Tessa sat motionless, watching as he grabbed his hat — which he'd taken off when they'd come inside — from the seat beside him and then stood. She couldn't bring herself to move as she watched him walk over to Rose, handing her some money before he walked right out of the restaurant.

Shit. He was her ride.

Figuring she had no choice but to follow, Tessa stood quickly, waved at Rose as she passed, and then followed him out into the parking lot. To her surprise, Cooper was standing by his truck, his hands braced on the bedside.

"Hey." She kept her voice low, unaffected. She was confused and probably annoyed that he'd walked out on her, but she was more interested in what had happened. Why was he acting like that?

"Tessa, I had no idea," he whispered as he turned to face her. She could see the anguish on his face, and her heart broke a little.

Tessa knew that was only a partial truth. He had known. Maybe not how much she wanted the land, but he had definitely known. But for some reason, she didn't hold it against him. "Don't," she told him. "Please don't feel sorry for me, Cooper."

"Sorry?" He laughed without mirth. "Darlin', I don't feel sorry for you. I feel like a selfish bastard. I walked in here and stole that land right out from under you."

She couldn't deny the truth, but for some reason, she wanted to comfort him. Although she'd been torn between wanting him and hating him for stealing her dream, there were other emotions that had been more prevalent recently.

Tessa moved in closer, planting her palms flat on his chest. His heart was pounding wildly, his golden eyes shadowed by the black Stetson on his head. It was her turn to grip his chin and make him look at her. When their eyes met, Tessa swallowed hard. "As much as I hate it, everything happens for a reason, Cooper. Considering we're both going after the same dream, I can't say I'm sad that you were able to buy the land. At least something good is going to come of it. Much sooner than I ever could've made it happen."

"Tessa…" Cooper's voice sounded strangled, his eyes weary. "I can't help but think that if I'd never shown up here…"

Breaking eye contact because she truly didn't want him to think that way, Tessa eyed Cooper's truck, and an idea came to her.

"Give me your keys," Tessa said firmly, releasing his chin so she could hold out her hand.

"What?" It was Cooper's turn to be surprised, but Tessa didn't want to explain more.

"Just give me the keys, Krenshaw."

When he finally handed them over, Tessa ordered him to get in the truck. She moved around to the driver's side and started the engine. A few minutes later, they were heading back to Devil's Bend.

Before Cooper had a chance to regret his decision to go after his dream, Tessa wanted to remind him what he had. And she knew exactly how to do that.

∞ ∞ ∞ ∞ ∞

He was such a selfish bastard.
Selfish, selfish, selfish.
Sonuvabitch!

Up until that moment when Tessa had laid out how her dream had evolved, Cooper hadn't given much thought to the fact that he was actually stealing her dream out from under her. And why? Because of something he wanted? Did it even matter that they both had the same goal in mind? Had he even considered how important Tessa's dream was to her?

The answer was a resounding *fuck no*. He knew what she'd wanted, but that hadn't stopped him. Hell, he had even been given the opportunity when Luanne decided to up the ante on the property. But then Tessa had selflessly pushed him to go after the land, to make sure that at least one of them could accomplish what she'd been working toward her entire life. And he hadn't bothered to think of anything except what he wanted.

He felt like a total ass. Here he was abandoning his entire life because he wanted to get away from it all and do something meaningful. And once again, he hadn't thought about anyone but himself. The irony was a brutal slap in the face.

"Where are we going?" he asked, knowing he sounded as angry as he felt.

"Just sit back, cowboy. Let me do the drivin'," she said, a smile in her voice.

He wished like hell he could force himself to smile. He wanted to. Just being around Tessa made him happy. Sitting beside her, even if she was driving his truck like a mad woman, should've been enough to erase all of the anger building in his gut. But it didn't. It didn't go unnoticed that she was taking care of him when he should have been the one putting her first. Realizing that only made him feel worse.

When they pulled up to Tessa's house a few minutes later, Cooper glanced over at her. So she wanted to go home? He actually couldn't blame her. Before he could get his door open, she turned on him.

"Sit right here. Don't you dare move from that seat. I'll be back in five minutes."

Cooper could hardly comprehend what she was saying because his own anger was like a hornet's nest in his brain, the buzz unbearable. She was coming back? He forced a simple nod and stared out the front window of the truck as she climbed out. As much as he wanted to, he didn't even watch as she made her way up her front steps.

Just like she'd said, Tessa was back in less than five minutes. Her arms were full, and he was about to climb out of the truck to help her when he saw her shake her head. What was she up to?

She walked around to the bed of the truck, tossed everything inside, and then moved back around to the driver's door. Once she was inside, she buckled her seat belt and put the truck in reverse, tearing out of the driveway once again.

"You gonna tell me where we're going now?" he asked, suddenly nervous.

"Nope. And you've asked more than your share of questions tonight, cowboy. Just keep your mouth shut and enjoy the drive."

If she was trying to improve his mood, she was doing a good job. Her feisty attitude was warming his blood like a pot on simmer. He couldn't take his eyes off her. She was so focused on driving that he allowed himself a few minutes to stare. And like every other time he had looked at her, his head swam with a jumble of thoughts and images.

He still had a perfect picture of the first time he'd seen her at The Rusty Nail, her tight black T-shirt molded to extraordinary breasts. Then later, when she'd inserted herself between two pissed off cowboys because it was her bar and she wasn't having any of their shit.

Of course, his mental scrapbook wouldn't be complete without the one of her standing on her front porch in those white shorts and tiny tank top…

The more the images flashed in his head, the more his anger subsided. Only now the blood that had been boiling in his veins was taking an immediate detour directly to his groin.

By the time the truck slowed, Cooper was looking around to see where they were. He watched out the front windshield as they passed his house, heading down the dirt path that led to the barn. He was just about to ask her what the hell she was up to, but her quick "uh-uh" shut him up.

And exactly why did her sudden authority make his dick that much harder?

They passed the dilapidated barn and continued through what would eventually be a pasture, down a bumpy decline until they were pulling up near a pond. He hadn't had time to check it out more than just a glance as he passed by, but he knew this was one of the three small stock ponds on the land, probably from when there were cattle grazing these fields at one point.

The truck turned abruptly and then Tessa was backing toward the water. He was just about to get nervous when she applied the brakes and then grinned over at him.

"Okay, you can get out now."

Tessa didn't wait for him, so Cooper climbed out on the passenger side and then headed around to the back of the truck, just a few feet from the water's edge.

The scrape of the tailgate lowering caught his attention, and he turned to see Tessa climbing up into the bed of the truck.

"What are you doing?" he asked, no longer caring to be kept in the dark.

"Just get in, would ya?" she called to him as she proceeded to throw a blanket down into the bed of the truck.

That's what she'd been carrying. Blankets and pillows. Oh, and a six-pack of beer.

Would she ever cease to amaze him?

Cooper climbed up into the bed of the truck, waiting until she sat down on one side before he lowered himself beside her. She popped the cap on one of the beer bottles with the skill of a professional and then handed it over. He grabbed the bottle but never stopped looking at her.

"Now relax," she commanded, fluffing one of the pillows up against the cab of the truck.

They both got situated, propping themselves up and staring out at the water.

Holy shit.

Out in front of him was nothing but darkness. Well, except for the white light of the giant moon as it reflected off the black water.

"Perfect, ain't it?" she asked, her voice quieter than before.

Cooper glanced over at her, thinking that she certainly was perfect. For him.

"I'm talking about the night, Cooper," she said with a chuckle. "Now be quiet and just breathe."

Cooper did as she instructed, drinking his beer and watching as the moon rose higher in the sky, the reflection on the pond shifting on the glassy water. Up above them, the stars shone brightly, and the warm breeze moved through the trees. Aside from the rustling of branches and the sound of crickets, there wasn't another sound.

So this was what peace was. A perfect night, a cold beer, and a beautiful woman. It was the antidote to all of the anger he'd built up just a short while ago. And exactly the place he felt he needed to be. After years on the road, nights spent in front of hundreds of people, singing his heart out, this was what actually filled Cooper with that peaceful serenity he'd been searching for.

He had no idea how much time had passed, but he didn't budge until Tessa shifted beside him, setting her beer bottle down as she moved to lie flat in the bed of the truck. Cooper followed suit, getting comfortable beside her, their arms touching as they stared up at the sky.

"I used to love to sit outside under the stars. Okay, that's not entirely true," Tessa said quietly. "I still love it. There's more light at my house, so the sky isn't quite this clear from my yard. Sometimes I'll grab a blanket and join Havoc and Harmony on the grass, just enjoying the peace and quiet."

Cooper wasn't sure he'd ever seen the sky so clear. A sea of black, dotted with bright stars and a brilliant moon overhead. He could imagine Tessa lying on a blanket beneath the stars, the two massive animals cuddled up to her side, seeking her protection and offering their own.

"This is what it means to slow down, Cooper," Tessa told him, her head turning to the side. He turned his head to face her, utterly in awe of her.

"I could get used to this." If she was beside him, Cooper was pretty sure he could get used to anything.

"Me too," she admitted, her eyes never leaving his.

The only thing better would be if he had her in his arms. And honestly, now that the idea had planted itself in his brain, he couldn't think about anything else.

CHAPTER SEVENTEEN

Tessa's heart was thumping against her ribs as she stared over at Cooper. Even in the darkness, his eyes glowed, and the way he was watching her made her chest swell with a strange feeling. One that she hadn't felt in years. Not since…

Knowing that she was the one to bring him here, to show him the place she used to love to come and watch the stars and that he enjoyed it as much as she did … well, Tessa felt more complete than she had in a long time.

This particular spot was one she loved to visit, especially in the summer when the water was warm enough to get in. That was what she considered being the perfect night — skinny-dipping under the stars, nothing to hinder her body or her mind.

When Cooper moved, propping himself on his side, and his warm hand cupped her face gently, Tessa wondered if tears would spring up to her eyes. Her emotions were running rampant, and the only thing she wanted right then was to be as close to this man as she possibly could. Only she couldn't get the words out.

"Tessa." The way he said her name sent a shiver across her skin, made her heart skip a beat or two as she waited anxiously to see what he was going to do or say next.

She hoped he could read her mind, could sense what she needed, because she was sure if she had to ask him, then she was going to lose a piece of herself that she so desperately wanted to keep securely in place.

When his mouth brushed over hers, Tessa slid her fingers into his hair, letting the warmth of him ground her. Whatever was happening between them right at that moment felt like something different. Something she wasn't sure she wanted but knew down deep that she needed.

It was a connection.

As his tongue caressed hers gently, easing into her mouth and tentatively exploring, she sighed. Keeping her touch gentle, she allowed the soft strands of his hair to tease her fingers while the heat of his chest seared her breast. The farther he leaned over her, the safer she felt, and she didn't want his touch to disappear.

"God, Tessa," he whispered against her mouth. "Darlin', I—"

She had no idea what he was going to say, but she was grateful that he locked the words up tight. Right now, she just wanted to feel. Words weren't needed. The moment was just right, his body was more than perfect against hers, and the lost look in his eyes told her that he was feeling the same thing she was.

When he managed to prop himself over her, one knee pressing between her thighs, she eased his T-shirt up and over his head, leaving her hands free to roam the taut, smooth skin of his chest. Her fingertips traced down his neck, over his collarbone, then over the muscled planes of his chest.

They were staring into one another's eyes, neither of them saying anything, their mouths not searching for the other because their eyes were saying more than anything else possibly could. Tessa knew she wasn't going to survive this experience with her heart intact. This man was quickly getting to her, embedding himself in her soul, which terrified her.

She reveled in the gentle scrape of his fingers as they deftly unhooked the buttons down the center of her blouse, moving ever so slowly. As each button escaped its mooring, his fingertips raised goose bumps on her sensitive flesh and her breath lodged in her throat.

"So pretty," he whispered as his head tilted downward, the heat of his breath brushing over the skin his hands had just warmed. "Baby…"

Another sentence left unsaid, causing Tessa to wrap her arms around him, her hands trailing over the rigid muscles of his back.

While Cooper worked to remove her shirt and bra without forcing her to let go of him, Tessa closed her eyes and inhaled his musky scent. The smell was like a drug, entering her bloodstream and instantly making her light-headed, yearning for more. The frenzy that ignited in her veins caused her to let go of him, wanting nothing more than to get him naked and feel him skin to skin. She maneuvered her hands between them, working to release the button on his jeans, letting him know how eager she was to get a move on. She needed him. Needed to feel his skin against hers, to take him inside of her, where she could get closer to him.

"Cooper." His name came out as a broken sob, and Tessa feared she was going to lose it. He was so tender, so sweet. There wasn't an ounce of the desperate passion she'd seen in his eyes the last time they'd been together. This time there was more. A connection that he was trying to make, and despite her resistance, her heart was answering the call.

"I want to make love to you, Tessa." The words were spoken against her neck, his breath a warm tickle over her skin.

"Please," she pleaded. What was she asking for? She didn't want to make love, didn't want to let this man get that close to her, but his emotional hold on her was unbreakable.

Finally, they both had to move in order to rid themselves of their clothes, but once they were naked and Cooper donned a condom, he was on top of her again. The weight of his body reestablished the safety and security she managed to find in his arms.

Their eyes met briefly before their lips touched. Tessa was tempted to deepen the kiss, to push this faster, but she couldn't. Her heart was controlling her body, and the slight tremble in her limbs was more than a desperate need for his touch. As he shifted her legs farther apart, Tessa made room for him until his thick, hard erection was pressing against her entrance.

The deep rumble from his chest as he pushed inside of her sent another bolt of electricity racing over her skin, her entire being lighting up from where their bodies joined.

Cooper adjusted their positions until he was resting on one forearm, his hand cupping her head while he held himself up with his other hand. His hips were moving ever so slowly as the heat built inside of her, their bodies melding together in a dance as old as time and as moving as the dawn of a new day. The thick, hard length of his cock teased every sensitive nerve ending inside of her. Slowly. Ever so slowly until Tessa's entire body was strung tight.

"Cooper, please," she begged.

"Please what?" he asked, his lips coming down to brush against hers. "Tell me, darlin'. Tell me what you need."

"I need you. I need you just like this," she admitted, scared of what that really meant.

Another deep rumble in his chest made Tessa's pussy clench tightly around him. The sensual way he loved her body, cradling her in his arms while he pressed inside of her, was too much. More than she'd thought possible. This was supposed to be sex, and without even wanting more, Tessa realized she was quickly getting attached to this man.

"Look at me, Tessa. Open your eyes."

She hadn't realized she had closed them, but Tessa managed to lift her eyelids, staring up into Cooper's handsome face, the soft, golden glow of his eyes captivating her, drawing her closer to him.

"Tessa... Baby... You're so hot. So sweet."

She barely heard his words as they were whispered against her mouth, and she wondered for a second if Cooper had even said them.

And then his body shifted, his cock burying deeper inside of her as she wrapped her legs around him, holding him as close as she could.

"I can't hold out much longer," he admitted softly, his eyes fierce with the same need Tessa felt growing inside of her.

"Then don't," she offered with a smile. Meeting his thrusts with her own, their bodies finally took over, seeking, searching, driving for that release that they both had been holding back.

"God, yes, Tessa. Baby, you feel so good." The dark, rich sound of his voice made the words all the more erotic.

Tessa's nails dug into his back as her brain went on the fritz, her body taking over completely. She bit her bottom lip to keep from crying out, but there was no way to stop the way her internal muscles locked down on him.

"That's it, baby. Come for me, Tessa," Cooper whispered.

Her head dug into the pillow beneath her, her neck straining as she gave into the orgasm that threatened to tear her in two. Heat, light, waves and waves of pleasure consumed her. Just when she thought she was safely crashing back to earth, Cooper's mouth crushed down on hers, his tongue thrusting inside as his body stiffened, his hips locking as he buried himself deeper. This time, the rumble in his chest reverberated through her, and another orgasm crested, the tremors felt all the way to her toes.

Tessa knew without a doubt, no matter how hard she fought and pleaded with her heart, Cooper was going to be the next man to break her. It was inevitable.

∞ ∞ ∞ ∞ ∞

Cooper had never been as content as he was right in that moment. Lying beside Tessa, her soft body pressed up against him while she slept, he was sure he would never find another place he'd rather be.

He wasn't sure what had happened between them a little while ago, but he knew she felt it too. While they'd made love, he had noticed something in her eyes. And it filled a hollow void deep inside him. In fact, she had filled it to overflowing, and he wondered whether she understood what that meant to him.

Not in as long as he could remember had Cooper felt such a powerful hunger for any one woman. And his need for her had nothing to do with sex either. This was deeper. Stronger.

However much Cooper wanted to tell her how he felt, he knew he needed to keep a lid on his emotions. He was smarter than that. He didn't doubt for one second that Tessa was going to fight him every step of the way. At least once they had to make their way back to reality. But right now, he just wanted to hold her and never let her go.

The moon had risen high in the sky, the soft glow sliding over Tessa's smooth, golden skin. Pressing a kiss to her shoulder, he pulled her closer as he inhaled deeply. This woman was getting to him.

Not that he deserved her.

He knew his time was running out. His reality was going to descend on him and this sleepy little town before long. There would probably be reporters crawling out of the woodwork. He didn't particularly care if they found him, but he knew once they did, they'd start digging around. They would want to know more about the people he was spending his time with. Namely Tessa.

As soon as word got out that he had found a woman, they would be itching for a story. And yes, he was certain they would find out about her, because even if he wanted to, he would never be able to deny what he was feeling for Tessa. Hell, it was probably written all over his face.

But he didn't want Tessa to get caught in the crossfire. Although she hadn't told him everything about herself, it was clear she was holding something back from him. Hiding something that she didn't want him to know about, and no matter what it was, she considered it big. Regardless of what that was, he knew the tabloids would have a field day when it came to digging into her past, dredging up the pain that she had been through already just because he was with her.

And again, his selfish side was roaring to the front. As much as he wanted to shield her from all of that, Cooper didn't want to let her go. He didn't want to risk losing her. But he knew Marcus was going to show up soon. Even if he didn't admit he was running, Cooper knew it appeared that way.

And they would find him. Which meant he better be prepared when that time came.

CHAPTER EIGHTEEN

By the time Thursday night rolled around, Tessa was grateful to be back at the bar. She had spent a lot of time with Cooper during the day. After their rendezvous in the bed of his truck, she had asked him to take her home. He had, but rather than dropping her off and kissing her good-night, he'd come in for a while, saying he wasn't ready to let her go. His sweetness was nearly her undoing. To her surprise, Cooper had gone home rather than stay the night.

She wasn't sure whether she was relieved or disappointed about the last part. Or both.

Either way, she'd woken up that morning to her phone ringing. When she'd answered, Cooper had advised her that she had half an hour to get ready because he was coming to pick her up. After a quick breakfast at a fast-food restaurant just outside of town, he had taken her back to his place, and they'd spent most of the day supervising the movers as they unloaded a huge moving trailer. Luckily, the movers had done most of the work, but after sitting idly by for about an hour, Tessa had no longer been able to sit still, so she'd pitched in.

Helping him to get situated in his house by relocating boxes to the appropriate place was not the only way in which she was introduced to a day in the life of Cooper Krenshaw. Tessa also had had the pleasure of seeing what it meant to be stalked by paparazzi.

Apparently, word was now out, and the fact that an eighteen-wheeler was delivering Cooper's personal items to Texas was big news in the country music world. And thus had brought about reporters who would do just about anything to get what Cooper referred to as a money shot.

Tessa was immediately turned off by the fact that someone would want to sit outside Cooper's house and watch him through a telephoto lens just to see what he could capture on film. Needless to say, they'd had to stay inside in order to avoid the reporters, and after a while, Tessa had begun to feel claustrophobic.

Aside from that weirdness, their interaction throughout the entire ordeal had been comfortable and easy, almost as though they had been spending the day together for quite some time. And true to form, Tessa found she was overthinking the whole relationship, starting at the beginning and trying to nail down where in the world she'd gotten off track. After all of the ways her brain had picked through the events of the last weeks, she still had no idea.

But now that she was back at work, she was hoping to figure out a way to put some space between them. Only because she feared she was getting too close too fast. And surprisingly, for the first time, she was more interested in not running Cooper off than she was worried about these feelings he was dredging up inside of her.

The sound of the microphone feedback had Tessa turning toward the stage. A smile snuck up on her as she watched Cooper move toward the front of the stage, grinning down at the handful of people already on the dance floor. She tried not to keep her eyes glued to him as he started to sing, but admittedly, that was easier said than done. She was enraptured by the man. It was no wonder there were people who'd pay decent money to watch him perform.

It wasn't until a customer caught her attention that she turned away. "What can I get ya?" she asked the well-dressed man who'd found a seat at the bar.

"Crown and Coke, if you don't mind," the man said matter-of-factly, his southern drawl distinct and obviously not from Texas.

"Sure thing," she answered politely as she moved to grab the Crown from the shelf and a clean glass. As she poured, she discreetly scoped him out, taking in his perfectly cut blond hair, his clean-shaven jaw. He didn't have on a hat, and the suit he sported looked totally out of place in her dimly lit bar.

Once the drink was made, she pushed the glass his way and gave him the price.

"Put it on Coop's tab." The brusque manner in which he replied sounded oddly familiar. When he turned his back on her again, she studied him, unable to come up with where she might know him from.

"Excuse me, what?" she asked, glancing over at Eric, who had just made his way behind the bar.

"You heard me, sweetheart. Just put it on Coop's tab."

"And you would be?" she asked, unable to conceal the irritation in her voice.

"Oh, sorry. I just figured you'd recognize me," the man said with an air of conceit, turning back to face her as though seeing his entire face would ring a bell.

Nope. Nothin'.

"Sweetheart, the name's Marcus Evergreen."

Sweetheart?

Tessa was more than familiar with being called all sorts of endearing terms; after all, she was the main one responsible for providing her customers with alcohol on a nightly basis, but something about the way this guy addressed her made her feel slimy.

Oh, hell.

Did he just say…?

Marcus the Manager.

Oh, Lord. The strange, empty feeling in her stomach had nothing to do with the fact that she hadn't had dinner and everything to do with why Manager Marcus was sitting in her bar.

Tipping her head at Marcus, as though she actually wanted to greet him, Tessa quickly shot a glance at Eric. Not necessary, it would seem, because Eric was already easing his way out from behind the bar. If she were lucky, he was about to let Cooper know he had company.

"So, what brings you here, *Marcus Evergreen?*" she asked, pretending the name didn't actually ring a bell. The man seemed a little full of himself; no need to give him the satisfaction just yet.

"You don't remember me?" he asked, a questioning look in his dark brown eyes.

"Sorry, should I?" She offered him a shrug.

With a huff, Marcus set his half-empty glass on the bar and focused his smarmy grin at her. "I'm here to take the talent back where he belongs."

"The talent?" Tessa didn't particularly care for the way Marcus referred to Cooper. After all, he had a name. And he was so much more than just mere "talent."

"Yes ma'am," Marcus answered with a tilt of his head toward the stage. "It's time for Cooper to go back where he belongs. He's had his fun."

"Sorry, I'm not sure I understand." Tessa knew she was laying it on thick, but she figured she would take the opportunity to get to know what this guy's agenda was while she had the chance.

"Marcus." The low rumble of Cooper's voice had Tessa turning to face him. She hadn't even realized he wasn't singing anymore.

"There he is," Marcus greeted Cooper as though they were best buds who were being reunited once again.

The hard lines etched across Cooper's forehead said he wasn't nearly as happy to see Marcus though.

"Why are you here?" Cooper asked, nodding his head at Tessa as though dismissing her.

Nuh-uh. She wasn't going to miss this for the world. After all, as far as she was concerned, she now had a stake in this. Cooper was managing the entertainment at The Rusty Nail. Without him, she would have to do the job herself, and there just wasn't enough time in the day for her to do anything more than what she already had on her plate.

Sounded reasonable.

"I figured you'd be happy to see me," Marcus added with that smirk that Tessa was beginning to realize was more devious than pleasant.

"Why would you figure that?"

Tessa felt like she was watching a volleyball match, her head bouncing back and forth as the two men spoke. Cooper was on the defensive, and Marcus was either too obtuse to realize he wasn't welcome or he just didn't care. Tessa had a feeling it was the latter.

"Oh, I don't know. I thought you'd prefer I be the one to find you rather than the press."

Too late for that, Tessa thought to herself.

"I really didn't care either way," Cooper said firmly.

Tessa pretended to be busy while she poured a beer and then handed it over to Cooper.

"Perfect," Marcus rumbled smoothly. "Have a seat. Let's have a drink. It's been a while. We've got a lot to catch up on."

Tessa noticed the way Marcus's eyes darted in her direction, and as soon as they did, Cooper growled but managed to collapse onto one of the bar stools near the bar.

"I'm not going back." Cooper's voice was low and eerily calm, but Tessa felt the anger radiating off him.

His reaction to his manager wasn't what she was expecting. She understood that Marcus was fighting Cooper about going back to Nashville, but the response didn't fit the situation. Clearly there was something she was missing.

"Tessa." Cooper turned to look at her. "Do you mind?"

"Well," she said in a huff, feeling as though Cooper had just slapped her square in the face.

Feeling like a sulking child, she stomped toward the opposite end of the bar, hating how she was acting. Forcing a fake smile, Tessa walked right up to another group and insinuated herself right in the middle. It was either that or go pout.

No matter what, she was damn sure not going to let Cooper see her pout.

∞ ∞ ∞ ∞ ∞

Cooper ignored the way Tessa stomped off, mainly because he was more concerned with why Marcus had just shown up in Devil's Bend. Completely unexpected.

Okay, so maybe not entirely unexpected. After all, Cooper had disappeared right off the grid, and until now, he hadn't come face-to-face with anyone who knew him. But for Marcus to get his arrogant ass on an airplane and fly to Texas, well, that meant he was up to something.

"You shouldn't have come here," Cooper told him, turning to face the bar. He gripped his beer, more worried about keeping his hands busy so that he didn't strangle the man sitting beside him than his thirst.

"Well, I figured someone had to do it. You've pushed your limit this time."

A grainy, red haze clouded Cooper's vision as soon as the words left Marcus's mouth. He was always hearing that, listening to Marcus act as though he were some unruly kid who needed to be reined in.

"Whoa, buddy. You need to just relax." Marcus's hand gripped his shoulder firmly, and that's when Cooper realized he was growling, his anger apparently trying to escape so that his head didn't explode.

Shrugging Marcus's hand from his shoulder, he took a drink of his beer, hoping to clear his head before he lost it right there in Tessa's bar. Hell, he'd already pissed her off, no need to make matters worse.

Cooper knew Marcus wouldn't be able to hold out for long before he would start to talk, so he kept his mouth shut. He had nothing to say, so it really wasn't a hardship. As far as he was concerned, Marcus's trip was wasted, and if he were smart, he'd hop right back on a plane home as soon as possible.

"So, where're you staying? We can head on over, get your things, and then head on back to Nashville tonight. All of this forgotten."

Cooper tipped an eyebrow, looking sideways at Marcus. Well, at least that confirmed his suspicion. The man didn't listen to a single thing he told him. Ever. Not to mention he was a liar. If the paparazzi had found him, then Marcus knew exactly what was going on in Cooper's life. So, for him to pretend he didn't know Cooper had officially moved seriously pissed him off.

"I'm quite content right here," Cooper mumbled, hoping he sounded more disinterested than pissed off.

"Look, man," Marcus began as he leaned in close. "I've lined up someone who you can talk to. They'll be real discreet, and we can get you some help."

"Some help?" Cooper asked incredulously, knocking his beer hard enough that it sloshed out of the glass mug and onto the bar top. Forcing himself to his feet, he peered down at Marcus.

Marcus looked around, his eyes scanning the area around Cooper quickly. "Man, keep it down. You don't want these people knowing your business, do you?"

"These people *are* my business," Cooper retorted. "I'm not sure what the hell you do when I talk, but listening clearly ain't it."

"Come on, Coop. You're gonna have to stop doing this," Marcus said quietly, and Cooper's back straightened.

He seriously wasn't bringing that up, was he?

Fuck.

Not wanting Tessa to get an earful of conversation that he knew she wouldn't understand, Cooper nodded his head and motioned for Marcus to follow him. They'd take this outside. At least then he wouldn't have to worry about everyone knowing his business.

Once they were outside, Cooper moved around to the side of the building, avoiding the few people who were wandering in from the parking lot. Since it was Thursday, the bar wasn't as packed as the weekend, but he knew they would keep coming right up until around eleven.

"You really need to go," Cooper told Marcus when they were out of earshot of anyone else. "I'm not leaving."

"You sure about that?" Marcus asked, his eyes narrowing on Cooper's face. The threat was there, he could feel it. Every time they had a disagreement, which was anytime Marcus felt he wasn't getting his way, they would go toe-to-toe.

"I'm sure," Cooper growled, making sure Marcus could hear the fury in his tone. He was done letting Marcus threaten him.

"How about this," Marcus said haughtily, jerking his suit jacket straight as he stared back at Cooper. "I'm going to give you one last night to enjoy yourself. You do what you have to do, but tomorrow I'll be right back here. You'll meet me here with your shit, and we're heading back to Nashville. I'm done playing games with you, Cooper."

Although every muscle in his body tensed, his hands curling into fists and his legs beginning to sway beneath him, Cooper managed not to hit the guy. He was so fucking tired of Marcus and the way he was treated. Shit, if it weren't for Cooper, Marcus Evergreen wouldn't have shit. And the high-handed approach had never been warranted. It was just the way Marcus was.

Nodding his head, agreeing that Marcus was leaving and nothing more — although Marcus had no way of knowing that — Cooper waited until his manager offered up that smug grin once again.

He didn't mind that Marcus believed he had won this round. There wasn't a damn thing Marcus could do to Cooper to hurt him. It was just time for Cooper to accept the fact that he held all the power and this business arrangement was about to come to a very abrupt halt.

Just not tonight.

CHAPTER NINETEEN

When two o'clock finally rolled around, Tessa was ready to sneak out the back door and let Eric close up himself. Since she had efficiently evaded Cooper for the last few hours, she figured the least she could do was skip out on an argument.

There would most definitely be an argument.

He had dismissed her as if she didn't matter.

And he'd hurt her feelings.

Not only that, but once he had come back inside — without Marcus, thank goodness — he hadn't paid any attention to her at all. His escape was in the form of the stage where he'd spent most of the night singing, not even interacting with the crowd much like he normally did.

So maybe he was in a bad mood. Still, Tessa felt she deserved more than the easy shrug-off that she'd gotten when he'd felt she was eavesdropping on his conversation. And what could they have talked about that he didn't want her to hear?

That had bothered her most of the night too. He was still a mystery to her. Getting to know him had been a slow-moving train when compared to how quickly their lust had caught fire.

Glancing over at Eric, Tessa contemplated sneaking out as originally planned, but before she could, Cooper walked up.

"I want to talk to you before you leave," he told her and then he headed back to the stage.

Knowing she wasn't going to get away that easily, she resigned herself to her closing duties, and half an hour later, she was finishing up.

"Need anything more from me?" Eric asked from the other side of the bar.

"No, I'm just about done here too."

"Awesome. I'll see you tomorrow then."

"Hey, would you lock the front door on your way out?" Cooper called from his perch on the stage.

What the hell was he doing? From where she stood, it looked like he was tuning his guitar.

"Sure thing," Eric yelled from the opposite side of the room as he left.

When Eric's car roared out of the parking lot a few minutes later, Tessa knew she was stuck having to deal with Cooper before she went home. Part of her wanted to know what he and Marcus had talked about and why he seemed so moody all of a sudden. The other part wanted to rip him a new one for treating her so callously when Marcus had been there.

"Where're you going?" Cooper asked as she tried to make a hasty retreat to the bathroom.

"The restroom. What? Do you want to hold my hand?" she snipped. She needed a couple of minutes to gain some of her composure, and then she'd be better equipped to deal with whatever he had to say.

She had a feeling he was getting ready to let her down easy.

Thankfully, Cooper didn't say anything more, and she disappeared down the dark, narrow hallway heading straight for the bathroom. The first measure of business was to splash cold water on her face. She could do this. She could.

"If he's going back to Nashville then that's what was meant to be," she told her reflection.

She spent a few minutes righting her clothes, making sure she looked more at ease than she felt. Frowning at her choice of outfit, Tessa fixed the sagging shoulder of her lightweight sweater. She'd actually dressed up tonight. Well, dressed up for her anyway. Her blue jean skirt and off-the-shoulder olive green sweater had made her feel pretty when she'd first put them on. The boots on her feet had made her feel normal.

Yet now, knowing that Cooper was waiting for her, she felt significantly overdressed. It would've been easier to face him if she had on her jeans and a T-shirt.

But there was nothing she could do about that now.

Taking a deep breath, Tessa flung open the door and shrieked when she ran right into Cooper's chest, face first.

"What the—"

Before she could finish the sentence, Cooper had her slammed up against the wall, his steel-hard thigh inserted between her legs pushing her skirt up high. The brutal way his tongue lashed into her mouth had Tessa responding with all of the frustration she had built up over the course of the night. Only her fury matched his, equally fervent, masking itself with the passion that burned bright and hot between them.

Tessa was torn between yelling at him for hurting her the way he had and pulling him closer, trying to wrap herself around him like a blanket. The hallway echoed with their combined groans and moans, the sound of their harsh breaths reverberating in the limited space.

"I need you, Tessa. Right here," Cooper groaned when his lips released hers, their breaths mingling as they sucked in oxygen.

Was he asking for permission? Would she give it?

"You don't deserve me," she countered, her irritation with the situation resurfacing, a vivid reminder of how he had brushed her off like she didn't mean a thing to him.

"You're right, I don't. I won't argue. It doesn't change how I feel," he said, his finger curling beneath her chin and forcing her head back so she couldn't look away. His eyes were hidden by the shadow from the brim of his hat, and Tessa wished she had her hat on. At least she could hide some part of what she was feeling. Even in the dim light of the hallway, she felt entirely too exposed.

"You blew me off," she bit out. "You acted like I didn't matter."

Cooper let go of her chin, planting his hands against the wall on each side of her head, his unyielding thigh still lodged between hers, making her painfully aware of the arousal slowly gaining momentum.

"You heard the way Marcus talks to me, Tessa. He treats me like a dog that's supposed to heel at his feet, and I'm the one who makes him the fucking money. How do you think he treats people who don't mean a damn thing to him? I wasn't about to let him talk to you like that."

Well, when he put it that way ... it did kind of make sense.

"You could've told me. I deserved that much."

"Yes. You did. He just makes me so fucking mad." The heat emanating off Cooper wasn't all from his animosity toward Marcus. He was still fuming, his anger bubbling out of control, but there was an underlying hunger.

Tessa wanted to be his release. Letting her own outrage at the way Marcus treated Cooper consume her, she gripped his head, dislodging his hat as she pulled his face down to hers. Crushing her mouth to his, she pushed him, his body slamming into the opposite wall. They didn't come up for air as the passion ignited like a firestorm in that narrow hallway as they all but devoured one another.

The next thing Tessa knew, she was ripping open his belt buckle and yanking the button free on Cooper's jeans. Pulling his cock free, she stroked him firmly with her hands as she pushed against him, trying to get closer. Cooper had different plans, because Tessa found herself back against the opposite wall, his cock slipping from her hands when he grabbed her wrists, lifting them high above her head.

"Don't move," he warned, the gleam in his eyes barely visible in the shadows. The grip he had on her wrist wasn't painful, but the position he put her in made her body burn that much hotter. She was helpless beneath his strength, and although she knew he wouldn't hurt her — she didn't know *how* she knew, but she did — Tessa wanted him to continue.

Cooper's rough palm slid beneath her sweater, scraping against her bare belly as he moved upward, shoving her bra out of the way until her right breast was freed. Only a second passed as the cool air brushed over her skin before the fiery heat of his mouth was on her. He sucked her nipple into his mouth, making her cry out as a bolt of pleasure-pain shot through her. When he nipped her with his teeth, her pussy clenched painfully tight, her clit pulsing with a need so fierce she thought her legs might give out on her.

Then his hand was gone from her breast, but before she could inhale, he was shoving her skirt up higher on her hips, his fingers eagerly shifting her panties to the side before she felt the sinful rasp of his finger through her slickness.

"Fuck *me*," he breathed against her ear. "You're wet, darlin'."

Just a little bit.

"Don't tease me, cowboy." Tessa was hanging by a thread, and if he wasn't careful, she was going to explode on impact.

"Or what?" he growled.

Cooper's finger thrust inside of her, and Tessa gasped, her pussy clamping onto the intrusion, her body instinctively working to increase the friction.

"That's it, baby. Fuck my finger. Just like you're going to fuck my cock."

Tessa knew she shouldn't like the vulgar words, but she did. She wanted him to tell her all of the lewd things he was going to do to her while he did them. But she couldn't think clearly with his finger penetrating her, curling inside of her at the perfect angle…

"Oh, God!" she screamed when his thumb pressed against her clit, forcefully grinding the swollen bundle of nerves.

Just when she was riding the high of the release that was building, Cooper's hand disappeared.

"You—" She was just about to call him a bastard when his grip on her wrists tightened.

"I'm going to fuck you. Right here in your bar. I'm going to fuck your sweet pussy until you scream for me. If you don't want me to, Tessa, I need to know right now."

"Yes." Her choked plea sounded strangled, but she was hanging on a razor wire of ecstasy so potent she was going to split right in two if he didn't fuck her.

"Leave your hands right there," he instructed and Tessa barely registered the sound of foil tearing.

Condom.

Thank God he was prepared.

She moaned, a garbled plea for him to hurry as she closed her eyes. And then he was on her, her wrists once again secured by his powerful grip, his cock lingering at her entrance long enough to line up, and then he was slamming into her.

"Fuck," Cooper groaned hoarsely, his body doing exactly what he said.

He was fucking her with wild abandon. The two of them the only people in the place, hidden in the darkened hallway while he fucked her into oblivion. Tessa would've been appalled at her behavior had this been anyone else, but what she wanted from this man defied logic.

And right now, she wanted every damn thing he could give her.

∞ ∞ ∞ ∞ ∞

Cooper was blinded by lust, his body moving of its own accord, his hips pistoning hard against Tessa's as his cock went deeper. His thighs were screaming from the position he was holding himself in, but fuck, the pain was so worth it. Her sweet pussy was wet, warm, and so damn welcoming he never wanted to stop.

He watched all of the expressions play across her face as he pinned her to the wall. Each one of them reflecting everything Cooper was feeling. His frustration and anger had built to a crescendo, and he'd sought Tessa's lovely body for release. He wasn't mad at her. The opposite actually. But he needed her. She was like a lifeline in the violent storm he'd been battling for the last few hours. And now, he felt a surge of relief, all of the pain and anger dissipating beneath the onslaught of her sweet passion.

"Cooper. Oh, God, Cooper. Make me come."

The way she begged made him harder, his hips driving against her painfully as his cock buried deeper. His balls were tightening, the electric current of warning starting at the base of his spine and slowly moving upward. She felt so fucking good, her pussy wrapped around his cock, slick, hot. He didn't want to stop. He could fuck her just like this all night if she would let him.

Cooper watched as Tessa's eyes opened, locking with his. The rich warmth he'd seen in her sparkling green eyes was replaced with a soul-deep desire. One that he wanted to fulfill.

"Fuck. Me." She didn't close her eyes as she practically yelled the command.

With one hand, Cooper held her wrists tightly, doing his best to ensure he didn't bruise her while his other hand gripped her hip. "Come on my cock, Tessa," he growled, slamming into her once, twice, barely holding the leash on his control as he waited for Tessa to let go.

Her head tilted back so erotically, the sleek column of her neck taut as her jaw thrust forward, her eyes closing. "Fuck yes!"

The high-pitched scream triggered Cooper's release, his body stilling as he erupted, his dick jerking as he filled her.

It could've been ten minutes, hell, it could've been an hour. Who knew how much time had passed after they'd given themselves over to the heat of passion in the dark hallway of Tessa's bar. But neither of them had moved. Not an inch.

Well, except for him releasing her arms, which she quickly threw around his neck, holding him against her. He rested his forehead against hers, desperately trying to draw air into his lungs.

"I think that was the best sex I've ever had," Tessa murmured.

Chuckling at the breathy way she said those words, Cooper's cock pulled out of her, and he immediately missed the warmth of her body. While she fixed her clothes, Cooper disappeared into the bathroom to clean up, returning with his clothes back in order only to find that Tessa wasn't in the hallway anymore.

Shit.

Ever since he'd gotten her soft, lush body against the wall, he had lost all common sense, not caring what happened because of tunnel vision. The only thought was of Tessa, needing her to ease all of the anger and frustration that he'd let consume him since Marcus had stepped foot in the building earlier.

Now he feared what he was going to find when he stepped out of the hallway. Wasn't like he could stay there forever, although the idea had merit. If he didn't go out there, he could pretend that she wouldn't have any regrets or wouldn't be overthinking. After all, she had declared that the best sex she'd ever had, and Cooper knew he couldn't argue with her there.

Did that qualify as makeup sex? The question made him smile, but he wiped the expression from his face as he stepped out of the hallway to face the music.

"You ready?" Tessa asked, the beaming smile on her face nearly knocking him backward.

Rather than giving her any ideas about being mad at him, he just nodded his head. They had taken separate trucks that morning, but he would be more than willing to leave his here if she had another idea.

"Follow me to my house?"

Or that worked too.

Nodding again because his mouth was suddenly dry, he turned and followed her toward the back of the building. Once outside, he walked her to her truck, waited until she got situated, and then went to his.

His body was slowly recovering from his orgasm, and now that he was following her back to her house, Cooper wanted nothing more than to toss her on her bed and love her for the rest of the night. Then they could sleep the day away tomorrow and come back to the bar when it opened.

Except he was going to have to meet Marcus tomorrow and tell the guy the grim news. He had probably put off firing Marcus because he wasn't fond of confrontation, but Cooper knew it was long past time to do the deed. He needed to hire someone who would take care of him, make sure he was getting what he needed. For Marcus, Cooper was just padding his wallet. You would think he'd be treated with at least a little respect, but he didn't get an ounce from Marcus. Never had.

By the time Cooper pulled into Tessa's driveway a few minutes later, his rage was returning, and he hated himself all the more for it. After ravishing Tessa's body, he should've been relaxed to the point of exhaustion.

"Come on, cowboy." Tessa's voice startled him when he realized she had opened his door and was standing just outside his truck. He had to glance around, barely remembering how he'd gotten there.

"Maybe I should go home," he told her, irritated with himself for his lack of concentration, but he knew he would be even more pissed off if he took out his anger on her.

Angry sex notwithstanding.

"Get out, Cooper." Tessa's tone left no room for argument as she turned and stalked off, obviously not letting him get away with the disappearing act.

Fine. But she asked for it.

CHAPTER TWENTY

When Cooper finally made his way in the house, Tessa dropped her keys on the table by the door and let Havoc and Harmony out for a few minutes. She wasn't going to let Cooper mope for long, so before she returned to the living room, she ushered the dogs in as soon as they did their business and sent them into the bedroom they had commandeered as their own.

Cooper was sitting on the couch, his head tilted back, eyes closed. She could see the strain on his face, and she decided exactly what she needed to do. Disappearing down the hall before he realized she was watching him, Tessa grabbed a couple of candles from the dresser in her bedroom and relocated them to the bathroom.

Hunting for a lighter proved to be challenging, but then she remembered she'd tucked one in her nightstand. Once the candles were lit, she turned on the shower and went back to the living room for Cooper.

"Come with me, cowboy," she told him, her tone just as firm as when she had dealt with him outside. Even after their bout of explosive sex, he was still incredibly tense, so taking control of the situation seemed like the only way she was going to get through to him.

He opened one eye, peering at her from the side before he sighed and then pushed himself to his feet. She waited until he joined her at the door to the hall. Grabbing his hand, she led him to the bathroom. Since it was an old farmhouse, she didn't have a master bathroom, unless the only bathroom in the house was considered a *master*, so this one would have to do. It wasn't pretty with the pale yellow tile and faded flower wallpaper, and it wasn't big, but the shower worked, and that's all that mattered to Tessa.

"Get undressed," she instructed.

She didn't waste any time removing her sweater and skirt, followed by her panties and bra. She noticed Cooper's hesitation as he watched her, and the passion that had returned to his golden gaze was hotter than the steam now billowing in the small space. Stepping into the long, narrow tub, Tessa pulled the shower curtain closed behind her.

The rustle of clothing being removed was barely heard over the sound of the shower, but knowing Cooper was getting with the program lightened Tessa's heart. It did funny things to her insides to know that he was spurred into motion by the sight of her naked body.

Once he climbed in with her, Tessa forced him closer to the shower spray, putting herself behind him.

"Put your hands on the wall," she said sweetly, trying to keep the anticipation out of her tone. It wasn't an easy thing to do.

Tessa had always been the take-charge kind of girl, ever since she was young, but this was pushing even her boundaries. Here in front of her was a glorious, naked cowboy, one who made her feel significantly small by comparison, although she wasn't a lightweight and he was doing what she instructed him to do.

Aside from a skeptical backward glance, Cooper did what she asked, leaning forward and placing his hand on the wall beneath the shower head. She turned the sprayer so that it ran down the tiled wall beside them and then grabbed a bottle of body wash from the shelf. Pouring a significant amount into her hands, she started soaping his back, making her way up to his shoulders.

The intention of this shower liaison was to get him to relax. Since sex hadn't accomplished that goal, she was going to work on him with her hands.

The low groan that echoed made Tessa smile. She kept rubbing, kneading her fingers into the tight muscles across his broad shoulders. The body wash actually contained baby oil, so her hands were slick as they moved easily over his wet skin.

A solid ten minutes had passed before Tessa reached around, offering the same ministrations to his chest muscles as she pressed her breasts against his back. "Does that feel good?" she asked as she let her hands wander over his sides. Reaching for the bottle again, she added more and then put her hands back on him.

"Like heaven," he groaned.

Well, then she would keep going.

Dropping to her knees, Tessa knelt behind Cooper, her soap-slick hands wrapping around his ankles, massaging the muscles as she moved upward, over his corded calves, then up to his rock-hard thighs. Considering how thick they were, she focused both hands on one before alternating to the other. She continued her upward trek until she reached his perfect ass, digging her fingers deep into the muscles once she was upright.

Another approving groan and then Cooper stood tall once again. Tessa grabbed one more handful of soap and then continued as she reached around him, letting her hands slide down his chiseled abs, then teasing the hair beneath his navel and following it as it trailed downward.

When she reached his cock, she wasn't shocked to find him thick and hard. Using what she had, Tessa wrapped her hands around his erection, her breasts pressed against his back as she stroked slowly, letting the slippery soap work in her favor.

"Tessa." Her name came out on a growl, and she laughed.

"You like that?"

"Too much," he moaned.

She didn't stop, just squeezed his cock in her hands, not too tightly but not too gently either. "Turn around."

Cooper's sudden movement made her giggle. Excited much? When he looked down at her, she was thrilled to see that the tension in his face had eased and that dark hunger was back in his eyes. Taking the shower sprayer from the wall, Tessa doused him with it, washing away the soap from his entire body and then spending an extra minute letting the water cascade over his cock.

She met his eyes and smiled. Now she was ready to send him over the edge.

∞ ∞ ∞ ∞ ∞

Cooper's eyes had damn near rolled into the back of his head when Tessa had dropped to her knees the first time. But now, with her eye level with his cock, he might just pass out altogether.

For the last ten minutes at least, he'd been enjoying the way she focused her attention on him. She had obviously known just what he needed to relax, because her determined touch, the way she kneaded the tension out of his muscles, had him feeling boneless.

Soft, wet hands gripped his cock, making his whole body jerk, and he put his hand on the wall at his side to keep himself from swaying. The shower was tiny, almost too small for both of them to fit comfortably, but the bathtub was at least long and narrow.

As Tessa's lips closed over the head of his dick, his muscles tensed up yet again, but not in a bad way. Shit. Her mouth was hot and wet and … and … and… *Hell, what was he thinking about?*

Oh, right. Torture. The gentle teasing of her fingers and the soft flicks of her tongue were fucking torture. She laved him with her tongue, her eyes continuing to watch him as he stared down his body at her.

She had the ability to hypnotize him at any given time with just a look, but there was something uniquely erotic about the woman as she knelt before him, her green eyes sparkling while she sucked his dick. Unable to help himself, he slid his fingers into the wet strands of her hair, holding firmly but not forcing himself on her. He let her explore him with her mouth, her tongue, the gentle scrape of her teeth along his shaft.

"Fuck, baby," he groaned, his balls tightening ever so slightly. Shit, he wished he could do this all night. The hot cavern of her mouth was excruciating in the best of ways. "Suck me, Tessa."

God, she was good at that. So fucking good.

One small hand cupped his balls, rubbing them gently for long seconds. When the pressure of her hand increased, so did the suction from her mouth, and Cooper's hands tightened in her hair.

"You want me to fuck your mouth?" He had no idea how far he was allowed to push this, but after their intense romp at the bar and the assertive way she was bossing him around when they got to her house, Cooper got the impression Tessa liked it a little rough.

She moaned, and as the vibrations sent a shockwave of ecstasy right up his shaft, he took that as a yes. Holding her hair tightly, Cooper shifted so that he could take control, pushing his cock deep into her mouth. He wasn't interested in gagging her, but he longed to feel her mouth on all of him. She sucked hard as he pulled out, then let him slide in again.

He continued to drive deep, maintaining the steady rhythm as more heat washed over him. After how hard she'd made him come earlier, he doubted he would be able to do it again, but it didn't take long for her to prove him wrong. Tessa squeezed his balls firmly as he fucked her mouth faster, his groans echoing off the tiled walls until he was coming with a rush. He watched as she sucked him dry, his body shuddering with all-consuming pleasure as she swallowed.

Shutting off the water, Cooper pulled Tessa to her feet and then dragged her out of the shower. Her giggles made him laugh. They were tromping down the hallway when she tugged on his arm, a blatant indication that she wanted to go back. He relented, letting her snatch two towels from the bathroom cabinet before she led him to her bedroom.

That would work too. He'd been heading back to the living room, but if she wanted to go to bed, who was he to argue?

Once in her room, he tossed one of the towels on the bed and then pushed her down onto it, making her giggle more as she bounced on the bed.

"You like when I'm forceful with you, don't you, darlin'?" he asked as he proceeded to dry her with the other towel.

"Maybe."

Maybe, hell. She loved it. And he loved her all the more for it. They had so much in common, both their interests and their goals, not to mention sex between them was an exploration of souls. She didn't fight him but rather embraced whatever he needed at the time.

He was a selfish bastard.

Before the thought could piss him off, Cooper focused his attention on her body, leaning over her. She was naked and soft and so responsive. He started at her neck, kissing her smooth skin as she squirmed beneath him. Once he reached her breasts, Cooper climbed up onto the bed and straddled her, trapping her legs beneath his body. "Am I hurting you?"

"Nope," she said, that expectant tone back once again.

"Good."

Sitting on his heels, his thighs bracing her hips, he stared down at her. Cooper rolled her nipples using his forefinger and thumb, watching as her eyes glazed over. Her back bowed beautifully as she pushed up against him.

"You're so fucking hot, baby. I love to watch you squirm beneath my touch."

He released one of her nipples and leaned forward, sucking her into his mouth. He teased her, holding the hardened point between his teeth as he lashed at it with his tongue until she was moaning, her hips trying to buck him off.

"Like that?" he asked when he switched, taking her other nipple in his mouth.

"Yes. Oh, yes!" she moaned.

When she continued to writhe beneath him, Cooper knew he had to push her over soon or she would get frustrated. That was one thing about this little cowgirl — her patience was thin when it came to her pleasure. Grabbing her hips, Cooper flipped them so that she was straddling his stomach. Once she was on top, he grabbed her ass and pulled her forward quickly, her hands grabbing the headboard to keep from falling forward. With her perched above him, her knees on each side of his head, he buried his mouth in her pussy, teasing her clit ruthlessly.

Tessa began fucking his mouth, grinding down to ensure he was right where she wanted him. Gauging how close she was by the moans that tickled his ears, he continued, focusing all of his attention on the little bundle of nerves. He had to shift so he could add his hand to the mix. When she realized what he was doing, she re-situated herself so that he could drive two fingers up inside of her while he continued to lick her pussy.

"Don't stop! That feels so good," Tessa moaned as she continued to push her hips down, impaling herself on his fingers while he latched his mouth onto her clit.

"Cooper!"

Her high-pitched scream told him she was close, and after the way she had taken care of him, he knew he had to send her over. But he wanted to watch her come, and he couldn't in this position. Sitting up, he forced her onto her back, never pulling his fingers from inside of her. Once she was beneath him again, he locked eyes with her and fucked her hard and fast with two fingers.

"Come for me, Tessa. Fuck my fingers until you come."

Tessa's hips were thrusting against his hand, and he was ruthless in his pursuit of her orgasm. She held off for longer than he thought she would, but then her head fell back, her neck straining as she groaned her pleasure, her pussy gripping his fingers as she came.

"So fucking beautiful," he whispered as he dropped onto the bed beside her, his fingers still lodged deep inside of her. "I don't think I'll ever tire of watching you come."

Tessa's eyes opened, the green even more vivid as she smiled. "I hope you don't."

Cooper pulled his fingers from her warm sheath and then dragged her closer. Their heads were at the wrong end of the bed, but he was too tired to care. Tessa nestled into his arms, her head resting against his chest, one silky leg thrown over his thigh, and Cooper closed his eyes.

Nope, he would never get tired of this.

CHAPTER TWENTY-ONE

Tessa woke up the following morning — or rather, afternoon — feeling incredibly sated but more than a little sore. So, apparently, ordering Cooper around equated to some highly imaginative sex. Even though she was fairly active, Tessa was going to have to get some exercise under her belt if she intended to keep up with him. The man only needed a couple of hours of sleep before he was ready to go again, and Tessa had been hard-pressed to keep up. Although she did her best, without argument.

"Morning," she greeted Cooper sleepily when she walked into her kitchen to find him sitting at her table drinking coffee and working on his laptop.

As if seeing him doing something so domestic in her kitchen hadn't been enough, when Cooper stood from his chair and made his way over just to kiss her good morning, Tessa was a hairsbreadth away from melting into a puddle.

God, she'd missed that kind of interaction. Loving someone was not easy. There were ups and downs, sure, but to wake up each day or go to sleep each night in the arms of the person who would undoubtedly cherish everything about you… Nothing was as heartwarming as the smile on his face.

Not that she loved Cooper.

She didn't.

"How 'bout coffee?" Cooper asked when he pulled away, leaving her staring after him. He wore jeans and nothing else, his delicious upper body chiseled and sleekly muscled. Letting her gaze travel over him, she stopped to check out his bare feet. Why were bare feet on men so damn sexy?

"Sounds perfect," she answered, forcing her feet to move forward. Reaching out to take the cup, she smiled up at him. "What's on your agenda for the day?"

A flash of the same vexation she'd seen on his face yesterday distorted his features briefly, but Cooper morphed back into his easygoing self almost immediately. "I've got to meet with Marcus later this afternoon."

They never did have a chance to talk about the actual conversation Cooper had had with Marcus the day before. Even though he had so rudely dismissed her at the time, her curiosity hadn't been diminished, so as she dropped into one of the kitchen chairs, she figured she'd ask. "How'd it go with him last night?"

Cooper's descent into his chair slowed as he stared back at her. From where she sat, he looked like he was holding his breath, but then time kicked back in and he sat down, his focus on the coffee cup in front of him.

"Not as good as I expected," he said, peering over at his laptop screen. "But that's not the worst of it."

Oh, crap. She didn't like the sound of that.

"What's wrong?"

Cooper shook his head as though telling her nothing was wrong, but then his eyes met hers. "Looks like the press has officially found me."

For absolutely no substantiated reason, Tessa glanced around her kitchen as though she might find some reporters hiding behind the kitchen counter.

"No, darlin', they aren't in here."

She knew that, but she looked anyway and then laughed at the way he regarded her as though she'd lost her mind.

Wait, he had specifically said *in here*. Did that mean they were…?

"No, I suggest you don't go outside dressed like that," Cooper told her, and Tessa glanced down at her tank top and boxer shorts.

"They're out there?"

"'Fraid so."

Tessa wanted to jump up and run to the front door to see if her lawn was littered with news vans and cameras, but she forced herself to stay seated. They were at *her* house. Not Cooper's. Which meant they knew *Cooper* was at *her* house. *Crap.*

"Do you think it has to do with Marcus?"

"Maybe. Doubtful, but maybe."

"Well, what are we supposed to do about it?" Tessa asked hysterically, wondering whether she was ever going to be able to step outside her front door again.

"We're going to go about our business. I've got a phone call out this morning. I'm not expecting Marcus to handle this one, so I'm going to have to take matters into my own hands."

Tessa wasn't sure how she felt about that. And what was business as usual if their small town was swarming with reporters? It would probably cause an uproar. Hell, just Cooper's appearance in town had brought people out of the woodwork.

"Don't worry about it, Tessa," Cooper said solemnly.

Tessa nodded just to placate him, sending a quick look his way. There was no way she wouldn't worry. She didn't know how to handle the spotlight, and she knew that when people started digging, they were going to find things that she didn't want them to find. And just like every other time, there wasn't anything she could do about it.

"I'm going to take a shower," she declared as she pushed up from her chair, nearly spilling her coffee. She needed a few minutes to think this through. And she needed to be alone.

Thankfully, Cooper didn't follow her to the bathroom, so she locked herself in and hurried into the shower. As she let the water cascade down her body, the memory of the night before flashed briefly, but she quickly pushed it away. Not that remembering how incredible the sex between the two of them was was a terrible thing, but Tessa really needed to get her head on straight.

What was going to happen when Cooper found out about her past? Was he still going to want to have anything to do with her? And she knew without a doubt that the press would easily be able to unearth her demons.

But they were a long time ago, she told herself. What she'd done as an unruly teenager didn't mean she was that same person. In fact, she had worked for years to lose that reputation, to ensure that her past didn't catch up with her. It was one of the main reasons she worked with troubled kids, wanting to offer them some help so they didn't end up in the same situation she had.

She remembered how easily everything had been brought back up when she'd broken up with Chad...

Shit.

Grabbing the shampoo, Tessa washed her hair and then followed it up with a glob of conditioner while her memories took hold, transporting her back to a time she didn't particularly care to revisit. Her heart never handled reliving the past very well.

"So, what are you in for?" A rough, melodic voice sounded from somewhere on the other side of the stable.

Tessa glanced around, noticing only a line of stalls, all but two containing a horse. "Where are you?" she called out, unable to see a human being anywhere in the near vicinity, and as much as she would like to find out that the horses were talking to her, she knew better.

"This side," the deep voice chuckled, and Tessa followed the sound.

She had to walk outside and then in through the other door to get on the far side of the stalls that lined the middle of the huge stable.

"You gonna tell me what you're in for? Or are you just gonna stand there?"

Tessa finally found the guy attached to the voice. He was in one of the empty stalls, shoveling manure with a big shovel into a backhoe sitting just outside the door. Exactly what she was supposed to be doing. Although she was trying to buy herself some time.

"Why would you ask that?" she questioned, curious as to what he was in for. It was true, she was there as punishment, but she wondered how he would know that.

"Most kids in here don't come for the fun." He chuckled.

No. She could clearly see how they wouldn't find shoveling horse shit a fun way to pass the day. She sure as hell wouldn't be doing it if she hadn't been caught.

"So I take it you find this fun?"

"I don't mind it," he said, a cute smile slipping her way from underneath the brim of his straw hat.

"So, you're not in trouble?"

"Nope. Come here every day after school."

"Why would you do that?" Tessa glanced around, wondering if she should grab a shovel and help him. Although he seemed to be doing a fantastic job all by himself. He was almost finished.

"FFA," he said simply.

Future Farmers of America.

Tessa had heard of the organization at her school.

"Oh."

"But that doesn't answer why you're here," he said as he turned toward her, carrying the shovel as he moved closer.

"Hey, I know you," she said, recognition dawning. "Richie Donovan, right?"

"Yep. And you're little Tessa Dryden. Adam's baby sister."

Tessa didn't make a snide remark, but she wanted to. She hated being referred to as Adam's baby sister. And she definitely didn't approve of being called little.

"So, why are you here?"

"Mr. Deluth didn't tell you?" Tessa asked curiously.

Considering Mr. Deluth had caught her red-handed when she'd brought his prize thoroughbred, Texas Shadow, back into his stall early that morning, she figured half the town would know what she'd done by now.

"Nope. Haven't seen him today," Richie said as he opened the adjacent stall door and headed inside, leaving Tessa to stare at him from just outside.

"I got caught bringing Texas Shadow back this morning."

Richie's head snapped in her direction, a deep frown on his face. "You stole Shadow?"

Stole was such a harsh word, Tessa thought to herself. She would admit she had snuck into Mr. Deluth's stable and taken the horse out for a ride, but to say she stole him would insinuate she'd had no intention of bringing him back. And she had brought him back.

"Technically, I brought him back," she said defensively.

Richie's face was a mask of concern as he stomped toward her, tossing his shovel onto the hay that lined the perimeter of the stall.

"Where're you going?"

"To check on Shadow," Richie barked, not looking back at her.

Tessa felt about two inches tall right then. Was Richie worried about the horse? She hadn't hurt him. She'd just taken him out for a ride. Granted, it had been dark, and after the tongue-lashing she'd received from Mr. Deluth, she now understood how dangerous that had been for both her and the horse.

But she'd just wanted to ride.

She had felt like there was a rope around her neck, chaining her in place, and she'd just needed to get out. Sitting on a horse, her hair flying in the wind, the power of the animal beneath her, the thud of hooves against solid ground... She hadn't found anything that was quite like it.

She'd gotten so tired of listening to her mother and stepfather argue because her mother was crying all the time, sometimes never getting out of bed for days at a time. They did it more often than not, and Tessa was beginning to wonder why the man even hung around. She was starting to believe maybe that was why her father had left.

Shaking off the thought, she jumped into motion, heading out of the stable and back in the opposite side toward the stall where Texas Shadow was kept. When she got there, Richie was inside, his hands roaming over the animal, his voice low and soothing as he talked to him. Tessa made eye contact with the horse, and her heart galloped almost as fast as he'd done last night.

Texas Shadow was one of the most elegant horses she had ever seen. Tall, broad, sleek. His lustrous black coat was soft, his mane long and coarse. She'd fallen in love with the animal the first time she'd seen him. Granted, she didn't visit Mr. Deluth's farm often because she and Luanne weren't friends anymore. Hadn't been since the beginning of their ninth grade year.

"You're lucky he's not hurt," Richie said angrily as he stomped past her, nudging her backward as he did to get her out of the stall.

Tessa took two steps back, watched as Richie closed and latched the stall door, and waited to see what he would say. When his piercing blue eyes landed on her, Tessa could see his fury, but right there in Mr. Deluth's barn, she fell in love with that boy. Just a little bit.

And a year later, Tessa was head over heels in love with Richie Donovan.

The shower water had turned cold, so Tessa turned it off before grabbing one of the towels hanging on the rack. She went to wipe her face, realizing she was crying, the salty taste of her tears on her lips.

God, she missed Richie.

He had been her saving grace. And he'd even stood by her when karma had paid her a visit several years later, punishing her for all of the things she had done as a rebellious teenager. The thought brought more tears to her eyes.

Holding the towel to her face, knowing the waterworks wouldn't shut off until they were ready, Tessa stood in the bathroom, dripping on the bathroom rug.

She knew she should've been grateful for the sequence of events that had led her to Mr. Deluth's door and ultimately to Richie, but the consequences hadn't been as easy for her. Or Richie.

Ultimately, Mr. Deluth had spared her. Had Jerry Deluth opted to punish Tessa for stealing his horse, she knew she would've been in a lot of trouble. Not only would she have been arrested, but in their small town, she never would've been able to get rid of the stigma associated with what she had done. As it was, there was a long list of indiscretions that she *was* responsible for.

Right up until her nineteenth birthday, or shortly thereafter, Tessa had been a free spirit. At least that's what Richie had liked to call her. She'd disobeyed every rule that was laid out for her. Hell, sometimes she even wondered how she was still alive with all of her ignorant stunts: drugs, alcohol, vandalism, even some petty theft, and although safe, she had been promiscuous when it came to sex. Tessa had pushed the envelope, tried to see what she could get away with.

By the time she was twenty-one, Tessa had settled somewhat, at least when it came to all of the illegal stuff. Alcohol was still her friend, although she was getting tired of it quickly. But she was still trying to garner attention wherever she could. Thanks to Richie and one of the youth counselors at her church, Tessa had realized she'd been acting out to get the attention of her father. The man who hadn't wanted anything to do with her or Adam since she was an infant.

Not that any of her craziness actually brought her onto his radar, but apparently that was part of why she was doing it. That and her mother. Sheila spent days and nights crying her eyes out, sometimes for no reason at all. Tessa never had tried to understand her mother. Never even attempted to understand what it meant to be depressed after her mother had been diagnosed. Not until she was older anyway.

Her punishment for stealing the horse had included only six months of working on Mr. Deluth's farm, doing the jobs most people hated to do, and turned out to be one of the only things Tessa found she enjoyed. That was just one of the things she and Richie had had in common. So after Mr. Deluth had freed her from her obligation toward the end of her sophomore year in high school, she'd asked to volunteer to help. And had done so for years after.

By the time Tessa's father left her The Rusty Nail when she was twenty-three, she had managed to get her life under control. Richie had gone to a junior college and then applied to the police academy, something he'd always wanted to do. During the years leading up to that, Tessa had grown close to Mr. Deluth. After all, Luanne had hated the farm, wanting to leave Devil's Bend altogether, so Tessa and Richie would spend time with him in the stables, or sometimes even riding.

Not going to college, Tessa had worked odd jobs, mostly secretarial work, but she had continued to work for Mr. Deluth because being confined to a desk was proving to be her worst nightmare.

Her marriage to Richie had been a long time coming, but Richie, being the level-headed one, had insisted they wait until they were financially stable. He knew that they would have a hard enough time at that point, and he wasn't willing to risk their relationship. She'd been working in the bar, and Richie had gotten on with the Austin Police Department, and life had been good for the first time in Tessa's life.

Then, the gift of all gifts had been given to them when Tessa had found out she was pregnant. Richie had been beside himself with joy, as had she. Even her mother had been excited about the baby. But four months into her pregnancy, karma had kicked her right in the face. The doctors had told her there was nothing she could've done differently, but the pregnancy had terminated itself. She and Richie had been devastated.

And almost a year to the day after that, Richie had been killed. Tessa accepted at that point that all good things came to an end, which was why she refused to get too attached to any one thing.

A loud bang on the door scared her so badly she clutched her chest. Realizing she was standing stark naked in the bathroom, tears still streaming down her face, she knew she had to get herself together. After all, there was no way she could let Cooper know what she was thinking.

There was no reason to ruin the good thing they had. At least not yet. At some point, she knew karma would return to ensure that he was yanked right out of her life as well.

She just wished she knew how much time she had.

CHAPTER TWENTY-TWO

Cooper pulled into the parking lot of The Rusty Nail, his mind still on Tessa. After her shower, she'd been closed off and entirely too quiet. He could tell she had been crying, but no matter what he'd tried, she wouldn't tell him why. He managed to get her to take a nap, or rather, she'd fallen asleep from sheer exhaustion an hour ago.

Knowing he had to meet Marcus, Cooper had left her a note and then gone home to shower and change. Now that he was back in front of the bar, he dreaded what was to come.

When he pulled into the parking lot, Cooper noticed Eric's fire-engine-red muscle car was already there, so he shut off the engine and slipped in through the back door. He would prefer to be the one to approach Marcus, rather than the other way around. Since The Rusty Nail hadn't opened yet, he knew his soon-to-be ex-manager wasn't there yet.

"Hey, Coop. What's going on?" Eric asked when Cooper approached the bar.

"Not much. I've got to talk to my manager, so I figured I'd come in early."

"Oh, that guy." Eric's exasperated tone put Cooper on edge.

"What's wrong?"

"Not a damn thing." Eric glanced at the front door and then back to Cooper. "Now anyway. The asshole was waiting out front when I got here. Once I got inside, he started pounding on the door. The man's kinda dense."

Cooper would agree with that assessment, but he didn't say anything.

"Anyway, I told him we weren't open, and he tried to invite himself in. When I refused, he got snippy. Don't be surprised if his nose is off-center when you see him. I slammed the door in his face, and he finally left."

Well, shit. That would mean Marcus was already primed for a bad mood. And what Cooper had to tell him wasn't going to make him happy anytime soon. Which, Cooper knew from experience, meant Marcus was going to retaliate. In probably one of the worst ways.

"Hey, didn't you say you had some big name playing tonight?" Eric asked as Cooper was setting up his laptop on the bar.

"Son of a fucking bitch!" Cooper had completely forgotten about that.

Nearly an hour later, Cooper watched as Tessa walked in through the back door. He had cued up some music after he'd updated the sign out front to display the live music talent he was expecting to show up at any minute. Now, as he watched her move across the floor, his heartbeat rivaled the thud of the music. The one thing he noticed was that she looked like she had put on a solid layer of armor.

Gone was the sweet girl he'd seen the night before in her short jean skirt and soft sweater. In her place was the no-nonsense woman who had caught his eye in the very beginning. She wore a form-fitting black T-shirt, jeans that accentuated her luscious ass, boots, and her cowboy hat that shielded her eyes. Her blonde hair curled down her back and over her shoulders, making Cooper want to reach for her and pull her close by wrapping his fists in the silky strands.

Not that he would. She looked like a woman on a mission. He felt better when she returned a smile as she passed by, but he decided to leave her be for a bit. The front door opened, and in walked just the man he had been waiting for. Before anyone could notice him, Cooper intercepted him in his path to the bar.

"Hey, man. Glad you could make it," Cooper greeted Dalton Calhoun with a hand held out to shake, but that was quickly thwarted by the infamous guy-hug that was little more than a couple of thumps on the back.

"So glad you invited me. Shit, man. This is cool," Dalton said as he checked out the interior of The Rusty Nail. "How the hell'd you land your ass all the way down here?"

Cooper tilted his head, a silent gesture for Dalton to follow him toward the stage. As he passed the bar, he held up two fingers for Eric and received a nod of understanding. "It's somethin', ain't it?" Cooper asked.

"So this is what's got Nashville all in an uproar. Your ass disappeared off the map to come down to BFE and sing in a little bar. Man, I don't know if I'm pissed off or jealous."

"Well, I'm glad you came down. You can give it a shot, see what you think." Cooper and Dalton had become close friends over the last few years, both of them living in Nashville, chasing their country music dream. Dalton had hit the big time a year or two before Cooper, so he had learned a lot from the man, although they were roughly the same age.

"That for me?" Dalton asked, tilting his head toward the stage.

"It's all yours tonight."

"Hot damn!" Dalton exclaimed, glancing up at the stage.

Eric walked up, two Bud Lights in his hand and a gigantic grin on his face. Cooper introduced the two men briefly. Before Eric sauntered off, he turned around and said in a mock whisper, "Just a warning. My wife's here tonight." And with that, he was gone.

Cooper laughed while Dalton looked back confused. "What the hell does that mean? I swear, I don't know his wife."

Cooper let out another roar of laughter before he slapped Dalton on the back. "I promise, when you meet her, you'll understand the warning. Hold up a minute, would ya?"

"Lemme run out to my truck and get my guitar. I'll be right back."

Cooper nodded and then headed across the bar to get Tessa. She was pouring a beer for a customer, and when she finished, he got her attention.

"What's up?" she asked, sounding more upbeat than she was when he'd left her house earlier in the day.

Leaning over the bar, he gave her an expectant look and waited until she leaned forward so he could kiss her. He didn't linger, and the smile that tipped her lips when she pulled back made him feel better.

"You got a minute? There's someone I'd like you to meet."

Tessa got Eric's attention and let him know she would be back. The bar was quickly filling up, which meant there wouldn't be much downtime from here on out. Thankfully, although Cooper had forgotten his buddy was coming in, he'd had the good sense to tell Tessa a week ago that she might want to bring in her cousins to help man the doors and fill in as bouncers. Based on the folks already coming in, he'd been smart in doing so.

Now it was time to introduce Tessa to the guy who was going to help Cooper get his farm up and running. Sooner rather than later.

Tessa had just gotten into a rhythm that helped take her mind off her emotional morning. Truth be told, she'd been hoping for a huge crowd at the bar so she wouldn't have to do much thinking at all. Based on the sheer volume of people flooding in through the front doors, she was going to get her wish.

As she followed Cooper across the room toward the stage, she tried to get a decent look at the guy Cooper had booked for tonight's entertainment. She hadn't been able to see the sign out front when she'd gotten in because there were actually cars in the parking lot already, which had surprised her.

"Who is this?" she asked Cooper, his hands flexing over hers.

As soon as they reached the mountainous cowboy, Cooper said, "Tessa, I'd like you to meet Dalton Calhoun. Dalton meet Tessa Donovan. She's the owner of The Rusty Nail."

Okay, so maybe she wasn't the biggest country music fan, but she definitely knew who that was. She'd have to be a hermit not to have seen or heard something about the guy over the last few years. She should've known. His name was mentioned with the likes of Jason Aldean, Kenny Chesney, and of course, Cooper Krenshaw.

Cooper's arm came around her, and he kissed the top of her head gently while she shook hands with Dalton. Glancing up at Cooper briefly, she then looked back at the guy who would be gracing her stage tonight. "Sorry, I'm not usually star struck, but…"

"Damn, Calhoun, I didn't even get that kind of reception from her." Cooper laughed, and Tessa blushed.

"See, that's where he's wrong." Tessa added, "I remember very clearly how this cowboy had his hands on me that night."

Cooper's roar of laughter made her heart leap. For the first time all day, she actually smiled, feeling his amusement all the way to her toes. The feeling made her feel significantly lighter than she had before.

"Should've known," Dalton said with a rusty chuckle of his own. "Well, it's a pleasure to be here."

Dalton's smooth country drawl rivaled Cooper's, and that was saying something. Tessa still found she liked the guttural sound of Cooper's voice better. But then again, she was sort of biased.

"It's our pleasure," Tessa said, trying to find her backbone. She wasn't the blushing type.

"Oh! My! God!" The familiar voice sounded over the low rumble of conversation taking place in the bar. The shriek that followed had almost everyone turning to the front door.

"Yep, that's Izzy," Tessa mumbled, laughing at her best friend.

"If you need any help" — Tessa turned to Dalton — "that guy over there is her husband. He can't control her much, but he might be able to protect you."

Cooper's and Dalton's rumbled laughter filled the space at the same time Izzy came running over. She stopped just a few feet away from Dalton, staring up at him as if he hung the moon. Lord. The woman was something else.

"You're Dalton Calhoun! Oh. My. God," Izzy said, barely containing her own excitement. "Eric! Did you see this? It's Dalton Calhoun!"

"Yep, baby. I saw him already," Eric's rich baritone echoed from across the bar, sounding amused.

"Can I touch you?" Izzy asked seriously, her eyes sparkling like stardust as she stared at the much bigger cowboy.

"Yes, ma'am," Dalton said after getting the go-ahead nod from Eric across the bar.

As soon as the words were out of his mouth, Izzy was plastered against him, her arms wrapped around him as she squeezed him tightly. When Izzy finally stepped back a solid minute or two later, she was beaming brightly at Tessa.

"Did you see this?" Izzy asked in a conspiratorial whisper that the entire bar probably heard.

"I saw. It's Dalton Calhoun," Tessa confirmed, her head turning as she caught Katie walking past them, toward the bar.

"Hey, Katie," Tessa called out to her. "Come over here and meet Dalton Calhoun."

Katie looked almost as star struck as Izzy had a few minutes ago as she approached slowly, her ponytail bobbing as if her energy was too much to contain and had to find an outlet.

"Go on, girl," Izzy encouraged. "You can touch him."

The group laughed, and Katie, with a brilliant glint in her eyes, moved up and put her arms tentatively around Dalton. The man actually put his arms around her in a very intriguing protective hug that nearly had Tessa's mouth dropping open.

"Nice to meet you," Katie said sweetly, her face almost as red as the glowing exit sign near the back door.

"My pleasure, darlin'," Dalton crooned in a low voice that had Tessa glancing up at Cooper. He seemed just as taken by Dalton's apparent interest in the pretty waitress.

And just like that, Katie was off toward the other side of the bar, followed by Izzy close on her heels, the two women chattering about Dalton. At one point, Katie actually glanced back, and that's when Tessa noticed that Dalton was still staring after her.

"Man, you all right?" Cooper asked his buddy with a loud clap on the back.

Dalton turned his head, a slow grin tipping his lips. "Never better. You ready to get this show on the road?"

"Always." Cooper turned and pressed his lips to Tessa's, making her blush like a schoolgirl before he sauntered back toward the stage, leaving her to stare in his wake.

Wow. The difference a few weeks could make. Tessa still couldn't believe how Cooper Krenshaw had crash-landed in her life and left such a monumental impression that she was standing here, staring at him as though she were a woman in love.

Oh, hell.

Tessa squeezed her eyes shut.

Yep, that trouble she'd known she was going to be in had finally caught up to her.

Shit.

CHAPTER TWENTY-THREE

Two hours later, the bar was jumping. The sound of two cowboys entertaining the rowdy crowd, singing like they'd been born on the stage, filled the room. The energy was significantly different from what Tessa was used to when they had a performer up there. These two guys had a rhythm about them that had nearly everyone moving. According to her cousin Shane, there was a line that wrapped around the building, and it looked like they'd all be turned away soon enough.

Izzy was behind the bar helping Tessa and Eric while Miranda had come in to help Katie. Jack was coming in to help, but Tessa hadn't seen him yet. They were fully staffed and at maximum capacity, yet Tessa hadn't felt a lick of stress since Cooper had gone up on that stage with Dalton. It was a sight to see, that was for damn sure.

When they broke out into a slower song, the bar settled somewhat, and there was another surge of people to the bar. Tessa had just finished preparing a handful of shots for Miranda to take to a table near the door when a familiar voice sent a violent shudder racing down her spine. Not the good kind.

Turning toward the sound, Tessa saw Chad standing at the edge of the bar with two women practically wrapped around him. Swallowing hard, an effort to maintain her composure, Tessa tried to force a smile but failed.

A quick glance around showed her that she was by herself because Eric and Izzy were busy with a line of customers, which meant she would have to deal with Chad herself.

"What can I get you?"

Chad's glare made Tessa's stomach churn painfully. She hadn't seen Jack yet tonight, which was probably the reason Chad had grown a set of balls and decided to come to the bar rather than order through one of the waitresses.

Tessa had never officially kicked him out of The Rusty Nail despite everyone's insistence that she should. Having attempted to be the bigger person, Tessa had hoped he would just keep his distance. Based on the glint in his midnight-blue eyes, she had a feeling he was about to push the boundaries.

"Three Bud Lights," the brunette on the left of Chad said sweetly.

Well, if Tessa only had to deal with the women, she might just be able to get through this unscathed.

"Thanks, darlin'," Chad said to the woman as Tessa moved off to get their beers. "That's the slut I was telling you to stay clear of."

Tessa's back straightened at the cruel words, but she forced herself to move forward. The man had pretty much called her every name in the book before today, so it wasn't like she hadn't heard it before.

"Her?" the other woman with Chad asked.

"Yep. Used to date her, but she got a little too freaky for me, if you know what I mean."

The women giggled, and Tessa's hands squeezed so tightly around the beer bottles she was carrying she thought they might just shatter in her hands.

"Freaky how?"

"She was always hanging on me, begging for sex. I sang in here a few times, and it got to be too much trouble because she was always up on me, ya know?"

God, had Chad always sounded so stupid? Tessa wondered to herself. Just listening to his bullshit story made her want to wrap her hands around his neck and squeeze until his eyes bugged out of his head. The guy was so full of himself. Had it not been for Tessa's generosity, allowing Chad to play in her bar on occasion, she was pretty damn sure he'd never have been allowed past open mic night anywhere else.

"God, I can't stand women like that," the blonde said, her hands plastered to the front of Chad's thick chest.

Tessa bit the inside of her cheek to keep from laughing. Okay, so laughter was good. At least it meant dealing with him was getting easier.

"Ain't that right, darlin'?" Chad asked as Tessa slid the three beer bottles toward them.

She told them the amount they owed and ignored Chad's question altogether.

"See, she's still bitter. I won't take her calls, so she has to pretend she's not into me anymore."

"I prefer men to boys," Tessa mumbled, ashamed that she was succumbing to his antagonism.

"That right? Sure don't seem like it to me," Chad snarled. Turning his head toward the blonde, he grinned. "Her nasty cunt is already chasing Cooper Krenshaw. I heard he's gettin' ready to hightail it out of town just to get away from her."

Tessa grabbed the twenty-dollar bill that the blonde placed on the bar and turned toward the register. Before she was two steps away, the deep baritone of Jack's voice startled her.

"See, son, that's where you heard wrong."

She turned abruptly to see Chad flinch while the women who'd been molded to his side were quickly moving away. Jack was standing behind him, one huge hand clamped down on Chad's shoulder, the impression of his fingers scrunching Chad's shirt.

"Fuck, man. Get your goddamn hands off me!" Chad yelled, ripping away from Jack's grip.

"This is your last fucking warning," Jack said slowly, his voice frighteningly low.

"Or what, man? You're just pissed that I didn't enjoy nailing the shit out of your sister. You didn't have a problem until I tossed her out like yesterday's garbage."

"Jack, stop!" Tessa screamed the instant her brother's hands gripped Chad's shirt, yanking him off of his feet as he got right up in his face.

Everything from that moment forward happened in a blur. Jack shoved Chad hard enough to send him sprawling on the concrete floor, forcing other customers to jump out of the way or be taken down like bowling pins.

"Out! Don't let me see your face in here again," Jack demanded, moving fast for a guy his size.

Chad was backing up on the floor but unable to get enough purchase on the slippery concrete to make it back to his feet. Tessa couldn't get out from behind the bar because Eric had moved close, keeping her sandwiched between him and the wood while Izzy stood by her side.

"Get up!" Jack growled.

Chad managed to make it to his feet, but as soon as he was upright, he was backing away while Jack was pursuing him like a cougar cornering its prey.

"She's a fucking whore, man. The whole fucking town knows it."

And that's when the shit hit the fan. Tessa was watching Jack, waiting to see what he would do next, when Chad was yanked backward, his legs barely managing to keep him up off the floor for a second time. Tessa glanced up to see Cooper as he pushed Chad toward the door.

"Not another fucking word," Cooper barked. "If you know what's good for you, you'll keep your fucking mouth shut."

Another chill raced down Tessa's spine. She'd never seen Cooper that angry, not even after he'd had to deal with Marcus face-to-face yesterday. Part of her was worried he was going to kill Chad.

"Hey, folks," Dalton's voice crooned through the speakers. "Y'all keep lookin' that way and I'm gonna get my feelin's hurt."

The distracted patrons laughed as Dalton effectively redirected everyone's attention back to him.

Tessa glanced down to see her hands were shaking. There was no way she would be able to keep her past a secret now. Not from Cooper anyway. She glanced toward the front door just in time to see it shut behind Cooper and Jack. She took a deep breath and wondered if she should make a run for it. After all that, she knew she didn't have it in her to try and explain herself tonight.

"It's all good," Izzy said, her hand rubbing up and down Tessa's back.

She momentarily allowed the motion to soothe her as she tried to figure out what she was going to do next.

"Don't worry about him. He's a jackass," Eric confirmed before stepping over to help the customers who had just had a front row seat to Tessa's humiliation.

Nodding her head in agreement, she remained where she stood, wishing like hell she could sneak out. Since the bar was so busy, she knew that wasn't an option.

"Just think of it this way," Izzy whispered. "The night can only get better from here."

∞ ∞ ∞ ∞ ∞

"What the fuck was that about?" Cooper asked Jack when they were heading back inside after Jack handed Chad off to Shane, one of the burly bouncers standing outside. His instruction to ensure Chad never stepped foot inside the bar again would be heeded, he was sure.

"Nothin'. He's a dumbass."

That didn't answer Cooper's question, and he realized Jack was deflecting. The dumbass part was a given, but what Cooper wanted to know was what the hell the guy had against Tessa. In all the time Cooper had been in Devil's Bend, he'd never met a single person who had said anything negative about her. Until tonight.

Grabbing Jack by the arm, Cooper stopped abruptly. "That doesn't tell me shit."

"It ain't your fucking business," Jack growled.

"The hell it ain't." Tessa was his business, and he'd be damned if anyone would talk to her like that.

"He's trash, man. Just let it go." Jack's tone dripped with disdain, and his emerald-green eyes shot sparks of fire.

Nodding his head because he knew he wasn't going to get anything more from Tessa's brother, Cooper moved to the door. Once he was inside, he made a straight line for the bar, moving people out of his way as he went. The only thing he cared about was seeing that Tessa was all right.

"Can I talk to you for a minute?" he asked when he approached her at the bar. Never mind that there were at least ten people standing in line waiting to get their drinks.

"Can't right now," she muttered but didn't look up at him.

Cooper glanced over at Izzy, who was watching him. When their eyes met, she shook her head slightly, as though signaling him to give her a break.

Fine.

He made his way to the wall, standing close to where the sound system controls were, and waited. Jack joined her behind the bar, and roughly twenty minutes later, they had managed to get the waiting customers down to a minimum.

By then, Cooper's temper had cooled, which he considered a good thing. As he moved toward where Tessa was now standing, he glanced up at the stage to see Dalton looking his way. A quick tilt of his head was the only nonverbal communication he needed to send because the next song that Dalton began was a slow one. Something to douse the remaining flames of the anger that had flared up inside of Cooper when that bastard had started talking shit.

Rather than asking permission, Cooper lifted the wood top and slid behind the bar to join Tessa. He walked right up to her, wrapped his arms around her waist from behind and whispered in her ear, "Come dance with me."

To his surprise, she didn't argue, and Cooper took her hand, leading her back out the way he'd come and over to the dance floor. Joining the group of other dancers, Cooper fell in step and pulled Tessa up against him, wrapping her in his arms and holding her tightly against his body. They didn't talk, but the way she wrapped her arms around him and pressed her cheek against his chest said everything he needed to hear.

Dalton ventured into another slow song, giving Cooper more time with Tessa, but he knew he would eventually have to let her go. When his buddy decided to take a break, Cooper released Tessa but grabbed her hand when she would've walked away.

"Can we talk for a few minutes?" he asked, nodding his head toward the back door.

When she relented, he realized just how much she'd been through tonight. Hell, today. After that morning, he knew something had upset her, but he hadn't been able to get her to open up to him. Hoping she might now, he took her hand and led her outside.

"What was that about?" he asked calmly once the door closed behind them, glad that enough time had lapsed for his temper to settle.

Tessa looked up at him briefly but then diverted her gaze as she stepped away. He waited patiently for her to answer, and to his surprise, she didn't make him wait long.

"His name is Chad."

"What's his deal with you?"

Tessa's head jerked back toward him, her eyes weary. "I used to date him."

Cooper nodded, hoping she would continue.

"It's been a year since I broke it off with him."

A year and the guy was still going crazy on her.

"Did you do something to him?"

Tessa's back straightened, and he noticed the moment her defenses went up. He wasn't trying to piss her off, but he knew that the sort of anger that man showed was usually triggered by something. That or he was just plain fucking crazy. Based on Jack's reaction to the guy, Cooper was leaning toward the crazy.

"I broke up with him, that's what," Tessa said defiantly, her hands going to her hips. "If you don't mind, I really need to get back to work. I don't have any desire to discuss Chad with you or with anyone else."

"Then do me a favor," he retorted, his anger slowly starting to build.

"What's that?"

"Stay away from him."

Tessa's eyes narrowed on him, and he felt the chill all the way to his bones. She obviously didn't take too kindly to his demand, but he couldn't help himself. He hated seeing that bastard talk to her that way. If Cooper had anything to say about it, the guy would've been leaving in an ambulance, but luckily for everyone involved, he had somehow managed to keep himself under control.

"In case you didn't notice, I own this bar," she said adamantly before turning away abruptly and heading back inside, leaving Cooper standing there, staring into the night.

Shit.

He hoped like hell this night didn't get any worse.

CHAPTER TWENTY-FOUR

A short while later, Tessa was standing behind the bar once again, making change, when Izzy's statement from earlier resounded in her mind.

"Just think of it this way. The night can only get better from here."

She hoped like hell Izzy was right. There for a few minutes, when she had been dancing with Cooper, she'd thought her friend might be on to something. Being in Cooper's arms for even that short period of time had been just what she'd needed to calm her nerves. The safety and security she found in his arms was such a welcome change from the chaos that had erupted not long before that. It was difficult to admit, but Tessa was actually getting used to him being there and the comfort that his nearness afforded her.

At least until he went and said something idiotic like he had outside.

Stay away from him.

It was almost as though he believed she had started the incident with Chad. She had seen the doubt in his eyes, known that he wasn't absolutely sure of her because of what had happened, but for the life of her, she hadn't wanted to argue with him. Especially not about Chad. She had no intention of talking about him. Ever.

"Can I get a Crown and Coke over here?"

Tessa's spine straightened as the voice registered, and she turned slowly to see Marcus Evergreen once again gracing her bar with his presence.

Oh, hell. Apparently, Izzy had spoken too soon. Tessa got the feeling things were about to go from bad to worse.

Tonight Marcus looked not much different than the night before, only this time, his suit wasn't gray, it was either navy or black, she couldn't tell in the dim light.

Nodding her head when he continued to pin her with his beady eyes, Tessa took her time getting the Crown from the shelf. There was no way she could warn Cooper this time. There were too many people there, too much going on, and quite frankly, she didn't want him to have to endure this guy just yet. For the first time since Tessa had met him, Cooper seemed perfectly at ease, like he was doing what he loved to do — the altercation with Chad notwithstanding.

Once she had the drink poured, she gave him the total as she pushed it toward him. And just like last time, he told her to put it on Cooper's tab.

"Sorry, no can do. Cooper doesn't have a tab here anymore."

Marcus's chocolate-brown eyes narrowed. Tessa felt as though he were examining her, trying to determine exactly what he needed to say. Or perhaps how he needed to say it. As she waited, refusing to walk away until he paid for the drink, the guy continued to make her uncomfortable.

"Fine," he said with a huff, standing from the stool and pulling his wallet from his back pocket. Slapping a ten on the bar, he told her to keep the change, and she offered a small smile in return.

"You mind going up there to let Cooper know it's time to go?" Marcus said, grabbing her arm just as she was turning to walk away.

Tessa's outrage at being manhandled nearly broke loose, but she managed to stare down at her arm, then back up at Marcus. "You're gonna take your hand off of me now." Her voice was low and calm, but she hoped he understood how deadly her statement was. She might not have the ability to kick this guy's ass, then again, she might. He was kind of puny, in her opinion. But there was a bar full of her cousins, not to mention her brother Jack was somewhere close, who'd do the deed for her if she just said the word.

Marcus's fingers slowly uncurled from around her arm, and Tessa pulled far enough back that he couldn't reach her. "And I'm not your messenger, so you'll have to go talk to him yourself."

"Oh, that's right," Marcus said, acting as though he'd just recognized her. "You're the gal he's hooked up with this time."

Tessa tried not to let the "this time" in his statement bother her. She failed. It'd been an emotional day; she was curious. "What do you mean, 'this time'?"

Marcus glanced away, his eyes searching the room before landing on hers once more. Tessa kept her mouth shut, waiting for him to answer when she wanted to grab him by the shirt collar and insist he tell her everything.

"It's just time Cooper goes back home. He's done this before."

A sour taste filled Tessa's mouth, and her stomach felt as though it might revolt. She gripped the edge of the bar, trying to convince herself that this guy was a liar and she shouldn't listen to anything he had to say.

Marcus sipped his drink, and after setting it back on the bar, he looked at her with a serious expression on his face. "Oh, sorry, sweetheart, I guess he hasn't informed you that this is a phase he goes through every now and again. Takes him some time to cool off, but he always comes back where he belongs. Sometimes I just need to give him a little push."

"What do you mean, 'a phase'?" Tessa asked, just for the hell of it. She'd already heard more than she needed to. A smart woman would've told this guy to fuck off, but something had Tessa rooted in place. A need to know more? To get someone else's opinion, maybe? Heaven knew she'd already gotten herself in over her head with Cooper.

"Oh, you know," Marcus began, acting as though she should already know what he was talking about. "Last year he ended up in Arkansas. Some backwoods town he took up residence in. Stayed there for a couple of weeks with some filly he picked up in a bar."

Tessa actually felt her heart drop from her chest to her stomach. She didn't want to believe this guy, didn't want to take him at his word. Not after all she'd learned about him, but he sounded so confident she was having a hard time.

Wanting to appear busy, Tessa grabbed a towel from beneath the bar and began wiping down the top slowly, staying close to where Marcus was sitting. Her gaze darted between the guy in the expensive suit and the cowboy who was now heading down the steps at the side of the stage. Cooper didn't look happy.

"It's about damn time," Marcus said with enthusiasm. "You sounded good up there."

Tessa watched as the men shook hands, Cooper's eyes darting back and forth between Marcus and her as though he were trying to figure out whether they'd had a conversation or not. Was he feeling guilty? Did he not think she'd learn that he did this frequently? After all, the topic of their conversation from the day before had gotten derailed every time she had asked about it.

She suddenly felt sick to her stomach. Really, really sick. Thankfully a customer walked up asking for a beer, and Tessa moved out of earshot to handle the request. Before she could finish, Cooper and Marcus were heading out through the front doors, obviously wanting to talk in private.

Well, she was more than willing to let them chat it up if they wanted to.

"Hey, Eric," she called out after she made change and the customer was on his way back to the table he'd been sitting at.

"What's up?" Eric's deep voice startled her, sounding much closer than she expected him to be.

"I'm not feeling well," she explained hurriedly, her eyes darting toward the front doors. "You think you can handle things tonight? Jack's here and so is Izzy."

When Eric didn't respond immediately, she glanced up to meet his eyes. "You know I can, Tessa. But I don't think—"

Interrupting him before he could finish, Tessa mumbled her thanks, grabbed her keys that she kept under the bar, and fled to the back door. Never looking back.

A few minutes later, she was driving out of the overflowing parking lot, not bothering to look around to see if Cooper was out there. She didn't want to see him. Not now. Hell, maybe not ever.

When she was halfway home, Tessa glanced down to realize she had her hand over her heart. It was aching. Physically hurting in her chest, but she knew it wasn't a heart attack. No, this pain was self-inflicted. All because she had been stupid enough to get caught up in Cooper's life. She should've known better.

Stupid. Stupid. Stupid.

Once she was home, Tessa continued to fight the urge to have a breakdown. He wasn't worth her tears. She knew that. And no matter how much she'd started to like him, she had worked diligently to keep some emotional distance between them. Even if he had seemingly tried to bridge that gap a time or two, Tessa had forced herself to stay back.

She was grateful for that.

That and her two huskies.

"Hey there. Did you miss me? Huh?" she asked Harmony and Havoc when they met her at the front door.

She wished they could talk, but since they couldn't, she settled for taking solace in the way their entire bodies wagged with their happiness. Making her way into the house, she went straight for the dog food, knowing that's the first thing they expected even though she was several hours early. Just as she was pouring the last scoop in Harmony's bowl, a knock on the door nearly sent her into hysterics.

Whirling around, she found Izzy standing on her front porch, staring at her through the screen door.

Damn that Eric. Why'd he have to be such a loyal friend?

"Eric send you?" she asked her friend as she motioned for her to come inside.

"Of course he did. And I came running."

Izzy was usually a big help when the bar was busy, but she knew Eric wouldn't hesitate to send her to make sure Tessa was all right.

"Want some wine?" Tessa offered.

"Nope. I brought something stronger," Izzy answered, revealing a bottle of Tito's Vodka.

"Thank heavens," Tessa exhaled on a sigh. Even if the bottle had come from her bar, she wasn't going to ask questions.

"Come on, let's go back outside."

Izzy knew her all too well. Tessa didn't do well being cooped up inside, no matter the time of day or the season. She'd much rather be sitting on the front porch, enjoying the weather. She never actually thought about why that was, but for as long as she could remember — even as a child — Tessa had always escaped outdoors.

She remembered back to when her mother was an emotional wreck because of Tessa's good-for-nothing father. Even years after the man had abandoned them, Sheila spent hours sobbing in the house. Rather than listen to her mother cry her eyes out, Tessa had found her solace outside. And if Adam ever came looking for her, he knew she'd be somewhere close, but always outside rather than in.

Izzy planted her butt on the porch swing and patted the cushion beside her. Tessa knew better than to argue, so she ventured over to her friend and plopped down beside her.

"Want to tell me what happened?" Izzy asked as she uncorked the bottle of vodka.

"Not really, no," she muttered, knowing Izzy didn't care one way or another whether Tessa actually wanted to talk. She'd be chatting it up before too long. Vodka was one thing that always loosened Tessa's lips.

"Tough." Izzy took a swig of vodka and handed it over.

This was going to be one of those nights. She could feel it.

Half an hour later, or hell, maybe it was just ten minutes, Tessa was feeling good. Better than good actually. The smile on her lips wasn't forced, nor was the numbness in her limbs.

"How serious is this thing with you and Cooper?" Izzy finally asked, and surprisingly, the vodka refused to allow Tessa to get defensive.

"I thought it was serious, but I learned he's…" Okay, so maybe she wasn't as loose-lipped as she'd thought she was.

"He's what?" Izzy asked, the words coming out as *heswatt*.

"Nothing. He's just not what I thought he was," Tessa slurred before grabbing the bottle of vodka again.

"So does that mean y'all aren't together anymore?"

Tessa wasn't sure what it meant. She'd listened to Marcus, and part of her brain had latched on to every word. The other part told her she needed to give Cooper a chance to explain himself. She considered that part vulnerable and stupid, so she refused to listen to it.

She was done with vulnerable and stupid. Done. Done. Done. "Izzy," Tessa began as tears formed in her eyes. "Why me? Why… I should mind my own business."

"What are you talking about?" Izzy asked, her full attention now focused on Tessa, making her feel like she had to say something.

"Trust. It's too hard to trust anyone. The only person I should've ever trusted was Richie." Nothing short of the truth. Richie had loved her, protected her. He had never hurt her.

"Remember that time when you and Richie broke up and you found him talking to Annie Metcalfe?"

Glaring over at Izzy, Tessa's mouth fell open. "Are you serious right now?"

Izzy stared back at her like she'd lost her mind. "You didn't trust him either, did you?"

Shit. No. Not after that. But they were just dating, and they were teenagers, and it didn't matter anyway. Her brain was getting carried away, the alcohol buzzing and making the memories fuzzy. Was that what it was? Were her memories of Richie just that fuzzy that she only thought he was perfect?

"He wasn't, Tessa. You and I both know he wasn't perfect. No one is."

Oh, crap. Had she said the words out loud?

"You've got to give Cooper a chance to explain," Izzy said, her cool hand on Tessa's arm a reassuring gesture.

"I gave him a chance, Iz," Tessa admitted a few minutes later. "He broke my heart, but I gave him a chance."

Izzy's arms flew around Tessa, and she let her friend hug her for long minutes. The pain was there, but the vodka had at least dulled it. Tessa knew it was only temporary, but for now, she'd take it.

There would be more time later to let the crushing weight of another broken heart consume her.

∞ ∞ ∞ ∞ ∞

Cooper pulled his hat off his head and thrust his fingers through his hair. He'd been standing in the parking lot with Marcus for the last half hour arguing with him. Not that it was doing a damn bit of good. If Marcus was anything, he was stubborn.

Then again, so was Cooper.

"I'm not going back," Cooper restated, unsure why Marcus couldn't just grasp the concept.

"Unacceptable," Marcus barked. "I'm tired of playing these fucking games with you, man. You're coming back to Nashville because we've got obligations. You can't just run away."

"Bullshit," Cooper growled, forcing his hat back on his head and closing the gap between him and his manager. "I can do whatever the fuck I want to do. I know what my obligations are, and I fully intend to take care of them."

"How?" Marcus exclaimed. "How the fuck do you plan to do that all the way out here in bumfuck nowhere?"

Cooper abruptly turned away. He had to calm down because the repercussions if he didn't certainly were not worth it. He was seconds away from planting his fist in Marcus's too-perfect face.

Obviously his manager understood he needed to give him a minute, because he let him be. Finally, when Cooper turned back to face him, he noticed the cocky smirk on Marcus's face, which was almost enough to send his fist flying.

"You don't have anything keeping you here," Marcus told him. The taunting smile on his face didn't disappear.

"I've got more here than I do in Nashville," Cooper told him. He had *everything* keeping him there. Namely Tessa. And the farm. After the last few days, Cooper wasn't sure he'd ever be able to go back to where he'd come from. Not if it meant he would risk losing Tessa for good. He couldn't even picture it in his mind.

"I do know that," Marcus said snidely. "You know that little girl in there that you've been making it with?"

Cooper's hands immediately balled into fists, but he forced them to remain at his sides. "Don't do it, Marcus. Don't you dare disrespect her like that," he growled.

"That's all moot, my friend," Marcus said with a bigger grin. "Ten bucks says she hightailed it out of there after she found out that this is a consistent thing for you."

Cooper's heart pounded against his ribs. Once, twice. The roaring in his ears deafened him as he stared back at the asshole manager he should've fired years ago. "You didn't."

"I did," Marcus confirmed. "It's a phase, Coop. You know it. I know it. Now she knows it. It's time to get back to reality."

Cooper's vision was hazy, a red film shading the world in front of him. "This is my reality," he ground out.

"Is that what you said last year? You remember the time, don't you, Coop? Does Arkansas ring a bell?"

Cooper turned away, pacing the parking lot and hoping like hell he could rein in his temper before he pounded Marcus into the gravel.

"That wasn't the same thing, and you fucking know it," Cooper declared, not bothering to look Marcus in the eyes.

God, he needed to get inside to see Tessa. He needed to talk to her. To explain. What happened in Arkansas wasn't the same as this. In fact, it was completely the opposite. Not that she would believe him.

"Ahhh, but see, the details are irrelevant," Marcus told him. "What's important is that you get back to Nashville, and we'll move on like this never happened. You've got an album to make, and you can't do that from here."

Cooper stopped pacing. He took a deep breath and turned to look at Marcus. "You're fired," he stated with every ounce of pent-up frustration that boiled in his gut.

Marcus's eyes widened, but for the first time since he'd showed up, the man didn't have a comeback.

Grabbing his phone off his belt, Cooper didn't wait for Marcus to respond. It was over. He should've fired him years ago. And now that he had, the weight of the world seemed to lift off his shoulders. He dialed the familiar number, listened as it rang twice.

"Hey, boy." David Krenshaw's powerful voice reverberated through the phone.

"Dad," he greeted his father. "Remember the last time we talked? When I said I might be looking for a new manager?" Cooper didn't wait for his father to answer before he continued, "You still interested?"

"You son of a bitch." Marcus's words echoed through the parking lot. "You're gonna regret this!"

Cooper didn't react to Marcus's rant, knew it wouldn't make a difference if he did. Marcus Evergreen was a vindictive son of a bitch, and yes, firing him was bound to have some repercussions, but at this point, Cooper would much rather deal with those than to deal with the man himself.

Focusing his attention on the conversation with his father, Cooper filled him in on what was going on. Both his mother and father knew exactly where he was. They both knew what he was doing even, and they'd been supportive ever since he'd called them when he had been on the road to Texas, not even knowing then what he was set out to do. In fact, Cooper had talked to them every day since.

After Cooper gave his father the specifics of his location, they hung up. At least his best interests would be taken care of at this point. Now, he just had to figure out how to fix what Marcus had already broken. And then he had to prepare himself for the aftermath that was sure to come.

"Where is she?" Cooper asked a seriously pissed off Eric a few minutes later. He had come inside the bar to find her gone. To confirm his suspicions, he had made a beeline for the back door. When he didn't find her truck, he knew she'd run away.

Damn that Marcus.

"You need to leave her alone," Eric ground out, his eyes spitting fire.

Cooper sighed heavily. He didn't want to do this right now. He appreciated the defensive friend routine, but he needed to talk to Tessa before she had time to come up with a million scenarios that weren't even close to the truth.

"I just need to talk to her," Cooper explained, trying to keep his composure. He was already pissed off; the last thing he needed was to go rounds with someone he would like to consider a friend.

"Give her a break." Eric's tone was almost pleading. "She's been down this road before, and I don't want to see her go through it again."

Down what road? Cooper doubted Eric had a clue what actually had gone on, but he wasn't going to hang around and try to explain either.

"I'm out," Cooper declared as he retrieved his truck keys from his pocket and headed back in the direction he'd come in. More than likely, Eric was going to warn Tessa that he was coming, but he didn't have much of a choice. If she wasn't at her house when he got there, he didn't have any problems waiting for her until she showed up.

Ten minutes later, he was pulling into Tessa's driveway. Her truck was there. And so was she, because he could see her sitting on the front porch. With Izzy.

Great. Not exactly what he wanted to have to deal with tonight. If Eric was defensive, he could only imagine what her best friend was going to be like.

Taking his time and trying to collect his thoughts, Cooper slowly got out of the truck. Not that it mattered, because the second his feet hit the ground, Izzy was standing directly in front of him. He ground his back teeth together, reluctant to say anything until he got the chance to talk to Tessa first.

"You need to talk to her," Izzy said, sounding surprisingly calm. "I don't know what happened, and don't ask me why, but I'm giving you the benefit of the doubt."

Staring down at the tiny woman, Cooper battled the urge to glance over at Tessa.

"You don't know all that she's been through, but I can assure you that it's more than she ever should have. I don't know what she is to you, but … just make this right, Cooper."

The plea in Izzy's voice clutched at Cooper's heart. He nodded his head in understanding, unable to find any words. He waited as she turned to go back toward her house, but before he moved even one step, Izzy was turning back to him.

"Oh! And she's drunk. So, um … good luck with that!"

Why did it sound like Izzy was laughing at him?

CHAPTER TWENTY-FIVE

Cooper didn't make any sudden movements. He took his time getting to the porch, petting the dogs when they came out to greet him. Surprisingly, Tessa was still sitting on the porch swing, but she had yet to look his way.

Drunk, huh? This was going to be interesting.

As he approached the porch, he said hello but was met with silence. So she was going to be stubborn as well? Why would that surprise him? Figuring he'd let her be the first to say something, he moved up the stairs and then propped himself up against one of the cedar posts that held up the roof over the porch. He never took his eyes off Tessa, unless glancing down to see the half-empty bottle of vodka sitting on the ground by her feet counted.

"Did you have a good conversation with Marcus?" she asked after several long minutes of silence.

"I don't think you could describe it as good, but yeah, I talked to him," he answered honestly.

"So when are you leaving town?" she asked, her words coming out slurred. She might appear to be stone-cold sober, but she was certainly intoxicated. That was likely the reason she hadn't stood up yet. He'd bet money that her world would tip sideways once she did.

He waited until she looked at him before he answered. "I'm not going anywhere, Tessa." It was the truth. As far as he was concerned, Devil's Bend was his new home, and he had no intention of leaving.

He was going to wait for his father to call him back next week to figure out the logistics, but he'd been adamant that this was where he wanted to be. Then again, if Tessa tossed him to the curb, Cooper might have to rethink that decision. As sure as he looked at her now, he knew that he probably wouldn't be able to spend the rest of his life in the same town as she was if he couldn't have her all to himself.

"Well, you should. Probably a nice woman waiting for you in the next town you sneak off to."

Cooper didn't say anything. That was the story Marcus had told her, and right now, with her being drunk, he knew it wasn't going to go well if he told her the truth. Which he fully intended to do. Tomorrow. When she woke up beside him.

"I've got some things to explain to you, Tessa," he began and held up his hand when she started to interrupt. "And I fully intend to explain, but not tonight. Not like this."

"So why'd you come here then?" she asked, her words running together more.

When she reached for the bottle of vodka, Cooper intervened, stopping her. She'd had more than enough. "This isn't going to help, and you know it," he told her, holding her hand in his as he leaned over her.

Without waiting for permission, which he knew he wouldn't get anyway, Cooper settled onto the swing beside her, pulling her against him. When she started to fight him, he held her tighter. "Don't," he commanded softly. "Just sit here with me."

The alcohol's effect was probably the only thing that kept her there, but Cooper considered it a win. He'd have hell to pay tomorrow, but for now, he was going to hold her. That's all he wanted to do anyway.

♥ ♥ ♥ ♥ ♥

Okay, so the morning after a vodka binge could not be categorized as a good time. Not that the night before was anything to write home about either.

Unwilling to open her eyes, Tessa snuggled into her blankets, wishing like hell she'd thought to take aspirin before she'd gone to sleep. But then again, she might have. She'd been so lit she didn't even remember coming inside. The last conscious memory was of Cooper showing up at her house, but she was pretty sure she'd sent him on his way.

When nature called a few minutes later, Tessa knew her morning was about to go from bad to worse. Why shouldn't it? That seemed to be a pattern for things these days.

She had to get out of bed, which meant the room was going to spin, and she was probably going to get to scrutinize her last cleaning job up close when she made friends with the toilet.

Forcing her feet over the side of the bed, she felt the mattress shift, and she knew then and there that it was worse than she'd thought. Once she was vertical, she grabbed on to her dresser and made her way down the hall to the bathroom. Someone must've been looking out for her because she didn't get sick like she'd thought. After doing her business, Tessa splashed cold water on her face as she stared at herself in the mirror.

"You look like hell, woman," she mumbled to the reflection, noticing the dark circles under her eyes and her crazy hair. "That'll teach you not to fall for a man. It never gets you anywhere. You should know by now that karma has it out for you."

When a throat cleared from the doorway, Tessa nearly fell flat on her face into the sink. She whirled around to see Cooper standing in the doorway of her bathroom looking impossibly sexy. He was shirtless, his jeans unbuttoned but zipped and his feet bare.

She had to blink twice before her brain accepted that what she was seeing was not just a figment of her imagination. Her mouth felt like she'd been sucking on cotton, but somehow she managed to force the words out. "Why are you here?"

Cooper didn't say a word, and that was when Tessa remembered what she'd just said. Out loud. To herself. Shit.

He'd heard her talking to herself. Glancing down at the floor, she contemplated what would happen if the tile would open up and swallow her. At least she wouldn't have to face him this morning. It seemed that the alcohol had diluted her anger, and now she was left with confusion.

She stared at the man standing in her bathroom door, watched as he walked over to her shower and turned on the water. Well, it was nice of him to make himself at home. Shouldn't he be leaving? And why was she having this conversation inside her head, rather than with him?

Before she could ask him directly, she felt his warm hand on hers as he pulled her closer. And just like that, all of her memories from the night before flooded back: her conversation with Marcus, hearing that Cooper was a serial runner who shacked up with various women from time to time when he felt like his world was overwhelming him too much… Crap.

"Don't," Cooper demanded, his voice hard and firm.

Tessa's eyes flew up to meet his at the same time her fight-or-flight instinct kicked in, and she was geared up to fight him with everything that she had.

"Don't you dare tell me—" She didn't get the sentence finished before Cooper had pulled her into the narrow bathtub with him, both of them fully dressed. Okay, not fully, Tessa realized as she glanced down, remembering that she didn't have on her jeans. She was confident she'd been wearing them the night before. If not, she was definitely going to have to lay off the vodka in the future.

Cooper disconnected the handheld sprayer from the wall and aimed it at her head, soaking her hair and making her sputter water. "What the hell are you doing?"

And then his mouth was on hers, his hard body pressed against her front while the cold tile met her back. Despite her brain's insistence that she push him away, her hands had other ideas. She found herself pulling him closer, the warmth of the water running over her skin while she attempted to devour him.

It was the alcohol. That's the only explanation she could come up with. The alcohol was obscuring her judgment, and she was temporarily out of her mind.

When Cooper pulled his mouth from hers, she looked up into his eyes. The usual golden-brown was darker, more intense than she'd ever seen it.

"So you fell for me?" he whispered.

It took a minute for the question to register, and that's when the starch returned to her limbs, effectively allowing her to push him away from her. There wasn't much space in the shower, but at least she managed to gain a few inches of distance between them. Not that it mattered; she still felt the heat of his body emanating from him.

"I did not!" she snarled.

"That's not what I heard."

"Well, you're delusional, cowboy." Tessa tried to turn away from him, but his hard hands brought her up short.

"Listen to me, Tessa," Cooper stated firmly, his grip firm on her upper arms, forcing her to stand facing him. "We're going to take a shower, as innocent as you'd like it to be. And then we're going to go into your kitchen, have coffee and breakfast, and I'm going to explain some things to you.

"No, wait, I'm not finished," Cooper growled when she was about to interrupt. "After I explain everything to you, then I'll let you make the decision. If, at that point, you want me to leave, I will. Not willingly, but I'll go."

Tessa felt the tears sting her eyes. Or maybe it was the shower water. No, damn it. Definitely tears. She remembered everything Marcus had told her, and the idea of Cooper using her temporarily was enough to make her heart hurt. Again.

"Understand?" he asked, and Tessa forced herself to nod. "Good, now come here."

Tessa allowed him to pull her closer as he removed her T-shirt and bra, then her panties. She felt numb, almost like she was outside of the shower looking in at the two people there. Not bothering to move when he managed to force his jeans down his legs, Tessa held her breath when he stood back up.

Damn him for being so fucking gorgeous. She didn't want him to be. She didn't want him to be anything. She wanted to hate him and send him on his way, but she couldn't. Her brain had misfired somewhere along the way, and it wasn't listening to reason.

Now that he was standing naked in front of her, she really, really needed it to listen to reason.

Shit.

Why did that damned persistent trouble always insist on following her?

∞ ∞ ∞ ∞ ∞

Getting Tessa naked in the shower might've been a lousy idea.

Especially considering Cooper genuinely wanted the opportunity to talk to her. Right now, he was having a hard time keeping his hands off her. The water was sluicing over her golden skin, and he was so captivated by the sight he couldn't focus on anything else. Including the raging hard-on he knew was on prominent display now that he was just as naked as she was.

Blindly grabbing the shampoo bottle off the shelf, Cooper kept his eyes trained on her breasts as the water cascaded over the pebbled tips. He wanted to put his lips there, to taste her, to feel her body writhe beneath the onslaught of his mouth. Filling his palm with soap, he moved forward, fully intending to wash her hair for her, but she quickly put her hand up and took a step back.

"Hold up, cowboy. You can't put that in my hair," she warned, a sudden gleam in her pale green eyes. Glancing over at the bottle he'd picked up, he noticed he'd grabbed the dog shampoo.

"Why the hell do you keep that in your shower?" he asked with a deep laugh as he let the water rinse the soap away.

She didn't answer him, but she did offer up the shampoo bottle, so he took it from her and tried one more time. This time he filled his palm and then turned her to face away from him. It was probably the only way he'd be able to focus. Looking down, he admired the perfect shape of her ass and knew he was mistaken. He couldn't suppress the growl that escaped, but he did his best to ignore his own needs.

Pulling her back against him, Cooper slid his hands into her hair, lathering up the soap as he massaged her scalp. He took his time, letting the sweet smell of strawberries fill the shower. He'd probably never look at strawberries the same again.

"I think my hair is clean now," she mumbled, her voice wavering.

"I'll be the judge of that," he answered, ignoring the demands of his body. He wanted to bend her over and slowly slide inside of her, let the warmth of her pussy grip him as he thrust deep and hard.

But there were two reasons he couldn't. One: he didn't have a condom. Two: he'd surely seal his fate and be forced to leave without having a chance to explain anything to this woman. And as much as he wanted to feel her sweet body sheathing his aching cock, he wanted to be able to look forward to it in the future as well.

He had to take things slow with her. At least right now.

Retrieving the shower sprayer from the wall again, he rinsed her hair, letting the soap run down the front of his body, the water teasing his cock, making him painfully aware of how much he was denying himself.

He observed the other bottles on the shelf and grabbed the conditioner, effectively lathering her hair once more before he picked up the body wash and the puffy thing hanging from a hook. He probably used more soap than he should have, but his brain was intensely focused on how he was going to accomplish this task without coming.

"I can do that," Tessa whispered as he began running the sponge over her breasts, keeping her back against his chest.

"Not this time," he said, his voice sounding strangled.

As if washing her body wasn't difficult enough for him, Tessa moaned as the sponge slid over her nipples and then louder when he reached the juncture between her legs.

Pressing his mouth to her ear, he said, "You keep doing that, and I can't promise you I'll control myself. This is hard enough for me as it is."

Tessa nodded her head, but Cooper had no idea what that meant, so he bit the inside of his cheek and slid down to his haunches, her gorgeous ass directly in front of him.

He managed to wash her legs, between them, and then made his way back up, returning to a standing position. He let the water rinse the sponge, but before he could use the sprayer to rinse her off, Tessa turned on him, grabbing it from his hand.

"I can only take so much," she warned, her eyes sparkling as she looked up at him.

He knew exactly what she was talking about. Just the thought of that sprayer directed between her legs made his dick throb.

When he thought she would climb out and let him continue by himself, Tessa surprised him. She took the bottle of body wash, but she didn't use the sponge. He watched in awe as she filled her palms and then planted them against his chest, the soap dripping slowly down his stomach as she started rubbing it in. The memory of the last time she'd massaged him right there in the very same shower assaulted him.

"Tessa." Cooper closed his eyes. "Darlin', I'm not a fucking saint."

Her chuckle made him groan. This was probably payback. Or even a test. He didn't know, but either way, he was about to fail miserably. When her hands went lower, gripping his cock firmly, Cooper fell back against the shower wall. "Fuck."

He was fucking trembling. An all-out vibration running through his body as she touched him.

Tessa didn't say a word, which was probably a good thing right about then. Only things took another turn when he opened his eyes and looked down to see her hands stroking him slowly, one on his cock, the other slipping lower to massage his balls. She was torturing him on purpose, and he knew he wasn't going to be able to hold off much longer.

"Tessa," he pleaded. "Baby. Fuck." Cooper was slowly losing control.

Her hands disappeared, and a spray of water hit his cock, making him jump. He figured that was her ultimate punishment, but then she dropped the sprayer, throwing her arms around his neck and pulling him to her until their bodies were melded together, lips, teeth, and tongues clashing as they sought the release that the torturous shower had been building toward.

"Tessa, baby," he said, trying to pull back as she shifted, aligning his cock against her entrance. "Tessa, don't."

Her eyes opened, and she jerked back, pain and rejection reflected back at him, and Cooper quickly pulled her closer. "I'd give anything to take you right here. But I can't," he explained. "I don't have a condom."

And wasn't that just fucked up.

"I'm on the pill," she blurted, but Cooper pulled back and looked down at her.

"That's nice to know, because it will come in handy in the future, definitely," he started, "but, Tessa, until you trust me unconditionally, I'm not going to take you without a condom. And, unfortunately, I know you don't."

He hated saying that out loud, but they both knew it to be the truth. He'd never once imagined he'd turn Tessa away, but Cooper had bigger plans in mind for them than just a quickie in the shower. She'd be hurt and confused later, and he didn't think he could handle that. Not until she gave him the chance to explain. If, at that point, she wanted him to fuck her right there on her kitchen table, he was all for it.

But right now, he had to settle for holding her in his arms and praying what he would tell her in a few minutes wouldn't send her running for the hills.

CHAPTER TWENTY-SIX

Although the temperature outside was hovering in the eighties, Tessa was tempted to put on sweatpants and a long-sleeve shirt. Anything to cover herself. Not that it would've mattered. Whenever Cooper looked her way, she felt like she was naked. The way his gaze caressed her made her want things she was supposed to be denying herself.

For instance, *him*.

So it was safe to say that the shower had been a terrible idea. His hands on her body had made her yearn for more, almost willing to beg. And she knew he'd felt it too, but the stubborn man had held back.

Something about talking and nonsense.

At least one of them was thinking with their brain and not other body parts. Had she had her choice, they'd have gotten down and dirty in the shower just a few minutes ago. Anything to drown out the pain that had started as a dull ache in the center of her chest when she thought about what Marcus told her.

Instead, he'd washed her, she'd washed him, and now she was going to join him in the kitchen where she smelled the heavenly aroma of coffee brewing. After wasting enough time, Tessa finally ventured in that direction.

"Hey, puppies," she greeted her huskies when they met her in the hallway that led from her bedroom to the main living room. They were pouncing around, but neither of them actually jumped on her — a feat that had taken her months to accomplish. Considering they both weighed upwards of sixty pounds, Tessa appreciated them staying on the floor rather than on top of her. "Y'all wanna go outside?"

Leading them through the house, she let them slip through the back screen door before she turned to face Cooper, who was standing in front of her stove.

Shirtless.

She wasn't sure which was more mouthwatering, the sight of him barefoot or...

"Hey, where'd you get more jeans?" she asked him as she realized he was partially dressed, but a few minutes ago he'd gotten in the shower with his jeans on.

"From my truck. I keep a bag there, just in case."

The thought made Tessa's stomach churn and not in a good way. Did he keep clothes on hand in the event he spent the night with a woman?

"Don't go there, Tessa. That's not the reason," he said with a firm tone before turning back to the food he was preparing on the stove. "Get some coffee, then sit. I'll finish up here, and we'll eat."

Not wanting to argue, mainly because she didn't want to even think about what had happened the night before, Tessa did as she was told. She prepared two cups of coffee and left his sitting in front of the coffeepot while she carried hers to the table. Staring down at the scarred wood, she allowed the events of last night to play out in her mind.

She remembered Izzy coming over with just what the doctor ordered. The bottle of vodka had been what she'd needed to muddle her brain enough that she didn't have to think about Cooper. Well, that was only partially true. The vodka had helped, but she'd never once stopped thinking about Cooper.

The rest of the night was fuzzy. At some point, she remembered Cooper arriving, and a strange excitement had filled her. Obviously she was getting too attached to him that she was glad to see him, hoping like hell he was going to tell her that Marcus was a liar.

Only he hadn't said that.

She didn't think he had anyway.

A plate full of food was pushed in front of her, and Tessa glanced up to see Cooper watching her. Rather than sitting down, he disappeared down the hall, returning a minute later with a couple of aspirin in his hand. After handing those to her, he left again, coming back with a glass of orange juice.

Why did he have to do that? Why did he have to think of everything? She'd much prefer him to be the asshole she expected him to be.

Like Chad.

Couldn't he just get defensive and blame everything on her? It would make things so much easier. More specifically, walking away would be easier.

"Eat," he commanded as he dropped into the chair beside her.

Tessa knew she should. She was famished, and the breakfast actually looked wonderful. Eggs, bacon, toast. Everything cooked to perfection and sitting in front of her, beckoning her. Only her stomach wasn't listening to her mouth.

"Tessa, look at me." Cooper's softly spoken words had her breaking her concentration and looking up at him. She felt like she was going to cry. The tears were threatening, and she knew any minute the dam was going to break.

"I can't do this," she choked out.

"Yes, you can," he argued. "Give me a chance, Tessa."

The statement brought back the memory of Izzy insisting that she do the same thing. Last night, she'd actually been surprised that Izzy hadn't jumped on board the hate train and rallied against Cooper after what Tessa had told her. That's what her best friend was supposed to do. But not last night. No, Izzy had been the voice of reason, begging her to let him explain.

And here they were, but Tessa wasn't sure she wanted to know. Hell, if Cooper wasn't willing to have sex with her because he didn't think she trusted him — which she didn't — then she knew what he had to say wasn't going to be good.

"Where's Marcus?" she asked, hoping to derail her thoughts for a few minutes. Grabbing the piece of toast, she nibbled on the edge, staring down at her plate.

"No idea. I fired him last night," Cooper answered, his fork clinking against the glass plate as he went to work on his food.

Tessa's eyes flew up to meet his instantly. "You fired him?"

Cooper nodded, his mouth full of food, but he kept his eyes trained on her.

"Why?" she asked, her voice unsteady. Had he done that because of what Marcus had said? Had Marcus lied to her and Cooper wasn't having any of it?

"It was time." That was all Cooper said before he dug back into his food.

Tessa allowed the silence to descend around them as she made a half-assed attempt to eat the food he'd prepared for her. It was good, she'd give him that. Although she wasn't sure her stomach was going to hold it down for long. Her nerves were suddenly jumping, and her fear of what he was going to say was getting the best of her.

When they were finished, Cooper grabbed her half-empty plate and carried it to the sink with his. Tessa stared at his back — his sexy, muscled back and smooth, sculpted shoulders. Why did the man have to look so good?

"More coffee?" he asked a few minutes later when he returned to her side.

She just nodded, her eyes still glued to his body. She'd apparently sat there watching him the entire time, and now her insides were starting a slow boil. Damn it. She was supposed to be mad at him.

"Come on, Tessa. Let's go sit on the porch, and I'll explain," Cooper stated, sounding defeated. He waited for her as she pushed out of her chair and then mindlessly headed toward the back porch rather than the front.

She had several chairs scattered on the porch, two of them the comfy kind that she loved to sit in and read on a cool evening. Because she could keep farther from him if she did, Tessa chose one of those chairs and dropped into it, taking the coffee he offered once she was seated.

Holding the cup close to her chest, she blew on the top, watching the steam as it drifted upward. She glanced over to see Cooper sitting in one of the hard-back chairs, his coffee cup resting on the railing as he sat with his elbows on his knees, his hands wrapped around his downturned head.

He looked so incredibly vulnerable like that. Invisible strings on her heart tugged painfully hard, forcing her to swallow. If this was hard for him, she couldn't imagine what it was going to do to her.

"Marcus said you do this often," Tessa said suddenly, unable to sit there and watch him any longer. This was getting to be too difficult. He really needed to spill it and then move on. It was the only way Tessa was going to survive with her heart intact.

Okay, *part* of her heart intact. A very small fraction.

∞ ∞ ∞ ∞ ∞

Hanging his head low, Cooper tried to gather his thoughts. Ever since he'd woken up that morning, Tessa's soft, warm body beside his, he'd been trying to come up with an easy way to explain himself. He knew no matter how he told the story, she wasn't going to be happy with him.

But he had no choice.

"Marcus told you about a woman in Arkansas," Cooper began. It wasn't a question, and he wasn't expecting her to answer him, so he continued, "Her name was Tabitha. She came to one of my concerts in a neighboring town, and at the end of the night, I found her in my tour bus. That had been a bad night for me." He remembered feeling helpless and alone that night, and he'd had half a mind to disappear at that time, but he had held tight and just gone out to the bus, hoping for some time to himself.

Cooper didn't look up as the memories of that night flooded his brain. "I was surprised to find anyone on the bus, but she seemed sweet enough, and I had learned to gently approach the fans who were brave enough to go to those lengths to meet me. We talked for what seemed like hours." Cooper looked up at her. "And no, before you ask, I didn't have anything to drink. Just three bottles of water."

Cooper turned his gaze to the yard, watching the two dogs as they sniffed through the flower beds that were just beneath the back porch. "She was the one who brought me the water, and honestly, I didn't think anything of it. At some point, I passed out. I didn't know it at the time, but she'd drugged me."

Cooper wasn't proud of the story. He knew it would sound as though he were making shit up, but he wasn't.

"The next morning, I woke up in my bed on the bus, completely naked, with Tabitha beside me. Just as naked." He couldn't bring himself to meet Tessa's eyes. "We parted ways after that. I was used to women like that, wanting to have a story to tell, so I didn't think anything of it. I didn't remember sleeping with her, but she told me… She confirmed that we had." Cooper wasn't going to go into details, but Tabitha had been particularly candid about what activities had occurred through the night.

"Three months later, I get a phone call from Tabitha. She got a hold of me through Marcus. Keep in mind, I hadn't heard from her at all since that night." Cooper dropped his head, staring down at the floor while he wrapped his hands behind his neck. God, he hated this story. "She told me she was pregnant. Told me she hadn't been with anyone else before or after me and that the baby was definitely mine."

Cooper remembered the phone call, and aside from being utterly shocked, there was something else. He'd found himself somewhat excited by the idea of being a father. It hadn't mattered that he didn't know the woman, couldn't even remember sleeping with her. But the part of him that had been searching for something more permanent, something that would allow him to settle down, had wrapped its hands around the idea and jumped up and down with joy.

"I went to Arkansas," he explained. "I bought an old house close to where she was, and we spent the next couple of weeks getting to know one another. I knew when the baby was born I was going to ask for a paternity test, but until then, I didn't see how it could hurt for me to get to know her. If she was the mother of my child, I wanted to be there for her."

Looking up, Cooper met Tessa's eyes for the first time, and he saw tears there. His heart constricted. She was going to hate him after this, he could feel it.

"I never slept with her, Tessa. Not after she told me she was pregnant and as it turns out, I had never slept with her before then either. She was pregnant when she'd come to my tour bus, but her asshole boyfriend had left her, and she wanted to find someone to help her take care of the child. Don't ask me why she picked me; I have no idea.

"One afternoon, the boyfriend approached me. At the time, I didn't even know he existed. He gave me the full scoop right there in a busy restaurant close to her house. I felt like an idiot. She'd blindsided me and lied to me about the whole thing."

"Does Marcus know the full story?" Tessa asked, the first words she'd said in quite some time.

Meeting her eyes, Cooper forced himself to his feet, pacing away from her. "Of course he knows the fucking story, Tessa." The anger was bubbling down deep. "He made sure that I was reminded of the incident for the next six months or so. He used it to hurt me as often as he could."

"Why did it hurt you?" she asked, sounding concerned.

Cooper stopped pacing and turned to face her. "I'm thirty-one fucking years old, Tessa. In all my life, I never imagined I'd be over thirty and single. For years I'd hoped to find the right girl, settle down, have babies," he explained, the fury frothing like acid in his gut. "And no, maybe it's not what most men my age are actively pursuing, but dammit, I want something of my own. I'm fucking tired of being alone."

He turned away, running his hands through his hair before resting his palms on the porch railing. He knew how the story sounded, knew that it made him appear weak and needy, but he wasn't going to lie to Tessa. In truth, he wanted what his parents had found nearly thirty-five years ago, and to this day, he never expected it to happen to him. So when Tabitha had tricked him into believing he was going to be a father, he'd been happier than he had been in years.

Cooper's body went rigid when he felt Tessa's hands on his back. He hung his head low, expecting her to tell him that he needed to go, he needed to go find someone who could give him what he needed because she wasn't that person.

But damn it, he wanted her to be. It wasn't very often that he found a woman who treated him like a normal man. Like he wasn't in the limelight. He liked the way she tried to keep her distance yet relented when he pushed, because no matter what, up until now, he knew she'd felt something for him too.

Cooper's back hardened when her soft, cool hands were replaced by her lips. She wasn't trying to seduce him, she was trying to comfort him, and when she wrapped her arms around him, her palms flattening on his stomach, he almost lost control of his own emotions. He couldn't remember a time when a woman had held him like that. As if she actually wanted to ease his pain.

If he hadn't already been falling in love with her, he certainly was now.

CHAPTER TWENTY-SEVEN

Tessa felt the thump of Cooper's heartbeat against her palms, the warmth of his skin against her cheek as she held on to him.

His story wasn't what she'd expected to hear, and the sorrow in his voice as he told it hit her in a strange way. As much as she wanted to deny the truth, the pained look in Cooper's eyes had told her he wasn't lying. And it helped to explain the sadness she'd seen when she had brought up kids before. Some of what he'd said was probably difficult for him to admit. Based on the way he stood stone-still in front of her confirmed it.

He wanted a family, and he'd been conned into believing he was going to be a father. Above all else, he'd done the right thing. Something many men wouldn't do. She had to admire him for that, even if her heart was breaking for what he'd been through. She wanted to find the Tabitha girl and claw her eyes out for hurting him like that.

Tessa was about to say something when her back screen door flew open, slamming into the wall, making her jump. She turned to see Jack barreling toward her and Cooper as if the house was on fire.

"Sonuvabitch! What the fuck did you do to my sister?" Jack growled as he moved closer.

Cooper's sudden movement caught Tessa off guard, and when she began to stumble, he righted her and then eased her behind him as he went toe to toe with her younger brother.

"Jack! Don't!" she yelled, trying to move around Cooper. He wasn't having any of it, and she was getting pissed off by the way he was trying to protect her.

This was her brother.

Slapping his arm away, Tessa moved around Cooper, watching as Jack got right up in Cooper's face. Granted, Jack was closer to six foot six, compared to Cooper's six-foot-two, so they didn't meet eye to eye.

"You bastard! If you hurt her, I'll fucking kill you!"

"You don't want to do this, Jack," Cooper warned, his voice calm but eerily low.

His body language didn't at all resemble the tone of his voice though. He appeared rigidly defensive, but he wasn't aggressive toward Jack physically.

"Nothing happened," Tessa told him, trying to push her way between them. "Dammit, Jack! Nothing happened!"

"No?" Jack barked, never moving out of Cooper's face. "Then why did I hear you went home last night after this shithead's manager stopped in? How do you explain that?"

Tessa grabbed Jack's arm and forced him back an inch. Not that she could've budged him if he didn't want to move, but he placated her.

"I didn't feel well," she explained. That was the truth. After she'd spoken to Marcus, her stomach had been churning painfully from her grief. But, in Cooper's defense, she hadn't given him a chance to explain himself.

Jack pinned his stare back on Cooper, who hadn't moved from where he was standing, his fists clenched at his sides.

"You hurt her, and I'll hurt you. Understand me?" Jack asked.

"You don't want to do this, Jack," Cooper repeated. "You're gonna want to take a step back."

Tessa could feel Cooper's ire as it radiated off him like a heat wave in summer.

"Jack, stop. Cooper didn't hurt me," she told her brother. She looked up at Cooper, waiting until he looked at her before she said, "He wouldn't hurt me." The sudden realization made her body tremble and tears rush to her eyes.

He wouldn't hurt her. He was one of the good ones. Even if she was scared senseless about what that meant for them. She didn't want to invite more heartache into her life, but she found that she trusted him. Something that she didn't do easily. After Richie died, leaving her utterly alone, and Chad had tried to sabotage her reputation because he hadn't gotten his way, rightfully so, she was jaded.

But just like Izzy had suggested, Tessa had managed to give Cooper a chance. And here he was copping to his innermost insecurities, and she knew without a doubt that he wasn't going to hurt her. At least not on purpose.

"Never," Cooper whispered, his eyes locked with hers. "I promise you that."

Grabbing Jack's arm, she applied as much force as she could, pulling him backward. "Now, go on. Thank you for wanting to protect me, little brother, but it's time for you to go."

Jack stood motionless, staring at her as if she had morphed into something alien right before his eyes. "Fine," Jack said quietly. "Just remember that I won't tolerate anyone hurting her. You get me?"

"Sounds like we've got something in common," Cooper answered, his brown eyes calmer than they had been moments ago.

Without another word, Jack turned and stalked back in the direction he'd come from. The screen door slammed once more, followed by the front door a few seconds later.

"I'm sorry about that," Tessa said, pacing away from him.

Cooper's warm hands stopped her movements as they rested on her shoulders. He turned her to face him, and Tessa's breath lodged in her chest. "Don't be sorry. I'm glad to know that he's got your back. I feel better knowing you've got someone in your corner."

Tessa nodded, fighting the tears that had suddenly appeared to cloud her vision. There was so much emotion churning inside of her she wasn't sure she'd be able to hold them back much longer.

That's when her feet were swept out from under her, and she found herself in Cooper's arms, a squeal escaping her as she tried to kick her legs.

"Hold still, woman. I've got you," he muttered as he started moving. "Barely," he said with a laugh.

Tessa slapped his chest as she laughed. "I figured you were stronger than that, cowboy."

Cooper managed to pull open the screen door as the dogs pushed their way into the house before he followed behind them.

"What are you doing?" she asked when he closed the back door and locked it.

"Keeping your brother out. I figure if he comes back, this way he won't interrupt. Lord knows what he'll do when he hears you screaming."

Tessa laughed, wrapping her arms around his neck tightly. "You plan to make me scream, cowboy?"

"More than once, darlin'. More than once."

"Promises, promises," she goaded him as he moved down the narrow hall to her bedroom.

Without any finesse whatsoever, he dumped her on the mattress, making her laugh again. The giggle quickly died when his hard body came down over her, his hips fitting between her thighs until she was wrapping her legs around him and trying to pull him closer.

"Seems like we've got on more clothes than necessary," Cooper said with a mischievous gleam in his eyes.

"Then you should remedy that," she taunted.

The mattress dipped, and she bounced slightly as he pushed up to his feet abruptly. She couldn't tear her eyes off him as he stripped out of his jeans in record time. Once he was fully naked, he grabbed her shorts and pulled them down her legs, panties going with them.

When he came back down over her, the only things she had on were her tank top and bra. "I think you forgot something," she told him seriously.

"Working on it, darlin'," he crooned in her ear, his tongue tracing the outer shell. "I promise, I'm going to have you naked soon."

His voice sent chills racing down her spine. His words reminded her of all of the times she had heard him sing in the last few months. His voice was like rich, dark chocolate coating her skin. Sweet, warm, delicious.

As though he knew she was thinking about his voice, he sang a chorus from one of her favorite songs of his.

From the first time I saw her
Her smile spoke to my soul
My heart found a home
Right there in the arms of my angel in blue jeans

"I love that song," she whispered to him, cupping his stubbly jaw as she looked into brown eyes that drew her in, held her close.

"I hope so," he muttered with a smile. "It's about you."

Tessa stilled. *About her?* "Seriously?"

"Yup," he answered, his fingers sliding under the material of her tank top, pushing it higher on her torso until he got it over her breasts.

A strange echo erupted in her chest, as if she had been hollow before and now, all of a sudden, there was something swirling inside of her.

He pressed a gentle kiss to her mouth before pushing up onto his knees and ridding her of her tank top quickly. Because she didn't want to wait, Tessa unhooked the front clasp of her bra and maneuvered out of it as fast as she could, her eyes never leaving Cooper's.

"So, what are you waiting for?" she asked breathlessly. "I want you inside me."

"Oh, darlin', that will all come in due time."

He shifted, and Tessa felt his hands on her butt, pushing her up the bed until she was closer to the pillows at the top. As he settled between her thighs, she glanced down at him, waiting with bated breath for him to do something. Anything.

"You're a frustrating man," she joked when she realized he was taking his time, staring between her legs as he parted her with his fingers. The warmth of his breath against her sensitive nerve endings was making her crazy.

"Hmmm, but it'll be worth the wait, I promise. I've waited to do this again for so long." His eyes traveled up the length of her body until they met hers again. "I crave the taste of you. I want to feel you squirm against my mouth while I fuck you with my tongue."

God, she loved when he talked like that. The eroticism of the words drove her wild. Something she hadn't thought would happen again. She had vowed for the longest time that she would never let herself lose control like that with another man. But with Cooper, it was almost as though she didn't have a choice. It was as if he insisted that she lose her inhibitions when they were together. And the pleasure he wrought from her body was so worth it she couldn't even try to control herself, even if she wanted to.

His thick fingers spread her wider as she watched. When his head lowered, she tried to focus on what he was doing, but the second the heat of his tongue trailed lightly over her clit, Tessa's head fell back on the pillow, a moan escaping. "I love when you do that," she admitted.

"When I lick your pussy?" he asked.

God, could he make this any hotter? Just his words alone... "Yes. Yes, when you do that."

"Say it, Tessa. Tell me you love when I lick your pussy."

Tessa tensed, her body straining to fight off what he was asking her to do. It was one thing to enjoy what he did, what he said, but to repeat it... She couldn't.

She felt his breath between her thighs once more, and she thought he was going to move on, but he didn't. "If you want me to continue, you'll tell me."

"You're incorrigible," she bit out.

"I'm many things, darlin'. Tell me."

Tessa groaned as his breath teased the sensitive tissue, her pussy begging for his touch. "I love when you lick me," she said, her words reflecting her uncertainty.

Cooper pushed her legs farther apart, his big hands flat on the insides of her thighs, holding her open to his gaze, and Tessa wanted to beg him to lick her.

"Lick you where? Repeat after me, Tessa. 'Cooper, I love when you lick my pussy.'"

Oh, God! She nearly came up off the bed as his tongue briefly touched her clit, an obvious attempt to torture her. "Cooper, I love — Oh, God! — I love when you lick my pussy!"

As soon as the last word left her lips, his mouth descended on her, and she screamed, the sudden heat against her needy nerve endings almost sending her over the edge. To her relief, he slowed his movements, his tongue searching, seeking, torturing her as he lapped at her over and over again. She was a writhing, moaning mess by the time he drove his tongue inside of her. "Cooper! Please!"

"Please what?" he asked, the smile in his voice evident.

"Please make me come." Now *that* she could say.

"My pleasure, baby," he growled, the vibration reigniting the embers, making the flames burn hotter until she was gripping the comforter beneath her hands, her muscles locking up one by one until she was thrusting her hips upward, pressing against his mouth. When he began flicking her clit relentlessly, her orgasm exploded like a violent earthquake, knocking her off balance as she tried to hold on to the last vestiges of her sanity.

CHAPTER TWENTY-EIGHT

As Tessa came, Cooper couldn't tear his eyes off her. When she settled back on the bed, he eased up her body, tasting her skin along the way, teasing one puckered nipple before continuing. There was a smile on her face that made his heart swell.

"I love to watch you come," he whispered against her mouth.

"Mmmm," she moaned.

"Feel better?" he asked, pressing his iron-hard cock against her lower belly.

"I will in a minute," she said, taking him entirely off guard.

"Well, that's not what I expected to hear."

Tessa's sudden movement surprised him, and she managed to flip their positions before he realized what was happening. He flopped onto his back, allowing the alluring, naked cowgirl to straddle him.

"I could get used to this," he told her.

"I'm sure you could. But that comes later."

He growled. She smiled.

As she probably already realized, patience wasn't one of his virtues, but it seemed like she always wanted to push his limits. He was about to warn her when she pressed her entire body against the full length of his, her tongue teasing his bottom lip. Figuring she wanted to take the reins, Cooper remained motionless, watching to see what she'd do next.

He tracked every movement, heard her uneven breaths mixed with his own as she moved down his body, her lips trailing blazes of heat over his skin. When she gently bit his nipple, he almost bucked her off him.

"Sonuvabitch," he growled.

Her head came up, and the little minx was smiling.

"Did that hurt?"

"Fuck no," he growled. It didn't hurt. It felt too fucking good and that was the problem. Ever since the shower that morning, Cooper had been hanging by a thread, and he wanted to be inside of her. If she was going to torture him, then he wouldn't be able to make it until then.

"Then lie back and enjoy it, cowboy," she said sweetly, her mouth lowering above his other nipple, teasing him with her breath before licking him.

She must've sensed he was going to say something, because her finger came up and landed over his mouth, making him laugh. He got the hint. He was supposed to be quiet. He could handle…

"Fucking hell!"

Her throaty laugh made his cock swell impossibly further.

"You bit me again," he accused.

"And the more you talk, the more I bite."

Okay, he didn't need to be told twice. Dropping his head to the pillow, he closed his eyes and tried to hold on to his control. He was just going to have to endure.

Her silky hair drifted over his chest as she moved lower, her mouth placing hot, wet kisses over his skin as she continued. As soon as his brain recognized what she was about to do, Cooper's legs locked up.

Smooth, soft fingers curled around his straining cock, moving ever so slowly, the sensations nearly too much to bear. It would be one thing for her to be aggressive, but this sensual torture was going to be the death of him.

He tried to compartmentalize the different sensations, hoping like hell he could ignore the subtle strokes along his cock.

Nope. Not happening.

Shit.

"Tessa. Darlin', please," he begged, his voice strained with how much he was holding back.

"I love when you ask so nicely," she teased, and then her hot, moist mouth was on him, the head of his cock slowly slipping between her lips, and he found himself gripping the blankets beneath him to keep from reaching for her.

"Oh, fuck, yes!" he roared, pushing up into her mouth.

Her small hands landed flat on his thighs, attempting to hold him down, and he gave in, forcing his body to remain flat against the mattress as her sweet mouth slid over him, her tongue teasing the flared head before taking him deeper. He squeezed his eyes shut, focusing on the heavenly feel of her mouth on him. She wasn't just sucking his cock, she was exploring him with her mouth, and he wanted to shout to the heavens. It was the most unbelievable feeling, her tongue stroking, teasing. When her lips closed around him and she sucked him deep, he groaned, his balls drawing up tightly to his body.

Unable to stop himself, Cooper grabbed her head with one hand, holding her still. "Uh-uh. I'm not coming in your mouth, Tessa. Not this time, baby." He wanted to be inside of her. He wanted her to come at the same time he did, and if she kept this up, he was going to lose all of his noble intentions.

He kept his fingers threaded in her hair, controlling her movements as best he could, enjoying the silky feel of her mouth as she sucked his cock, bathing him with her tongue until he couldn't take any more.

"Come here, Tessa." Adding a bit of demand to his tone, he kept his fingers wound in her hair, pulling gently until she was doing as he asked. Once she was over him, he flipped them again, wanting to feel her beneath him. "Remember what you said earlier?"

Tessa nodded, her wide eyes locked with his. "I'm on the pill," she said. "I swear to you, I'm on the pill."

The fact that Tessa understood his pain from earlier made his chest swell. He appreciated her reassurance, and he believed her. Hell, he'd believed her the first time she had told him.

"I'm clean, Tessa. I have routine checkups, and I use condoms."

Tessa's eyes darted away briefly and then back to his. "I'm clean too. I don't have sex. The last time — before you and me — was a year ago. With Chad. We used condoms, but I was tested anyway."

Cooper's gut twisted with the mention of the bastard's name, but he ignored the jealousy and nodded his head.

"Do you trust me? If we're going to do this, I want to know that you trust me. That you won't run from me if things get tough." He paused, swallowed. "This is just the beginning, Tessa."

"Yes," she said on a sob. "I trust you, Cooper."

Her cool fingers rested against his cheeks, and Cooper leaned down, pressing his mouth to hers. The kiss started gently but quickly escalated, infused with the molten heat that they generated when they were together. Shifting until he was right where he wanted to be, Cooper didn't break the kiss, inhaling Tessa's gasp as he thrust into her hard.

As much as he wanted to go slow, to make love to her the way he had in the bed of his truck under the stars, the thread on his control was too frayed. Pulling back, he stared down at her. "Put your hands on the headboard," he ordered.

Her grin made his heart melt. She easily lifted her arms, her hands wrapping around the bars on the headboard.

Cooper pushed up onto his knees, gripping her hips as he lifted her slightly, pushing deeper and then retreating slowly. Her breasts swayed as he began a slow, almost gentle rhythm. He could only maintain slow for so long, because the hot, wet grip of her pussy was too much. Without the latex barrier, she was scorching him, and the slow glide through her slick heat quickly morphed into punishing thrusts of his hips as he slammed into her, her arms locked as she added resistance against the headboard.

"Cooper," Tessa groaned, her eyes closing as her head tipped back against the pillow.

He was unable to say a word; his body spoke the only language he knew at the moment as he continued to pound into her. He refused to come until she did, but she seemed to be holding out on him. He released her hips and took one leg, lifting it high on his shoulder as he leaned into her, providing the perfect angle…

"Fuck, baby." Cooper paused, taking a deep breath as the pleasure overwhelmed him. "Tessa, you feel so fucking good. So damn tight." He was rambling, but it was the only thing he could do to keep from slamming into her and coming with a vengeance.

"Cooper! Don't stop! Oh!" Tessa screamed as her pussy gripped him like a velvet vice, clamping down on his cock until he had to give himself over to the pleasure.

"You do know we have to get up at some point today," Tessa told Cooper a couple of hours later when they awoke, cuddled up next to each other in her bed.

A disgruntled sound came from Cooper's chest, and she curled into him even more.

"Shit!" he exclaimed and pushed up, glancing over at the clock.

"What's wrong?" she asked, pulling the sheet up over her bare breasts as she sat up.

"I left Dalton at the bar last night. He was supposed to stay with me," Cooper told her, a smile replacing his frown.

"Oh, crap."

"Yeah," he answered, crawling out of bed and walking naked toward the bathroom. "There's no telling what kind of trouble that boy got himself into."

Tessa fell back on the bed, staring up at the ceiling. She remembered the way Dalton had been watching Katie and wondered for a minute... Surely not. She wasn't sure Katie could handle a cowboy like Dalton. Hell, she wasn't sure Devil's Bend could handle him, especially if he was anything like Cooper.

He peeked into the bedroom a minute later, smiling at her. "You mind coming to the house for dinner tonight? I'd like you there when I talk to Dalton about the logistics of the farm."

Tessa nodded, her heart constricting in her chest. He wanted to include her in his discussions about the farm. She knew he'd been working on getting a plan together, bringing in some volunteers to help with the barn. There was a lot of work to be done before he could purchase horses though.

The sound of the shower came on, and Tessa let her eyes close as she thought about everything that had happened since last night. Just when she'd thought her world was crashing in on her, Cooper had gone and thrown her for a loop. His story had broken her heart, and at the same time, she was angry at Marcus for trying to make Cooper sound like a serial womanizer.

Still, there was a tiny part of her that was scared to open up to him completely. Even if she trusted him, her past didn't allow her to embrace any sort of happiness. Her path seemed paved with roadblocks that would keep her from a life of happiness. Granted, she had no one to blame but herself. Had she not been so out of control...

When Cooper appeared a few minutes later wearing only his jeans, Tessa pushed all of her negative thoughts to the back of her mind and focused on him.

"I better head out and see if I can track him down. The last thing Devil's Bend needs is that man on the prowl. I'll see you in a couple of hours?"

She nodded, watching as he moved around the room, pulling on his shirt.

"Hey, do me a favor," he said to her as he sat on the edge of the bed, leaning over and focusing on his boots. "Tell Izzy and Eric to come tonight, would ya?"

That got Tessa's attention, but she didn't say anything. Cooper must've realized she was surprised by his request, because he crawled up on the bed, hovering directly above her.

"I'd like to see what they think of the plans. Maybe they can give us some ideas."

His explanation made her feel better, and she laughed. "You don't know the half of it." Izzy wouldn't hesitate to add her two cents, especially if someone was asking for her input. "Are you sure? I don't want Dalton to panic if she's ogling him from across the table."

"I'm sure he can handle her. If not, I doubt Eric has any problems keeping her in line."

Tessa laughed so hard tears came to her eyes. "Right. You don't know her well, do you?"

Cooper grinned, and the crooked smirk made her bones turn to mush. When he leaned closer, his mouth pressing to hers, she put her arms around him. "I wish we could stay here a little longer." The thought escaped through her mouth without her permission.

Opening her eyes, she met Cooper's intense gaze, and what she saw there had her heart leaping in her chest.

"I promise, we'll be doing plenty more of this in the near future," he replied, his rough finger trailing down her jaw. "I don't think I'll ever get enough of you, Tessa."

God, she really hoped that was true.

CHAPTER TWENTY-NINE

Cooper didn't have much time to do anything productive when he got home. After leaving Tessa's, he had called Dalton to find out that the guy had, in fact, slept in his truck, in front of Cooper's house the night before. He apologized profusely for leaving him stranded, but when he met up with Dalton at his house, the grin on Dalton's face had assured him he didn't mind. Apparently, he'd gone out for an early breakfast with Katie after The Rusty Nail had closed.

Cooper had spent an hour or so trying to straighten the house as best he could, considering he was still living out of boxes. It wasn't that he didn't have the time to unpack, but with everything else going on, he had pushed that to the lower part of his priority list. He still didn't consider it important, except that he was expecting company and wanted to ensure his guests could move around when necessary.

"You get the stuff on the list?" Cooper asked Dalton when his buddy walked in the back door.

"Got it," Dalton said matter-of-factly.

Grabbing two of the overstuffed paper bags from Dalton's hands, Cooper started putting things away. When Dalton just stood in the kitchen staring back at him, Cooper turned to face him.

"What's up?"

"You mind if I invite someone tonight?"

"Not at all. Who'd you have in mind?" Cooper had a pretty good idea, but he didn't jump to conclusions these days.

"Katie," Dalton replied shyly.

Interesting. Cooper wasn't sure he'd ever seen Dalton act like that when it came to a woman. In fact, Dalton had never been the type of guy who went out with the same girl more than once. At least Cooper didn't think he did.

"Not at all. Izzy and Eric are coming over as well." Tessa had called to let him know she had to run a couple of errands, but she had confirmed that Izzy and Eric had accepted his invitation for dinner.

Glancing over at the clock on the stove, Cooper knew he needed to kick it into high gear or he'd be the worst host in the history of the planet. Taking the steaks from the bag and the sauce he had asked Dalton to get, Cooper got down to business.

A few minutes later, the steaks were marinating in the refrigerator, and he was sitting on the back porch with Dalton drinking a beer.

"So, when are you gonna have that thing torn down?" Dalton asked, his head tilted toward the old barn that was an eyesore more than anything.

"I've got a demolition crew coming next week to knock it down and haul it away. There are a few other things out in the back forty that need to be hauled off." Cooper hadn't had the time to go over the land with a fine-toothed comb yet, but he'd hired someone who would go out and see what all was out there.

"You plannin' to move quickly with this?" Dalton asked as he stood from his seat, moving to lean against the rail that wrapped around the outer portion of the porch. Cooper's mind drifted to the night Tessa had come over. He wasn't sure he'd ever be able to look at that railing without thinking of her.

"Hopin' to," Cooper confirmed. "I want to do a lot of the work myself, but I'm not gonna lie, I need help."

"Well, that's what I'm here for." Dalton glanced his way. "From what Katie tells me, that lady of yours has a lot of resources too. Did you know she's a youth counselor down at the church?"

Yes, Cooper did know that. However, he wasn't sure how happy he was that Dalton had been in town less than twenty-four hours and he knew as much, if not more, about Tessa than Cooper did. "I know her goal was to build a farm to work with disabled children and troubled youth."

"That's what I heard, too. Pretty noble, if you ask me. Does she live on some land now?"

The question was a sore spot for Cooper. No, Tessa didn't have property to do what she had been planning to do because Cooper had come in and stolen it right out from under her. He busied himself with drinking his beer so he didn't have to answer the question. Thankfully, Dalton moved on quickly.

"The two of you serious?"

Well, shit. More personal wasn't the direction Cooper was hoping this conversation would go, but he didn't want to shrug Dalton off. His buddy had come down from Nashville with the intention of helping him get this dream off the ground, so to speak. Singing at The Rusty Nail was just a bonus — for both of them.

"I'd like to think so, yeah," Cooper answered, staring out at the barn that would soon be replaced with something much more modern. He could actually see himself sitting out here with Tessa on warm summer nights or working in the stables alongside her during the day. Indefinitely.

"I heard her husband died a few years ago," Dalton said, seemingly ignorant to the fact that he knew more about Tessa than Cooper because he had spent time with one of the women who worked for her.

"He did." Cooper didn't like talking about her when she wasn't there, felt like it was a sort of betrayal, but this was his closest friend. Despite their lifestyles and how often they were on the road separately, Cooper and Dalton kept in touch often. They were each other's sounding boards when it came to music, and ultimately, Cooper knew Dalton was a loyal friend. "He was a police officer. He died in the line of duty."

Cooper hadn't actually done any digging to find out more about Tessa's husband's death. He didn't want to invade her privacy, but now that he thought about it, he wondered if he should have. Getting to know her had been a slow process, and there were so many things he felt she was keeping from him.

"Sucks, man." Dalton paused. "Katie told me they lost a baby." Dalton's voice reflected the sadness one would expect with a story of loss.

Cooper tried to keep his expressions masked, but he knew he couldn't do it. Pushing to his feet, he forced himself to move. She'd lost a baby? She'd never told him that. The idea of Tessa having to go through anything so painful tore at his heart. He wanted to hold her and protect her from all of the cruelties that the world had to offer.

Then again, she'd done the same for him earlier that morning. When he'd thought he was going to be a father, he'd been elated. Not even the awkward situation had been able to deflate the joy that had filled his heart. And to find out from the jackass boyfriend that Tabitha was lying to him had been a crushing blow.

Would Tessa want to try to have kids again? She was young and healthy, and he couldn't see why not, but he knew from his own experience how hard it could be to get emotionally attached and have it pulled from his grasp.

"Man, I'm sorry. I thought you knew." Dalton's firm tone caught his attention, and Cooper realized he'd been pacing, his hand thrust in his hair.

"It never came up," he explained. He paused briefly, staring out at the countryside and then back to his friend. "She's the strongest woman I know, Dalt. I've never felt like this before."

And maybe that was more information than he should've shared with anyone, but he felt better saying the words out loud.

"I can tell." Dalton's voice was louder, as though he'd moved closer. "I think the two of you might have something here."

Dalton knew what Cooper had been through. And apparently he knew what Tessa had been through as well. So to hear someone confirm that they might stand a chance renewed his faith that something might come out of this. Well, if he could get Tessa to jump on board with the idea, it would.

"What time is everyone coming over?" Dalton asked, obviously trying to change the subject.

"Six." And that wasn't going to come fast enough.

"Well, you've got about fifteen minutes to get this place spruced up. What can I help with?"

Fifteen minutes? *Shit.*

Cooper pulled his cell phone from his pocket and glanced at the time as though he didn't believe Dalton. Sure enough, fifteen minutes until six.

"We should get the grill fired up," Cooper stated firmly as he turned back toward the house. "You get that started; I'll grab the rest."

CHAPTER THIRTY

Tessa was enjoying Cooper's impromptu party more than she wanted to admit. They had finished eating about an hour ago and found themselves sitting on the back porch watching Havoc and Harmony trample around the yard, checking out the new scenery. She had hated leaving them home alone, so she'd called Cooper, and to her delight he had agreed she should definitely bring them.

When she'd arrived, she'd been almost stunned to see Katie there with Dalton. Not that she didn't want Katie to find all the happiness in the world, but she wondered whether the woman knew what she was getting herself into. Tessa didn't have a lot of experience, but she had dated Chad. And now Cooper. Granted, those two guys were like night and day, from what she could tell, and she had to wonder whether the fact that Cooper had actually made a name for himself in country music was the difference.

Chad never had made it big, although his ego seemed to be one step ahead of reality. Even the nights he would sing at The Rusty Nail hadn't been all that profitable, because they never brought in the crowds like he had insisted they would. But that was about the time Tessa had realized he was using her.

Not wanting to dwell on that painful part of her past, Tessa focused on the conversations going on around her. She had taken a seat on the steps that led down into the yard while everyone else sat up on the porch. They must've realized she needed some space, because no one had yet to join her. Not even Katie or Izzy.

Now that she thought about it, Katie had been acting weird ever since she'd showed up. At first, Tessa had thought she was just nervous, but her interactions with Dalton seemed friendly and not as reserved as Tessa would've thought.

She heard the group talking about how Katie had gone out with Dalton after The Rusty Nail had closed, which meant they had apparently ventured to the IHOP in the neighboring town because nothing in Devil's Bend stayed open that late.

"How long have you two been married?"

Tessa turned to glance behind her, noticing that Dalton was talking to Eric and Izzy. Obviously. No one else was married. The thought actually depressed Tessa, but she didn't want to bring down the mood of the party, so she turned back to focus on her dogs as they sniffed the ground around the porch.

"Almost six years," Eric answered easily. "We got married a few months after Tessa and— Oomph!"

Despite her heavy heart, Tessa smiled, picturing Izzy elbowing Eric in the ribs to get him to stay quiet. "It's okay, Izzy," she called out, not bothering to look back.

"Sorry, Tess." Eric's apology wasn't needed. Her friends had loved Richie as much as she had, and although talking about him was still hard for her, she wanted him to be remembered.

Twisting to lean against the tall post so that she could face the group, Tessa pulled her knees up close to her chest. "Eric and Izzy got married two months after Richie and I did. The only reason they waited was because high maintenance over there insisted on this huge wedding."

The group laughed, including Izzy. "So not true," she said in a mock defensive tone. "He's the one who wanted a big wedding."

"Okay, so that was mostly true," Tessa added with a laugh.

"Do you guys have kids?" Dalton asked, his attention still focused on the couple sitting across from him.

Tessa immediately glanced out at the yard, her heart pounding erratically. The pain of losing her baby was still there, although she tried to ease the discomfort by telling herself that Richie was cuddling their little one up in heaven these days. It helped, but not nearly as much as she would like it to.

"No kids. Not yet. We've been talking about it though."

Tessa's head jerked back to Izzy. They were? She'd had no idea. The idea made her heart double in size, happiness filling her for her friends. "It's about time," she told them. "I've wondered if you two would ever get with the program."

The solemn look on Izzy's face told her exactly why she hadn't known about this. Her friend was so careful to ensure she didn't hurt Tessa's feelings or rouse memories that would make her grieve. But that was life. As much as she didn't want it to sometimes, it moved on. Her losses, although she felt they were cruel and pointless, had made her a stronger person. Even if she would prefer to be weak if it meant she hadn't had to experience them.

"Do you want to try to have kids again?" Dalton asked.

For a second, Tessa didn't realize he was talking to her. Her head felt like it was attached to her body by a bungee cord as she swung her gaze in his direction.

How did he know? Oh, God. She looked over at Cooper and noticed the sadness in his eyes. Or was that pity? Did he feel sorry for her?

Pushing to her feet, Tessa all but ran from the porch, heading around to the front of the house in a full-on panic attack. Her dogs, loyal followers that they were, fell into step beside her. She had to get out of there. Her chest felt like it was caving in.

How did Dalton know? And Cooper?

Tessa had to stop, unable to drag air into her lungs. She was leaning over, her hands resting on her thighs as she fought for breath, when strong arms came down on her shoulders. She refused to cry, but the tears were trying to ignore her specific instructions to stay back.

"Darlin'," Cooper said as he turned her and pulled her against him.

She was angry and hurt and confused. She hadn't wanted him to find out about how miserable her life had been. Not only had she lost their baby, but she'd lost Richie as well. And she knew it was her fault. All of it was her fault. She'd been rebellious and foolish, and no matter who'd tried to talk to her, she hadn't been able to stop herself. There for a while, she had even convinced herself that her father had left because of her.

"Tessa, look at me." Cooper's voice was a loud crack in the silent night.

Tessa jerked her head up, realizing she was still heaving, trying to force oxygen past the immense boulder resting on her chest.

"Stop it!" he ordered, and she stopped cold.

"I'm so sorry," she whispered.

"What are you sorry for?" he asked, confusion lacing the words.

"It's all my fault." Why was she doing this? He didn't need to know about her life before him. She was supposed to be enjoying the time they had together, knowing full well that Cooper would move on with his life, and she would be left to pick up more pieces than had been there before he'd arrived.

His strong finger curled beneath her chin, and he forced her to look up at him.

"We can't control the outcomes, Tessa," he said softly.

"That's not true. Everything I've done in my life has brought me to this place. If I'd been…" She knew she shouldn't be telling him this, but she suddenly couldn't stop herself. "If I had walked the straight and narrow and not been so reckless, none of this would've happened."

"You really think that's true?" he asked, the incredulity in his voice making her shudder.

"Yes," she said without conviction. She had no idea what she believed. When it came down to it, she knew everything happened for a reason. She had done so many things wrong in her life, and losing everything was her punishment.

"How'd you meet Richie?" Cooper asked.

Tessa jerked away from him, not wanting to tell him. The answer to that question would give away even more about herself that she wanted to keep hidden from him.

When Cooper laced his fingers with hers and pulled her back toward the house, Tessa tried to break free.

"Stop fighting me, Tessa," he warned. "We're going to sit right here." He was pointing to the front porch, so she let the fight drain out of her arm. At least she wouldn't have to face everyone else.

Glancing up, she noticed there were several cars parked out on the main road. Reporters, she knew. They were stalking Cooper.

Once they were seated on the steps, Cooper pulled her against his side, his arm a comfort she needed more than anything right then.

"Ignore them," he whispered against her hair. "Talk to me. How'd you meet Richie?" he repeated.

Tessa swallowed hard. With the press in town, there was a chance that all of this would be dredged up anyway, so Tessa decided she might as well come clean. She didn't know what it would mean for her relationship with this man, but at least she'd be the one to tell him. If he walked away from her, she wouldn't have to guess as to why.

"I was a sophomore in high school," she began, her head resting against his shoulder. "One night, I did something incredibly stupid." No one knew that she had stolen Texas Shadow except for Richie and Mr. Deluth. Luanne hadn't even known the details. Mr. Deluth had been too worried about the legal consequences if the sheriff found out, so he'd told her to keep quiet. As for Richie, well, he'd never told anyone either.

"Mr. Deluth caught me and my punishment was to work in his stable for six months, taking care of the horses."

"What did you do?"

Tessa swallowed hard. No one would ever find out the details of what she'd done; she knew that. If she just kept her mouth shut, no one would know, because Richie and Mr. Deluth had died with her secret. But for some reason, she felt like Cooper should know. It would help him to understand why karma was such a heartless bitch to her.

"I took one of his horses. I came out here after dark, took Texas Shadow right out of his stall, and then rode for hours that night."

Cooper didn't say anything, so Tessa continued. "When I brought him back the next morning, Mr. Deluth was waiting for me. Needless to say, he was livid. Rather than call the law on me, he worked out a deal that I would take care of the horses for six months."

Tessa took a deep breath and burrowed closer to Cooper. "Richie worked for Mr. Deluth. He was a senior in high school and part of the FFA. When he found out what I'd done, he was so mad at me. But then we had to work together for the next six months. The rest is history."

"They forgave you." It wasn't a question, but Tessa didn't know what Cooper was getting at.

"I guess."

"But you've never forgiven yourself? You were what? Fifteen or sixteen?"

"Fifteen."

"And you've carried this around for half of your life, never forgiving yourself?"

"That's not the only thing I did, Cooper. That was probably the worst of it, but it certainly wasn't the only thing."

"Do you still do those things today?"

"God no!" she exclaimed, trying to pull away from him but unable to maneuver out from beneath the steel band that was his arm.

"Don't move," he ordered, glancing down at her.

Tessa stopped pulling away, all of the wind leaving her sails in an instant. She had never shared this story with anyone. At least not all of it. Izzy didn't even know. Well, she didn't think she did anyway. Tessa couldn't imagine they would still be friends if she did. Although her best friend had stuck by her through the years, she didn't think Izzy knew the worst of what she'd done. The alcohol, sure. But not the drugs or the theft.

"Look at me, Tessa." Cooper's tone was soothing, not an ounce of anger in the words, and Tessa glanced up slowly. "You were a kid, darlin'. We all do stupid things when we're kids. That doesn't mean you have to pay for it for the rest of your life."

"But it does," she retorted. "I lost my baby. Richie died." *I lost my land.* She kept the last part to herself, not wanting to hurt Cooper.

Cooper's hand cupped her jaw, his thumb beneath her chin forcing her head back farther. "It doesn't. You couldn't have stopped those things from happening, Tessa. You told me yourself that things happen for a reason."

Yes, she had told him that. And she believed it too. Which was why she blamed herself.

"You've got to let go, baby."

"It's not as easy as you think it is," she said snidely and then immediately regretted her rebuttal. Cooper had told her his story just that morning. "I'm sorry."

"No need to apologize, Tessa. I can't imagine the pain you've been through. My circumstances were different. And yes, they hurt, but I'm not comparing my life to yours. I hate that you've had to go through all of that, and if it were in my power to change things, I would. But, Tessa" — Cooper's hand tightened on her jaw just a bit — "everything that's happened to you has made you who you are. And you're a remarkable woman who has the biggest heart of anyone I've ever met. I wouldn't want that to change."

A tear leaked down her cheek, and Tessa wanted to brush it away, but Cooper did so first, his thumb caressing her cheek. Was it even possible that he didn't hold all of this against her? Would he change his mind after he had time to think it over?

They sat in silence for a few more minutes, Cooper's strong arms around her, making her feel safe, secure for the first time in as long as she could remember. Maybe it was the night or the man or possibly both, but Tessa suddenly felt the urge to talk.

"Richie was always the sensible one. The guy who liked to have fun, but he walked the straight and narrow. When we fell in love, I think he was worried about what that meant, because I was hell on wheels. No matter how hard he tried, he couldn't keep me in line.

"We broke up several times during the years we dated, especially when I was still in high school after he graduated, but I think we both knew that we'd eventually be together forever." The tears were steadily streaming down Tessa's cheeks, but she didn't try to wipe them away. It would've been pointless. "By the time I was a junior in high school, my mother had already been diagnosed with depression, but she didn't take her medicine like she was supposed to. I hated being at home, seeing her like that."

Tessa still felt like the worst daughter any mother could have because rather than trying to help her mother, she'd managed to put distance between them.

"So, I was gone from home more than I was there, and much of the time, I would stay with Richie, even though he had to sneak me in his window at night. I knew he hated doing that, because his parents would've been devastated to know their son was lying to them, but he did it anyway. For me.

"I hated working for other people, didn't do well with authority of any kind, so after I graduated from high school, I would jump from job to job. As much as I hated my father for not having anything to do with me or Adam, when he died and left us The Rusty Nail, I knew it was an opportunity I couldn't pass up. After talking to Richie, I decided I would go for it. I didn't go to college, both because I was broke but also because I didn't want to. I hated school, but I still managed to graduate. I just couldn't see myself sitting in class again, so I refused.

"Taking over the bar was supposed to be easy, or at least that's what I told myself. I mean, it's a bar, right? How hard could it be? Well, I soon learned that it wasn't just serving drinks. There was the inventory and accounting, taxes and licenses. I learned real quick that I couldn't just sit back and hope it worked out. So, I took Richie's college textbooks, and I studied them." Tessa laughed and sobbed at the same time. "He never even knew I did it, but I wanted to successfully run the bar, and I knew I had to learn somehow. So, between his textbooks and the Internet, I taught myself the accounting software. I found out I was pretty good at it."

Cooper's arm tightened around her, and Tessa relaxed. For the first time in as long as she could remember, she felt lighter all of a sudden. Everything she'd held inside for so long was spilling out, and she felt as though Cooper wasn't judging her.

God, she prayed he wasn't judging her, because she couldn't bring herself to stop talking.

CHAPTER THIRTY-ONE

Cooper held Tessa close; the only thing he paid attention to was the sound of her voice and the heartbreaking story she was telling him. He wouldn't interrupt, because as hard as he knew it was on her to talk about her past, he knew she'd bottled everything up inside for so long that she needed to get it out.

"When Richie finally asked me to marry him, I was ecstatic. I felt like I'd finally made him proud of me. So, needless to say, we got married. It wasn't anything elaborate, and my mother didn't even come to the wedding, not that I had invited her. Richie's parents were there, and so was Adam since they were friends."

Cooper couldn't imagine his parents not being at his wedding. The thought of Tessa getting married without the love and support of her family there with her made his heart hurt.

"We'd only been married for a couple of months when I got pregnant, and the idea of having a baby was the most wonderful thing that could've happened to me. To us."

Tightening his arm around her, Cooper pressed his lips against the top of her head as another shudder wracked her body.

"I was only fourteen weeks when I started spotting and cramping really badly. We went to the doctor, and he said I was miscarrying, and there wasn't anything that could be done."

When her body started to shake uncontrollably, Cooper felt his own tears forming in his eyes. She was breaking his heart right in two, and he wanted to ease her pain, but he knew there was nothing he could do but let her get it all out.

"I-I wanted my baby more than anything in the world." Tessa hiccupped. "I begged God, pleaded with Him to let me have my baby."

Tessa's sobs wracked her body, and she couldn't speak for several minutes, but Cooper didn't rush her. He held her, letting her feel the warmth of his body against hers, waiting until she was able to continue.

"After that, I refused to get pregnant again. I couldn't handle losing another child. Richie and I managed to get through each day, but things weren't easy between us for a while. I probably wouldn't have made it through it without him. He always made sure that I knew he loved me, that he was there for me. Until him, I had never known that kind of love. Never had someone to ensure I understood just what I meant to them."

Cooper made a vow right then and there that Tessa would always know exactly how he felt about her. She'd had that love only once in her life, and it had come from her husband. He'd never be able to compete with the first man she'd loved, and he would never try to. But Tessa had so much more love inside of her, and Cooper wanted to be the man she gave the rest of her heart to.

When she was silent for long minutes, Cooper shifted so that he could look down at her face. Her eyes were closed, the tears leaving streaks on her pale cheeks. Lifting her face gently, he pressed a soft kiss against her mouth. "I'm here, Tessa. I've got you."

Another round of sobs shook her, but when Tessa's arms wrapped around him and she held on for dear life, Cooper's world shifted on its axis. He loved this woman. Heart and soul.

Cooper had no idea how long he and Tessa had ended up sitting outside the night before. He'd held her until his ass was numb from sitting on the ungiving wood porch, but he would've endured hours more if she'd have needed him to. They hadn't moved an inch until Izzy and Eric had come around the house to let them know they were heading home. Tessa had felt terrible and told them as much, but her friends had told her not to worry. Cooper knew she had anyway.

After checking in with Dalton, Cooper had taken Tessa inside, making sure the dogs had a place to sleep before he took her to his bedroom. At that point, they'd talked for several more hours, and this morning, as he lay with Tessa in his arms, he felt as though he knew her better than he knew anyone else. And vice versa.

They'd been open and honest with one another, more so than Cooper had expected. She'd answered every question he'd asked, and he'd done the same. They'd talked about high school, friends, enemies, and even some of the rowdy things they'd both done at that age. And she was right — according to her stories, she'd been hell on wheels as a teenager, but then again, so had he. The difference between them was that he had come from a loving home where he'd been the center of his parents' attention. Hers was the opposite. And he understood her better now.

He didn't pretend to know what it felt like to grow up the way Tessa had, but he assured her that it wasn't her fault. He'd been just as rowdy, and he didn't have his parents to blame. Cooper wasn't sure Tessa would ever fully forgive herself for the things she'd done, but he tried to summarize all of the ways she had turned herself around based on everything he knew about her.

She had explained how she volunteered as a youth counselor at her church, how she had continued to work for Mr. Deluth — for free, mind you — years after her punishment had been lifted. She'd told him how she still helped with the Austin Police Department's Blue Santa program every year around the holidays and how she selflessly helped at one of the no-kill animal shelters in the neighboring town, which was, in fact, where she'd found Havoc and Harmony.

Tessa was the most generous person he'd ever met. Every single thing she did was for someone else, because she had this illogical belief that she had to pay everyone back for the things she'd done as a teenager. Cooper admired all of the things she did, and finally, he had convinced her to see that she did those things because she wanted to, not because she had to. For once, she had agreed with him.

And at that point, even though they were both exhausted, Cooper wasn't sure he'd be able to let Tessa sleep. When he gave in to the urge to put his hands on her, she'd been too worried that Dalton would hear them, so he had held off on tormenting her, choosing rather to make love to her only once before they'd crashed just after four in the morning.

And now as they lay in his bed, Tessa stirred in his arms, the silky strands of her hair tickling his arm when she moved. Leaning down, he kissed the top of her head and waited to see if she was awake.

When she didn't rouse, he figured he needed to get up. The sunlight was just beginning to come in through his windows, and he knew his parents would be there soon. They had called him the day before to let him know they were driving down to visit. And yes, he had knowingly kept that a secret from Tessa. No sense in worrying her even more.

After making a pot of coffee, Cooper let the dogs out the back door and joined them on the porch. Sliding into one of the plastic chairs, Cooper stared out at the land in front of him as the sun continued its remarkable ascent into the sky.

"Mornin'." Tessa's drowsy voice came from behind him a second before her arms wrapped over his shoulders and around his neck.

"Mornin', baby," he greeted her, his hands landing on her arms, enjoying the softness of her against him. "Sleep well?"

"Not too bad," she answered, and he heard the smile in her voice.

A loud bark had Tessa pulling away. "Thanks for letting them out this morning. You should've woken me up."

"They're easy to manage," Cooper told her, glancing at her over his shoulder. "And anyway, you needed the sleep."

Tessa's knockout smile made his heart lurch in his chest. He'd spend the rest of his life trying to make her smile like that if she would let him. However, he knew now wasn't the time to try and push that issue. One day at a time was what they'd agreed to, and he was trying damn hard to stick to his word. It was a little harder now that he knew he loved her.

Grabbing her arm, he pulled her around in front of him and then down onto his lap. Placing his hand on her bare thigh, he smiled. "My dad and mom will be here in a bit," he warned her, taking in the fact that she was wearing only his button-down shirt. Since it came to her knees, he knew she was modestly covered, but she probably wouldn't appreciate meeting his parents for the first time dressed like that.

"Here? Today?" Her voice was high and thin, and if he wasn't mistaken, there was a hint of fear in her eyes.

"Yep. So, go on in and take a shower. You've got time."

"But Coop—" She started to argue as she rose to her feet.

"No, 'buts,' Tessa. Just do it." He laughed as he smacked her on the butt. "I'll handle the dogs and Dalton will be up shortly."

Without another word, she disappeared inside. Maybe he should've warned her in advance that his parents were coming, but Cooper truly wanted her to meet them. He knew Tessa, and if she had any sort of advance notice, she'd probably have come up with at least one excuse. Probably more.

Half an hour later, Cooper had just finished frying the bacon and scrambling enough eggs to feed a small country when there was a knock on the front door. His father's booming voice was the first warning, followed by the excited barks of Tessa's dogs.

"Come in," he hollered over the loud barks.

After scooping the eggs on a plate and tossing a paper towel over them, he ventured into the front room, where his parents stood petting the dogs as if they'd been friends all their lives.

"Momma," Cooper greeted his mother, giving her a kiss on the cheek when she stood. "How was the trip?"

"Oh, you know your father," she teased. "Sometimes I worry that his foot's on the brake and not the gas."

"Oh, hush, woman," his father belted out as he stood to his full height, which was eye level with Cooper. "Too fast. Too slow. It'd be easier if she'd just tell me how fast she wants me to drive and I set the cruise control."

"Why didn't you mention that before? That would make it so much easier," Becca Krenshaw teased as she poked her husband in the ribs.

"Watch it, woman," David said with a smile. "So, this is the house, huh?"

Cooper glanced around the room, trying to see the house through his father's eyes. "Yup, this is it. It needs some work, but I like it."

"It's charming," his mother said as she moved through the open living room. "Open, airy, just like a country house should be."

Cooper bit back his laugh. His parents lived in a four-thousand-square-foot cabin in the Smoky Mountains, so this was like a cardboard box in comparison to their three-story retreat.

"Is that food I smell?" David asked, his hand landing firmly on Cooper's shoulder.

"Yes, sir," Cooper answered, glancing down the dim hallway as they made their way toward the kitchen. He was surprised Tessa hadn't appeared yet. Then again, if she had her way, she would probably hide out in his bedroom until she thought the coast was clear.

Not that he was going to let her.

When the back screen door opened and then shut, Cooper turned abruptly to see his angel in blue jeans standing in the doorway, a shy smile on her face. Sneaky woman. She must've snuck out the back door when his parents had arrived so she wouldn't be caught coming out of his bedroom.

Cooper saw the dogs running down the back porch steps, which meant she had done exactly that when he had been greeting his parents.

"Hey, darlin'," Cooper said, heading straight for her. "Mom, Dad, this is Tessa Donovan. Tessa, this is my mother, Becca, and my father, David."

"Oh, she's a beauty," Becca swooned as she moved in close, grabbing both of Tessa's hands in hers and then pulling her in for a hug. That was his mother. She didn't have any respect for personal space whatsoever when it came to the people in her life.

"Woman, let her be," David said with a laugh after a good thirty seconds or so.

"Why don't y'all head on out to the table on the back porch, and Tessa and I will bring the food out." Cooper held the door open for his parents as they disappeared outside.

"Dalton up yet?" he asked Tessa when he turned back to face her.

"I heard him moving around, but I haven't seen him yet. Want me to go get him?"

"Nah. Once he smells the food, he'll come runnin'."

By the time the four of them were sitting at the table on the back porch, Dalton came cruising out the back door, sniffing the air with a grin on his face. "Mornin', Mr. and Mrs. Krenshaw. Tessa. Thanks for calling me for breakfast, jackass." Dalton aimed the last jab at Cooper, making the entire table laugh.

"Dalton," David greeted. "Good to see you, boy."

"You too, sir." Dalton grinned as he pulled out the chair between Tessa and Becca. "Y'all saved me the best seat in the house."

Definitely a charmer, that boy was. For the next few minutes, everyone ate, the conversation surprisingly comfortable. Tessa joined in when the questions were directed at her, which a lot of them were considering Cooper's parents were obviously interested in getting to know her. Surprisingly, she didn't seem at all bothered by answering them.

"Tessa, would you like to help me clear the table?" Becca asked once all of the plates were emptied and pushed away, signaling everyone had gotten their fill.

"Yes, ma'am," Tessa said with a grin.

"I'll get it," Cooper offered, pushing his chair back to help.

"No, sir," his mother said, pinning him with a glare. "You boys have stuff to talk about. We girls will be fine."

Cooper nodded, his attention redirected at his father. This was the reason they'd shown up unexpected. Maybe not entirely unexpected because Cooper had fully anticipated his father coming to see him soon. He didn't spend a lot of time away from his parents, usually stopping in to visit at least once every two weeks when he wasn't on tour.

"Tell me more about this equestrian center," David insisted as the three men sat at the table, glancing out to see the dogs rumbling in the yard.

"See the barn out there?" Cooper asked as he pointed in the direction of what was left of the old barn.

"Ain't that a little close to the house?" David asked, leaning back in his chair with his hands resting on his flat stomach. At fifty-one, the man was still in top form.

"It is. I'm looking to tear it down and rebuild farther out. I've got just over two hundred acres to play with, so I think I can make it work."

"How far out? What about that direction?" David asked, looking out toward the tree line that hid the pond Cooper and Tessa had made love by a couple of weeks ago.

"Yeah?" Cooper asked, interested in what his father had to say.

"I think we put in a road over there, that'll keep the traffic away from the house."

"Traffic?" Cooper asked, glancing between the two men.

"You know once the media gets wind of this, they're gonna descend on you. If they know the boys you've got helping you out, it'll be sooner rather than later." David added, his expression serious.

True. And thanks to Dalton and several phone calls, they had more volunteers than they needed. The materials were on order and would be delivered in the next week, coming in by the truckload. Although he and Dalton had only briefly talked about the plans, the man had run with the idea. He'd even spent Sunday nailing down the help they would need.

When Dalton Calhoun got involved, things moved pretty quickly. Cooper's original concept of an equestrian center focused on working with disabled children and adults had come from one of their more in-depth conversations, he knew Dalton was fully on board with the idea.

"All right," Cooper agreed. "I'm game."

For the next half hour, the three of them talked about the logistics, even mapping out the location on a copy of the land survey to ensure they had everything placed within the appropriate boundaries.

When Tessa came back out with Becca and a full pot of coffee, Cooper was already missing her. Before she could take her seat in the chair she'd commandeered earlier, Cooper pulled her onto his lap. When she started to squirm and tossed him a look that guaranteed retribution later, he put his hand on the inside of her thigh, and she immediately stopped squirming.

Exactly how he'd planned it.

"What are you boys up to?" Cooper's mother asked as she returned to her seat.

Tessa couldn't believe that Cooper had trapped her on his lap, but each time she tried to move, his hand moved up higher on her thigh. She knew no one could see beneath the table, but she wasn't about to risk him making her turn bright red. Not in front of his parents anyway.

"What's that?" Tessa asked when she noticed the land survey sitting on the table in front of her. There were some red marks on it, clearly marking the location of the various outbuildings needed to support the farm, including the stables and a separate barn.

Pulling the paper closer, she studied it for a moment before glancing up at the others at the table.

"Look good to you?" Cooper asked.

"Would you mind if I make a couple of suggestions?" she asked, suddenly feeling as though all eyes were on her. Which they were, obviously.

"Not at all," David said, leaning forward. "What's your take?"

"See this here?" She pointed to one of the buildings on the paper. "I think you need to bring in the road from this side." With her finger, Tessa circled the road that ran along the south side of the property. "That'll keep Cooper's house off the beaten path. No matter how you design it, there will be people who want to insinuate themselves into his life, even if he tries to keep them off the property. Being that the center will be open to the public, that's not gonna be all that easy."

Tessa could feel Cooper's eyes burning into her, and she turned to look at him. The smile he gifted her with made her heart beat rapidly, probably heard by everyone at the table. "What?" she asked, wondering what he was thinking.

"I think that's a brilliant idea," David answered for Cooper. "Never even thought about that. That way Cooper will have one way in and out from his house while the public can come from the other direction. Good idea."

For some reason, David Krenshaw's approval made her feel light-headed. Granted, she'd given the plans for this center, as well as the farm, a lot of thought over the years, and because it now belonged to Cooper, she wanted to provide insight if they'd let her. With a renewed sense of self-confidence, Tessa leaned forward and outlined for David and Cooper all of the ideas she'd had. When they were finished, they had used about fifty percent of her suggestions and come up with several more collaboratively.

"Can I talk to you for a minute?" Cooper asked, sounding serious as he took her hand in his and stood, pushing her to her feet.

Tessa glanced at his parents and then back at him, her confusion probably more than obvious.

"Excuse us for a minute," Cooper said to his parents and Dalton before leading her inside.

Once they were in the darkened hallway, Tessa was about to apologize for monopolizing the conversation when she found herself pressed up against the wall, Cooper's hot mouth on hers. The moan that escaped was followed by her arms going around his neck automatically, holding him closer.

"Woman, I'm not sure I've ever wanted you more than I do right now," he whispered in her ear, making her clit pulse as she thought about him taking her right there in the hallway.

Feeling a tad rebellious and a whole lot lighter because of last night's conversation with Cooper, Tessa leaned her head back, lining her mouth up right by his ear and whispered, "Prove it."

Cooper's body hardened beneath her hands, and he pulled back, his whiskey-brown eyes pinning her in place, a smile tipping the corners of his mouth. When he grabbed her around the waist, pulling her against him and then turning so they were just inside his bedroom, Tessa had to swallow her squeal.

"I'm going to make you wear skirts in the future," he growled as he unbuttoned her jeans while she toed off one of her boots. Without letting one another go, they managed to ease her jeans from one leg while Cooper shoved his down over his hips.

"Turn around," he growled against her ear, and Tessa quickly turned to face the wall, her hands flat. "Just remember, you have to be quiet, or my parents will hear you."

The warning sent a shiver down Tessa's spine. Last night had been hard enough knowing Dalton was in the house. But what if his parents came inside? What if they heard them?

When he kicked her foot out to the side, widening her stance as he put his hand on the middle of her back and forced her down slightly, Tessa wasn't sure she could wait until he was inside of her so she would just have to be quiet. His rough touch set a fire inside of her unlike anything she'd ever felt before.

Sure, she felt desired when they made love, but never like when he wanted her fast and hard. Like the man couldn't wait another second to have her. This was beyond explosive, and she wanted nothing more than to have him inside of her.

Luckily, she didn't have to wait much longer. His fingers were teasing her pussy seconds before his cock slid home, driving into her and forcing her to hold herself away from the wall. When he leaned over, his mouth brushing against her ear, she turned her head slightly.

"Fuck me, Cooper," she whispered so low she barely heard herself, but his answering growl had her pussy spasming.

"Tessa." Her name on his lips sounded like a warning, and when he stood back up, gripping her hips before slamming into her, she braced herself.

She felt the tingles in her core almost immediately, and they slowly radiated outward, growing stronger as they went until she was sweating and hanging by her fingernails to the fragile edge of an orgasm that was going to rock her to her very core.

"Darlin', I could do this forever," Cooper growled, but he never slowed, slamming into her as she pushed back against him.

She had to grind her teeth together to keep from crying out as her orgasm detonated, making her legs weak and her arms even weaker. She barely managed to remain standing as he slammed into her once, twice, three more times before his body was motionless behind her, his fingers gripping painfully on her hips. The pain disappeared abruptly as he filled her.

"Darlin', you do that to me much more and I'm not sure I won't have a heart attack," he joked, his voice still just a whisper so no one else could hear them. "Go get cleaned up and I'll meet you back outside."

With that, Cooper pressed a light kiss to her cheek, lingering a second before he pulled out of her and disappeared out the door. She heard the door to the other bathroom close, and she smiled before limping into the surprisingly spacious bathroom that was in Cooper's bedroom.

Being an old farmhouse, and one that Mr. Deluth had never wanted to remodel, Tessa was surprised to see that, at some point, they had made some significant changes to the bathroom. Tessa never had met Mrs. Deluth — she had passed away when Luanne was just a baby — but she knew from her talks with Mr. Deluth just how much he had loved her. Didn't surprise her that he'd made a change like that for the woman he loved.

Tessa knew all too well just what lengths one was willing to go through for love.

When she stood in front of the mirror, she froze, noticing the woman whose smile was radiating from her flushed face, her hair a tangled mess. She looked different. Well fucked, maybe? No, that wasn't it. Tessa felt different too. As if the weight of the world had been lifted from her shoulders. As if she was … in love.

Tessa was beginning to think that life was finally taking a turn for the better. Right where she'd always hoped it would be. And, for the first time, she actually thought she might have a chance at finding the happily ever after that had been eluding her for so long.

CHAPTER THIRTY-TWO

The following Saturday night turned out to be the equivalent of an unchaperoned teenage dance.

A full week had disappeared quickly, everyone busy, including Cooper's parents, who had remained in town for several days to help Cooper get things in order.

Thanks to his mother, his house was in much better shape. And thanks to his father and Dalton, they had everything on order to get the fences mended, the concrete poured for the new stable as well as the barn, and they had an outpouring of volunteers coming the following week to help with what was needed.

And somewhere along the way, Dalton had decided to do a benefit concert, donating all proceeds to various organizations that Tessa worked with. Maybe the guy felt guilty that his questions had spurred her breakdown, or maybe Dalton was just being Dalton, Cooper didn't know. But either way, trying to keep up with the man wasn't easy.

On Thursday, Dalton had informed him that he was working with the local radio stations to announce the benefit concert in order to garner more attendance.

Because The Rusty Nail could only hold so many, Dalton had asked Cooper if they could set things up on his property. After learning that Dalton had targeted radio stations that spanned three counties, he hadn't had much of a choice but to agree. There was no way to handle it otherwise.

So, after Friday was spent setting up a sound stage and various tents for a BYOB party, everyone was enjoying the fruits of their labor.

"Where's Tessa?" Cooper asked Eric when he managed to break through the horde of women and men currently surrounding the stage, where Dalton was gearing up to play. With a full-blown band.

The guy had pulled out all the stops tonight, including an entire tent that was being manned by a couple of famous locals whose sole focus was on collecting money. The concert was free with a donation. Cooper didn't even want to think about what it would look like tomorrow when everyone left. Thankfully, he had some time to kill before then.

"She said she needed a break," Eric told him, his voice raised to be heard over the ruckus.

"Thanks," Cooper mouthed and then headed back through the sea of bodies until he reached an empty space on the other side of one of the tents.

"There you are," he said when he found Tessa pacing back and forth, her attention focused inward. "You all right?"

"Never better," she said with a huge grin. "This is amazing."

"You're telling me," he agreed. "That's Dalton for ya. The man doesn't do simple and easy."

"I see that." Tessa peered over her shoulder where they could see the crowd growing. "I've called in backup. My cousins usually fill in as security at the bar, so they said they'd help us out here. Tonight they're bringing their friends. They assured me they had it covered."

Cooper nodded, pulling Tessa up against him. "I had no idea he'd do this, I swear."

"Well, since it's for a good cause, I'm not sure I can complain. But I will say I'm looking forward to a few quiet hours after this."

"Quiet, huh?"

"Yes. You know … you, me, a truck bed, and a starlit night. How does that sound?"

"Like heaven. Can we just sneak out now?"

"Not a chance, cowboy," Tessa said, placing her hands on his face and forcing him to look at her. "But I promise to make it worth your while afterwards."

Cooper's entire body heeded her words. He wasn't sure he could wait that long. He knew for damn sure that he didn't *want* to wait that long.

"Are you going to sing tonight?" Tessa asked as she took a step back.

"I'm thinking about it," he answered simply. Dalton had asked him to, and honestly, the scene was getting into his blood. The excitement was filling him, and he craved it.

"Well, good luck. I'll be listening for you."

Cooper leaned down and kissed her, gently at first, and then he couldn't stop himself. Tessa amazed him in so many ways, and he found that he looked forward to seeing her every minute of every day. To the point that he wanted to make it permanent. Only he was scared. Not of what that meant, but of what Tessa's reaction would be if he suggested it.

They'd certainly mended some rifts between them in the last couple of weeks, but he knew she was still scared. Tessa had spent more years than not trying to atone for her mistakes, and even though he could tell she was getting better, she was still holding herself back.

Shaking off the thought, Cooper broke the kiss and stared down at her, running his finger down her jaw. "I'll check on you in a bit. Try to stay close to Eric," he told her. "Oh." Cooper grabbed her hand before she could get away. "I don't care what happens, don't talk to any reporters."

Tessa's eyebrow cocked in question and Cooper smiled. "You shouldn't have to deal with them. I'm not worried about what you'd say, but I don't want them hurting you."

Her subtle nod didn't reassure him that she understood his reasoning, but at least she agreed for now. Planting a quick kiss on her lips, he pulled a strand of her hair gently and turned to leave her in peace.

Two hours later, all hell broke loose.

Cooper had just come off the stage when he noticed two guys near the donation tent going toe to toe. He couldn't see much, but based on the crowd gathering, he knew he wasn't going to like what he found. Glancing around, he glimpsed Eric at the same time the man noticed what was going on. The two of them made a beeline for the fight, both of them coming from different directions.

After forcing himself through the wall of bodies forming a circle around the fight, Cooper came up short just a few feet away from Jack.

"Stop, Jack! Please. Stop!" Tessa was screaming at her brother, who had some guy pinned to the ground by his throat. That wasn't what had Cooper's breath heaving in and out of his lungs.

Tessa was holding her shirt closed because it had clearly been ripped, her hair was halfway out of her ponytail, and there was a mark obscuring the side of her face. Big and red…

"He's not worth it, Jack!" Tessa screamed, her eyes wild as she tried to pull her brother off the man.

"Nuh-uh." The voice, along with a firm hand, pulled Cooper up short before he even realized that he was moving in closer. "You get her," Dalton said fiercely. "We'll take care of the rest."

"Bullshit," Cooper growled.

"Both of you, out of here." Eric's stern voice caught Cooper's attention. "Get her, Coop. See if she needs medical attention."

Cooper was trying to rein in his rage, and Eric's statement did just that — as efficient as a gallon of ice water would've been. He was just about to move to get Tessa when the guy that Jack had pinned managed to deliver a low punch, effectively doubling Jack over. As soon as the guy was free, Cooper got a good look at who it was. Chad. The bastard he'd thrown out of Tessa's bar.

Although Chad seemed to be struggling to breathe, he lunged at Tessa, slamming her backward. Before Cooper could get his feet in motion, Chad grabbed her by the hair.

The roar that escaped was probably heard for miles, but Cooper heard nothing except for his blood thundering in his veins. He hit the asshole at a fast clip, sending them both flying to the ground. As much as he wanted to beat the hell out of Chad, Cooper knew he'd spend the night in jail, and at this point, this guy was going to get the honors if Cooper could just keep himself in check long enough.

Pushing to his feet, he kept his eye on the man on the ground, but the bastard didn't try to move. He just started yelling.

"She's a stupid fucking cunt!" Chad spat toward Tessa. "Fucking whore! Don't think your famous boyfriend won't find out the truth about you! Fucking bitch!"

The group that was now gathered, the noise, everything faded as Cooper's world narrowed down to the guy throwing obscenities at Tessa. He'd fucking hurt her, and his nasty insults weren't slowing. And that's when Cooper let loose, his fists flying, his anger unstoppable. Chad never knew what hit him either. It wasn't until someone — make that several someones — pulled Cooper off that he stopped.

"Out of here now!" Eric barked, pulling Cooper until he stumbled backward. When the noise and the lights assaulted his senses, Cooper realized where he was, and he immediately searched for Tessa, finding her as Jack was leading her away.

Apparently the bastard now lying in the dirt must've gotten in a few solid punches because Cooper felt as though he'd been run over by a truck. He managed to limp toward Tessa, gently pulling her into his arms as Jack moved to clear the area.

"Take him back to the house," Jack ordered Tessa, referring to Cooper. "Don't come back until I tell you."

The next thing Cooper knew, they were in his truck, tearing across the back pasture toward his house. Once they were locked inside of his house a few minutes later, he took stock of her condition. Yep, that was going to be a nasty bruise on her jaw.

"What the fuck happened?" he asked, realizing how cruel he sounded. He was doing his damnedest to get his temper under control, but the only thing he saw was when that bastard had knocked her down. And Cooper knew full well that his anger was obscuring his common sense, but he couldn't rein himself in no matter how hard he tried.

"You don't want to know," Tessa said as she inhaled deeply, her bottom lip already swelling.

"I told you to stay the fuck away from him, Tessa." Cooper growled, forcing himself to stand up straight although his ribs protested as he did.

Tessa glared at him, her anger matching his. "You *told* me?"

"Yes. I fucking told you to stay away from him." Moving closer, he lifted her chin, forcing her to look at him. When she flinched, he felt like an asshole, but he couldn't help himself. He checked out the mark on her cheek as he waited for her to answer him.

Tessa pulled away, walking to the other side of the room.

"What the fuck made him hit you?"

Tessa shrugged, and Cooper's anger was like a wildfire roaring to life again, gaining momentum as it barreled through dry brush. "You don't know? This is the second fucking time he's gone after you. Did you start the fight, Tessa?"

Her incredulous expression pinned him in place, but Cooper was long past sane at the moment. "Did I not tell you reporters would be here? Are you fucking trying to draw attention to me? As it is, they've probably got it all on video. Shit, it may be all over the television by now."

Obviously she didn't like the question or his tone of voice because her hands balled into fists at her sides, her eyes shooting daggers.

"Why would you ask that?" she asked, her voice much stronger than minutes before.

"Is there something I should know?"

Tessa's body straightened and her eyes narrowed on him. "Yeah, you should know that I'm just the town whore as far as he's concerned. That make you feel better?"

The words were like a slap to the face and Cooper actually recoiled. How the hell had this conversation turned in this direction? "*What?*"

"You heard me," she yelled. "I need to go."

Before he could stop her, Tessa disappeared out the front door, and she was making a run for her truck. He tried to follow her, but his ribs protested, forcing him to stop and breathe through the pain. With no choice but to let her go, he watched until her taillights disappeared at the end of his driveway.

Sonuvabitch!

A few minutes later, Dalton and Jack came inside the house.

"Where is she?" Jack asked as soon as he stepped into the living room.

"Hell if I know."

"What do you mean you don't know?"

"Just what I fucking said," Cooper yelled, taking a step closer to Jack.

"Hold on now," Dalton stated, pushing an arm between the two of them. "Tempers are hot right now. You two need to calm down."

"Fuck you, Calhoun." Cooper turned his wrath on his friend.

"Chill the fuck out, Coop. This ain't helping, and you know it."

"She was defending your sorry ass," Jack stated, his voice low and laced with venom.

"What?" Cooper's head jerked back toward Jack as though his neck were a rubber band. "Defending me? What the hell did *I* do?"

"Nothing. That's the damn problem."

Cooper felt like he'd been sucker-punched. Again.

Jack thrust his hands through his hair as he turned to pace the room. "His name is Chad Harper," Jack said by way of explanation a minute later.

"*Chad Harper?*" Dalton asked incredulously, his tone causing both Cooper and Jack to turn to face him.

"You know him?"

"Not personally, no. He was supposed to open for a friend of mine. Some sort of favor or something. The only reason I know is because they said the bastard was crazy."

"Yeah, you could say that. The asshole thinks the world owes him something. It doesn't surprise me that he'd go off half-cocked. *Again.*" Jack glared at Cooper.

Why the fuck hadn't Jack told him all of this last time Chad had pulled this shit at the bar? If he had, maybe Cooper could've protected her.

Sonuvabitch!

"What the hell does he have against Tessa?" Cooper asked.

"Chad spent almost a year in Tessa's bar, bragging about his *almost* fame. He never actually made it. My sister dated him for a while. About a year or so ago. She said he didn't beat on her, but sometimes I wonder. He was abusive in every other way that I could tell. When she finally kicked him to the curb, he started talking shit about her. Being this is a small town, and considering Tessa's past" — Jack's eyes went to the floor — "the rumors flew, and people swallowed them whole. Wasn't a good time for anyone there for a while."

His heart felt like Jack had just seared him with a cattle prod. Why did Cooper have to be such a dumbass?

Only now, as some of the anger subsided, could he rationally see how his behavior was beyond aggressive, and he hadn't even understood what had happened. Realizing he'd all but accused Tessa of starting the fight only to find out she had been defending him, Cooper turned his attention to Jack and asked, "What started it tonight?"

"Chad likes to talk shit. From what I gathered, there's some news crew out there asking questions. It's no secret that the two of you are *hanging out*. Hell, I heard the reporter myself. They've been stalking her house and yours." Jack's expression hardened. "My guess is Chad thought this might be his chance at another fifteen minutes of fame."

"Fuck."

"That about sums it up," Dalton added, pushing himself off the wall. "I'm going to see if I can help the guys get things settled down." Dalton turned to Jack. "Let me know if I can do anything."

"Let's just hope the bastard doesn't press charges," Jack added as he followed Dalton out of the house, leaving Cooper standing there staring after them.

Spending a night in jail was the least of Cooper's worries at the moment.

Tessa could barely see through the tears to drive. She continued to wipe them away as fast as they fell, but she never managed to get them under control.

Her face hurt, but worse, her heart ached from Cooper's reaction. Had he really assumed she was the one to start the fight with Chad? Why would he think that? And did he honestly think she'd want to draw attention to him? She'd been standing up for him, and this was the thanks she got.

Her jaw was swollen, but she didn't think it was broken. Thankfully — if there was anything to be thankful about — Chad had hit her with an open hand rather than his fist.

Pulling into her driveway, Tessa immediately looked around, making sure no one else was there. Not that she expected anyone to be. If Cooper was a smart man, he'd stay far, far away from her after his accusations. She didn't care if he'd been pissed or not, they were supposed to have established some trust between them. Hell, she'd given it a try, had actually fallen for the man.

That would teach her.

The second she walked in her front door, every ounce of Tessa's strength drained right out of her. After letting her dogs out and back in, she locked the doors, ensuring she wouldn't have any uninvited guests, and went straight for her bedroom.

The ringer on her cell phone was the next thing to be taken care of, and when the icon showed silent, she tossed her phone on the nightstand. Stripping off her clothes, she fell into bed, pulling the blankets up to her neck as she rolled into the fetal position.

Unfortunately, sleep didn't come nearly as easily as the tears had. And now, as the morning sun peeked through the narrow slats of the blinds, Tessa felt as though she'd been run over by a freight train and then hit by a military tank. Twice.

Every single muscle in her body hurt. Including her heart. And now, morning was upon her, and she had nothing to look forward to, except for the aches and pains. Rolling her head to the side, Tessa eyed her phone, wondering whether she'd missed any calls. Figuring she was going to look at some point anyway, she grabbed the offending piece of machinery and tapped the screen to life. Her heart lurched into her throat at what she saw.

Five missed calls.

Ten missed text messages.

Flipping through the screens, she saw that three of the calls were from Izzy, two from Jack. The same went for the texts: five from Izzy, three from Jack and two from Eric — probably Izzy as a last resort to get her to answer.

Not a single text or call from Cooper.

Dropping her phone on her pillow, she rolled over, hugging herself, closing her eyes and wishing sleep would take her.

Unsure why she'd expected Cooper to come after her, Tessa was more than disappointed by the fact that he hadn't. Then again, she'd walked out on him. Rather than staying to talk, she'd run. After accusing Cooper of running from something, Tessa had done essentially the same thing. And the fact that he didn't care enough to call was probably what she deserved anyway.

Ten minutes later, when sleep wouldn't come, Tessa embraced the fact that the tears had stopped. Her tear ducts were probably dry, because heaven knew she didn't feel any better. Forcing herself out of bed, she made her way to the living room, meeting her rambunctious dogs along the way and letting them out. While they were out sniffing and searching, she opted to take a shower. That should help her to feel better.

For the rest of the day, menial tasks never helped her mood, but at least she felt more human. The bruise along her jaw notwithstanding.

After her phone continued to ring and the texts continued to stream in, she responded to both Jack and Izzy, letting them know that she was fine but that she wanted to be alone. Neither of them seemed happy with her response, but Tessa didn't have it in her to argue, so she turned her ringer back off.

Once again, Tessa felt entirely, miserably alone.

CHAPTER THIRTY-THREE

One week later

Cooper was dripping sweat as he moved another pile of boards, wondering just when summer was going to take a backseat to fall. He was in Texas, and he'd been warned by more than one person that summer generally morphed directly into winter, but that wasn't until February. So, based on his calendar, he still had another four months of hell to go through.

But the back-breaking work was good for him. It kept his mind focused. The barn and the stables were under way, the concrete foundations poured and curing. Once that was done, the next step was getting the structures up. He was looking forward to the final product, needing something to keep his mind occupied. Right now there were no horses, no tack. Nothing to show what his plans were. But it was coming together.

For the last few days, he had contemplated his plans for the farm. Hell, for a couple of days there, he had even considered packing his shit up and going back to where he'd come from.

Only that wasn't what he wanted, and a phone call with his father had reminded him of that. He had plans, and although part of those plans had been ripped right out of his hands thanks to his own sanctimonious attitude, he still had something to prove to himself.

During the days since the benefit concert, Cooper had spent his time consumed by back-breaking work. By his own choice. When he wasn't doing something outside, for at least a few minutes each day, he would have a phone conversation with his father, who was now his manager, trying to lay out a plan for his career. Now that they had worked out a deal, Cooper had set his schedule accordingly, and soon enough, he would have to start working on his next album.

Feeling like he was running out of time, he knew where his focus needed to be. He only had a month to get things in order at the farm. Not that he expected a finished product, but he wanted to at least see progress. He had more help than he knew what to do with. Between Dalton remaining in Devil's Bend until things died down and the generous folks in town, the work didn't seem quite so overwhelming. But there was still a lot to do. The road into the farm was going to be laid in the coming weeks, but until then, there was only so much they could do.

Since the debacle last Saturday, Cooper had worked at the bar two days — Thursday and Friday — having missed Monday because he had still needed time to cool off. If it hadn't been for the promise he'd made Adam, Cooper might've called it all off, because seeing Tessa but being unable to speak to her, to hold her in his arms, Cooper was slowly going out of his mind.

He had no one to blame but himself for that either. He'd all but accused her of drawing attention to him. Even if she hadn't meant to, that's exactly what had happened. The fight with that jackass Chad Harper had been just the beginning. It was a damned miracle Cooper hadn't ended up in jail, but thanks to Jack, Eric, and Izzy, the bastard hadn't pressed charges. But neither had Tessa.

For now, everything seemed to be simmering down. The reporters were finally getting bored. He had refused to talk to anyone, and from what he heard, Tessa's friends were keeping her shielded from their onslaught. His father had made a public statement that if they wanted a story, they would have to come to Nashville and talk to him. Surprisingly, no one had heard from Marcus, which Cooper did not consider a good thing.

Sure, Cooper was grateful that his father was willing to take the heat off him, but he knew he should've faced the music. Not only with the press but with Tessa as well. She deserved so much more than he'd given her. Part of him wanted to explain why he hadn't made a single attempt to talk to her in the past week. Because he had wanted to, even if he thought she would tell him to go to hell.

He was being an ass, proven in the way he'd reacted to her, the way he'd ripped her world apart, all but stealing her dreams, and then the way he'd thrown it all back in her face.

He'd managed to talk to Izzy once, but she wasn't as forthcoming as he would've hoped. Tessa's friends were a protective bunch, and he both appreciated and hated that fact. As much as he wanted to know that Tessa was being taken care of, he also wanted to know how she was doing.

A couple of times, he'd had to stop himself from going over there just to see for himself. But more than their relationship was at stake at the moment. At the bar, she rarely even looked at him, and she didn't speak to him. Everything she had to say to him — and vice versa — was handled through Eric. Or Jack.

Cooper wiped the sweat from his forehead with the T-shirt he had shrugged off an hour ago and grabbed the jug of water that was now half-empty. In another hour or so, he would have to go in and eat, or he risked passing out in the heat.

He was downing what was left of the water when he noticed dust blowing up along the driveway, the identity of the vehicle obscured momentarily. He watched as an old red Ford came into view, and he dropped the jug on the ground as he moved at a rapid pace toward the truck.

"What's wrong?" he asked Izzy as soon as she jumped out of her truck, making her way toward him like her ass was on fire.

She was out of breath when they met in the middle, and he grabbed her arms, holding her upright as he stared into her eyes. "What the hell's the matter?"

Panic was filling him, and she hadn't spoken yet.

"It's— It's … Tessa," she huffed, trying to draw in deep breaths. "I need you to … just come … with me, okay?"

Cooper grabbed her arm, all but dragging her along with him. Once they were back at her truck, he reached into his own and grabbed the extra T-shirt he'd left in there the day before. Pulling it on over his head, he made his way to the driver's door, effectively forcing Izzy to scoot over because there was no way he was riding shotgun. She'd be able to explain as he drove.

"Talk to me, Izzy. Where am I going?"

"To The Rusty Nail!" she squealed. "Just drive!"

277

Cooper glared at Izzy momentarily but then refocused his efforts on the road. His heart was pounding like a bass drum on steroids, and his hands, which were currently gripping the steering wheel, were white-knuckled and shaking. He wanted to press her to talk, but he was more interested in getting to Tessa. Even if he had no idea what he was walking into.

After taking several turns on two wheels, Cooper hit the straightaway that would lead directly to town. When the truck hit sixty, the piece of shit started to shake, so he had to let off the gas. Izzy really needed to get a new truck.

"Holy fuck," Cooper growled when the parking lot for The Rusty Nail came into view. There didn't appear to be a single empty space throughout the entire lot. The satellites were up and aiming skyward, antennas were like skyscrapers hovering high above the mayhem.

Glancing over at Izzy, he saw that her eyes were just as wide as they had been earlier. "What's going on, Izzy?"

When she turned to look at him, her gaze went from worried to burning mad in an instant. "She's being hounded. Your fucking manager gave an exclusive to the press this morning announcing that you two have severed ties. I hope you're happy, but her entire life story is front-page news."

Ex-manager, he thought to himself. Cooper sighed heavily, then put the truck in park, leaving it on the side of the road because there was nowhere else to put it.

"But that's not the worst of it, Cooper," Izzy said, her hand landing on his forearm.

His head jerked toward her as he waited for her to continue.

"You can't see the sign out front, but as of this morning, The Rusty Nail is for sale."

"What?"

"I didn't stutter, big guy. She's put the bar up for sale, and she's moving."

Cooper knew his mouth was hanging open, but for the life of him, he couldn't get any words out.

Izzy leaned over, her eyes narrowed to slits. "You better make this right, Cooper. I will *never* forgive you if my best friend leaves. Until you, she's never run from anything in her life, and you and I both know she hasn't had it easy. She's spent her entire life chasing her dreams, not running from them."

Cooper knew exactly what Izzy meant. He'd spent his life doing the same thing. Chasing dreams seemed to be the only thing he knew how to do.

Forcing himself out of the truck, Cooper walked around to stand in front as he glanced through the crowd. So many reporters that he recognized, most of them national news, but he did see some local station vans.

Shit.

This was not going to be fun. He had hoped for just a little more time.

Pulling his hat lower on his head, Cooper tucked his hands in his pockets and started through the cluster with his face pointed down toward the ground. Considering he was filthy from working outside all day, he hoped no one would recognize him. At least not until he got to Tessa.

"Is it true that Cooper Krenshaw got another woman pregnant and then disappeared on her?" The reporter didn't sound familiar, but there were so many people trying to talk, he wasn't sure he'd recognize them anyway. The question, however, wasn't anything new. He was used to the lies and the made-up stories.

When there wasn't an answer, he considered that a good thing. At least Tessa wasn't giving in to them.

"Is it true, Ms. Donovan, that your husband was killed in the line of duty?"

Oh, fuck. It was one thing for them to question her about him but something else entirely for them to target her personally.

"It's true." Tessa's voice sounded weak and uncertain.

"And is it also true that, since his death, you've been known to hook up with various country music singers who play in your bar?"

What. The. Fuck.

"No, that isn't true," Tessa answered quickly.

"Do you have a relationship with Cooper Krenshaw?" A male voice sounded from somewhere in the back.

"Is it true that Mr. Krenshaw stole your property from you? That he came in and decided to take over your plans to build a horse ranch?"

"No, that is absolutely not true," Tessa said adamantly, and Cooper stopped in his tracks to look at her. He hadn't yet made it through the masses, but her response to the question had brought him up short.

"Cooper … I mean, Mr. Krenshaw moved to Devil's Bend with the intention of doing something exceptionally special. Mr. Krenshaw and his manager are working to build an equestrian center that will be used to work with the disabled, both children and adults. This was Mr. Krenshaw's dream, and the town of Devil's Bend is blessed that he chose this as his place to start his venture."

Cooper's heart swelled. The way she defended his reputation, knowing full well that what the reporter had asked was nothing short of the truth, didn't surprise him. Tessa Donovan never sought the limelight. As a matter of fact, she always seemed to be the one in the shadows.

"But it is true that you were purchasing the land that he came in and bought?"

"Mr. Krenshaw had the funds necessary to complete the sale long before I would have. And it wouldn't have mattered anyway, because hearing of his intention for the property, I would've bowed out gracefully anyhow."

"This wasn't just my dream," Cooper said loudly, his voice carrying over the group, several people whirling on him, microphones being tossed in his direction almost instantly. "I might've been the one to buy the land, but once I met Tessa, I knew that I couldn't do this without her. In fact, this was her dream. She's the one who helped Dalton round up volunteers to help build the center and to implement the programs."

Cooper was moving closer to Tessa, but she was backing away, her head shaking back and forth as though telling him to be quiet. He was done being quiet. A solid week had passed since he had talked to her. Here she was defending him when she should be cursing his name for the way he'd waltzed into her life, taking over all of her good intentions.

"Cooper! Cooper! Can you tell us more about Tabitha Johnson? There was a rumor that you are the child's father. Is that true?"

Cooper fought to keep his face expressionless as he stared at Tessa. He'd told her the story, but he could still see the hurt in her eyes.

Feeling as though he needed to defend himself, Cooper was about to answer when a gruff voice sounded from behind him.

"It's not true."

Cooper turned abruptly to see his father standing a few feet away. The relief that flooded him was almost enough to steal the air from his lungs. He'd been waiting for this, stalling for time, and here his father was. Which meant…

"Thank you all for coming out today, folks. I'm not sure why you're here, but now that you are, I'd be happy to answer any questions that I can. In case you don't know who I am, my name is David Krenshaw. I am Cooper's manager."

"What happened to Marcus Evergreen?" one woman called from the group.

"Mr. Evergreen and Mr. Krenshaw decided to part ways. It is my understanding that Mr. Evergreen has decided to pursue other artists, and I'm sure he'd be more than happy to answer any questions you have. I, however, cannot speak for him."

Cooper slipped into the bar as soon as his father had gained the attention of the horde of reporters. He fully expected to see Tessa because he'd lost sight of her when his father had caught his attention. Unfortunately, the bar was empty, with the exception of Izzy and Eric.

"Where is she?" he asked in a rush, letting his eyes adjust to the dim light of the bar.

"Where is who?" Eric asked, turning to face him.

"Tessa. She was just outside. Where'd she go?"

"She didn't come this way," Izzy said, concern lacing every word.

Cooper turned back and reemerged in the crowd, trying to see over them. That was when he saw her sneaking around to the back of the building. Without worrying about who saw him, Cooper took off at a flat-out run, his boots skidding on the gravel as he turned the corner. He caught up with her just as she was getting into her truck.

"Tessa, don't," Cooper commanded, but she appeared to be ignoring him. He caught the edge of the door seconds before she would've slammed it closed. "We need to talk."

"No, *Mr. Krenshaw*, we don't," Tessa stated with remarkably little emotion in her voice.

Gripping her chin between his thumb and his forefinger, he turned her to face him, aware that he was being the aggressor but unable to stop himself. "We are gonna talk."

"There isn't anything more to say. I did my best out there. They've been hounding me for a week, so I'm not sure why you care now."

"A week?"

"Yeah. I guess you've managed to keep yourself pretty isolated out there all by yourself. They're camping out on the street in front of my house. Hell, I can't even let my dogs out front anymore."

Shit. How the hell hadn't he known about that? Her friends had said ... whatever Tessa wanted him to hear. *Fuck.*

"I think they know more about me and my life than I do. But that's okay. This town clearly isn't big enough for both of us, so I'm going to do you a favor."

"Move over," Cooper demanded, pushing himself into the truck, forcing her to scoot to the center of the bench seat or he was going to sit on her. This was not the time or place to have this conversation.

"What the hell are you doing?" she squeaked, trying to keep from moving, but luckily she wasn't much of a match for him.

"I'm getting in. Now give me the damn keys." Holding out his hand, he waited for her to hand them over. He didn't have to wait long before she was slamming them down into his palm.

Ouch. "Thank you."

It was time they hash this out, and he knew exactly the place to take her to do that.

CHAPTER THIRTY-FOUR

Tessa was somewhat tempted to fling herself out of the passenger door to avoid having to talk to Cooper. Only she wasn't interested in doing any more damage to her body than she'd had done to her in the last week. But she certainly did not want to talk to Cooper, so the idea was almost too tempting to pass up.

Somehow she had managed to move on with her life. The last seven days hadn't been a party, but waking up each day and going to sleep each night were getting easier. Life was at least back to normal. Even if normal had a new definition. The reporters who had taken up residence in front of her house didn't add a whole lot of charm to the place, but she hadn't been able to do anything about them.

She was hoping they would get the hint because of the lack of information they were receiving. Not only was she not talking, but the rest of the town had gone radio silent as well. That was one thing Tessa loved about her small town. They rallied together, and as soon as word got out that they were harassing her and Cooper, people everywhere stopped talking.

It would seem the press had another spur in their behinds these last couple of days though because they weren't budging, even when Tessa didn't comment. She hadn't intended to say anything that morning either, but when she'd gone to put the For Sale sign in front of the bar, she'd obviously been followed. Before she'd known what was happening, they'd been descending like bees, buzzing all around her until she couldn't go anywhere.

Then the questions had started. She hated the questions, especially those that were about her personally. She had managed to give answers to a few about Cooper, retelling the stories she'd heard David Krenshaw tell but adding her own perspective. At first, she'd hoped that would get them to forget about her personal life.

The worst were when they talked about Richie. Which they did often. Dredging up her pain had apparently turned into a hobby for these people, and Tessa wasn't sure how much she could handle. Which was why she was leaving Devil's Bend.

Tessa bounced on the truck seat, her attention drawn to where they were. That was when she noticed Cooper was driving down the dirt path that had been rutted out between his house and the pond just a couple of hundred yards from where the foundation for the new barn and stable had been laid.

She took a minute to admire the area. It was going to be a beauty, much bigger than she had expected it to be. Even the area for the outdoor arena had been sectioned off, and soon enough, the electrical for the floodlights would have to be run. Dropping her head, Tessa studied her hands as she clasped them tightly in her lap. She hated that she wouldn't get to see the finished product, but getting away was her only option at this point.

When the truck came to a stop, Tessa turned to Cooper instantly. "Talk. Then let me go home." She tacked on a please at the very end in her attempt to be polite.

"Get out," he ordered as he did the same, leaving her staring after him.

Looking at the ignition, she realized he'd taken the keys, so her chances at a sneaky getaway were thwarted. Damn him.

Taking as much time as she could, Tessa climbed out of her truck, shutting the door easily and taking deep breaths. As much as she wanted to be angry at Cooper, all of that had dissipated, leaving nothing but a big, empty void in the center of her chest. The same void that she'd felt after Richie died. And truthfully, Tessa didn't know which was worse, not being able to ever tell Richie how much she loved him because he was no longer on the earth, or not being able to tell Cooper how much she loved him even though he was just a few miles away.

Technically, now he was only a few steps away, but the last thing she was going to do was to tell him her feelings hadn't yet changed. She wanted them to, kept hoping each morning when she woke up that she'd forget all about him and move on with her life. Up till now, she'd had no such luck.

The creak of the tailgate as it lowered drew her gaze, and she watched as Cooper sat on the edge, his feet hanging down. Unsure what she was supposed to do, she opted to mimic his stance when she climbed up onto the tailgate, but she maintained at least a foot of space between them. To her surprise, Cooper didn't look at her.

"Do you remember when you first brought me out here?" he asked after a few minutes of uncomfortable silence.

She nodded rather than answering. He didn't seem to require an answer though.

"Do you remember *why* you brought me here?"

Tessa stared out at the calm water. "Because I wanted you to see what made this place so special," she admitted, her legs swinging as her heart constricted in her chest and her throat started to clog.

She was not going to get emotional. There'd been more than enough time for that in the last week. She could not let Cooper see her break down.

"And I understood what you were showing me," he began, his voice strong yet gentle. "But it isn't the breeze or the stars or even the moon that makes this place special for me."

Tessa swallowed hard, his voice sliding over her like velvet.

"*You* are what makes this place special to me."

Tessa's head snapped his way. She didn't miss his use of present tense. He wasn't talking about how he'd felt in the past. He was...

"That was a long time ago," she muttered, watching him closely.

"No, it wasn't," he answered, pushing himself back to his feet.

When Cooper moved around to stand in front of her, Tessa's hands began to shake, and tears formed in her eyes. She had dreamed about what it would be like to be this close to him again. When he tilted her chin up, she met his eyes, trying to blink the tears back.

"You accused me one time of running," he whispered. "And maybe that was the truth. But it didn't make sense to me until I talked to Izzy earlier."

Tessa swallowed the lump in her throat, her eyes locked on his, the turbulence of his emotions evident in his shimmering brown gaze.

"She told me that you've spent your life chasing your dreams. And I knew just what she was saying. I've done the same thing. Only now, I know where I belong."

Tessa glanced away, unsure where he was going with this, but it wasn't where she'd thought it was. "And I'm still on that path," she assured him. "If I keep chasing, I'll catch them one day."

"That's where you're wrong, Tessa. This is where you're supposed to be." Cooper's finger curled under her chin, forcing her to look at him again.

"You're right, Devil's Bend is my home. I never thought I'd leave—"

"Not Devil's Bend, Tessa," Cooper stated, his voice louder, sharper. "Here. Right here. *With me.*"

Tessa closed her eyes. Opened them. Although Cooper's face was blurred through her tears, she knew he was real, but for some reason, she felt like she was stuck in a dream. Her anger started bubbling in her belly, moving outward until her whole body was consumed by it and the tears were dried up from the blazing heat that had engulfed her.

"For one week, Cooper. One solid week I haven't heard from you. Not a word. And you want to sit here and tell me that I'm supposed to be with you? Where the hell were you when I was crying my eyes out? I never heard you tell me you were sorry or that you didn't mean to accuse me of trying to draw attention to you when I was doing nothing more than defending you."

She saw the muscles in his arms tense as his hands fell to his sides. Tessa was trapped by his golden gaze, but she wasn't finished. "I'm still trying to get over you. It doesn't work like this, Cooper. You can't just decide you want to be with me when it's convenient for you!" she screamed.

"It's not fucking convenient for me, Tessa!" Cooper yelled, his voice echoing out over the water and bouncing off the trees. "I don't fucking deserve you, don't you get that? You're better off without me. I'm a selfish bastard, and that's not gonna change. I go after what I want, and I get it no matter the cost."

"You didn't go after me," she said sadly.

"But I did, Tessa. I did go after you. Until I hurt you. Until I couldn't see past my own self-righteous attitude, and then I let you walk away. You deserve so much better."

This time Tessa was the one to touch him, grabbing his face between her hands and forcing him to look at her. "I do deserve more than you showed me the last time we talked. I'll give you that."

"See. That's exactly what I'm talking about. I was so blinded by my anger, furious that you were hurt, but I turned it around and blamed you."

"That was one time, Cooper. That means you're passionate about your feelings; it doesn't make you selfish. You're not a selfish man. If you were, I wouldn't have fallen in love with you. Look what you've accom—"

Shit.

Shit. Shit. Shit.

She so did not want to admit that out loud, but now the words were out there, and the look on Cooper's face said he'd heard them loud and clear.

"Say it again," he pleaded, his work-roughened hands coming up to cup her jaw. "Tell me, Tessa. Say it again."

Even through the haze of her own tears, Tessa could see the moisture building in his eyes, and the fact that he was breaking down just as easily as she was took the last of her control. "I love you, Cooper." Clearing her throat, Tessa continued, "I've prayed that it would be easy to stop loving you. I don't *want* to love you." The tears were coming faster, Cooper's thumbs brushing over her cheeks as he tried to stop them, to no avail.

"I never thought I'd hear you say that," he choked out. "I never thought you'd understand how hard or how fast I fell for you. I was just grateful to have you in my life, but then you were gone."

Tessa wanted to hear him say the words back. To admit in three little words everything he was telling her. When he didn't say anything more, she pushed his hands away. "I'm not gone yet. But I will be."

"No." Cooper's voice thundered in the thick, humid air. "I don't want to lose you again. Tessa, I don't even know how to say the words. I spend my days playing songs about love, but I can't figure out how to express what I feel for you. It's so much more than love."

"But you didn't realize it until I was leaving. What does that say about us, Cooper?"

"It says that I'm an idiot. I should've never let you go. But I needed to give you space. I wanted you to want me as much as I want you. I needed you to love me, Tessa."

"I do love you, Cooper. But I don't think it's enough."

"It's more than enough. It has to be enough because I love you. I've loved you since I first laid eyes on you in the bar. From the first time you fell into my arms. And from the first time I closed my eyes and dreamed about you. I don't want to lose you. I promise, I'll be better."

"Better than what?" Tessa didn't want him thinking he had to change for her. She didn't want that. "I don't want someone else. I want you. Just like you are. I think we're looking for the same thing here," she said, the beginnings of a smile tipping her lips for the first time since she'd woken up that morning.

He'd said he loved her. Her heart had doubled in size as soon as he had said the words, and then it'd cracked wide open. "I think we just have to figure out how to stop running. How to stop hiding. If we can do that, I think we'll have it made."

Cooper's lips were on hers in an instant, and Tessa couldn't resist him. Her entire body was trembling from the mountain of emotions crumbling inward, threatening to bury her alive.

And for the first time in a week, she wasn't willing to let it all come tumbling down on her. She wanted to dig herself out.

∞ ∞ ∞ ∞ ∞

Cooper had no idea where everything had gone wrong, but with Tessa in his arms, he felt like he could right everything again. He'd spent the last week wishing that he could hold her, wanting nothing more than to feel her in his arms and to inhale her sweet, fresh scent. And now she was here.

He couldn't help but wonder how long that would last though. She sounded just as optimistic as he felt, but they both needed the reassurance that they would stick it out.

As hard as it was to tell her his feelings, he needed to know that she wasn't going to run. How he'd managed to stay away from her for this long was beyond him. It could've been his desperate attempt to give her some semblance of peace after he'd come in like a whirlwind and toppled everything in her path, leaving her to clean up the mess.

Only her peace hadn't come, and he hadn't been the white knight to come in and save her. At least she wouldn't think he had. Because he had a secret that he'd yet to share with her.

Releasing her mouth, Cooper stood in front of her, his hands still cupping her jaw as he watched the passion and lust recede from her gaze.

"What do we do now?" she asked, her voice muffled.

"In the past week, have you heard from Marcus?" he asked because he needed to know.

She seemed stunned by his abrupt change of subject, which made sense. He'd easily gone off on another path, only this one actually led right back to where they were.

"Not…" Tessa closed her mouth, opened it again, but she didn't say anything more.

"Tell me."

"Not since the first day after we broke up."

Cooper hated the fact that they'd broken up, but he loved the sound of it when Tessa said it. Only because for them to break up, they would've had to be a couple in the first place. As much as he wanted to believe they were, he still wondered how far away she was keeping herself. Now he knew.

She'd been right there with him but probably too scared to admit it. After everything she had lost, he couldn't necessarily blame her.

"Why?"

"Did he come see you?" he asked, taking a step back and pulling his Stetson off his head so he could run his hands through his hair. He was sweaty, and he needed a damn shower, but this was more important.

"Yes," she said slowly. "He came to see me that next Monday at the bar. The night you didn't come in to work," she explained. "He didn't stay for long, but he told me he was there to meet with Chad."

Her frown made his hands ball into fists. The memory of what she'd looked like that night after that bastard had hit her… He could hardly stand to think about it for fear he'd lose his temper.

"He came to see me that night too," Cooper admitted, pacing slowly in front of her. "He said he spoke to you, but he didn't tell me what y'all talked about. He did tell me that he had met with Chad earlier that day, and he had something that might be of interest to me."

"What could he possibly have?" she asked, just as bewildered as Cooper had been that night. He hadn't understood what Marcus's angle was, but he'd known it wasn't good.

Cooper swallowed hard and turned to face her. "Pictures."

All of the color drained out of Tessa's face right there in front of his eyes. Figuring he had better give her the whole scoop, he continued, "He told me that I had two choices. He was going to leak the photos to the press, or I was going to hire him back and head back to Nashville immediately."

"Oh, God." Tessa's words were but a whisper. "Oh, God. Oh, God. You're still here. That means…"

"No, that's not what it means, Tessa. There aren't any pictures."

"But—" she argued.

"I had to placate Marcus for a while. I told him I didn't give a shit about the pictures and gave him the story of how we broke up. I knew it was a risk, but I've known him for a long time. Most of what he says is bullshit, and I was banking on this being bullshit too.

"As soon as the opportunity arose, I went to talk to Chad. We had a nice long chat, and yes, Dalton was there to supervise so I didn't kill him. He confirmed that there weren't any pictures. Marcus had told Chad he'd be working on a record deal for him if he could produce something. Luckily, I was able to intervene when I did. Or rather, my father was.

"I had to stay away from you. I needed Marcus to believe that there was no chance of us getting back together. I was banking on the press keeping the story hot, although I had no idea they were hounding you. So, for the first couple of days, I kept an eye on Chad, and my father kept an eye on Marcus. Once we had enough on Marcus, my father had planned to confront him. My father coming here means it has all been taken care of.

"Marcus won't be working in Nashville any longer, and you don't have to worry about Chad. Now that he's out of the way, the press will likely leave on their own or at least drop the story."

"So there weren't any pictures?"

"No, darlin'. No pictures." Cooper tilted his head, studying her for a minute. He had no idea about the relationship she'd had with Chad, but he didn't like her reaction. "Should there be pictures, Tessa?"

She glared up at him, but just as quickly as the defenses went up, they came down. "Not that I know of. None that I would've allowed willingly," she admitted. "I swear, Cooper. I'm not like that."

"Tessa, you don't have to explain yourself to me. I know how you are. I know *who* you are. I know you're a very passionate woman, and I wouldn't have it any other way. It's his loss that he was too stupid to know what to do with that."

Tessa looked down at the ground for a long time. Cooper wanted to give her some time to process what he was telling her. He hadn't stayed away because he wanted to. And he'd just been waiting for his father to give him the go-ahead. The fact that his dad was back in Devil's Bend told him everything he needed to know. Everything was taken care of. And not a minute too soon.

"So you didn't stay away from me to hurt me?" Tessa continued to look down at the ground, and it broke his heart to know how much he'd hurt her.

Marcus was the only reason he had stayed away, even though Cooper had tried to convince himself that she deserved better than him. He still felt she did, but… Well, even if Tessa said otherwise, Cooper *was* selfish and he didn't want to give her up.

"I hated that I couldn't tell you, but Tessa, I had to protect you. I didn't want to stay away, but until I was sure I could get Marcus under control, I wasn't willing to risk you." Cooper kept his eyes on her as he paused.

The sad truth filled his chest as he watched the most amazing woman he'd ever had the pleasure of meeting. She was so strong, so resilient, and so deserving of every happiness in the world. "I still think you deserve better than me."

When a genuine smile formed on Tessa's mouth, Cooper's insides churned. He still hadn't learned to be patient, so waiting for her to say something was killing him.

"I don't want better," she said, and he caught the humor in her tone.

Moving in closer, pushing his body between her thighs, Cooper cupped her face and locked his gaze with hers. "That's good because from here on out, you're stuck with me, Tessa."

"I think that might just be a punishment I can handle," she whispered back as Cooper leaned forward.

He didn't care how she looked at it, as long as he had Tessa, he intended to spend the rest of his days doing his damnedest to make her happy.

"I love you, Tessa."

"I love you too, cowboy."

CHAPTER THIRTY-FIVE

"Don't you think we should probably get out of the house at some point today?" Tessa asked Cooper the following afternoon when they were still cuddled together in her bed.

Cooper's sexy growl sounded from behind her and she smiled. Ever since they'd said the L word to one another the day before, Tessa had been as high as a kite, better than any drug in the world. And the hours they'd spent making love the night before, proving just how deep their feelings were for one another, had left her even more invigorated, despite the lack of sleep.

Because of all of the hoopla that was going on with the press, she and Cooper had gone to work at The Rusty Nail on Saturday night. Although they had expected the worst, the night hadn't been as bad as she had expected. Luckily, Dalton had come in to yank everyone's attention right off them and over to him. The man was good at that.

Well, him and David, Cooper's father. To her surprise, David and Becca had showed up at the bar, and when all was said and done, the reporters had been settled somewhat.

Tessa wasn't sure the press would ever get tired of following Cooper around, but then again, why would they? She knew just how amazing he was, so it only made sense that everyone else knew it too. That didn't mean she wasn't happy when she and Cooper were able to sneak into her house and lock the rest of the world outside for a few hours.

But now those hours were up, and she really needed to get out of bed. Just when she was going to roll over so she could get the day started, Cooper pinned her back beneath him, a huge smile on his face as he loomed over her.

"Where do you think you're going?" he asked.

"Hmmm, I was thinking breakfast might be in order."

"Breakfast?" Cooper asked as he glanced over at the alarm clock on her bedside table. "It's a bit late for that, don't you think?"

Tessa tilted her head to read the numbers on the clock. Okay, so he was probably right. Three o'clock in the afternoon meant breakfast was more like supper.

"I need a shower," she teased as she pretended to try and push him off her. She knew as well as he did that if he wasn't willing to move, he wasn't going anywhere.

"Is that an invite?"

The devilish gleam in Cooper's eyes said he was ready for another round, but the aches in her body said she needed a little time to recuperate. "Sorry, cowboy, you wore me out last night."

"Darlin', that was nothin' compared to what I plan to do to you later."

"Later?" she asked, groaning as though the thought were distressing. In fact, Tessa looked forward to later. As long as she could lie next to Cooper every night for the rest of her life, she was more than willing to endure whatever he could dish out.

"Yes, later. Like tonight."

"To—" Before she could get the question out, Cooper's finger was pressed against her lips, effectively shutting her up.

"Tonight. Tomorrow night. The night after that…" Cooper leaned in, replacing his finger with his lips as he pressed a sweet, gentle kiss to her mouth.

"Hmmm, I like the sound of that," she whispered.

"In fact, I intend to wear you out for the rest of our natural lives."

Tessa's body stilled, the urge to panic rising in her chest, but before she could say or do anything, Cooper grinned down at her.

"You're learnin'." Cooper laughed, kissing her again.

"Learnin' what?" she asked, confused.

"Not to freak out on me."

Oh, she wasn't so sure about that. Keeping herself closed off to everyone was a conditioned response, one that would take time to get past. Granted, when it came to Cooper, her heart had been freed from the chains she'd had it locked in for all these years, but that didn't mean her first instinct wouldn't be to hide within herself.

Cooper's eyes darkened, his brow furrowed as he studied her for a minute. When she thought he would push her to talk, he surprised the hell out of her by rolling off her and climbing out of bed.

"Where're you going?" she asked, suddenly nervous that she'd upset him.

"Shower. Isn't that what you said?"

Tessa watched as he padded across her bedroom and then out into the hall. She heard the sound of the shower coming on and she sighed.

What the hell just happened?

Knowing that talking to the ceiling wasn't going to get her any answers, Tessa forced herself out of bed. Grabbing Cooper's T-shirt, she pulled it on over her head and then made a beeline for the kitchen. While he was in the shower, at least she could make coffee.

Tessa met Havoc and Harmony in the hallway, their tails wagging, their big, furry heads looking up at her with such love she felt her heart swell even more.

"I bet y'all are starving," she told them as she made her way past.

"I fed them this morning," Cooper called from the bathroom.

He'd fed them? When had he gotten out of bed? Rather than going to the food bowls, she opened the back door and let them out to do their thing. A few minutes later, she had the coffee on and was heading back toward her bedroom.

She passed Cooper in the hall, the comfortable feeling of him moving around her house so easily both unsettling and … welcome. There was no other way to put it. After the last week, being without him had been the most difficult thing she'd had to endure since…

"Shower. You. Now," he ordered with a swat on her butt that made her jump.

"Gettin' kinda bossy, are ya, cowboy?" she teased, relieved that he had redirected her thoughts.

"We've got somewhere to go, so make it quick. I'll have your coffee ready for you."

Before she could ask him what they had to do, he was around the corner and into the kitchen, leaving her standing in the hallway to stare at the empty space he had just vacated.

Where could he possibly be taking her?

∞ ∞ ∞ ∞ ∞

Cooper waited patiently — yes, he was actively working on the patience piece — for Tessa to get ready. While he sat on the back porch watching the dogs in the yard, he shot off several texts and waited for the responses. It was later than he had wanted, but thankfully everything was still moving forward as planned.

When she finally emerged from the house, he was sitting on the edge of the chair wondering just how much longer he'd be able to hold out. A short whistle had the dogs running up to the house as he turned and went inside. Grabbing the travel mug that he'd put Tessa's coffee in, he handed it off to her and ushered her out through the front door with the dogs alongside them.

"Where're we going?" she asked, but Cooper just smiled. She would figure it all out soon enough. Maybe. Until then, he planned to keep a lid on the surprise.

A few minutes later, Cooper was pulling his truck down the long dirt road to his house, a smile permanently plastered on his face. Although the trip had been a short one, he had managed to evade all of Tessa's questions. He couldn't help but think about how she sounded just like Adam the last time he'd had breakfast with the man. Seemed like just yesterday that her brother had grilled him about his plans to stay in Devil's Bend but still felt like months had passed at the same time.

"What's going on, cowboy?" Tessa asked sternly when Cooper parked his truck beside the spot where the new stables were going in. Nothing more than a concrete foundation for now, but he could pretty much picture the entire setup in his mind already.

"Come on," he told her as he climbed out.

While he waited for her to join him, Cooper let the dogs out of the bed of the truck and then moved around to her side.

Taking her hand, Cooper started walking, forcing her to fall into step beside him. He had to give her credit, she wasn't asking any more questions. Then again, she was probably too stunned to speak considering the people who were waiting for them.

Nodding his head toward Izzy, Eric, Katie, Miranda, Jack, Dalton, David, and Becca, he didn't say a word. Once he and Tessa had joined them in the middle of what would soon be the equestrian center, he stopped and turned to face her.

Still holding her hand, he felt her tremble, and he only hoped she wasn't shaking from fear.

"Tessa," Cooper said when he looked down at her, taking both of her hands in his. The afternoon sun was shining down on her, blonde hair glistening like gold, green eyes sparkling back at him, and a measure of uncertainty written on her face that made his heart twist.

"What's going on?" she whispered, the tremor in her hands evident in her voice as well.

"I…"

"Wait, hold up!" Dalton yelled as he took off running toward his truck.

Cooper couldn't help but laugh, as did the others. Everyone except Tessa, who seemed to be trying to figure out what was going on.

"Sorry, man." Dalton was out of breath when he returned, but he was grinning, his hands behind his back.

It was Cooper's turn to want to ask questions, but he focused on Tessa, the main reason they were all there.

"Tessa," he began again, his heart clenching in his chest as he smiled down at her. "Since the—"

The sound of a horn bleating from up near the house had everyone turning that direction. Cooper was beginning to sweat, and it had nothing to do with the afternoon sun and everything to do with his nerves. The interruptions weren't helping.

"That's…" Tessa said, her hand squeezing Cooper's. "That's Adam's truck."

Oh, thank God. Cooper was hoping her older brother could make it. Unsure how much longer he would be able to hold out, Cooper sent up a silent prayer that Adam would get a move on so he could continue before he lost every ounce of nerve he'd worked up over the last hour.

Adam's big white Silverado came to an abrupt stop next to Cooper's truck, and even though the sun was glaring off the windshield, Cooper could tell there was more than one person in the vehicle, but he had no idea who Adam could've possibly brought with him. This had been a spur-of-the-moment deal. Well, the scheduling part had been. The actual event had been on Cooper's mind for some time now, but as it turned out, not everything in his life went according to plan.

Tessa's breath hitched, and Cooper squinted in order to make out the other people with Adam. He didn't recognize the big man who climbed out of the passenger side, but the woman who Adam was helping out of the backseat looked vaguely familiar, although Cooper was certain he'd never seen her before.

"Mom? Michael?"

Well, that explained why the woman looked familiar. She was an older, taller version of Tessa. And as it turned out, Adam had managed to do what Cooper thought would be impossible.

"What's going on?" Tessa asked when she looked back at Cooper, reminding him why he was there.

Squeezing her hands gently, he stalled for a moment while Tessa's parents joined them. Once they were standing with the others, Cooper smiled down at the woman he loved.

"Tessa…" Wow, he was tongue-tied. For a man who wrote love songs, he found it difficult to come up with the words to express to this woman exactly how he felt about her. Then he thought about the first time he'd laid eyes on her, and the words began tumbling out of his mouth.

"Since the first moment I saw you, when your eyes met mine from across the room, I felt something. A connection that I had never felt before. At that moment in time, I never would've imagined that I had just looked into the eyes of the woman I would soon fall in love with.

"And from the first time you fell right into my arms" — Cooper smiled, the memory so vivid he could practically smell the scent of beer and sawdust — "I knew you'd be the biggest challenge I've ever come up against."

The group behind them chuckled, but Cooper continued. "I knew that walking away from Nashville was going to change my life, but had I known just how much … I would've come to Texas a lot faster than I did."

"Nobody's perfect," Jack muttered, and everyone laughed.

"Hey, he got here, didn't he?" Izzy retorted. "Not everyone can be lucky enough to be born here, you know."

Cooper's gaze never strayed from Tessa's face. He could see a shimmer of tears in her eyes, and he forged ahead. "I admit when I came here, I was chasing a dream, but little did I know that what I had set out for wasn't what I thought it was. Building this" — he glanced around and then back to her face — "it's what got me here, but you, Tessa, are the one who kept me here. It all comes down to you. You're my dream, Tessa. You're everything I've wanted, everything I've prayed for."

A tear leaked down Tessa's cheek, and he paused.

"Get on with it, cowboy," Tessa whispered, making him laugh.

"We're two souls after the same thing. We're dream chasers, and I think it's high time we stop chasing those dreams and realize we've found what we're looking for," he said, his throat tightening. Taking one step back, Cooper lowered himself to one knee.

Releasing Tessa's hands, he retrieved the ring that had been burning a hole in his front pocket. "I love you, Tessa Donovan. More than I ever thought I could love anyone. You're my heart, my soul … my everything. I want to spend the rest of my days making you happy." Cooper had to swallow hard. "Will you marry me, Tessa?"

Cooper held his breath as he stared up at Tessa, his heart stuttering in his chest as he waited for her answer. Her tears flowed steadily now, and he couldn't stop the fear from clogging his throat. He wanted her to be his wife, to spend the rest of her days beside him, loving him. And letting him love her.

"Yes," she whispered. "I'll marry you, cowboy. Yes."

Cooper barely heard the words, but his heart didn't have any problem understanding what she said. Now his hands were shaking, but he managed to slide the engagement ring over Tessa's finger, his eyes never leaving hers. Pushing up to his full height, he couldn't stop the tear that escaped, nor did he try to.

"I love you, Tessa."

"I'll never get tired of hearing you say that, cowboy."

When Tessa flung herself into his arms, Cooper grabbed her up and held her close, his mouth finding hers. The group that was gathered behind them started to clap, several piercing whistles got the dogs excited, and then a booming "Yeehaw!" sounded, causing Cooper to look over at Dalton.

The man was holding the For Sale sign that Tessa had put up at The Rusty Nail. He grinned and then spun the sign around. On the other side was a handmade sign that read:

Dream Chasers
Equestrian Center

"It's perfect," Tessa said on a sob. "Absolutely perfect."

"Yes, you are," Cooper told her, squeezing her tightly. "You certainly are."

EPILOGUE

Tessa was a bundle of nerves and Izzy's excitement wasn't helping much. Her best friend was all but bouncing around the tiny room, a grin on her face as she continued to work on Tessa's hair. Getting all "prettied up," as Izzy referred to it, was proving to be a time-consuming ordeal.

"Are you almost finished?" Tessa asked.

"Yes!" Izzy squealed. "There! All done."

Tessa turned her head back and forth, studying the woman in the mirror, admiring the up-do that Izzy had spent the last forty-five minutes working on. Had Izzy not been so jittery, it would've probably only taken twenty.

"It's beautiful, Izzy," she said admiringly.

"No, you are," her best friend said on a sigh. "God, Tessa. I'm so excited for you."

Tessa could tell. If she hadn't been a nervous wreck, she would've been jumping up and down with her friend.

After all, she was getting married.

Today.

In fact, the church was quickly filling up, and Tessa knew they didn't have much longer before the ceremony started. As much as she wanted to hide out in the bridal suite for another, oh, say, two days, she knew she needed to get this over with.

Not the wedding per se. She was beside herself with joy at marrying Cooper. It'd been six months since he'd proposed, and they had been counting down to this day together. They'd kept the wedding simple and made a list of everything that had to be taken care of. With Izzy as her matron of honor and Dalton as Cooper's best man, everything had taken shape without much effort on their part.

In fact, getting to this point had been relatively easy. Not much stress involved when they spent most of their time enjoying one another. They'd had the opportunity to talk things through and had decided exactly how they saw their future. The one thing they agreed on … whatever they did, they wanted it to be together. Just the two of them.

Which meant Tessa had to let go of some of the ghosts from her past. So, last week, Cooper had taken her to visit Richie's grave, which had been harder than she'd thought it would be. Thankfully, Cooper had held her tightly both at the gravesite and then later that night when she'd fallen apart again. He had offered a comforting shoulder and let her say what needed to be said. She hadn't been to Richie's grave since the funeral, and she'd hated herself for that, but now that she had, she felt as though they both might be at peace. As much as they could be anyway.

Tessa would never stop loving Richie, and Cooper seemed to understand that. But, Tessa knew she would never stop loving Cooper either. In a matter of minutes, he was going to become her husband, and she was finally ready to take this next step. She had officially evicted the negativity from her life, and she'd learned to hope as much as she dreamed.

And all of her dreams were coming true. It hadn't been long after Cooper proposed that she had moved in with him. Days, in fact. She had been blessedly surprised that her need for independence hadn't been another obstacle they'd had to overcome. Cooper gave her as much space as she needed, and Tessa found on those few nights he was gone for something music-related she missed him terribly.

They seemed to have found exactly where they were supposed to be. The equestrian center, which they had justly named Dream Chasers, had become as much Cooper's passion as Tessa's. Although he was the one who put the dream within reach because he had the resources required to build it, they'd both turned it into what it was today. Then, of course, there was the farm. Thanks to the high school kids lining up to volunteer, it was thriving. And yes, Tessa got her petting zoo.

So, their days were long, and their nights were longer, but Tessa wouldn't have it any other way.

It was true, chasing dreams was something she'd been doing for as long as she could remember. Now that she'd lassoed them and pulled them in, she couldn't wait to get on with the rest of her life. And to know that she would be sharing that with the one man who shared her dreams as well… Well, that was more than she ever could've asked for.

It would seem that everything did happen for a reason, and although the pain endured along the way could be enough to knock you down, Tessa knew it was all about getting back up and moving forward. Now, as she stood facing the door that would lead her into the church, Tessa was going to do just that.

Two hours later, Tessa was standing beneath one of the enormous white tents that had been set up next to the barn, with Izzy, Miranda, and Katie. The four of them were watching as a group of guys got a little crazy on the makeshift dance floor thanks to Cooper and Dalton singing one of those fast country beats they used to rile up an audience.

The wedding photographer was moving in and out of the fray, risking his life, as far as Tessa was concerned. The day had been perfect. The wedding beautiful, but the reception… It was unexpected.

The barn wasn't big enough to hold everyone, so tents had been erected close by, one containing food and drinks, another the dance floor, and another still that contained more tables than Tessa could count.

Considering how intimate the wedding had been, Tessa had had no idea Izzy and Dalton had conspired with their families to throw a huge reception. And technically, huge was an understatement. Tessa's entire family was there, including her mother, her stepfather, both brothers, all of her cousins from her mother's side who lived in or around Devil's Bend.

And, as if that weren't enough, there were even some she hadn't seen in, well, forever. Despite the fact that Tessa's father hadn't been a part of her life, his sister, Lorrie, had always made a point to keep in touch with Sheila over the years. The Walkers lived in Coyote Ridge, a small town about half an hour away, and Tessa had no idea how Izzy or her mother had convinced them to come, but most of them were there. Admittedly, the cousins she spent time with regularly were intimidating enough, but Lorrie's seven sons took intimidating to a whole other level.

Cooper's parents were there, along with some of his friends. Yes, that's how he referred to some of the biggest names in country music — friends. Needless to say, invitations had had to be guarded once word had gotten out, but thanks to her cousin Shane, they didn't have to worry about security.

So far there hadn't been any altercations, everyone was having fun, and as far as Tessa was concerned, that was what mattered most.

"Hold up, y'all." Dalton's voice sounded over the speakers, and Tessa turned to look at the stage set up on the far side of the tent. "It's time for the bride and groom to share their first dance."

Tessa's breath lodged in her chest as she caught sight of Cooper moving her way, the seductive grin on his face making her skin tingle. The man was eye-catching in a pair of boots and jeans, but sporting a tuxedo, he was mouthwatering.

And he was hers.

Without a word, he took her hand and led her to the dance floor, his golden-brown eyes trapping hers, mesmerizing her with all of the love she saw reflected there.

"I'm sure y'all have heard this one on the radio recently. This is Cooper's chart-topping single that was just released, 'Angel in Blue Jeans.' He wrote this one for his beautiful bride, and he's allowed me the honor of singing it here tonight."

Tessa's eyes filled with tears as she let Cooper pull her into his arms. She could still remember the first time she'd heard the song when he'd sung it at The Rusty Nail, not realizing then that he'd written it for her. Since then, he had released the song as the first single from his next album, and to their delight, he had topped the country music charts with it.

"You doing all right, Mrs. Krenshaw?" Cooper whispered against her ear as he held her close, his head tilted down toward her.

"Never better, Mr. Krenshaw," she answered, squeezing his hand tightly. "It's still a little surreal."

"Well, you better get used to it, darlin'. This is only the beginning."

Tessa glanced up, met his eyes as she smiled. "I'm going to hold you to that, cowboy."

"Good," he said as he leaned down and kissed her gently. "Because I'm going to start proving it tonight."

Tessa laughed. "I certainly hope so." Glancing around briefly, she met his eyes again. "Think we can sneak out early?"

∞ ∞ ∞ ∞ ∞

Cooper would've endured the wedding and the reception one hundred times over just to marry Tessa, but he had to admit that this was what he'd been waiting for.

"Where're you at, cowboy?" Tessa's sweet Texas drawl echoed within the cavernous barn.

Cooper leaned his head over the edge of the hayloft and smiled down at her. "Up here, so get your pretty little ass up here with me."

Tessa chuckled, and he watched as she shuffled the items in her hands around so that she could make it up the ladder. Once she was within reach, he helped her by retrieving the items and setting them to the side. Wine, two glasses, cheese, crackers. The woman was optimistic, wasn't she? As far as Cooper was concerned, there wasn't going to be time to eat.

"Oh, wow," she said on a breath.

That was exactly the reaction he'd been hoping for. "Do you like it?"

Cooper glanced over at the bed he'd made over the straw, ensuring that it was soft enough for his gorgeous bride. He'd had to sneak the items up last week when she wasn't expecting it just to surprise her. And apparently that had worked.

He wasn't able to bring candles because of the hay, but he did bring strings of white lights that he'd hung from the rafters above them. The area was lit with a soft, golden glow, and as Cooper had been stringing them up, he had envisioned how beautiful his bride would look laid out naked right there so he could admire her. Tonight, he was going to get to see the real thing.

"When did you do this?" she asked, crawling to the bed before lying back and staring over at him. "It's lovely."

He grinned, unwilling to divulge all of his secrets. He happened to like the idea of sex in the hayloft, and he planned to confirm just how much before the night was over.

Unable to resist putting his hands on her, Cooper crawled his way over until he was kneeling on all fours above Tessa, smiling down at her. "You're so beautiful, Mrs. Krenshaw."

"Awww, shucks, cowboy," Tessa said with a mischievous grin. "You're not so bad yourself."

Cooper laughed, and Tessa reached up and cupped his face, her hands gentle and soft. He was wondering how she was going to set the tone for the night. He was all for making love to his wife on their wedding night, but he knew how much she enjoyed other aspects of their sex life just as much. Cooper never knew what to expect, but the way she was caressing his cheek made him think she was looking for slower tonight.

"But I think you're definitely overdressed," she said, smacking his cheek gently and making him laugh.

"Is that right? What about you?"

"Oh, this old thing?" Tessa asked as she pushed herself to a sitting position, forcing him to move or be knocked backward. Right in front of his eyes, Tessa gripped the hem of her frilly dress and lifted it up and over her head.

"Lord have… Holy hell, woman." There before him was the naughtiest woman wearing the skimpiest nightie he'd ever seen. Hell, there was more material in her normal underwear. Not that he was complaining. The red silk ensemble made his mouth water.

"Now what did you have in mind?" he asked, his breath coming in rapid pants. Her pussy was on full display for him even though he was pretty sure those were supposed to be considered panties.

"I was thinking we could set a precedence for our marriage."

Darting his eyes from between her silky-smooth thighs up to her face, Cooper tried to pay attention to what she was saying. "What does that mean?"

"It means I'd like you to show me just what I do to you, cowboy."

"Yes, ma'am," he groaned as he moved forward, obviously faster than she expected because she fell back onto the hay as she giggled. Sliding his hand between her legs, he slipped two fingers deep inside her and matched her mischievous grin when she moaned.

"You like when I do that?" he asked, leaning forward to press his lips to hers. "You like when I fuck you with my fingers?"

"I like when you fuck me, period." She laughed. "I still think you've got too many clothes on."

Cooper remedied that quickly, undressing and tossing his clothes to the other side of the loft, not caring where they went or if they'd be there when he was done. His mind was fully focused on the hottest woman he'd ever laid eyes on and that skimpy red thing that seemed pointless since it didn't cover a stitch.

Taking his position over her once more, he smiled as he lowered his head to her breast, teasing her gently at first before sucking her firmly into his mouth and using his teeth to scrape Tessa's pretty pink nipple.

"Oh!" Tessa's body bowed beneath him, her hands coming up to latch into his hair and pull him down to her. He thought about restraining her for half a second, but Cooper wasn't going to be able to make it that far.

Ever since she'd come walking down the aisle toward him, minutes before they'd made their vows to one another, he'd wanted to get her beneath him. And now that he had her there, he wanted to bury himself inside her and make her scream his name over and over.

Cooper alternated sucking and nipping each breast, applying suction and a tiny bit of pain as she writhed and moaned beneath him. His cock throbbed, but his heart did a crazy dance every time she said his name — which was quite a bit, he realized.

Releasing her breast, Cooper pulled his fingers out from between her legs and proceeded to lick them clean while her eyes widened, the lust burning bright and hot.

"Tell me you love me, Mrs. Krenshaw," he commanded as he shifted between her thighs.

"I love you, Mr. Krenshaw," she said softly, her hands resuming their place on his cheeks.

"What's that? I don't think I heard you. And this time, lose the mister."

Tessa laughed, placing her wrists on his shoulders and cupping his jaw again, their eyes locked on one another. The words weren't necessary anymore because Cooper knew just what he meant to this woman, and he made sure she knew the same. That didn't mean he wouldn't enjoy hearing her say them for as long as he lived.

"I love you, Krenshaw," she teased. Cooper pinched her nipple roughly. Her scream of shock was followed by an uncontrollable giggle.

Shoving his cock deep inside of her, he watched Tessa as her breath locked in her chest, her eyes wide with surprise.

"Try again," he ordered, trying to keep the demand in his voice. Cooper didn't move while he waited, letting her slick pussy sheath him in heat, making his body break out in a sweat.

So, so worth it.

"I. Love. You. Cooper." Tessa's words resounded through him, and he smiled.

"That's better, baby. I love when you say my name."

"I thought you liked when I screamed your name?" she asked playfully.

"Oh, trust me, that comes next." Cooper pulled out and slammed home. Then again. He didn't stop pounding into her, their eyes locked, her hands still cupping his jaw as every ounce of love they felt for one another was transferred not only where their bodies were connected but also through their hearts.

"Tell me one more time, Tessa."

And this time, as Tessa said the words, he drove into her, punctuating every word with a punishing thrust while Tessa's body bowed, her hands moving behind his head, her fingers finding their way into his hair.

"Now come for me, darlin'."

"Cooper!"

Yep, that was exactly what he'd been waiting for.

ACKNOWLEDGMENTS

To my amazing husband: First and foremost, you are what motivates me each and every day. Your love and support is more than I ever could've imagined. You are the love of my life and my soul mate. I love you.

To my readers: Every day I receive the most amazing emails and letters from those of you who have read my books. I'm moved in more ways than you will ever know by your kind words and your stories. It is a blessing that I can do this, and I have every single one of you to thank for it, but to have the opportunity to interact on a more personal level is the most wonderful feeling in the world. Thank you.

Nicole-Nation: As always, you ladies keep me going every single day. The compassion and love that you show me and each other is inspiring. I love you all from the bottom of my heart.

ABOUT THE AUTHOR

New York Times and *USA Today* bestselling author Nicole Edwards lives in Austin, Texas with her husband, their three kids, and four rambunctious dogs. When she's not writing about sexy alpha males, Nicole can often be found with her Kindle in hand or making an attempt to keep the dogs happy. You can find her hanging out on Facebook and interacting with her readers - even when she's supposed to be writing.

Website: www.NicoleEdwardsAuthor.com

Facebook: www.facebook.com/Author.Nicole.Edwards

Twitter: www.twitter.com/NicoleEAuthor

Nicole also writes contemporary/new adult romance as Timberlyn Scott.

Website: www.TimberlynScott.com

By Nicole Edwards

The Alluring Indulgence Series
Kaleb
Zane
Travis
Holidays with the Walker Brothers
Ethan
Braydon
Sawyer
Brendon

The Austin Arrows Series
The SEASON: Rush
The SEASON: Kaufman

The Bad Boys of Sports Series
Bad Reputation
Bad Business

The Caine Cousins Series
Hard to Hold
Hard to Handle

The Club Destiny Series
Conviction
Temptation
Addicted
Seduction
Infatuation
Captivated
Devotion
Perception
Entrusted
Adored
Distraction

Writing as Timberlyn Scott
Unhinged
Unraveling
Chaos

Naughty Holiday Editions
2015
2016